Ex Marks the Spot

Ex Marks the Spot

GLORIA CHAO

VIKING

VIKING

An imprint of Penguin Random House LLC

1745 Broadway, New York, New York 10019

First published in the United States of America by Viking,
an imprint of Penguin Random House LLC, 2024

Visit us online at PenguinRandomHouse.com.

Library of Congress Cataloging-in-Publication Data is available.

ISBN 9780593692714

1 3 5 7 9 10 8 6 4 2

Printed in the United States of America

BVG

Edited by Jenny Bak
Design by Opal Roengchai
Text set in Iowan Old Style

Also by Gloria Chao

When You Wish Upon a Lantern
Rent a Boyfriend
Our Wayward Fate
American Panda

For Anthony, for making my life beautiful.
And for those searching for adventure,
whimsy, and love.

The journey of a thousand miles begins with a single step.

—Laozi

Step 1 (pun intended): Make sure you're facing the right way.

—Gemma Sun

More important step 1: Make sure you're not on the edge of a cliff.

—Xander Pan

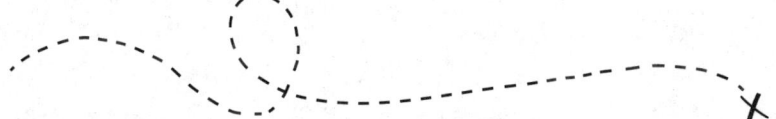

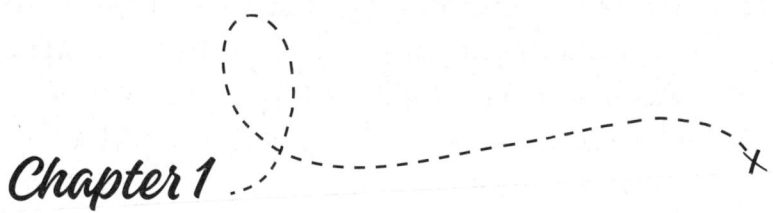

Chapter 1

Graduation is I-want-to-lie-down-on-the-ground boring. It doesn't feel like the end of an era or the entrance into adulthood. Everyone isn't being nice and nostalgic and writing funny things in my yearbook or throwing their caps in the air simultaneously after the best valedictorian speech in the world. Granted, we haven't gotten to the cap part yet, so that may turn out to be true, but the best-speech-in-the-world part is wrong. In fact, I would go so far as to say that the speech being given right this second is the *worst* speech in the history of the world. And I am not just saying that because it's being given by the worst person—Xander Pan, my ex and, as bad luck would have it, the one with whom I'm sharing the co-valedictorian title.

"High school is like a box of chocolates," he says, and it takes all my strength to not roll my eyes since I'm up on the stage too. "Marcus Price is the chocolate that's gone bad. Remember Donutgate, everyone? Lincoln Holmes is obviously the coconut one—"

Everyone but me bursts into laughter before Xander even finishes the analogy. I don't understand a single one of his references.

That's what happens when you've been dealt a crappy hand in life and spent all your time working two after-school jobs to help your mom keep the lights on. Or studying hard in order to get college scholarships as a possible way out—or up, I should say. Which only makes it more infuriating that this person who tied me for the valedictorian title not only doesn't need it as much as I do, having grown up with two doctors as parents, but has priorities that are, in order, (1) what others think of him, and (2) having fun. When the principal told us we had matching GPAs and I felt like I'd lost a battle, Xander deadpanned, *"What a dream come true to be co-valedictorian with my best friend!"* I sacrificed my free time, so much sleep, and my true passion, art, to chase a title that's just a joke to him.

"Even though you will eventually come to the end of a box of chocolates, the joy it brings can last you a lifetime," he continues.

I swear, someone in the audience dabs their eyes with a tissue.

How does no one else see? That not only is this metaphor terrible but it's all fake, an act, so transparent that they should be seeing through it, not laughing at the cheap jokes or crying at the forced sentimentality. This is why I call him Xander Pander—just in my head, of course—because that's what he does, to everyone.

But I'm the only one who sees him this way. Everybody else? They call him the Whole Package. Not sure if the double entendre is intentional . . . There might be a rumor floating around about it, but I wouldn't know the answer—we dated in ninth grade when we were two shy fourteen-year-olds. I called him Alex then, before he became Xander and somehow elevated himself to a plane no one else in the school could reach. Let alone me, the one they call Encyclopedia Yellow.

The only thing that gets me through the rest of the speech is catching the eye of my best (and only) friend, Valeria Gonzalez. From her place among the G surnames, she and I converse almost telepathically with only facial expressions—the human version of texting solely in emojis.

She begins by scowling at the podium while waving her hand. *Oh my god, what is wrong with Xander, can someone get him out of here?*

I widen my eyes and look at Xander, then up at the sky. *Is there anything more cliché than using the box-of-chocolates metaphor?*

Val points at me, looks through her imaginary box of chocolates, and smiles. *You're the chocolate caramel, my favorite.*

I smile and subtly return her gesture. *You're the dark chocolate, my favorite.*

She distracts me so well that I startle when I hear Xander say my name.

"And Gemma Sun, my co-valedictorian. Yi shan bu rong er hu."

I clench my fists so hard my fingernails dig tiny crescent moons into my palms. The words sound nice, but they were designed to tear straight into my Achilles' heel.

I'm embarrassed—ashamed, even—of how I don't know Mandarin or basically anything about Chinese culture despite my blood being 100 percent Chinese. And Xander has been rubbing it in since learning my kryptonite during the China unit of World History when I turned red every time the teacher asked me to add extra insight, of which I had none.

"One mountain can't tolerate two tigers," he translates for the audience and, of course, me. "But we proved them wrong, didn't we?"

Xander looks over to where I'm waiting in my co-valedictorian chair to give my speech after him—of course he got to go first, curse you, alphabetical order—and he winks at me like we aren't exes, like we haven't been enemies throughout most of high school.

"After years of fighting, even mashed-potato fighting"—the other kids in our class laugh, no doubt thinking about that fateful day Xander stole the class-president election from me on popularity alone and Val threw the first fistful of spuds at the back of his head—"it comes down to this. A tie. I guess this particular mountain will have to settle for the two of us. Because it's over. Today, finally . . ." His grin fills the pause. "We graduate!" he yells, and the entire class whoops and hollers with him.

That opportunistic, infuriating phony. How is he on his way to Harvard after this? That's right, because he stuck his nose up their ass by creating a summer program with a ridiculous name—TARP, for Taiwanese American Roots Pursuit. All the acronyms in the world and he chose that one.

I'm still seething when Principal McGrail announces, "Thanks, Xander, for the entertaining speech and the perfect segue to my introducing Gemma Sun, co-valedictorian!" That *co* hits my ears like nails on a chalkboard.

I walk up to lackluster applause. The story of my life. Why was Xander's applause so much louder?

I try to put that out of my mind and focus on the public speaking tips I memorized.

Don't clear your throat.

Don't think about how everyone loves Xander.

Don't breathe too loud.

Don't think about how Xander always breathes too loud yet somehow the microphone didn't pick up on it.

Don't smack your lips between words and sentences.

Don't think about how your hair is probably messy AF but Xander's looks like he's about to be photographed for a magazine.

Everyone is staring at me. *Everyone.* How does Xander thrive in a spotlight this suffocating?

I force a smile. It's creepy, definitely creepy, but I try to own it anyway.

"If high school's like a box of chocolates, then Blue Hill Regional High School is the two-for-one box left on the shelf two weeks after Valentine's Day" is what I think but don't say.

Instead, I read off the printout in front of me. "Principal Mc-Grail, faculty, staff, colleagues, family, what an honor it is to stand before you today."

Then I pause and look up.

Eyes are glazing over; yawns are spreading through the crowd like watercolors in a puddle.

Karma for making fun of Xander's speech sure caught up to me fast. And, I suddenly realize, this is the last time I'll be in Xander's presence. I can't have it end like this, not after years of trying to prove that I'm better, that I don't miss Alex, that I don't care how much our breakup hurt me.

For the first time in my life, I decide to wing it and just be honest.

"I don't know why I'm up here when I haven't figured anything out. I just had less of a life than the rest of you." A few laughs ring out—mostly from Val, I think.

And with those words, it occurs to me that much of my existence up until now has been about getting into a good school and . . . beating Xander. After today, it'll be over. What will be left after that?

I suddenly feel empty.

With no clue of where I'm going with the improv version of my speech, I smooth the printout with one hand and robotically read the rest of what I prepared, my mind blanking as autopilot takes over. Boring is better than wild card.

I finish to—what else?—lackluster applause. As lackluster as Xander's was enthusiastic. Honestly, the amount I get feels like too much for what I delivered.

Xander wins this one. And so what? Who cares? I'm never going to see him again. The idea is both thrilling and confusingly overwhelming.

I sit down in a daze.

Val glances over at me and mouths *fantastic*, then blows a kiss. She's a keeper.

Then the fact that we're going to be headed for opposite coasts next year sinks in. I've been so happy that she got into her top choice, USC, for game development, that I haven't thought about what it would be like for us. Maybe we can sit on video chat nonstop, but that isn't the same as physically being together.

I close my eyes, willing the tears away. I conjure up an image of the pentomino puzzle Val and I are currently stuck on in our latest video game, and thinking through possible solutions calms me.

The rest of graduation is somehow even more boring than the speeches. When else would you ever want to listen to someone read out hundreds of names? The only silver lining as students are called up one by one to receive their diplomas is that a few of them try to have fun with their moment in the sun, doing silly things like throwing confetti, streamers, whatever they could find at home—

even uncooked pasta. And in the case of Noah Jenkins, the class clown, he pretends to flash the crowd, only to be wearing an inflatable He-Man suit beneath his robe.

I yell out Val's name when she's up, though she doesn't need me to. She has her own cheering section that's much louder than shy little ol' me.

Xander athletically glides across the stage with a cadence that implies he's simultaneously confident and also doesn't give a shit. And suddenly I remember why I care so much. It's because he's the worst. It's because after six months of dating (which feels like six years at age fourteen), he accused me of being no fun, then chose a cardboard dog over me. Seriously. We were teammates for the ninth-grade science project, in which we had to keep a ball bearing moving for as long as possible, and while I desperately needed a good grade, he insisted on using a toilet paper tube as a connector that was, of course, accompanied by a three-foot-tall cardboard dog using a toilet next to it. Right before our presentation, I switched it out for a funnel, but he swapped it back. And then, just like I predicted, the toilet paper tube collapsed, preventing our ball bearing from even making it to the back half of our project. My first C, and all because Xander Pander had to be funny. Who cares about grades or our future? We broke up the next period, fighting so loudly that multiple teachers got involved and I was slapped with my first detention to accompany my first broken heart. Then later that week, even though I'd been looking forward to the ninth-grade formal— and especially having Xander as my date—I didn't go, not even to hang out with Val. It hurt too much.

As I watch Xander reach for his diploma, I will him to trip or mix up which hand grabs it and which shakes Principal McGrail's. But I can't even have that.

When it's my turn, I do not bask in my moment in the sun. I jokingly rationalize it's because I'm always in the sun, being a Sun. As I scurry across the stage, I tell myself it's fine, but it disheartens me that my soundtrack is minimal clapping. Val, Xander, and many other classmates have parents, siblings, grandparents, aunts, uncles, and even cousins here. But it's always been just my mom and me, my father having run when he heard she was pregnant, my grandmother having died in childbirth with my mom, and my grandfather passing away soon after I was born. I love my mother— she's my whole world—but sometimes I wish my world were just a little bit bigger.

When the ceremony finally begins winding down, an unexpected wave of nostalgia floods through me. I've done it. In a few short months, I'm going to Amherst College, an hour and change away from here. And as withered as my heart sometimes feels, today is significant. How did I get this jaded? As much as I don't want to admit it, Xander might be right—maybe I don't know how to have fun. But he doesn't get to judge me when he doesn't know what it's been like. It's impossible to have fun when your home situation forces you to grow up early. But I'm here today, having secured the next step of my future. And I will show him just how fun I can be at the appropriate times—which, mind you, Xander, is not all the time, especially not during a science project.

"Okay, everyone!" Principal McGrail is saying into the mic. "And now we've reached the part of the ceremony where students traditionally throw their caps in celebration."

I stand, yank my cap off my head, and throw it in the air with epic exuberance. I've always been scared of whooping—do you actually say the word *whoop* or is it more of a yell?—but I force myself to put my fear aside, and I whoop at the top of my lungs.

My cap arcs in the air beautifully, traveling vertically and horizontally because I pitched it at an angle, and it lands at Xander's feet.

It's Dead. Ass. Silent.

I'm the *only* one who has thrown their cap.

Principal McGrail forces a cough, then continues, "But this year, we won't be doing that in solidarity with Madeline Bridges, who can't take her cap off due to sun sensitivity. Madeline, we are so proud of you for being such a great advocate for alopecia awareness."

Oh no.

Maddy Bridges is trying to hide her face. She didn't ask for this.

Regardless, I look like the asshole. And everyone is glaring at me, as they should, even though it was an honest mistake.

I knew there was a reason I was wary of whooping.

"Sorry, Maddy," I squeak.

And with that, graduation has moved from the Boring category into Most Embarrassing. In my life, it always seems to be one or the other. What I wouldn't give to move this back into Boring.

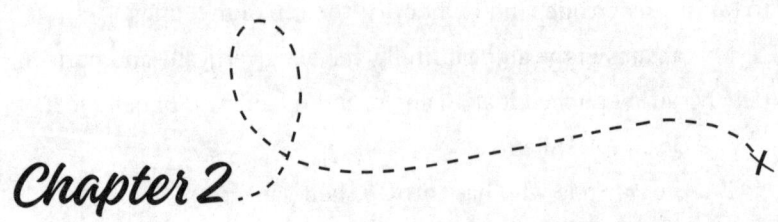

Chapter 2

"It wasn't that bad," Val is currently saying to me, but she's always been a terrible liar. We should be talking about our favorite memories from the past four years, but no, we're talking about the one moment I decided to have fun only for the universe to take a wet dump on me.

The ceremony is over and everyone is in pockets greeting their families, but I haven't found my mom yet.

Val adds, "At least it wasn't one of your wavelength things? This was a mistake anyone could've made."

Her words only remind me that when I have a "wavelength thing," it's not a mistake anyone could've made. For as long as I can remember, I've had this difficulty in social situations where I seem to be on a separate wavelength from everyone else. I somehow hear things a little differently, interpret words in another way, or need an extra second to process. Like how I became the president of the astronomy club. I'd walked in hoping to convince a few of them to vote for me for class president and somehow came out having been voted *their* president. I of course served dutifully, but I, to this day, don't know how it happened.

Val usually tries to make me feel better by saying the wavelength thing is where my puzzle and art superpowers come from—because I see things differently than others—but I'd rather be like everyone else, thanks. While the Great Graduation Cap Incident doesn't fall neatly under the wavelength umbrella, it's close enough.

I spot Maddy in the distance and am about to approach her to apologize, but she shakes her head and mouths *it's fine* to me. I manage to mouth back *sorry* right before she turns away.

"Don't worry," Val says, her eyes following mine. "At least you didn't compare all of us to chocolates."

"He couldn't have been just a little original? Even changing it to cookies or something would have been better." I groan. "Why does he infuriate me so much?"

"Because he's your ex. Your ex, X." In any other circumstance, I would have loved that play on words. Val and I first bonded in junior high over our love of puns, riddles, and puzzles. "And you're physically attracted to him but repulsed by everything else, so that's confusing."

"I am not physically attracted to him!" I almost yell.

"You dropped something," the most annoying voice in the world says from behind me.

I whirl around to see a grinning Xander holding out my graduation cap, which I snatch from him. Half of me hopes he heard what I yelled, and the other half wants to hide in a hole.

"Didn't know you had such an arm on you, Shi Tanzi."

As usual, his words have underlying teeth. First, because I don't know what his nickname for me means, and second, because he's making fun of how unathletic I am. That's almost as legendary as the mashed-potato fight, thanks to the time I accidentally threw a softball right into Mr. Marashio's crotch.

I want to call him Xander Pander, but I'm worried it's funny only to me. So I say the one dig I've ever thought of for him, which is barely a dig at all. "Hi, Alex."

He looks away, and I hope I've struck a nerve. Maybe even reminded him of before, when we would study in the library during free periods, draw rebus puzzles for each other, and share contraband hot chocolate because he didn't care that others thought it was only for little kids. But his gaze returns quickly, and there's a gleam in his eyes. I look over to Val for support, but that's when I realize she's been pulled away by her enormous family. I'm on my own for whatever's coming.

"Glad you're trying to have some fun," he says. "*Finally*. Though I think you need some guidance. Is that also what happened there?" He points to the fruit-punch stain peeking out above the collar of my too-large graduation gown. "Red always was your color."

How dare he.

Not just the joke—which is also rude—but how dare he not remember where that stain came from. Or does he remember and he's being extra dickish?

He is the reason I've had to wear a stained dress to presentations, award ceremonies, and now graduation. Not only did he tank our science project, but during the presentation, while he was trying to show off the cardboard dog like Vanna White, he waved his arms so wildly he knocked the cup of fruit punch right out of my hand and onto my only nice dress.

And he doesn't even remember?

I'm tempted to remind him of that terrible day, maybe find a cup of fruit punch to throw on him now, but I don't have the chance. And for the best reason.

My mom's long, straight hair dances in the wind behind her as she tornadoes into me, hugging me so tight I can't help a soft *ooph*. She could pass for my older sister, having had me young, at eighteen.

She's so emotional her voice is a husky whisper when she says, "I'm so proud of you, my Gemma-Bear. My sun."

Those words make me hug her closer. They also make me feel like I'm a child again, waiting at 5:00 p.m., before she left for her second job, to hear my favorite bedtime story, the one she made up about a sea slug named Slugger who wanted to gift her mother the best treasure in the world. The other slugs made fun of her, but then she did it. She found the best treasure. She gave her mother the sun. She found a special spot on the ocean floor where the sunlight shone through, and since sea slugs photosynthesize, it was the best treasure in the world.

To us, the sun represents family, the most valuable treasure. It's why my mother wears a necklace with a sun carving on it and why she named me Gemma—because it has the word *gem* in it, and as she always says, I'm her best treasure. And right now I feel that more than ever as my mom's arms embrace me tightly and her tears soak through my hair and onto my scalp.

Our beautiful moment is interrupted by Xander's family coming over. About twenty Pans, ten times as many as we have in our kitchen. They shake Xander's hand formally one by one, no tornadoes or hugs.

"Congratulations, Xander," my mother says, unaware of the extent of our history. I never told her about our romantic relationship, for the opposite reason as most kids, especially Asian kids. She would have been too excited. She'd want to do my hair and makeup and give me money she didn't have for dates, and Xander and I weren't that kind of couple. I had wanted to spend time together outside of school, but I couldn't afford to go on normal dates, and whenever I asked Xander to hang out at one of our places, he declined. *Just as well*, I thought at the time, since I was embarrassed to show anyone our shoebox-size home.

So my mother's kind words to Xander aren't unexpected, but her next words are. "An-Shun," she says brusquely, nodding in Mr. Pan's direction. "Congratulations to you as well."

I wasn't aware my mom knew him, let alone was on a first-name basis. She could never attend any of my award ceremonies and I took the bus to and from school, so I'm not sure when they could have crossed paths.

Even more surprising is Mr. Pan's curt response. "Hi, Jing."

I know that's my mom's legal name, but I've never heard her go by that before. She's always had a we're-American, let's-assimilate-as-much-as-possible attitude, which is why I know nothing about Chinese culture.

"Jean," my mother corrects in a tone implying that Xander's father should have already known that.

My eyes ping-pong back and forth between my mom and Mr. Pan, trying to read beneath the familiar names yet icy-cold exteriors.

"Ayi hao," Xander greets my mother in—of course—perfect Mandarin. Or at least, I assume it's perfect. The only Mandarin I grew up with was my mom asking me "Bian bian?" in public when I was little instead of saying "Do you have to poop?" so others wouldn't understand.

"No need for that, Xander," my mother says with a wave of a hand.

"Xander, lai, you have family to ying jie," Mr. Pan says suddenly, grabbing his son's arm and pulling him away from my mother and me like we're trash. A gesture I'm familiar with, unfortunately.

"Let's go," my mother says as she places her hands on my shoulders and steers me away. Before we're out of earshot, she whispers intentionally loudly, "I can't believe he's the one you tied with."

With a flick of two fingers in my direction, Xander yells after me, "See ya, Shi Tanzi! It's been fun!"

As fun as cleaning mashed potato out of your bra.

"They're so annoying," my mother mutters.

"How do you know Mr. Pan?" I ask, not thinking too much of it, but then she says, "I don't." And her eyes are not meeting mine, searching for something—a distraction, I realize.

"Really? Because it seemed like—"

"Ah, look! The Gonzalezes," my mother exclaims, dragging me to Val's family. My mom loves Val as much as I do, and I know she's grateful for all the times Señora Gonzalez stepped in to help us, like that time I broke my arm and required extra care for a few weeks, and when we were evicted and needed a place to stay while we sorted everything out.

As soon as the Gonzalezes spot us, they yell and sweep us into their giant group like we're family, which we are—*found* family. I make a mental note to bug my mom later about the weirdness with

Mr. Pan; then I let myself enjoy the warmth and hugs around me.

"Your mama and I will be so sad when you two leave for college," Señora Gonzalez says, and she and my mom pretend to cry on each other's shoulders.

Val giggles as she playfully rolls her eyes, and as I turn to her to roll mine back, I spot a middle-aged white man in a gray suit hustling toward us, waving frantically with one hand and gripping a briefcase with the other.

I assume one of the Gonzalezes is his target, but Val asks, "Who's that?" just as I'm about to ask her the same question.

"Gemma Sun!" he calls out as soon as he's within earshot.

My head instinctively turns to my mother, whose eyes are on him and widening with recognition, shock, and a fleck of anger.

"Mom, what—"

But she doesn't even let me finish before she grabs my arm. "We have to go."

Then she remembers her manners and yells to the Gonzalezes, "Felicidades! Lovely seeing you, as always! Let's get together soon and celebrate our girls!"

But even as she's saying all that, she's jogging away, dragging me with her in the opposite direction of the gentleman. She seems scared, which makes me scared.

"Who is that?" I ask, panting because she's picking up speed.

"It's no one."

"Mom—"

"It's . . . the town pervert, okay?"

"What? Come on—" She shoots me a look. Two can play at this game. "Well then, shouldn't we tell someone?"

"No, he's harmless."

"A harmless pervert?"

"Did I say pervert? I meant drunk."

"But—"

"Stop asking questions!" she uncharacteristically snaps. "Just trust me, okay?"

I look behind us at the man. He's given up the chase, leaning over his knees and shaking his head, likely cursing my mother under his breath.

Who the hell is he? And when did my mother start keeping so many secrets?

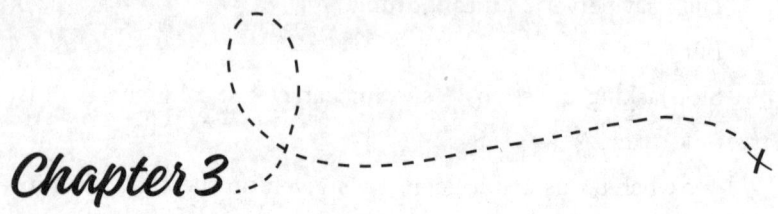

Chapter 3

The secrets taint our celebratory dinner almost as much as my cap throwing tainted graduation. I want to enjoy this rare time we have together when she's not rushing off to work or we're not sweating over finances, but I can't get the mysterious man out of my head.

"Seriously, Mom, who was that guy?" I ask as I dish casserole onto our mismatched plates. Everything Casserole is my mom's favorite—it uses up our leftovers, and while cheap, it's also delicious. And I think she loves how American it feels, like we're on one of those sitcoms she grew up envying, where a big family with two parents and lots of kids would sit down over a casserole and tell each other how their day was.

For me, I can't help thinking about how if my mom weren't so insistent on assimilating, maybe we'd have made fried rice instead. I'm sure Xander's family would have made fried rice for their scraps dinner, but they're probably celebrating right now at some fancy restaurant with the whole extended family.

"I already told you," my mom answers with a rare finality to her tone.

"*Town pervert* is not an answer, not without an explanation."

My mother, the one who has always insisted on an open-door policy, doesn't respond. Which only intensifies how bright red this flag is. We overshare about everything. Periods, butt moles—how is this secretive woman the same person who told me she accidentally sent the cute HR guy a photo of her butt mole instead of her passport because she'd saved them both as *Important Pic*?

As my mother brings our plates to the table, my mind wanders to the worst places. "Do I need to worry? Is this about money?"

"Of course not," she says as we sit down. I'm inclined to believe her mostly because I help with the bills and that doesn't feel like the kind of secret she would keep.

I can only think of one other possibility. "Is that an ex-boyfriend?"

She laughs. "When would I have time to date?"

As relieved as I am that an ex-boyfriend isn't stalking her, the words catch me off guard. Is she lonely? Does she want to date?

My mother raises her mug of ginger ale, and I instinctively follow.

"Gemma-Bear, my treasure, my sun, my little Slugger, I'm so proud of you. Amherst, my goodness!" She squeals. "You deserve this, my smarty-pants. You've worked so hard."

I want to bask in her words, but all they make me think about is the herd of tap-dancing elephants that have taken up residence in a room that has never had any before. Not only is she avoiding my questions about the mystery man, but college feels like a catch-22. I worked my butt off for the best chance of a future where my mother wouldn't have to spend her days cooking in a nursing home cafeteria and nights cleaning offices, and while I'd gotten in, even with financial aid and scholarships, school is expensive. Like, absurdly expensive.

My mom and I haven't talked about it because there isn't a solution. I have no idea where the tuition and living expenses are going to come from for next year, let alone the three after that—or two if I can manage to finish early. And now, with graduation, with this dinner, with her toast, the clock has officially begun.

The pressure is suddenly so heavy I can't breathe.

My mother is oblivious to the death spiral in my head—or maybe she's aware but doesn't want to talk about it—and she digs into her casserole while asking, "What's up with you and Xander?"

This is the mother I know. The one who always wants the latest tea, especially mine.

"Nothing. We're just . . . bitter rivals."

She raises an eyebrow. "That's it?"

I lower my eyes to my very American casserole. "Yup."

If she can keep secrets, then so can I.

The dangerous part about secrets is that they're not just yours to keep. The next morning, as I'm home alone stressing over tuition and picking my first-semester classes, a knock sounds at the front door.

We don't have a peephole, so I go to the kitchen and peek out the only window that overlooks part of the front stoop.

And I see a gray suit and briefcase.

A mess of thoughts rushes into my head.

This is the supposed town pervert.

He knows something I don't know, something my mom doesn't want me to know.

He's a stranger and I'm home alone.

My mom is scared of him.

What's my next move?

Another knock sounds.

"Gemma Sun?" he calls out from the other side of the door, and I jump away from the window, worried he can see me. "My name is Daniel York. I'm your grandfather's attorney."

My grandfather died right after I was born. Why would his attorney reach out now? This smells fishy.

I startle when I hear a noise under the door, then look down to see that he's slipped something underneath. A business card. With his name and title written in fancy font. I grab my phone and do a quick search for *Daniel York, Esquire.*

On the screen, the man from yesterday stares back at me, arms folded across his chest, an assured look on his face. Seems professional and lawyerly enough. And his firm appears legitimate. It would be quite the scam to set up a webpage, LinkedIn, and several articles about cases he's been involved in.

I have a bad feeling about this. I just can't figure out if it's because Daniel York is trouble or because my mom's lies might be much bigger than I previously thought.

Another shuffling sound spooks me. A pile of paper has been pushed beneath the door.

A last will and testament. It looks real. My mother's name—her

legal name, Jing—appears under next of kin, along with mine. Or-
dinarily, this would be enough to sway me, but in light of meeting
Mr. Pan yesterday, maybe she tells everyone her legal name when
I'm not there.

My world feels upside down.

I have to know what's going on. But safely. So first, I text Val the
details—Daniel York's name, number, photo, website, and that he's
here claiming to be my long-dead grandfather's attorney.

Then I open the door.

Hello, drunk pervert. I make a mental note to keep my distance at
all times just in case.

"Hi," I say awkwardly. "Uh, come in."

I lead Daniel to our secondhand sofa, then sit at the kitchen
table a few feet away. "Do you, um, want anything?" I try to think
of what refreshments we have. Tap water and the expired Pedialyte
my mom saves from the nursing home for when one of us gets sick.
It's practically the Ritz here.

But luckily, Daniel shakes his head, barely looking at me as he
sets his briefcase down.

Then, suddenly, he stills, looking at me with concern. The air
turns cold. Whatever's coming, it isn't good. I brace myself.

"Ms. Sun . . . I'm sorry to be the one to tell you this, but . . . your
grandfather passed away."

"Yes, I know," I say cautiously. Is this a practical joke? Is this guy
actually a drunk pervert I should be wary of?

He gestures to the papers I'm already holding. "I'm the executor
of his will."

"And you're coming now?"

"Well, I tried to contact your mother two weeks ago, but she . . .

ended our first call abruptly and refused to take my subsequent ones."

"Two weeks ago?"

"Yes, I called as soon as I heard the news."

"Wait, what?" Nothing makes sense.

Daniel is looking at me as if he's not sure I have a brain. "Your grandfather passed away two weeks ago from natural causes in Taipei, where he's been living for the past year. He wrote this will when he was still living here in Massachusetts."

"*What?*" This has to be a joke. There are cameras somewhere, right? Maybe Mom set this up to earn some needed cash for the college fund?

Daniel's eyes are filled with concern, but he doesn't understand where the disconnect is. "He left something to his next of kin, and after we go through the paperwork and dot the i's and cross the t's, it will be yours and your mother's."

I somehow find my tongue, which is completely dry and feels too big for my mouth. "Are you sure you have the right person?"

"Gemma Sun, granddaughter of Yong Ping Sun." That name holds no meaning for me. But then he pulls a photo from his briefcase and shows it to me.

The old man in the photo has the same nose as my mom and me. The Sun nose, apparently. Straight, narrow, with a rounded tip. And his lips. Thin on top, full on the bottom. Could just be a coincidence, but the way his smirk rises on just the right side to reveal the tiniest dimple in his cheek—that's my mom. And his ears that look almost too small for his head? That's me.

"He was . . . alive?" I ask. "Until two weeks ago?"

"Yes." He doesn't seem to know what else to say.

But suddenly, I have a million questions. The picture has untied my tongue and flooded my brain. My phone buzzes, but I ignore it—whatever it is can wait.

"Did my mother know?"

"I'm not sure, but she didn't seem as, um, surprised as you when I told her."

There's no way. Yet, at the same time, after her strange behavior yesterday, maybe? Or maybe I shouldn't believe what this stranger in front of me is saying.

Daniel breaks into my thoughts. "May we proceed?"

I blink at him.

"I assume you want what he left?"

Right. I forgot about that. A brief spark of excitement shoots through me, followed by a current of guilt for caring about money at a moment like this, even if we have almost nothing.

I'm in a daze as Daniel goes over the will with me, nodding despite the legal jargon not making sense. But I'm grateful for his interpretation.

I scan the text as he explains, and a few colored sections jump out. Always seeing the patterns first. Pointing, I ask, "Why is this part of the text blue?"

Daniel sighs. "Your grandfather insisted we do that. I don't know why—I tried to dissuade him, but he wouldn't have it. He was an, um, eccentric man."

His words rub me the wrong way for some reason, but I push past it.

Twenty minutes later, I've dotted the i's and crossed the t's—metaphorically, that is, since there are no i's or t's in *Gemma Sun*.

Daniel reaches into his briefcase and retrieves a medium-size wooden box. He hands it to me, then stands. "Lovely meeting you, Ms. Sun."

"Wait. This is it?"

He nods, already making his way to the door.

It's a beautiful hand-carved box with cranes flying among clouds and koi swimming through water below, but it's just one box that fits in my lap. Could it contain . . . a thick wad of cash? A cashier's check? It's too light to hold jewels or gold bars. I frantically open it and paw through.

Old newspaper clippings. That's what's inside.

"What is this?" I ask Daniel, who has one foot literally out the door.

"I don't know, Ms. Sun. He didn't tell me, and my job is to deliver it to your mother or you, which I've done."

The door shuts behind him.

Disappointment floods through me. And with that, I realize I was hoping for magic. Fulfilled dreams. A Cinderella story come to life but somehow with an Asian lead—that should have been my first red flag that it wasn't going to happen. I fell down a whimsical *Alice in Wonderland* hole imagining money for tuition and having all my problems solved, but reality is now crashing in.

There's no money. No magic.

Nothing but junk.

Somehow, I'm feeling even more distant from my grandfather, this random person who, well, seems like he was an eccentric man. Why does that word bother me? *Eccentric* isn't bad. I'm plenty eccentric compared to almost everyone I know. But . . . it's a part of me I don't like, and it feels weird to think that about someone I don't know. My mother has always refused to talk about him, saying it was too painful, and I stopped asking long ago.

Suddenly, I hear keys in the door. I check the clock. It's four hours too early for my mom to come home.

She starts yelling before she's even come inside. "Why didn't you answer your phone? How could you let a stranger, a man, into the house?"

"How did you know he was here?" It isn't the most pressing of questions given everything that just happened, but it simply burst out.

"Mrs. Levy told me." Our kind septuagenarian neighbor whose trash cans we bring in every week. Our tiny houses are so close they're practically on the same property. "I ask her to keep an eye on you when I'm not here."

That shocks me. I'm used to looking out for myself and didn't realize my mom was finding her own ways to protect me even when she wasn't around. But I guess she's been doing that my whole life, starting with Lilliput Day Care when I was small, which I was able to go to only because it was run by a generous acquaintance of Mom's.

She points to the wooden box. "Is that his? Is that all he left?"

"So you knew," I deduce. "You've been lying to me?"

She opens her mouth, then closes it.

I fill the silence. "How could you?" She's never lied to me before. But I guess I should amend: she's never lied to me before *that I know of*. Maybe the complete openness she insists on only goes one way.

"How long have you known?" I ask. I'm not sure if she found out because Mr. York tried to contact her or if she's known all along—

meaning, her lie was either two weeks (forgivable) or my *entire life*. How would we move past it if it's the latter?

I can't breathe as I wait for her response. She takes too long, and I can't hold it anymore.

"Mom, please."

"I was protecting you."

"From what? Him?"

She nods.

I hope for more, but nothing else comes.

"Mom . . ." My voice is desperate now, begging. "How long have you known?"

Her eyes plead with me, telling me the answer. But I need to hear her say it. My eyes plead right back.

It doesn't work. Instead, she comes over and runs a tender hand through my hair. "Do you know how much you mean to me? When did you get so mature? I feel like I blinked and you were eighteen."

I'm not going to hear her say it. And I can't keep the rest of the questions in any longer. They burst out, a gushing wave of emotion. "Why did you lie to me?"

She sighs. "He was not a good father. It's better he wasn't in our lives."

That's it? I wait, but she seems to be done.

"What did he do?"

"Oh, Gemma-Bear, it's all in the past. I don't want to relive it."

She's still not telling me, even after it's come to light. The frustration and lack of control erupt inside me in a full-fledged fire, and it takes all my self-control to keep from lashing out. I manage to soften my tone but not my words. "I can't believe you did this to me. I didn't get to know him. My *grandfather*. The only other family we have. You didn't give me a choice. And now you won't even tell me why."

I know what's coming before she says it. "Am I not enough for you?"

What if the answer is *sometimes*? What if I do crave a bigger family? Am I so terrible for wanting more people to love? From the way she talks about it, yes, it makes me a villain.

So I don't answer.

Then she says something that pushes me over the edge. "Well, what does it matter anyway? It's too late now, so the point is moot. Let's not argue anymore."

How dare she. I clench my fists hard, harder, hardest, until it's too much and I have to release them. I need to stay in control. Nothing is accomplished with my mom when I let my emotions take over.

"I have a right to know," I say calmly but with grit. "Aren't I an adult now? He's my family too. And you are now my only conduit to knowing anything."

My words chip the smallest piece into her armor. I grab the nail and try to hammer it home. "I want to get to know you better too, Mom. Understand where you came from."

Instead of saying, *I'm from here. We're Americans*, like she usually does, she stares at me for a second, then slowly nods.

"Okay. Mother-daughter tea. Just for a minute."

For us, the *tea* refers to both our drinks and our conversation. I run and make us two cups of ginger-honey rooibos, her favorite. While she would never admit it, it's a perfect melding of her Taiwanese and American sides.

At the kitchen table, she slowly begins to open up. "I was an only child growing up, like you. And as you know, my mother died soon after having me."

Did she really? I want to ask but don't. Instead, I clench my teeth, not wanting to react, lest it stop the flow of information. I force myself to also resist the urge to grab her hand and ask if she ever wishes for a bigger family like I do.

"It's hard to explain what it was like for me growing up, Gemma. He grew up there, in China and Taiwan, and I was born here. But he didn't respect that at all. I was surrounded by American ideals, but he expected me to be the perfect child *he* wanted, according to traditions I didn't understand."

Traditions I don't even know, I can't help thinking. How ironic. She pushed her culture away, and that's all I've ever wanted.

She must know what I'm thinking because she says, "You claim you want to know that part of you, but you don't. I promise. This whole time, I've been protecting you."

That's always been her argument, but why wasn't I allowed to figure that out for myself?

She continues, "He tried to control my life. I wasn't allowed to date or do anything other than school, violin, or whatever activity he chose for me. He even planned my future career."

There's no way his choice of career for her was an underpaid, underappreciated, overworked nursing home cook/office cleaner. I sit patiently, hoping for more.

"I rebelled!" she exclaims as she throws her hands in the air. "What else was I supposed to do? Once I had you, I had to protect you from all that. And I did. It's always been you and me against the world."

Those same words used to make me smile and feel like she and

I were partners, a team, a family, but right now I see red. "So you kept him from me just because he was tough on you?" It doesn't feel like enough.

"It's not like he fought for us either. Which just shows that I was—"

"Protecting me, I know, I know," I say, exasperated. "But did it ever occur to you that he might've been different with me? Aren't grandparents usually different with their grandkids?"

"I wouldn't know."

"Me either." *Because of you* goes unsaid.

"Gemma." She looks like a child begging me for forgiveness.

"You're the reason I feel so messed up, why I don't know anything about where I come from. You could've chosen to share at least a few things—you didn't have to keep *everything* a secret! I hate that I don't speak the language, I hate that Xander knows so much more than me, I hate that I feel incomplete, and I hate that you kept my grandfather from me and now it's too late" are all the words I think but don't say. I can't, not when she's looking at me like that.

It's all too much, so I push away from the table, run the three steps to our shared bedroom, then slam the door behind me.

For the millionth time, I wish that my world were a little bigger. Because if I had a sibling or grandparent or another parent, maybe someone would understand how I feel.

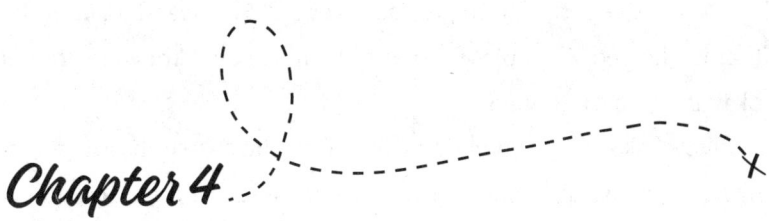

Chapter 4

There are too many thoughts in my head. The worst of which is *Did my mother lie about anything else?* Because now that she broke my trust once, I don't know how to get back to where we were before.

I don't even get three minutes alone.

A soft knock sounds, followed by my mother calling through the closed door, "Gemma-Bear? I have to go back to work."

"Okay," I yell, hoping she'll leave without coming in. I don't want to see her right now.

But of course, she continues knocking with one hand while slowly opening the door—that thing I hate because it's not asking for permission if you're coming in anyway.

I'm flopped on my twin bed, my back to her. I don't turn around.

"We can talk more about it tonight when I get back," she says. "But that's everything, okay?"

How could that be everything? We barely said anything.

She walks over to my bed and sits. The wooden box is in her hand. "Is this all he left us?"

I nod reluctantly, annoyed that my desire to know more trumps my desire to punish her. "Does it mean anything to you?"

"No. Leave it to him to give us garbage." She abandons it at the foot of the bed, then places a hand on my ankle. "Are you sure it's okay if I go back to work?"

She's asking, but no matter how I feel, the answer has to be *yes*, like always. Because she doesn't have a choice, and neither do I. I know it's not her fault, but frustration flares through me.

I manage a nod. My mother squeezes my ankle, and then she's gone without a backward glance. How convenient for her that she gets to escape.

Once I hear the front door close, I roll over. I'd been uncomfortable, my arm cramped beneath my shoulder, but I didn't want to adjust while she was there, as if moving would be equivalent to letting her win.

Nothing makes sense anymore. I sit up and stretch, jostling the wooden box at the foot of the bed, which bounces, then flops to the side, spilling the newspaper clippings.

With a sigh, I collect them to return to the box. They're all in English, except for one that's in Chinese. The headlines appear random, though a couple of them are funny.

SPLISH-SPLASH! COWS HAVE ADVENTURE OF A LIFETIME AFTER FENCE BETWEEN FARM AND WATER PARK FALLS DOWN

SURPRISING TWIST: CAT BURGLAR IS ACTUALLY A DOG IN SOCKS!

My mom was right; it's just trash.

As I'm about to return the pile to the box, a small pop of color catches my eye. The word *adventure* in the first headline is underlined in blue ink.

I riffle through the other clippings. Random words are underlined on each one. *Adventure* and *of* in the cows one, and *is* from the cat burglar.

It looks purposeful—a bold, straight, intentional line. Perhaps even drawn with a ruler, unless my grandfather had an incredibly steady hand. Are they random, or do they hold meaning?

The blue ink is the same shade as the blue text in the will.

Your grandfather insisted we do that, Daniel had said.

But also, *He was eccentric.*

I retrieve the will and return to the bed, hugging a pillow as I skim through.

Just like the newspaper clippings, the blue sections appear to be completely random. There's no equal spacing between them, no common theme or words or length. But as I look more intently, I notice that each section is labeled, starting with numbers, then moving to letters for the first subsections indented beneath, and then returning to numbers again for the next subsections. And the kicker that I didn't see until now: the numbers or letters labeling each blue section are underlined. It's subtle since it's just one character, but once I'm looking right at it, it's all I can see.

Underlined, just like the newspaper clippings.

I start flipping through the will faster, and I write down the underlined numbers and letters on a scrap piece of paper—a past-due bill, so not exactly scrap, but I'll make sure not to throw it out.

24U2N0ME

Then the last section is different. The number in front, *35*, isn't underlined. But one random line in the middle is—my grandfather's address in Taipei. The rest of the text mentions how he left some possessions behind and lists the contact information for his landlord so we can arrange logistics—something the lawyer had already gone over with me.

I add this last underlined bit to my notes, then stare at it.

2 4 U 2 N O M E Taipei apartment address

I read it out loud. Then feel ridiculous. What am I doing? But also . . . *4 U 2* sounds like *for you to*. As I continue staring at the line, my brain automatically puts a space between *NO* and *ME*. And then it hits me.

"For you to know me . . ." I have to go to his Taipei apartment.

Is this real? Or am I seeing things again? It's related to the wavelength thing, how I think and see everything differently, my mind always latching on to other meanings first or seeing patterns in places where there are none, like how the electrical wires on the highway look like angry faces to me. When I see numbers, factors and multiples just appear in my brain apropos of nothing. God knows why, it's just how I seem to be wired. I once asked my mother if she did any of that, and she didn't know what I was talking about.

I'm just seeing things again. I have to be. Especially because that 2 at the beginning doesn't make any sense.

This is ridiculous.

I push the will aside, shaking my head repeatedly. I'm so desperate for something more I'm imagining things.

I force myself to lean back on the bed. I just need to reset my brain, give myself a minute or ten to process everything that has happened—my mother lying for a bajillion years, my grandfather being alive until recently, and the fact that I'll never get to know him. All that is too much for anyone to learn in thirty minutes.

But as I sink back into my propped-up pillow, I spot it. The wooden box is splayed out in such a way that I notice a small number one carved in the corner, complete with serifs on the top and bottom so there's no mistaking it.

I snatch it up, feeling the grooves with my fingertips to confirm it's there. As I do so, my other hand holding the box passes over a small unexpected ridge on the back. I turn it over to see a tiny protruding square.

A button, my brain immediately says.

I push it—what's the harm?—and hear and *feel* a click from within.

I eagerly remove the lid and peer inside.

The inside back panel of the box has popped out, revealing it was a false side. And out spill . . . two more newspaper clippings, again with a couple of underlined words in each heading: *examine* and *the* from one and *next* and *will* from the other.

With only four words, there are only so many possible arrangements, and I immediately rearrange them to *Examine the will next* or *Next, examine the will.*

My heartbeat quickens. I'm not sure exactly why at first, but then the pieces begin clicking together so perfectly in my head I can almost hear the clicking sound the box made when the panel popped off. The four words make sense of the number one carved on the box and the number two in front of the hidden message in the will. Combined, they imply an order. A sequence. Like in a treasure hunt. The first two of many clues. I simply found them out of order, and this clue—clue number one—is directing me to the next puzzle I already solved in the will.

I'm so excited I have to press my fist into my mouth to keep from screaming.

I grab the original newspaper clippings and fan them out on the bed. On the paper, below the *4 U 2 N O M E*, I write out the underlined words: *adventure, of, is, the, end, the, at, the,* and two Chinese characters I don't know, 太陽.

The anticipation is overwhelming. I'm practically hyperventilating as I arrange and rearrange the words until I get:

The 太陽 is at the end of the adventure.

Just my luck that the two most important words are in Chinese. But thank god for translation apps. I download one, pick traditional Chinese, and aim my camera at the 太陽 characters in the headline. The print is too small and smudged to produce anything. I aim the camera at my handwritten copy. But it's so bad the app still doesn't recognize it.

Of course. Xander would have gotten it on the first try.

Frustrated—at myself but more at my mother—I try to perfectly imitate the exact shape of the characters. My strokes are unsure and a little wobbly, just like how I feel.

But then I realize—don't think of them as unknown words. They're shapes. I'm just drawing. This time, when I mimic the lines, they're smooth and bold. Thick, thin, and sharp in all the right places. Writing Chinese feels like drawing.

The app translates this version immediately, and a bud of pride blooms as a small thread connecting me to my heritage appears.

Sun.

The sun is at the end of the adventure.

The first thing that comes to mind is our last name. Which could be a possible interpretation. Is my grandfather still alive and at the end of this hunt? Then why make me jump through all these hoops to get to him, and why fake his death?

It can't be the literal meaning of *sun.* Not unless we're like Slugger, finding an actual sunny spot on the bottom of the ocean.

Wait. Slugger.

For us, the sun represents family, the most valuable treasure.

Again, with that interpretation, the sentence could mean that family is at the end of this adventure—maybe my grandfather's siblings or their kids or some long-lost cousins. That would certainly be a treasure worth discovering.

Or . . . it could mean *actual treasure.* An inheritance, family heirlooms, other valuables.

But did my grandfather know the Slugger story?

It had been such an integral part of my childhood. I always assumed my mother made it up, but now that I think about it, she never explicitly said she did. It's possible she was *retelling* it to me. After all, the story would have applied to her too.

I'm so jittery I almost drop my phone, but I manage to call my mom. I feel bad since she's at work, but I can't wait.

She picks up on the second ring. "Are you okay?"

"Did your father used to tell you the Slugger story?"

Her breath catches in her throat. "Yes. Why?"

"And did he like puzzles?"

"You're interrupting me at work to ask that?"

"Just tell me, please."

There's chatter in the background. She's distracted. I'm hoping that will benefit me since she'll want to get through this conversation faster.

"Yes, he loved them. Why?"

Is it possible that I'm not making this up? Did my grandfather intentionally leave puzzles sending us on a treasure hunt?

"Was he rich?" I ask.

"Of course not. He lost everything during the Communist Revolution. Left everything and everyone behind when he went to Taiwan. He had to start over completely."

Which could explain why he hid his treasure. Maybe his past made him distrustful. Is it totally out of the realm of possibility to think a man with that experience would hide what wealth he had accumulated since that time, then leave a coded map that only his family could solve?

"When you say *everyone*," I follow up, "does that mean there isn't any other family left? No siblings, cousins, whatever?"

"No, no one."

It's an inheritance hunt—I can feel it in my bones, bones that share DNA with the eccentric man who planned it.

"Is that it, Gemma? I'm really busy."

"Yeah. Sorry. Love you."

"Love you."

I'm barely listening as she hangs up. I'm staring at the newspaper clippings.

This can't be real, can it?

How could it be? It's too ridiculous. And if it's real, why wouldn't my grandfather have made it clearer? Included a letter, some instructions, or told his lawyer.

But . . . I figured it out, didn't I?

No, it's too implausible.

And even if it weren't, how would I do this? Following the clue from the will means I'd have to find a way to get to Taipei. Impossible.

But . . . what if there is an inheritance? What if my Cinderella/ Wonderland fantasies could be real? We need the money, desperately. For tuition, for bills . . . and there's a ticking clock over our heads. My first payment to Amherst is due soon.

Even if the chances of this being real are infinitesimally small, I have to try.

Maybe I can be Cinderella. Just a different kind. One who isn't after love because there's more to life than that and I'm just eighteen. I'm after education and a better life for me and my mom.

I'm going to find a way to go on this adventure no matter what it takes.

9:23 PM ET

Val

OMG I JUST SAW THE PHOTOS YOU SENT

!!!!!

YES THAT IS SO A PUZZLE, CLUE, WHATEVER YOU WANT TO CALL IT!!!

HOLY SHIT A TREASURE HUNT

Gemma

Are you sure?

Yes, I'm sure!

What do you think is at the end?

Gold? One of those rooms filled with treasure like in a movie?

A giant pile of money we can dive into?

Scrooge McDuck style?

No way! He dives into coins, ouch! We're going to dive into bills like classy ladies

Together, right?

Do you even have to ask?

Ride or die

For life.

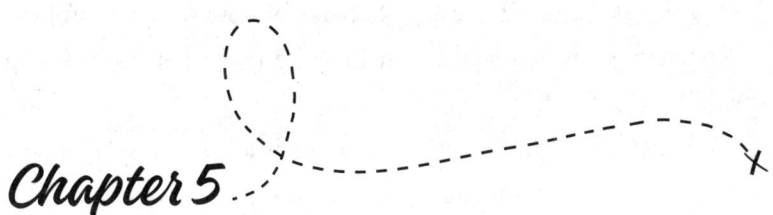

Chapter 5

"Stop seeing things where there's nothing, Gemma!"

My mother does not believe that my grandfather left an inheritance hunt for us.

"It's too much of a coincidence," I argue. "It *has* to be something. And you said yourself he loves puzzles."

"*Loved,* Gemma. Past tense. Just because you learned one fact doesn't mean you know him. Putting together an inheritance hunt that brings you to the other side of the globe is too much even for him."

"How would you know? You haven't talked to him in decades. And it references Slugger!"

That's when I see it. A crack in her armor. And it takes me a second to realize what's causing it.

Grief. Of course. Just because they were estranged doesn't mean she isn't sad to lose him. He was her *father*. And she thought about him more than she let on. Why else would she have told me the Slugger story every night growing up?

"Mom, are you okay? It's all right to mourn."

That snaps her out of it. "That's not what I'm doing."

She's always pushed me to share every feeling, but she's never been great at it herself. Perhaps because of how she grew up, I'm now learning. She's grieving, but I'll have to let her do it on her own terms.

"I'm just trying to bring you back to reality," she says. "Not only is it preposterous, but he didn't have anything to leave us."

"You don't know that. The Communist Revolution was so long ago." I pause, not sure what else to say about something I don't understand, thanks to her.

"He lost everything again more recently than that. When I was a child."

"What happened?"

I hold my breath. This is her chance to show me she's changed since the person who told me my grandfather had died long ago.

"It's not imp—" she begins, but then she sees my face. She sighs and starts over. "He . . . had a business partner who betrayed him. Took everything he had. He was never the same after that. Hardened. Distrusting. Sad."

Maybe distrusting enough to hide whatever he had made from that point forward? If it was when my mom was young, that's still almost four decades of life before he passed.

"I'm sorry," I say, and I'm not sure if I mean for her or my grandfather.

I've heard so little about him, and it already seems like too much for one person to go through in a lifetime. It only deepens my desire to have known him, to have heard about his experiences for myself, to comfort him. What if the thing he was missing was family? Just like I feel sometimes.

I reroute the conversation back to my original objective. "Even if there's no puzzle, I want to go to Taipei. See where I come from."

"You're from Massachusetts."

I play the ace I've been hiding up my sleeve. "You kept him from me. This is the last chance for me to learn about him."

"Except it's not. I'm telling you, there's no trail for you to follow."

"Well, someone needs to claim his things in the Taipei apartment."

She shakes her head. "It's just more junk, like the newspaper clippings."

I feel like I don't know the person in front of me. "How can you not want to go?" *And how was it so easy for you to cut him out when he was the only family you had?*

"I made my peace with everything a long time ago."

Except she hasn't. She's struggling, meaning her heart isn't as hardened as she's pretending.

"Is there something you're not telling me?" I ask.

My mother dodges the question. "What about your jobs?"

"I won't be gone for that long; it's not a big deal," I lie through my teeth. I can't say what I'm really thinking, which is that I'm taking a risk for a bigger payout, like playing the stock market. It's not like I make that much anyway, though the lost wages will hurt if there's absolutely nothing at the end of the so-called adventure.

Luckily, my mother is too prideful to bring up how much we need every cent. Instead, she argues, "Gemma, even if I agreed to let you go, how are you going to get there?"

It's a fair question. We've never taken a vacation, let alone traveled to the other side of the freaking world. I don't know how much plane tickets cost, and maybe I shouldn't check because I might throw up. But I have a plan. One she won't suspect, which is to my advantage.

I load up the question I prepared beforehand. "If I find a way there, can I go?"

She laughs. "Fine. If you do—and I'm not paying a dime—then you can go."

Step one, check.

Now I just need a favor from the last person on earth who wants to give me one.

Easy peasy.

Chapter 6

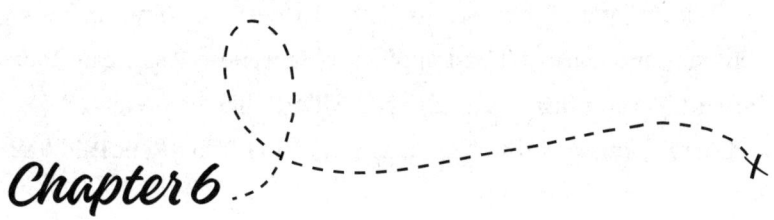

"Hey, best friend."

I expect Xander to respond with an irritating joke, but he's so surprised by my appearance, especially in this location, that he just gawks at me for a second. I feel like I won even though it's a dig at how little I belong here on the track, where he jogs five miles every morning because he sucks.

At least he stopped running. I was worried he wouldn't—*this six-pack doesn't just appear out of thin air*. Okay, he wouldn't say that. I have no idea how to come up with the witty things he says. Not that he's witty. Nor am I thinking about his six-pack, which I only know exists because other people at school talk about it.

At that exact moment, he lifts the edge of his T-shirt and wipes his forehead, giving me a glimpse of said abs. I try not to look at them or the V that disappears into the top of his shorts.

He's the bane of my existence, the most infuriating boy, the reason I no longer drink fruit punch or eat mashed potatoes, but when he covers his smirking face up . . . I mean, I still have eyes and hormones. Why couldn't he have looked like that when we were together?

"The program," I blurt out. Then I remember how to form a sentence and clarify, "I just applied to Taiwanese American Roots Pursuit." I can't bring myself to call it TARP like he prefers.

He raises an eyebrow. "You mean the Trip Airfare Rent Paid free-loader program, according to you?"

Why did I have to carp about TARP? Why couldn't I just keep my mouth shut for once? Though that's *precisely* the reason I'm applying.

Then he adds, "It's a little late to be sticking your nose up Harvard's ass alongside me, isn't it?"

Whoops. I stand by those words but wish I knew when I said them out loud how much it would come back to bite me in *my* ass.

"That's not what this is."

"Then what is it? The deadline was months ago."

He looks ready to start running again. My time is limited.

"I just realized how . . . cool it was. Your program." That line physically hurt to say.

He laughs, which adds fuel to my perpetual fire toward him. "I didn't know your acting was on par with your cap throwing."

I double down. "I'm not acting. I mean it. TARP"—I have to force the name out—"is such an amazing opportunity. I'm dying to be a part of it. I'm sorry for all the things I said before."

I hate how much I mean those words, how much power he holds over me at the moment, how I'm practically ready to drop to my knees and beg—or worse, give him the truth and a window into my most guarded treasure, my heart. I swore four years ago to never let him get close again.

His eyes drill into mine as if he's trying to see into my soul. I force myself to not look away.

Suddenly, he breaks eye contact. "I don't believe you."

Then he starts running.

Against all my better instincts, I follow. He picks up the pace.

"Wait . . . slow . . . down . . ." I say between pants. He doesn't listen. "What . . . can . . . I . . . do . . . to . . ."

He takes me out of my misery by answering before I finish my question. "It's just not possible. The slots are filled."

And of course he speaks as if he's sitting still, not speeding around the track like a mongoose running for its life. People do this for pleasure?

I can't keep up anymore. I stop abruptly, hands on my knees, stitch in my side, barely able to breathe as my heart beats in my ears.

What now?

"What now?" Xander says when I interrupt his cooldown. He's covered in sweat as he stretches his calves, then hamstrings, both of which look defined even when he's not flexing them.

After leaving him earlier, gulping down water from the fountain for two minutes straight, and then pacing in circles inside the gym, I've come back to dance with the devil again. Only because four of the words he said continued to ring inside my head.

I don't believe you.

He was right not to. Why does he have to know me so well? The only way forward is to tell him something true. And I'm just desperate enough to do it now.

"I want to know where I come from. To pursue my roots. Isn't that exactly your mission? It's in the name—"

"The very clever name. Best name ever."

I grind my teeth. Luckily, he doesn't make me agree with him. But he does tilt his head to peer at me as he says, "You've never cared about that before."

That's not true, but I take solace in the fact that I've been acting convincingly. *Acting on par with my cap throwing* my ass. And I will never tell him that I learned from him—pretending not to care is strong armor.

"What, so I can't change my mind?"

"What made you change it?"

I look him in the eye as I lie. "Starting the next step of my life. Graduation was so momentous and made me look at everything in a new perspective." He's narrowing his eyes at me, not believing me, so I start blathering, hoping that something will fly out of my mouth that convinces him. "I meant it before, this program is such a great opportunity. And the name is so great too—because a tarp is a waterproof covering, and, um, that's so on brand for you. It's the opposite of a wet blanket. And like I said, I have a new perspective now, so I want in. I want to be a"—I swallow—"TARPer."

I assume he's not going to understand the weird thing my mind just came up with, but he beams. "I'm glad you're finally trying to lose your nickname, Shi Tanzi."

That's what he's been calling me this whole time? Wet blanket? I didn't think he could make me hate that nickname any more, but I should've known better than to underestimate his ability to be annoying.

Oblivious to my processing the meaning of my nickname, Xander continues, "But I wasn't making that up before; the slots are filled."

"Aren't you the creator and organizer and god almighty of TARP?" The words sound pandering, but they're sarcastic in my head.

Amusement flickers in the corner of his eye. "And what am I supposed to do as TARP god?"

"I believe in you, Xander. You can come up with something."

He stares at me for a few seconds. Then he smiles. "Okay."

My heart soars, but I remind myself not to count my chickens yet. I learned that the hard way, even literally. During a junior high group science experiment, I almost failed because so many of my eggs didn't hatch.

But I can't help the excitement bubbling up. "Okay? For real?"

He nods. "If you admit that the dog cutout with the toilet paper roll was the right decision for our ninth-grade science project, I'll see what I can do."

"No!" I blurt immediately. What's wrong with me? He's extending the opportunity I want—at a price, but how costly is it really? I just have to say what he wants to hear. I don't even have to mean it.

But at the same time . . .

Instead of just getting it over with, I can't help asking, "Do you truly believe that? Even after we got a C?" And . . . *even after it led to our breakup?*

"I didn't say it was the right decision for the best grade. But maybe it's good to have some fun in life, no?"

"Maybe you need to take things more seriously sometimes."

That cardboard dog not only represents our breakup but the *why*— we couldn't be more different if we tried.

"Well, I see you've made your decision." Xander turns.

"Wait!"

He turns back.

I can do this. Easy peasy.

I swallow down saliva, maybe even a little bile, and definitely my pride as I say, "The . . . dog—"

"And the toilet paper roll."

"The dog and the toilet paper roll . . ."

"Yesss?" Xander says, drawing the word out in encouragement.

He's smirking at me. *Smirking.* Enjoying this moment. And that maddening right-side lift to his lips makes the vein in my forehead throb, makes me remember exactly how I felt four years ago fighting with him over the science project.

"I can't." I shake my head so hard my ears ring. "I hate that dog. And I'm not going to lie. That freaking dog . . ."

"That dog didn't hurt anyone."

Is he serious? Does he really believe that? His cocky grin is too much. It reminds me exactly why I've been playing this game with him for years. Why I need to beat him, why I need him to know just how great I am and how great I'm doing.

I try to calm my mind and tell myself I can't let him know how much I still think about that dog.

"Go screw yourself. You're just as ridiculous as that dog" is what I plan to say. But what chooses to come out of my mouth with the full force of my emotions is "That dog broke us!"

I turn and run, the hurt and embarrassment pushing me to do the impossible—I run even faster than I had earlier on the track.

Five days later

Gemma

I've spent days searching for other programs, scholarships, anything, and no luck.

What am I supposed to do?

Val

That disgusting piece of expired chocolate, it's all his fault

I swear I'm going to find him and throw mashed potatoes at his head until he caves

Mess up that precious swoopy hair of his, barf

OMG!

I know, I would pay to see Xander with flat hair

No, he just emailed me.

Forwarding to you now.

!!!!!!!!

What???

OMG!!!

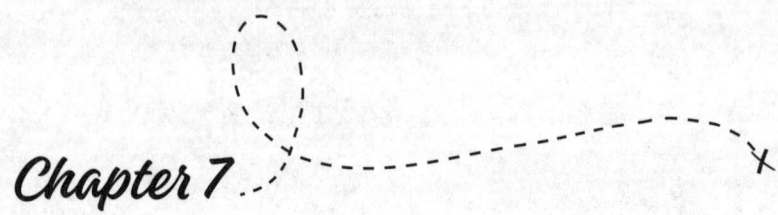

Chapter 7

Out of nowhere, Xander emails me a form letter accepting me into the program. No pleasantries, no explanation, nothing personal except my name inserted in the greeting. I read the email three times just to make sure, but there it is in black and white, with *Gemma Sun* at the top. I have no idea how he managed to do this or why, and I don't care.

I squeal, flail my arms in excitement, then text Xander.

> Gemma
>
> Thank you!!!
>
> Seriously, this is amazing, thank you.

> Expired Chocolate
>
> Someone dropped out so it's not a big deal
>
> You were just a last minute replacement

Well, that could have been nicer. But whatever. I'm *in*. I am going to *Taiwan*.

And after I officially confirm my attendance to the TARP email address that probably just goes to Xander, I jump into high gear. Given that I have less time than everyone else, I have to put on my type A hat to make sure everything will be ready by the time I leave.

With determination, I open the email attachment with the to-do list. Luckily I already have a passport because my mom makes us keep them up to date, though for a sad reason. Because of the state of the world, she finds comfort in having tangible proof of our Americanness. And maybe it also relates to her issues with her father and identity and et cetera, I'm realizing now.

Even with my passport ready to go, there's a lot to get done: getting my plane ticket, packing, making sure all the funding with the organization is squared away, downloading an app so I can video chat with my mom and Val whenever I have Wi-Fi, ordering some Taiwanese currency from the bank so I don't have to worry about it when I land, getting a travel credit card for emergencies . . .

And the biggest problem specific only to Gemma Sun: my mom. Even though she promised I could go if I figured out how, I know it's still going to be a fight.

Case in point, when I tell her about the program, her first words are: "You're going to *abandon* me to chase this nonexistent puzzle? You're seeing things!"

I guilt her at first, bringing up her lie. But that doesn't seem to be changing her mind, only riling both of us up.

New plan. I slowly chip away at her with:

"This is the opportunity of a lifetime. It's an amazing way to make friends and unbelievable memories, to see a new place." I leave out that it's not just any place, but where our family came from.

And "I'm not only getting to travel—leaving the state *and* country for the first time—but the costs are *covered.*" Which, now that I think about it, why didn't I apply sooner? People talk about love goggles, where they can't see a loved one clearly, but I have the opposite. Hate goggles. When they're on, I can't see past Xander's annoying personality or our history to the value beneath. With how many other things has that happened?

I consider also bringing up the inheritance to my mom but don't since she doesn't believe it exists.

And I have answers to all her questions: the program gives a per diem, so she doesn't have to worry about the cost of food or transportation; there will be chaperones on the trip; the program will provide us with new SIM cards so we can use our phones there; no, I don't need to get ahead on my coursework now—the syllabi aren't even up yet. For that last one, I leave out the thought that swims through my mind: *What's the point of thinking about coursework when we don't even know how we're going to afford the tuition?*

Eventually, she runs out of arguments. And her objections turn into warnings.

"Don't go out after dark."

"Don't go out alone."

"Don't talk to strangers."

I try to lighten the mood. "Do have fun?"

I can't help hearing Xander in my head. *But maybe it's good to have some fun in life, no?*

My mother frowns. "We've never been apart for more than a few days."

"I'm going to miss you too, Mom."

When she accepts my hug and grasps me so hard it feels like the Heimlich, I think I've done it.

And I know for sure when she comes home the next day with a new phone for me.

"I've been saving up," she says as I open it with cautious fingers. "I wanted you to have this for college; might as well give it to you a few months early. I'll feel better with you across the world—aiyah, maybe you shouldn't do this? It'll be better if you have a phone with good battery, good signal, and a working maps app."

I've never heard her say *aiyah* before. Maybe she's never been this stressed.

This time I hug her so hard it feels like I'm giving *her* the Heimlich.

I'm doing this. I'm getting on an airplane for the first time, I'm traveling to *the other side of the world*, I'm going to see where my family is from, and I'm starting the adventure of a lifetime. Nothing will ever be the same after this. A freaking treasure hunt!

Well, if it's real. I'm still not sure. At least right now, I have hope. I cling to it like a lifeline, and I dream of what I might find at the end of the rainbow: gold, stocks, a classy Lady McDuck pile of cash, a secret bank account.

I don't ever want to wake up.

8:45 PM ET

Val

I CAN'T BELIEVE YOU'RE GOING TO TAIWAN!!!

Gemma

Me either!

My mind still hasn't processed it.

I'm gonna miss you

Same, obviously.

Obvs

You're going to be at coding camp anyway.

And you're going to be in FREAKING TAIWAN

HOW IS THIS MY LIFE?

You deserve it!!!

Chapter 8

The program has a group chat with all the attendees, and I'm self-conscious about being the last-minute addition. But I force myself to at least say hello and give a few personal facts. I manage to refrain from typing out something embarrassing like, *I'm going on this trip for treasure hunting, arr!* Instead, I list the most basic things—I'm going to Amherst College in the fall and I'm from Podunksville, Massachusetts, among the cows (cows who are likely still waiting for their adventure of a lifetime, unlike those from my grandfather's newspaper clipping). And then . . . I decide to add something I normally wouldn't have before my world was turned upside down. I tell them I like to paint. I feel like a fraud typing out those words—how can I be a painter without paintings to show for it? I haven't had the time or resources to create artwork in years. But no one asks for proof or makes fun of me or whatever I thought might happen.

I'm grateful I stepped out of my shell and joined the chat for several reasons, and on the day of departure, I'm glad to know that the other nine attendees are from all over the country, so none of them will be at the Boston airport and I don't have to look for them. We'll all meet in Taipei at the local university that's kind enough to let us stay in their dorms while they're empty over the summer.

But of course the eleventh attendee (or maybe he should be number one since it's his program, as much as I hate calling him number one in anything) will be on my flight. There's a chance I'll just see him in passing, though.

I expect my mom to drop me off, but she's as nervous as I am and insists on accompanying me as far as she's allowed. Together, we navigate the confusing parking lot, board the shuttle, and trudge our way to the right airline to check in.

"Are you absolutely sure you'll be okay?" she asks me for the ten thousandth time.

I'm not sure—this has turned out to be harder than I thought, and I haven't even left the state yet—but I smile. "Don't worry about me."

"You've got your new phone?"

I nod, that simple question enough to make my throat close with suppressed emotion. How am I going to get through parting from my mom without crying? I thought I was cried out from saying bye to Val yesterday, but nope, apparently not.

When we enter the terminal, Xander has just finished checking his bags and is in the middle of saying goodbye to a horde of family members. Okay, there are three of them, but still. Why so many just to bring him to the airport? And why am I so jealous?

"What're they doing here?" my mom asks.

"TARP is Xander's program."

"Why didn't you tell me that?" She's pissed, which is just as confusing as her and Mr. Pan being on a first-name basis.

"Why does it matter?"

"Because," she sputters. "You lied to me."

"I really didn't. You're the only liar here."

A brief silence descends.

"I'm sorry," I say, only because I'm uncomfortable. In reality, I don't regret my words, and I'm upset that she not only lied but we still haven't really talked about it.

She sighs. "No, it's fair." Then she takes a second to compose herself. "I'm sorry about that. I should've said more, especially because I had to rush back to work that day, but I couldn't bear to bring it up again. You're right, though—we need to talk about it."

The loud, bustling terminal doesn't seem like the ideal place, but here we are.

"I shouldn't have lied to you. I should have found a way to tell you the truth years ago. It's the only thing I've lied to you about, and I hope you can find a way to forgive me. And I hope we can rebuild our trust."

"I forgive you," I say automatically, mostly because I don't want to leave things this strained between us.

"It's okay if—" my mom starts to say, but we're interrupted by the Pans storming over.

"What are you doing here?" Mr. Pan booms.

My mom shields me with her body. "Don't talk to my daughter like that!"

Xander is trying to drag his parents and aunt away. He looks just as confused as I do, that crease appearing on his forehead as it often did in AP English—I basked in those moments, the only time Xander seemed to struggle with anything.

My mom's words seem to have gotten through because Mr. Pan

now begins yelling at his son. "You stay away from her!"

Does he know about our history? Did Xander lie about our breakup? That would be hilarious, the idea of me breaking Xander's heart. I'm tempted to tell Mr. Pan that he has nothing to worry about and I will be staying away from his son, who is the bane of my existence, but I don't think that's what he's looking for either.

Mr. Pan talks to Xander like we're not even here. "Do you know what their family did to ours?"

I look at my mom. "What's he talking about?"

Mr. Pan suddenly spots my passport in my hand. "Is she in your program?"

Xander's face isn't fazed, but his hand grips his boarding pass tighter. "Yes, Dad, what's the big—"

"How did she get in so late?"

"Someone dropped—"

Mr. Pan interrupts in Mandarin, his volume rising with every word.

My mother pulls me to the side, away from the ruckus, to *calmly* explain (making me suddenly appreciate her all the more). "Remember how I told you your grandfather lost everything a second time, more recently?"

"Yeah, the business partner who took everything."

"That was Xander's grandfather."

My eyes bug out. I can't help staring at the Pans, who are still talking loudly and gesturing.

My mom *just* told me she hadn't lied about anything else, and now I'm finding out another huge thing she kept secret? But before we can unpack that, there are more pressing questions to ask, especially because I don't know what to believe from her now. "Why did

Mr. Pan say that our family did something to theirs?"

The briefest pause tells me my mother registered my distrust of her, but she pushes past it quickly. "They think they were owed the money and didn't do anything wrong."

Well, that explains the tension at graduation.

Everything sounds so messy—he said, she said, and whatnot. But doesn't the fact that the Pans grew up with so much and we so little point to the truth? As if I needed yet another reason to loathe Xander.

"Why didn't you tell me this sooner?" I ask my mom.

"I don't know," she says with a shrug, and it's the first time I'm sure she's being honest. "It just didn't seem important, especially given that you didn't even know your grandfather—which again, I'm sorry about—and you already seemed to hate Xander."

"You knew that?"

She tucks a strand of my hair behind my ear. "Of course, I'm your mother."

My face softens, though just for a moment.

Because she then asks, "Is there anything else you want to tell me, maybe about him?"

The hypocrisy is not lost on me. I know I've kept things from her too, but I want to hold on to my secret out of principle since I just have one and she's had too many to count.

I don't get a chance to respond. Xander and his family have been raising their voices this entire time. As people begin to stare, Xander seems to reach the end of his rope, turning suddenly and jogging into the security line. His dad tries to follow but is stopped by a TSA agent. Furious, he turns and starts making a beeline for us.

Crap.

My mom attacks me with a viselike hug. Quickly, she whispers into my hair, "You've been the best adventure of my life. I wouldn't change any of it for anything. Remember that, okay? I love you, I trust you. Now have your own adventure."

She pushes me toward the airline check-in. "I'll take care of this." She gestures toward Mr. Pan stomping closer.

I'm touched by her words, and I'm surprised her speech didn't end with any warnings, but then she calls out to me, "Be safe, honey! Text me all the time. If you think it's too much, I promise it's not enough."

I can't help a small chuckle as I step up to the check-in desk and don't look back.

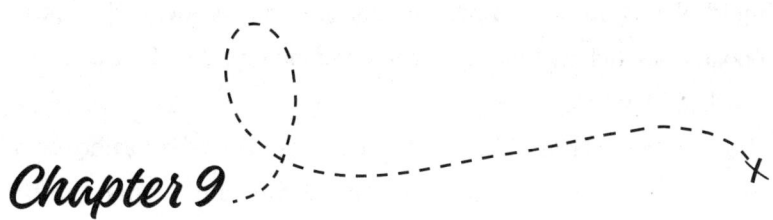

Chapter 9

I'm still processing everything that just happened, so I avoid my gate until the last possible moment. My pits are soaked as I board because I spent the last twenty minutes stressing about missing the plane. But it was still better than having to see Xander.

The plane is almost full, and when I reach seat 19B, I see that Xander is 19A.

So I just almost gave myself a nervous breakdown for no reason. And I could have started my full day of travel with dry armpits. For a second, I almost wouldn't mind some BO because then Xander would have to smell it. But I don't get any. I looked it up, and it turns out that some East Asians have a gene that makes them produce a different kind of sweat that doesn't attract the BO-causing bacteria. When I learned of this, I was not only thrilled to not have to worry about my armpits, but also weirdly happy because it was one of the few things that made me feel tied to my roots.

I keep my arms close to my sides as I sit down. It may not smell, but the deep stains are mortifying.

"Hi." My voice is as stiff as my posture.

"Cutting it close—that's out of character for you."

Like he doesn't know why I waited until the last minute. My mind blanks on how to respond and instead wonders whether he booked our tickets together or if someone else did. Or maybe it's just bad luck.

Once I get settled, the flight attendants begin their safety demonstration. I've never been on a plane before, and I listen like the nerd I am, telling myself it's not embarrassing because it's life or death—even though it hopefully won't matter, better to know where the life jacket is, right?

"You okay?" Xander asks me, looking up from his phone.

Guess we're doing this—addressing the giant elephant somehow sitting between us on the tiny armrest that barely supports a quarter of my elbow.

"I mean, as okay as I can be after finding out . . . all that about our families. Are you okay?"

Xander shakes his head. "I meant, you look kind of pale."

Maybe I sweated too much and I'm dehydrated. Or maybe I'm scared of flying but don't want to admit it.

The flight attendant walking down the aisle pauses next to us and motions for me to put on my seat belt.

For the plane ride or the emotional roller coaster I'm currently on? I can't help thinking.

It's straightforward and simple, I know, but with the flight attendant and Xander watching me—not to mention my sweaty palms—connecting the two straps suddenly becomes rocket science.

"Do you need—" Xander starts to ask, but I whip my hands and the seat belt away.

Him buckling me in like a child would be Most Embarrassing to the point of Humiliating.

I brute force it and almost whoop when I hear the click.

The flight attendant moves on. The plane continues to taxi. Xander and I fall into silence mostly because I can't focus on anything other than the foreign noises around me.

I feel it the second the plane begins to climb. My stomach drops. "Oh my god," I whisper.

How is everyone else so nonchalant? My fingers grip the armrest so hard my knuckles turn white.

I'm staring at the seat in front of me when a tiny sliver of silver pops into view.

Xander's handing me a piece of gum.

I take it and chew, grateful for the distraction. Then I'm grateful when my ears begin popping and the act of swallowing clears them.

"Thanks. But your dad would be mad at you for that," I try to joke.

He doesn't respond. I can't tell what he's thinking, but I'm shocked by the lack of a return joke. My curiosity gets the best of me and I start to say, "So, earlier—"

But he interrupts. "I don't want to talk about it."

Is that because the Pans are the bad apples? No way his dad just came out and said, *Your grandfather took everything from them, but they deserved it*, right?

I can't help the frustration that fills my throat. It was hard enough thinking the universe had simply dealt my mom and me a bad hand, but if there was a reason for our hardships?

That spurs me into saying, "Well, my mom told me that your grandfather took everything from mine."

A pop of color appears on Xander's cheeks. But he stays his unflappable self as he says, "Well, my dad told me the same about yours."

Of course he did.

Only one of our stories can be right, and it can't be theirs.

Except your mom's been lying to you, a tiny voice says in my head, which I squash immediately.

"Aren't you . . ." Upset? Angry? Seething? What exactly am I feeling?

"Am I what, mad? How can I be when I don't know the details? Maybe it was a misunderstanding. Maybe the Everything he took was the name of a pet fish or the title of a book, or maybe it referred to bagel seasoning."

Of course he's joking around. "Well, I came on this trip to get to know my grandfather. Maybe I'll find out more." *Like what your grandfather truly did to mine since the evidence—our lack of "everything"—points that way.*

At this, Xander's brow furrows. "I thought you said you came to pursue your roots."

"Well, isn't that part of it?"

"Then why didn't you tell me that on the track?"

The real question is, Why did I tell him just now?

"You know," he deadpans, "I had to set up a meeting with the program founder to get you in. The least you could do was tell the truth."

I roll my eyes. "Ha ha."

"No, seriously. This might affect your status as a TARPer. Unless you find a way to pay homage to the cardboard dog. You might think he's long gone, but I know exactly where he is."

If that cardboard dog were in front of me right now, I'd pay homage to it, all right. I'd throw it in the trash, where it belongs. "Don't you ever get tired?"

He smirks at me the way I hate, like he's Teflon and everything slides right off him. "Don't you?"

Always the oil to my water. "We just heard from our families that our grandfathers may have done something terrible to each other, and you're making light of it."

"What would you prefer? That we become mortal enemies because of something that might have happened decades ago?"

"Become?" Now it's my turn to laugh.

But for the first time, Xander isn't laughing.

"What?" I ask him, confused. "You're joking, right? Like always? Of course you are. You never take anything seriously." Not our relationship, not our rivalry. "Though you did get surprisingly worked up at the airport. What were you and your family fighting about, anyway?"

"None of your business." All the mirth has drained from his voice and face.

"For once, it feels like my business. It was clearly about our grandfathers, or about me—"

"You know what, Gemma? You've been avoiding me for years—"

"Not that you cared." And was it avoiding when I was loathing and competing?

"Do you really believe that?" He looks surprised, but how could he be?

"I mean, yes, though maybe my hate goggles were getting in the way." When he stares at me blankly, I blather, "You know, the opposite of love goggles—not that we ever . . . never mind."

Xander shakes his head in disbelief. "Wow, hate goggles—great, Gemma, just great. I see you're as charming as ever. Well, your wish is granted. Your *hated* mortal enemy will stay out of your way this entire trip, and after that, we won't have to see each other ever again."

I open my mouth to say something—*Splendid? Thanks? Sorry?*—but he pops his earbuds in, folds his arms across his chest, and closes his eyes. His entire torso is leaning away from me to ensure we don't touch, not a single cell. And we don't speak to or look at each other again for the rest of the flight to New York.

At the airport, I buy my own pack of gum (for way too much), and then we're on our way to Taipei. We're flying EVA Air, and our aircraft is the Hello-freaking-Kitty plane, with Sanrio characters painted on the outside of the aircraft and adorning every seat cover and pillow inside. Xander and I are seated next to each other again, but he doesn't acknowledge me or the ridiculous cuteness around us, which I want to squeal about with someone. But not him.

So I hold everything in as I play Hello Kitty games on the seatback monitor and eat my Gudetama-themed Chinese meals (which are delicious—who knew airplane food was so good?).

When the flight attendants come around to pass out Hello Kitty playing cards, I try extending a single olive branch in honor of him letting me into the program. I hold my deck up to Xander, who's putting his away in his backpack. "Do you want—" I start to say, but he cuts me off.

"I thought you couldn't stand when I try to have fun."

Before I can respond, he rolls over and closes his eyes.

I know he's not sleeping—his breathing is measured and he won't stop fidgeting—but message received.

Xander Pander is not pandering anymore.

Good riddance.

Chapter 10

When Xander and I arrive at the dorm, I'm so consumed by how hot and humid and *bleh* it is and how there isn't any AC in the building that I don't notice the handful of TARPers hanging out in the common area. Not everyone is here yet, but the ones who are yell out to Xander and me.

I only have a profile photo to go off of for each of them, so while I can figure out who's who, it's still so much nicer to see everyone in the flesh (sweaty flesh, I note, and I'm glad I'm not the only one with pit stains). Most of the attendees used their senior photos, but Brett used a picture of himself competing in the curling national championship, and Jax is doing *American Ninja Warrior* in his. Their pictures made me feel both dorky for using a selfie in front of a blank wall and also grateful that I wasn't the only one not using a senior photo, which I didn't purchase because they cost so much it felt like a scam. The one thing missing from their photos, though? A clear view of just how attractive they are, with Jax's muscled arms practically straining against his shirt and Brett's massive height making me need to crane my neck to look at his light brown eyes and lopsided grin. I have to tell myself not to let my gaze linger for too long on either of them.

Xander joins and immediately melts into the group like he's been there all along, doing the half handshake, half hug with the guys, and full hugs with the girls, some of whom might be trying not to let their gazes linger too long on him, ew. I'll let them figure out for themselves just how annoying he is.

Case in point, he suddenly yells "TARP!" then throws a fist in the air. I expect him to shoot me a pointed look, but he doesn't. Guess he meant what he said on the plane. I'm not even worth needling anymore. I should be happy, but I feel invisible, just like he intended. Who could have ever predicted I would miss the old Xander? Joke's on me, universe. You win.

The other TARPers begin chanting, "TARP! TARP! TARP!" and I half expect them to lift Xander in the air, but they don't. The chanting is plenty, though, and a sign that this program won't be too different from high school, especially with them sucking up to Xander as the program founder/leader/whatever.

Because I joined the program late and barely said anything in the chat, I hover at the edge of the group, worried they won't be as welcoming to me. But then one of the girls lying on the couch with her head, back, and shoulders hanging over the armrest points to me. "The painter!"

I don't recognize her, because her head is currently upside down, but once she flips around, I place her. Daphne, who I find both amusing and terrifying. Amusing because she was always joking in the chats, with a tendency to chime in with a perfectly placed "That's what she said," "Your mom," and even a "For me to poop on!" And terrifying because after Felix told the group three times that he wanted to avoid activities involving heights, she messaged everyone that she had a phobia of being close to the ground. A joke, sure, but Felix never brought up his concern again. I admire how she's the opposite of Xander Pander, yet I fear being on the receiving end of her honesty. And I now remember their names with the mnemonic *Felix fears and dodges Daphne.*

Before I can decide if I'm going to dodge or befriend Daphne, Jax surprises me by putting an arm around my shoulders.

"Long flight?" He leans toward my armpits, sniffs, then makes a face. "Phew! Smells like it!"

I jump back in horror. Did he actually just do that? Why did I ever wish for BO, even jokingly, for one second?

A smile spreads across his face. "Just messing with you, obviously. Don't sweat it." He pokes me. "Get it?"

I shrink away from him, still appalled. I like puns but not this one.

Brett rolls his eyes, comes over, and punches Jax on the arm. "If that's how you flirt, you'll need me as a wingman." He pushes an embarrassed Jax to the side and then winks at me.

I have never had this kind of attention before, even Jax's apparently bad flirting. Xander was so young when we dated, still pre-pandering, just the shy, sweet, innocent boy I still think about from time to time. So what's good flirting? Brett? That wink certainly made my stomach flip. Or maybe I'm just hungry.

As if he can read my mind, Brett says, "Go drop off your stuff! It's almost dinnertime. How about we all go grab some niu rou mian?"

Jax groans and nudges Brett's shoulder. "No, man, xiao long bao tonight!"

I let them debate what food we're going to eat while I hurry to find my room. And I try to tamp down the jealousy I feel that they're so comfortable talking in Chinglish. I hope I don't feel totally out of place here.

I leave the door open and survey my new home as I drag in the suitcase Mom borrowed from a coworker. A twin bed with clean blue sheets, a thin blanket, and a pillow is against one wall. A desk, chair, dresser, and bookshelf are along the other.

My own room. For the first time.

I push the curtains open and look out at Taiwan.

I'm here. On the other side of the world. In a huge city. Taipei is all tall buildings and busy streets, the opposite of home. And the most opposite? The Chinese writing everywhere. Obviously I knew to expect it, but it's still different to see it with my own eyes. Thank god for my phone—my new, functioning lifeline of a phone with maps and translation abilities. I clutch it in my palm, so grateful to my mom. I miss her even more than I thought I would.

A knock sounds behind me. I turn to see a petite girl wearing a T-shirt with—what else?—Chinese writing on it.

"Trisha, hey," I say, remembering her photo and the brief introduction a second ago. She had seemed sweet and encouraging in the chats, always the first to chime in on questions like whether or not we should be packing swimsuits (yes, because there are beaches close by), or to offer support, like when Daphne complained that trying to close her suitcase was like trying to squeeze into Spanx four sizes too small. Trisha even offered to share toiletries or anything else anyone might need, which made me immediately want to be her friend.

"Are you tired?" she asks, which, even though I don't know her, feels like a very Trisha thing to say. "How was your flight?"

Terrible. Emotional. Confusing. Xander and I didn't speak a word on the long cab ride over either. "Good, thanks. A little tired, but also hungry."

She gestures toward my suitcase. "Need any help?"

"No, but thanks." Unpacking will come later.

Daphne pops her head in. "The boys are about to eat the couch. Ready?"

I nod and quickly leave so she doesn't have a chance to comment on my suitcase that has BOB HERMAN written across it in Sharpie.

When we join the rest of the group, Brett says, "Okay, we took a vote. Right now, niu rou mian and xiao long bao are tied. What do the two newcomers want?"

He looks at me first, and I panic. I don't know what those are, and I don't want to ask. "I'm fine with anything."

Xander grins. "It's gotta be niu rou mian for me. Bring on the spicy!"

"You know, I wasn't sure what to make of the TARP founder and leader, but we're certainly getting off on the right foot," Brett says as he flings an arm over Xander's shoulder.

Of course Xander Pander said the right thing (and knows what niu rou mian is).

And we're off.

Niu rou mian is beef noodle soup. We trek on foot to a hole-in-the-wall that only makes that single dish, and we put two tables together for the seven of us—me, Xander, Brett, Jax, Trisha, Daphne, and fearful Felix, who seems to be succeeding in dodging Daphne by showing up right before we left and sitting on the opposite end of the table from her now.

Surprisingly, as I'm about to sit, Brett swoops in to pull the chair out for me. I've never had anyone do that, and after experiencing it, I don't get it. The seat of the chair pushes into my legs, basically forcing me to sit—or fall—and I'm left with a sizable gap between my body and the table.

"Um, thanks."

"Anytime." He winks at me again, then bumps Jax aside to take the seat next to me.

"So how'd you know about this place?" I ask him.

"It's one of the most famous niu rou mian spots in the world. My brothers and I used to come here every other day when we were visiting family growing up."

No one takes our order—they just bring each of us a giant bowl. I close my eyes and inhale. My first meal in Taiwan. It smells hearty and warm, like how I imagined my grandparents' or great-grandparents' kitchens to be.

With the steaming bowl in front of me, sweat drips down my face. There's no AC, just four plastic fans in the corners, and not even ice water to drink.

No one hesitates as they simultaneously fill their Asian spoons with soup while scooping up noodles with chopsticks. I grew up with both utensils—mostly because they're better for the cheap ramen that is a staple in the Sun house—and I take a moment to appreciate that they're here and everyone is using them the same way. It's such a small, silly thing but significant to me.

I scooch closer to the nearest fan, sighing a little when my right side receives the blast full-on. And I tell myself it's only about the fan and not because I'm now slightly closer to Brett.

Then, finally, I dive in.

The spicy, aromatic soup pairs perfectly with the chewy, thick, made-from-scratch noodles. The bits of scallion and pickled vegetables add just the necessary pop. And the beef is so tender it falls apart with the slightest touch. But the surprise favorite? Cilantro. Mom and I don't cook many dishes with it, and I've heard people hating on it or saying it tastes like soap, but I can't get enough of the fresh, clean flavor, so much so that I add a few extra spoonfuls from a plastic container on the table.

The group's content slurping is first interrupted by Brett asking, "So what's everyone most excited about?"

"The fact that the chaperones don't give a shit what we do," Daphne answers, and everyone laughs.

Oh right. The chaperones aren't even here. When Trisha sees me looking around, she tells me, "They're college students here for the free trip. They're out on their own right now."

This isn't at all the trip I thought it'd be. It's better.

Brett's eyes meet mine, and it takes me a second to realize he wants me to answer his question.

"Um, everything?" That makes me sound nerdy and sad, but he smiles as if it's endearing.

"First time?"

I nod. So many firsts—first time in Taiwan, first time eating niu rou mian, first time flirting, first treasure hunt.

Jax glances at me, then Xander, who chose the seat as far away from me as possible, just like Felix with Daphne. "Why does it look like you're trying to avoid each other? Aren't you both from Blue Hill?"

"Ooh, nepotism," Daphne taunts.

That idea is so ridiculous I burst out laughing. The others stare, confused.

"Yeah, no, none of that here," I say. But then I run out of words. How am I supposed to explain without telling them we can't stand each other and I'm only here because of a combination of begging and someone dropping out?

"She earned her spot," Xander says, and I'm momentarily relieved that he's backing me up. "Nobody works harder and has less fun than her."

His delivery is deadpan, of course, and no one can tell if it's a joke or not. Then Xander smiles, easing the tension, but I know he meant every word. Maybe the rest of them know too, because Daphne says, "Definitely not nepotism, then."

I'm glad the record was set straight, but also, he couldn't have found a better way?

"Anyone think this could use a pop of heat?" Jax asks, and I'm so grateful for the change in topic I could hug him. He reaches for the jar of chili peppers on the table, and as soon as he scoops a spoonful into his bowl, Brett grabs the jar from him and scoops two. Then Jax goes for three.

Daphne raises an eyebrow. "I could save you some glasses of milk by getting a ruler so you can just whip them out and measure."

At Daphne's comment, Felix chokes on his soup, the first sound he's made since we sat down. Trisha pats his back sympathetically from the adjacent chair.

After he recovers, his face is red from both the choking and the embarrassment, so I try to divert attention by asking him and Trisha, "Have you had beef noodle soup before?"

Felix shakes his head. He doesn't seem like he wants to be here. I can't decide if I should leave him alone or try harder.

Trisha says, "Yes, but only in New York, which was good, but holy moly this is a whole other level."

"Have you been to Taiwan before?" I ask them.

"A few times," Trisha says. "But we were always here seeing family, so it was different, you know? This'll be my first time with the freedom to explore."

Felix just shakes his head again. I'm disappointed not to get more out of him, but I'm relieved by his answer. I'm not alone. It's a sign that my self-consciousness is in my head and I should be focusing on my journey.

New discovery: I love niu rou mian. Three new Mandarin words and a new favorite dish. Not bad for my first hour in Taipei.

Chapter 11

I'm so exhausted from not sleeping much on the plane that after niu rou mian, I return to my dorm and fall asleep for an embarrassingly long time. Despite the heat, I sleep like a rock, no dreams, completely out, and confused about where I am when I wake. The good news is that my jet lag moving forward should be manageable. The bad news is that I slept through the first program event of visiting Longshan Temple.

But clearly the chaperones don't care, because no one came to get me. Or maybe they tried and even someone shouting in my ear wouldn't have woken me up.

Even though this is a good opportunity to complete the next step on the inheritance hunt, I feel an unexpected pang. I knew going in that I would miss out on activities and getting to know the others, but I didn't expect how much I would want to be a part of TARP once I got here.

But there's no time for that. The clock is ticking and Amherst is waiting. Which is also why, I tell myself, I don't have time to call my mom and instead, I send her one quick text to answer her seven.

Then I focus on the next part of the hunt: going to my grandfather's apartment. Before I left the States, I sent an email to the
landlord in both Mandarin and English (thanks, translation app!),
letting her know the dates I would be in Taipei. Though I still
haven't heard back, I feel better that I tried. At the very least, I hope
she read it so less conversation will be needed when I arrive.

To save money, I take the subway and eat a granola bar from
home on the way. With the help of my phone and the ability to
match up Chinese characters by sight, I arrive twenty minutes later
at a small, slightly run-down apartment building.

I take a moment out front. This is where my grandfather lived.
But I don't feel anything, no threads connecting me to him.

For you to know me . . . The sun is at the end . . .

Those words carry me forward, and I press the landlord's buzzer,
crossing my fingers that she's home. And that she knows English.

"Wei?" says a voice through the speaker.

I quickly type into my translation app, making it tell her who I
am and what I'm doing here. The app's pronunciation doesn't seem
great, but it's better than mine.

"Qing jin," the voice says.

A buzzing noise sounds from the now unlocked front door. I
enter and find her apartment on the first floor, the door already
open, a woman in her seventies with white permed hair waiting
for me.

"Ni hao."

I smile and repeat her greeting in a bad accent.

Sensing we need reinforcements, she calls into the next room.
"Mei mei! Keyi lai bang wo men ma?"

A middle-aged woman enters and smiles. "Hi! I'm Mira, her daughter. Can we help you?"

Thank god. I try not to let the relief show too visibly on my face. "Yes. My grandfather, Yong Ping Sun, used to live here, and his will said—" I don't know how to finish. I don't even know if this hunt is real, and even if it is, they don't care about that.

"Are you here to collect his things?"

I nod.

"Everything's packed up in the basement. I'm sorry for your loss."

As Mira leads me down the stone steps, I ask her, "What was my grandfather like?"

"Your gong gong was a very nice man. He kept to himself."

I guess those last four words said everything—she didn't know him much better than I did.

I latch on to what she called him, *gong gong,* and wonder what it would've felt like to have met him and called him that. Or would I have called him Grandpa? Or some Chinglish mix?

Mira brings me to a corner of the basement where Gong Gong's belongings are piled. There's some furniture I won't be able to take, and, reading my mind, Mira says, "Keep what you like, and anything you leave we'll donate for you."

"Thank you."

As soon as she leaves, I collapse into the nearest chair, which is so worn it leans to one side and almost spills me out of it.

I didn't realize it until she left, but I'd been expecting more from her. Some stories, a warm welcome—not that it wasn't warm, but I thought it would last more than two minutes.

And it's overwhelming down here. There's just so much *stuff*, and I'm alone and I don't know what I'm looking for.

I was a fool to come here chasing treasure. Maybe my mom was right—there's nothing but junk here. Maybe this is all a joke. For all I know, my grandfather could have been a prankster and wanted me to fly around the world to clean out his clutter.

But I'm here and the clock's ticking, so, like always, I shove my emotions aside, take a deep breath, and dive in, robotically sorting belongings into donate, trash, and keep piles.

Not having fun has its benefits, I think as I tear through.

Several boxes in, I gasp. Out loud.

Treasure.

Not *the* treasure, but treasure to me.

Paint supplies. My whole life, we couldn't afford brushes, paint, or canvases, and now, suddenly, here they are, right in front of my face for me to take.

For the first time, I feel a tiny thread tying me to my grandfather. Maybe I got my love of art from him. Simultaneously, I feel a regretful pang in my stomach that we didn't get to meet, talk about art, share paint supplies.

Both the thread and the longing grow stronger when I find his paintings. They're classic and stunning—all flowing strokes that demonstrate his skill, confidence, and talent. Most are landscapes painted in the traditional Chinese style, with rolling mountains, textured bamboo, or bodies of water. Some feature horses, cranes, koi. Others highlight temples or pagodas—old buildings with stories and secrets.

I clutch a handful of brushes to my chest while trying to get the bitter taste out of my mouth. So many things he could have taught me.

That thought spurs me to search harder and faster.

Fifteen minutes later, I cry out in joy.

There, on the lower right-hand corner of a silver photo frame, is a blue hand-painted 3. The picture inside shows my grandfather with my mom as a child—maybe five or six years old? And side by side, it's easy to see their physical similarities.

I take the frame apart eagerly. Between the backing and the photo, a folded slip of paper falls out. I unfold it gingerly, almost reverently. At the top, in melodic handwriting so consistent it looks like its own font, is the following riddle:

> If you give λ a stick and a rock—
> (when drawing, simplify to a dash and a blot)—
> thus sets homo sapiens apart from the flock,
> and helps λ create me that is hot.
> What am I?

What is that caret thing?

Is this actually a puzzle or just the scribblings of an eccentric man?

I take a closer look at the photo. Nothing appears to be related to the riddle. My mom has a backpack on, maybe on her way to or back from school. The focus is a bit blurry, and the edges are worn from age. Gong Gong isn't smiling, but he's not frowning either. Just . . . stoic.

I dive back into the cardboard box that the frame had been packed in, but there isn't anything of significance inside. Just a smattering of clothes, a small desk lamp, and some old bills. The outside of the box has writing on it in Sharpie, but it's in Chinese.

That's it!

The TARPers speak in Chinglish. So it wouldn't be unreasonable to think that Gong Gong might too, having spent part of his life in the US and part in Taiwan and China. Meaning, the caret is a Chinese word.

I pull out my app and translate 人 to *person* or *people*, which makes sense. The riddle mentions homo sapiens. I reread it with this new knowledge in mind.

> If you give 人 a stick and a rock—
> (when drawing, simplify to a dash and a blot)—
> thus sets homo sapiens apart from the flock,
> and helps 人 create me that is hot.
> What am I?

People plus a stick and a rock make me think of fire, and that's certainly hot. The ability to make it also sets homo sapiens apart from other animals, but what is that second line about simplifying to a dash and a blot? Does it even matter if I think the answer is fire?

My eyes focus on the 人, and on a whim, I look up *fire* in the translation app.

It hits me like hurled mashed potatoes.

The Chinese character for *fire* is 火. Add a dash and a blot to 人 and you get 火. I can't help smiling looking at that character. Now all I see is a stick person holding a stick and a rock to make fire. A quick internet search tells me that 火 is a pictograph of what fire looks like and has nothing to do with the 人 character, but I like my grandfather's version just as much, if not better.

So what's the point of all this?

火. Fire.

Oh my god. The rest of the page beneath the riddle is blank. I need fire. Or any heat source.

I almost trip over myself as I rush to drag a chair beneath the light bulb hanging down from the ceiling. It takes some trial and error of piling cushions and finding the right-size book to stabilize a wobbly chair leg, but I'm finally able to reach the bulb. I try to be patient as I hold the paper up to it.

Very slowly, text begins to appear.

First, the answer, 火, on its own line. Then, another riddle below.

> 火
> goes with water, wood, metal, and <u>earth also</u>.
> Find the wall crack, then follow down and <u>below</u>, so
> that you can locate the item that you now seek,
> in the southwest corner of the room with a peak.

I'm not sure why *earth*, *also*, and *below* are underlined. I start there, and since I can't find any patterns in English, I try translating each word into Chinese.

土也下

That doesn't tell me anything. But I write them next to the puzzle anyway.

I reread the riddle. The last three lines have to be referring to Gong Gong's apartment.

Feeling a little ridiculous, I return to Mira and her mom's place.

"All finished?" Mira asks when she answers the door.

"Actually, um . . ." How do I explain why I need to see his apartment? "So my grandfather . . . likes puzzles and riddles and stuff. And in his will—no, that's too far back. Um . . ."

I look down at the paper in my hand, trying to find the right introduction to it, and she follows my gaze.

"Do you need help with the Mandarin?" she asks, pointing to my handwritten Chinese characters for *earth*, *also*, and *below*. "That's di xia."

"What?" My translation app gave me three different pronunciations for each of those words, and *di* wasn't one of them.

"Di xia," she repeats, pointing to first 土也 and then 下.

"Is that one character?" I ask, covering up the 下 and leaving only 土也 showing.

"It can be. And that's the only way it makes sense with the *xia*."

Of course. *Earth also* was underlined together, a signal to combine the two to form a different word.

"What does *di* mean?" I ask.

"Ground. Or floor."

Oh my god. I have to get in there. "Is it possible to see my grandfather's apartment?"

Mira hesitates. "Why? It's empty."

Do I keep explaining and tell her that I think my grandfather hid something under his floor? Or—

"I guess I don't see why not," she says, likely realizing there's nothing in there to steal.

I follow her to the top floor and exhale when she leaves me alone inside.

The apartment's so small. Would someone who lived here have treasure to leave behind? Or did he have plenty because he lived like this?

I try to picture some of the furniture from the basement throughout this space. I try to visualize him in here, going about his day, but I can barely conjure up an image of his face. I hold up the photo of him and my mom, but it's too old and blurry to help.

I don't know why, but I thought I might feel closer to him coming in here. Maybe even closer to myself. But this is just an empty apartment.

Focused on the mission now, I examine every room, which doesn't take long. And the last room I check, the bedroom, has a sloped ceiling.

Room with a peak.

I quickly use my phone to locate the southwest corner.

Find the wall crack, then follow down and below.

My anxiety spikes when I'm standing in the corner looking at perfectly smooth white walls completely absent of any abnormalities. They must have repainted and fixed the place up. The wall crack—if it ever existed—is long gone.

Frustration runs through me, but I force myself to push past it. My eyes dip down from the wall, and I focus on the floor instead. The wooden planks appear to be flush with each other and the walls; no obvious secret hiding places.

With a sigh, I kneel to inspect closer. Seeing nothing, I feel the edges of the planks with my fingertips and try to ignore the chalky debris I'm picking up.

As the seconds tick by, I feel more and more ridiculous. Whose bright idea was this again? Oh right, mine. I am the sole one responsible, having begged (*cringe*) both Xander and my mom.

I plop backward onto my butt, suddenly exhausted. The force causes the plank beneath me to wobble.

Could it be? I turn and push on the wood in the same spot. The plank shifts again.

My nerve endings buzzing, I press my fist along the length of it. The closer I get to the edge, the more it wiggles. When I reach where it meets the wall, it's loose. This has to be it.

Unfortunately, I'm not sure how to pry the plank up. It doesn't move enough for me to slip my fingers in, and I can only push down on it, which doesn't help.

I need a tool of some sort. Something to wedge in there just enough that I can start lifting it with my fingers.

Praying that Mira is in her apartment and won't see me, I leave Gong Gong's door open and run back down to the basement. Quickly, I tear through his things, pocketing anything that might work. I've squirreled away a pen, a pair of scissors, and a butter knife when I reopen the box of art supplies. And it's almost like a spotlight from heaven is shining down on the paint spatula. I grab it and hustle back upstairs two steps at a time.

The spatula is about twelve inches long with a wooden handle, and the otherwise smooth blade has some scratches on it. I try it in a few different spots wedged between the wall and the plank—carefully, not wanting to break it. And I know when I've found the right angle because the wall scrapes the spatula along the small grooves that are already there. This was exactly what my grandfather used to lift this plank!

Everything swirls together in my mind just like this spatula swirled paint for my grandfather. How many times did he sit in this exact spot using this exact spatula to do what I'm doing now?

I slip my fingers beneath the wood, bracing for splinters or dust, but I don't find either. As I search blindly, I feel like I'm in a real-life adventure game. I had to find the spatula, put it in my inventory, and use it on this plank.

My fingers hit something soft. Dear god, please don't let it be a dead animal.

I grab a corner and pull.

When I see what it is, I start laughing. It's a dead animal. Sort of. It's a faux-leather notebook.

Is it a diary?

I open it.

On the first page is a numbered list. Next to number one, the words *Wooden box* are written. Next to number two, *Will*.

"Oh my god," I breathe when I realize what this is.

It's an index of all the puzzles.

Tears fill my eyes. "I was right," I whisper. Even though I pulled strings to make it here, even though I was so confident when I talked to my mom, I didn't fully believe the inheritance hunt existed until this moment.

A tear drips onto the index. I soak it up with the corner of my shirt.

It's real. The inheritance hunt is *real*.

And my life is about to change.

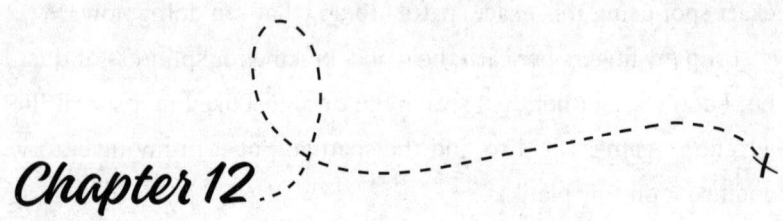

Chapter 12

Now that I know for certain the hunt is real, I realize the thread tying me to my grandfather was there the moment I saw the puzzle in his will. My weird way of looking for patterns, being on a different wavelength that my mother doesn't understand? I get it from Gong Gong. He saw the same underlying twists and turns and connections I do. *And* he was an artist.

The regretful pang in my stomach grows. I will never meet him, this man who shares parts of me no one else does. Sitting on the floor of his apartment, I grip the notebook tighter in my hands as if that will help me better hold on to this hunt, this last piece I have of him.

He must have also been type A like me, making an index for the hunt.

The index!

When I realize that the index is for the *entire* journey, the curiosity grows too overwhelming and I skip to the last item on the list. I'm not sure if I'm hoping to bypass everything in between or if I'm just looking for a hint of what's to come, but I can't help myself.

X Marks the Spot

That's all it says. Next to the number *13*.

I immediately take a pic, edit the photo to circle those four words, and text it to Val. She's asleep—it's after midnight for her right now—but she'll see it in the morning and appropriately freak out.

Unfortunately, there's not much I can do with that information. It's like reading the last page of a book. But thirteen puzzles, that seems doable, right? Even with the ticking clock of this TARP trip? I mean, I already have three in the proverbial bag.

My eyes find *3. Framed Photo* in the index and dip right below it.

But instead of finding number four, there are *a* and *b* parts listed for number three. Next to *a* are the words *Answer to first riddle*, followed by a colon and blank space. Next to *b* are the words *First line of second riddle*, again followed by a colon and blank space.

I don't know the purpose of these, but I dutifully fill in the blanks.

3. Framed photo
   a. Answer to first riddle: 火 / **fire**
   b. First line of second riddle: 火 **goes with water, wood, metal, and <u>earth also</u>.**

Leaning into my type A–ness—*A-ness* because I'm so *anal*—I use the edge of the spatula to neatly cross out the completed items in the index.

Then I look past the *k* to the next line.

5. Journal

Where's number four? I glance down the rest of the list, which is in order, one through thirteen, with only the number four missing. Unsure what it means, I put it aside for now and focus on the word *journal*. I flip through it, noticing that the rest of the pages are blank. Maybe this is where I'm meant to take notes, work out puzzles, and overall document my adventure. I run my fingers over the unlined paper. Maybe even to sketch.

As I reach the end of the journal, it falls open to reveal two pieces of folded paper tucked inside the back cover.

Of course. Since the journal is the next index entry, the next puzzle is in it.

Oddly, the outermost piece of paper has a crossed-out number 4 written on it in handwriting I now recognize. Beside it is the number *5*.

This explains the missing four in the index, but why?

I unfold the pages. On the first, there are two paragraphs. The top one is a riddle:

> *Listen, this won't be an easy journey for you.*
> *Sometimes it's as clear as—the sun goes with the moon.*
> *Other times, it's a mountain climb for the next clue.*
> *Add up the parts, line by line, and you'll be there soon.*

More underlined words, just like in the previous puzzle.

The second paragraph says:

If that isn't clear enough, try the following:

25, 1, 14, 7   13, 9, 14, 7   19, 8, 1, 14

That . . . is not clear enough either.

On the next page, separate from the puzzles, is an instruction:

To know my heart, you must go to the start.
Look for the Sun when you get to No. 1.

Below that, there are more seemingly random numbers.

Even though I have enough experience with puzzles to know not to do this, I immediately feel discouraged and want to give up. It's just that, after having such elation—*The hunt is real! I feel closer to Gong Gong!*—feeling overwhelmed by this next step sends me crashing down from very high up.

I try to remind myself that I'm not going to solve the puzzles within one second of finding them, especially not when I'm hungry and jet-lagged, and need to focus on a more immediate task: figuring out what to do with Gong Gong's stuff.

When I return to the basement, none of his possessions seem like trash anymore. What if everything is part of the hunt? Those newspaper clippings certainly looked like garbage. What if there's something hidden inside the chair cushion and I don't know to look until puzzle twelve, after it's been donated? But I also can't take it all back with me. And a quick scan of the index doesn't help me narrow down what I might need.

I end up taking what I can, which includes the boxes filled with art supplies, books, valuables like his wedding ring, and of course his paintings. I want to display them, study them, imitate them. Maybe if my paintbrush travels the same roads as his, I'll understand a new layer of him. I also take some practical items, like an electric fan for my dorm room and a map of Taipei. My gut tells me the map might also be a part of the hunt because it's hand drawn, with various locations illustrated. Maybe those are his favorite places? Unfortunately, most of the pictures don't make sense, like an arch of black-and-white birds—is that a landmark?

I leave the clothes, kitchenware, cleaning supplies, and furniture. But for good measure, I check them thoroughly for lumps, openings, restitched seams, or alterations. And the last step: I take photographs from several angles just in case.

Feeling pretty good about my decisions, I go to thank Mira, who calls a cab for me.

It ends up costing more than I planned for, but such was needed to transport everything back.

By the time I return to the dorms, it's late afternoon and my stomach is growling.

I'm used to budgeting my meals, but I've never done it in another country before. After shoving all of Gong Gong's things into corners, the closet, and under my bed and desk, I venture out in search of a late cheap lunch.

I pick an arbitrary direction and walk a few blocks, choosing to explore instead of using my phone. And I'm so glad I did because I stumble upon a guy in a chef hat cooking on a grill that juts slightly into the road. There's a sign above that I can't read, a Chinese-only menu written on the wall, and only two tables inside. The menu has about ten things total, and everything is listed as costing between 25 and 150 Taiwan dollars (TWD). Which—I quickly do the math in my head—is all less than five US dollars? How is that possible?

I'm not sure if I can order off the menu, but it doesn't matter because he's currently making only one thing, and it smells heavenly. I point, and he holds up a two and then a five. Twenty-five TWD. Less than a dollar US. I happily pull out two ten-dollar coins and a five-dollar coin. He uses tongs to slip one of the thick circles with green flecks into a paper bag.

I nod in thanks, trying to grab the steaming-hot paper in a spot where it won't burn my fingers. A scallion pancake, it seems, but not cut into triangles like in the US and not as thin. No soy sauce either.

After blowing on it a few times, I rip a tiny piece off with my fingers and pop it into my mouth.

Salty, crispy, flaky deliciousness. It doesn't need sauce or anything else. If it weren't so hot, I'd gobble the entire thing up in a second. How does he get this so perfectly crunchy on the outside yet chewy on the inside?

My phone buzzes with a text. I hope it's Val (to whom I also sent the new puzzles while I was in the cab), though I know it can't be because of the time.

It's just as good. Trisha is asking where I am and whether I want to go to Taipei 101 with other TARPers.

A tiny part of me feels guilty for not focusing on the treasure hunt, but the other part—the one noshing on my new favorite street snack—can't wait to see more of Taipei with my new friend.

Absolutely! I text back.

1. ~~Wooden box~~
2. ~~Will~~
3. ~~Framed photo~~
   a. Answer to first riddle: 火 / **fire**
   b. First line of second riddle: 火 **goes with water, wood, metal, and <u>earth also</u>.**
5. Journal
Destination:
6. Metal Box
   a. Need A:
   b. Destination:
7. Wall
8. House gate
Instructions, first line:
9. Address
Number:
10. Poem
11. Beginning
12. Watch
13. X Marks the Spot

Chapter 13

Taipei 101 is the 100—or 101—emoji brought to life. Mostly because I've never been in a building higher than ten floors, and this has *a hundred and one*. It was the world's tallest building from 2004 until 2010. I love everything about it: the modern luxurious feel, the fact that it vaguely looks like Chinese takeout boxes stacked on top of each other (architecture is a form of art, after all), the incredibly fast elevators that make me feel weightless, the heavily air-conditioned interior, and the adorable and clever logo that looks like old Chinese coins.

Some of the other TARPers call it *yi ling yi*, meaning *101*, and I tuck those new words away.

I guess the only less-than-ideal part is that the public space is just a six-story shopping mall, but I can't think of what might be better—a museum? The rest is office space, which, how cool would that be, to get to work here?

I'm in the elevator with the same TARPers from niu rou mian, minus Felix and plus one of the chaperones, Belinda. I worry Felix will be missing out until Belinda presses the button for floor 89. With his fear of heights—not to mention the presence of Daphne—maybe he made the right choice passing on this one.

As Belinda reaches into her purse to retrieve the group tickets the program prepaid for, she says, "Of course the observatory deck is on floors eighty-eight and eighty-nine."

I feel left out but am too embarrassed to ask. Then I remember—eight is a lucky number. Where have I heard that before? A TV show? Online somewhere?

"My mom works for Verizon and got a cell number with six eights in it," Daphne says. "She tried for eight eights, but it's good she couldn't get it or else she'd be getting calls all the time from people looking for an accident lawyer or cash for their car."

"At least she didn't get four eights!" Belinda says, and again, I don't know what she's talking about.

The missing number four in Gong Gong's puzzle pops into my head just as my eyes roam over the buttons on the elevator panel, immediately noticing what doesn't fit the pattern: there's floor 43 followed by 45, no 44.

I point to it, and Belinda nods as if sharing the joke with me. "Unlucky number forty-four. Surprised they have floor four, though."

A quick search on my phone tells me that the Mandarin word for *four* sounds like the word for *death* and is thus unlucky, feared, and avoided. Tetraphobia.

Was Gong Gong superstitious? Or did he skip the four because it's just what you do? Or is it somehow a joke, like how Daphne and Belinda talked about it just now?

I can't find any additional information on forty-four specifically, other than that it sounds like *die-die*. My first thought is that if you add up the digits, you get eight, which is lucky. But maybe my mind is the only one that works that way.

"Is it Lover's Day already?" Jax says from beside me as he points to an ad on the elevator wall covered in hearts, delicious food pics, and a sample image of how the mall will be decorated for the holiday. "It's so hard to keep track. I remember it's the seventh day of the seventh month, but who knows what that translates to on the lunar calendar, you know?"

"Lover's Day?" I pipe up, wanting to know more. How come I've never heard of it?

Jax puts a hand on my shoulder. "I'd be happy to introduce you to your first Qixi."

I'm so surprised I forget all words for a second. Is he implying what I think he is? Or am I on a different wavelength again? Luckily, Daphne responds and all I have to do is give Jax a small smile.

"It's in, like, a few weeks, yeah. Not that it means anything. It's like Valentine's Day in the US, all commercialized. Everyone forgets it's a celebration of Niulang and Zhinu. Do people even go out and look at the stars anymore? Or even talk about the folktale? It's our version of *Romeo and Juliet*, yet no one seems to tell it anymore, at least not in the States."

I don't respond because I'm just proof of not knowing any of it. Though I make a mental note to remedy that—the stars part alone has me intrigued.

On the eighty-ninth floor with 360-degree floor-to-ceiling windows, the view takes my breath away. It's so dense. It's a *city*. Big and tall and bustling. And from up here, beyond the packed buildings, I can also see winding rivers, mountains, and the ocean in the distance. It seems like there's some of everything on this tiny island that's anything but tiny from this vantage point.

Up until now, my world has been so small. The actual world is so huge, and I've barely seen any of it. At least I'm finally taking a first step.

I glance around to see if anyone else's mind is as blown as mine, but I just spot the backs of the other TARPers (minus Trisha) grouped around Xander. Why do people gravitate toward him? I liked him better when he was the shy nerd who cared more about rebus puzzles than what others thought of him, but apparently I'm the only one.

Trisha appears from around the corner and gestures for me to follow her to a section in the middle where, I'm not kidding, it looks like there's a massive golden ball below us suspended at four points. I read about it on the surrounding signs, learning that it's a mass damper, a.k.a. a four-million-dollar steel pendulum that essentially sways to offset movements in the building caused by strong winds.

The damper seems like such a simple answer, but a genius one that, according to the signs, can withstand typhoon winds and earthquake tremors.

Sometimes the simplest answers are the best ones. I make a mental note to remember that as I continue the inheritance hunt.

A few minutes later, Trisha and I return to the perimeter of the observatory deck to stare out at the city. I feel weirdly comfortable with her already, like we don't always need words.

I suddenly feel a bulky arm draping around my shoulders. I

tense instinctively. When I realize it's Brett, my muscles tense even more, not because I don't want his arm there but because this is unfamiliar territory. I don't have guy friends, and Xander—I mean, Alex—and I had been all longing glances, brushing fingertips, and *oh my gosh, we're sipping out of the same cup, like we're almost but not at all kissing.*

Brett's arm feels warm, comforting, and heavy, and I suddenly understand the appeal of a weighted blanket. But this is a friendly arm, not a flirty arm, right? How do I tell the difference?

"If you think this view is nice, just wait," he says mischievously.

"For . . . ?" I ask, my voice as stiff as my posture.

He waggles his eyebrows as he bites his bottom lip—which feels intimate, like he's giving me permission to look. Then he dips his head down closer to my ear, his nose grazing the side of my head as he whispers, "It's a surprise."

The sudden and unexpected contact startles me, and he interprets my muscle contraction as something else. "Are you cold?"

I'm wearing a tank top and shorts because of the heat, but the AC is cranked up in here, explaining why he would think that. But my insides feel warm from his proximity.

"May I?" he asks.

I have no idea what he means, but my body is sure that the only logical answer to his question is yes, so I nod.

He shifts his six-foot-something self from beside me to behind, then wraps both arms around my collarbone. His chin rests gently on the top of my head. I've never felt so cocooned. I give in to my urges and lean into him, my back pressing into his abs and my hips resting on his thighs.

This is romantic. Right? It has to be.

And then it happens.

The sunset. Gorgeous, vivid pinks and oranges streak the sky and clouds. The city is aglow, with mountains turning into erupting volcanoes and buildings twinkling like magic.

My breath catches in my throat.

Brett's arms tighten around me, and I feel like I'm melting from the inside out despite the AC. Trisha shoots me a knowing smile, then slips away.

Definitely romantic. Just like the sunset before me.

As darkness seeps in, the city gradually illuminates with lights dotting the expanse as far as the eye can see. They're so distant and small from up here that the pops of brightness almost look like fireflies—static ones that don't move because they like exactly where they are.

Maybe I relate to that right now. I feel like I'm exactly where I'm supposed to be.

10:58 PM Taiwan Standard Time

Val

I HATE TIME DIFFERENCES SO MUCH

I have no clue about that riddle

But I'm like pretty sure that code is a simple alphabet one where 1 = A and 26 = Z, which would give . . .

Yangmingshan

Which is a National Park near Taipei

Gemma

You're a genius!

Ahh you're still up! Video chat?

<Val is trying to video call you . . . >

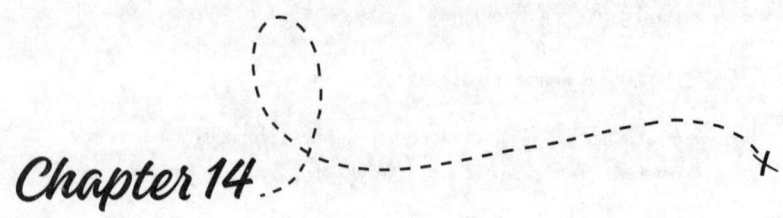

Chapter 14

An alphabet code, of course. Just like the damper, sometimes it's the simplest answer.

Seeing Val's face and hearing her voice are exactly what I need. But for some reason, I don't tell her about Brett. Partly because I know she'll make a big deal about it (and I'm scared I'm already reading too much into nothing), and partly because, well, I haven't let anyone in romantically since Xander, the biggest mistake of my life.

After the call, I look up *Yangmingshan*, learning that it translates to *Bright Sun Mountain*. And it's enormous. Just like all of Taiwan, the park seems to have a little bit of everything—hot springs, cherry blossoms, hiking trails, even a dormant volcano. Though I want to see all of it, I don't have enough time, so I focus on the second part of the puzzle, hoping it will narrow down my destination.

To know my heart, you must go to the start.
Look for the Sun when you get to No. 1.

The first thing that jumps out at me is the capitalized *Sun*. Is it referring to the *Bright Sun* in the mountain's name? Or does *the Sun* mean *treasure* here?

I focus on the *No. 1* next. Interesting that it's *No.* instead of a hashtag or *number*. Could it even be a *no* with a period, or *know*, like in the will?

I try searching for *Yangmingshan No. 1*.

And I jump in my seat when the results appear.

The top result: *Yangmingshan No. 1 Public Cemetery*.

And immediately the rest of the instructions make sense, everything going together as clearly as the sun and the moon.

To know my heart, you must go to the start.
Look for the Sun when you get to No. 1.

I have to look for a grave. A Sun grave. Is this where Gong Gong is? But the clue says to go to the start. Gong Gong's grave feels like the end.

After pondering for another moment, I realize I'm likely looking for the grave of a relative. Maybe his parents? Because to know Gong Gong, I have to go to the start of his story, which begins with them.

Gong Gong's promise is already starting to come true even though I'm not at the end of the adventure yet. I'm going to find the Sun tomorrow.

Instead of going with TARP to the trendy Ximending neighborhood with shopping, street dances, and pop-star meet and greets, I trek to Yangmingshan. When I arrive at No. 1 Cemetery, I show the first employee I see the string of numbers below *Look for the Sun when you get to No. 1*.

And as I suspected, they're a way of locating the grave. I'm directed to the right building, where another employee awaits.

"English?" I ask, but he responds in Mandarin.

I show him my paper, and he nods. From a row of long, thin keys with rounded ends, he selects one and hands it to me. I take it and stare, not sure what to do next, but then he gestures for me to follow as he leads me through the rows and columns of what appear to be closed cabinets.

It's a columbarium, I realize. A place where urns of cremated bodies are stored.

After enough zigs and zags for me to lose orientation, the employee gestures to a specific niche in front of us at chin level. Then he bows slightly. I bow back, hoping that's enough to show my thanks for his help. A whole conversation managed without a single word, amazing.

As soon as he leaves, I use the key to open the niche. Inside, the fairly roomy space is divided into two parts. The majority of it contains two plain gray urns with no carvings, decorations, or labels. To the side is a smaller space—perhaps for personal items or mementos?

My fingers reach for these immediately, coming away first with a folder. Inside, in the right pocket, is a piece of paper.

All in Chinese. Of course. A strike to my Achilles' heel.

I retrieve my app and begin the painstaking process of holding the phone steady until it translates each section.

I slowly read what turns out to be an obituary. The translation isn't perfect, but it's enough to give me a sense of my great-grandmother and great-grandfather, whose ashes are before me. In 1949, during the Chinese Communist Revolution, my great-grandfather had a seat on a plane out of Qingdao because he worked for the Kuomintang, but instead of taking it, he gave it up so that his son could leave. Gong Gong went to Taiwan alone and never saw his parents again—they died in China before the borders reopened. Gong Gong eventually returned when he was much older to visit their graves, and he brought them back here to Yangming-shan. There isn't much else about their lives, likely because Gong Gong didn't know any of it.

My hands are shaking, and it's not just because I've had to hold my phone steady. How could Gong Gong go through something like this and come out the other side? He would've been a teenager at that time, younger than I am now. I panicked about going to a foreign country for two weeks on my own with modern technology, a stipend, a way home, and a preplanned summer program, while Gong Gong came here alone *for the rest of his life*. He lost everything, not just money and belongings, but his entire family.

Being away from my mom has been hard enough—I can't imagine having to say goodbye forever. I often feel like my family isn't big enough, and Gong Gong had no one.

My heart is heavy as my eyes dip below the obituary to a sticky note at the bottom.

Pay respects by appreciating the other sun.

Other sun . . . another relative here? Except *sun* isn't capitalized like in the other clue. So if it's not a person, the other sun must be referring to *the* sun, the one and only. Right?

I return the obituary to the folder. Then I reach back into the mementos space to retrieve the last item: a ten-inch square metal box with tiny holes everywhere—which, upon first glance, do not seem to yield any meaningful pattern. But they're also not uniform in size or placement, so there must be something special to them.

I stow everything in my backpack, then face the urns. Unsure what to do, I bow my head. *I wish I could have met you*, I think to them. Then I relock the niche.

I manage to take only four wrong turns on my way out, which feels like a success.

After returning the key, it's time to go find the sun. Except isn't the sun visible *everywhere* on this Bright Sun Mountain?

Speaking of, is that why Gong Gong brought his parents here? Because we're Suns and we belong on Bright Sun Mountain? Honestly, that's the kind of wordplay I love. Are Gong Gong and I alike, or am I finding meaning in nothing, like Xander and his box of chocolates? I guess that's a question I'll never know the answer to.

The sunlight hits me the second I step out. In all directions, as far as I can see, it's shining down on lush green grass and rolling hills and steep inclines. The sun is somehow more beautiful here, but it's also much hotter. Being outside without AC or shade makes me feel like I, Gemma Sun, have become one with the sun.

Now what? None of this feels like paying respects.

There's a path leading away from the columbarium, and I follow it to an exquisite, well-kept garden with purple, red, pink, and white flowers in the shape of concentric swirls. In the center sits a pagoda just large enough for a circle of benches. The layout is luminous and intentional, creating a breathtaking, almost otherworldly visual.

Since this is the only other significant landmark within sight, I spend the next fifteen minutes examining the garden, taking photos, and searching for clues. When the heat becomes too much, I retreat to the shade of the pagoda.

With a gradual incline to the top, the pagoda sits higher than the rest of the garden and columbarium. It feels like I can see everything from here, yet I can't seem to find whatever it is I'm looking for. Am I in the wrong place? But beyond this garden, it's open greenery as far as I can see, nothing else.

I take a deep breath. It's silent except for the chirping of birds, the buzzing of bees, and the wind gently passing through flowers and leaves. This feels like the epitome of the word *Zen*. Almost transcendent, like if I closed my eyes and meditated, I'd be in another plane of being.

Right before my eyelids completely shut, I snap them back open. I'm wasting time.

Feeling like I must have missed something, I grab the folder again to reread the sticky note. And this time, my eyes catch on the left pocket. Nothing's peeking out, but I dip my hand in and my heart rate spikes when I feel two small items beneath the flap. The first, a photo. Old, black and white, and almost fuzzy because the resolution is so bad.

The camera is focused on the two East Asian males in it, which makes it difficult to discern the setting other than blurry water in the background. I recognize Gong Gong's Sun nose first, then confirm it's him by the full lips and small ears. He's young here, late twenties maybe. Handsome, full head of hair cut short, and the thing that jumps out at me most—a full smile that squinches his eyes and creates a dimple so deep I feel like I could sink my pinky into it.

When was the last time I saw my mom smile like that? Or me, for that matter? And this contrasts heavily with the stoic photo of him with my mom, sadly. Was this taken before he was hardened by the world?

As for the other person in the photo, I don't recognize him. He and Gong Gong are standing a few feet apart, but they're familiar with each other. Comfortable. Gong Gong is looking at him as he smiles, and the other person is doubled over in laughter. I wonder what Gong Gong had said right before the photo was taken. A pun? Wordplay?

Am I supposed to figure out who this other person is? Could he be a sibling? He looks younger, maybe early twenties. They don't have any resemblance to each other, so likely not a blood sibling. He could also be a friend Gong Gong made here. Found family.

I flip the photo around just in case, but the back is blank.

Next, I examine the second item, which is a four-by-six piece of cardstock. In familiar handwriting, there's a loopy number 6 (puzzle number six already!) and the following directions:

Open Metal Box. Need A Pan

Right. The metal box. I retrieve it from my bag. In addition to the holes making it look like retired target practice, there's a six-digit combination lock (*six* for puzzle number six!) on the top, which I missed before because it had been facing away from me. Is a pan supposed to help me open it? I don't see how it could, other than using it to smash it open. Is there a special pan hidden on this mountain that I'm supposed to find, maybe one with six numbers on it?

This is the most ambiguous clue thus far. The last one even told me the numbers needed to find my great-grandparents' resting place. There have to be further instructions somewhere that I'm missing.

The photograph. It hasn't served a purpose yet. I turn my attention back to it, searching for numbers or a six-letter word or anything else.

Nothing.

With a sigh, I grab a granola bar from my bag and eat as I look at the photo, then the box, then the clues, then out into the sea of flowers in a frustrating, unending loop. When I've finished every crumb, I stand and begin searching the garden again.

Soon, I can't take the heat anymore. And I need additional sustenance. As much as I don't want to, it's time to take off.

Except . . . how can I leave without knowing if I successfully appreciated the other sun? Just the thought of having to trek back here because I missed something is almost enough to give me a second wind. What stops me is not having a new lead to explore. It would take the rest of my trip and then some to scour this entire mountain.

My stomach is uneasy as the cab pulls away. I can't help running my eyes over every inch I can still see, hoping for an epiphany.

This is going to be a recurring problem for me, isn't it? I am not

known for going with the flow, winging it, or ceding control. I need
to know—and right now, please—if I've done everything I need to
at Yangmingshan.

All I can think as I'm taken farther and farther away is that my
brain might be wired for treasure hunts, but my personality is not.
It's going to be a stressful two weeks.

1. ~~Wooden box~~

2. ~~Will~~

3. ~~Framed photo~~

   a. Answer to first riddle: 火/**fire**

   b. First line of second riddle: 火 **goes with water,
wood, metal, and** <u>**earth also**</u>.

5. ~~Journal~~

Destination: **Yangmingshan**

6. Metal Box

   a. Need A: **Pan**

   b. Destination:

7. Wall

8. House gate

Instructions, first line:

9. Address

Number:

10. Poem

11. Beginning

12. Watch

13. X Marks the Spot

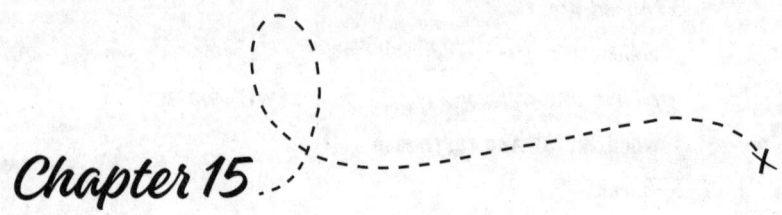

Chapter 15

Hunger gnaws at my stomach, but nowhere near as much as the unsolved clue gnaws at my mind. *Open Metal Box. Need A Pan.* Six words. Puzzle number six. Six-digit combination. I'm seeing all the patterns except the one I need, and the clock only continues to tick.

After devouring a paper bag of pot stickers from the scallion-pancake guy (now scallion-pancake-and-pot-sticker guy), I return to my room and dip into Gong Gong's art supplies. It's hard to put the puzzle aside, but after seeing that garden today, I have to paint it while it's fresh in my memory. Selecting a medium-size canvas, I take a deep, almost spiritual breath, and I begin. I want to see the image through my paints, and I also want to forever remember how that garden made me feel for that one brief Zen moment. Maybe if I capture it well enough, I can take that moment of meditation now.

I lose myself in the rhythmic strokes. Using a different part of my brain feels like coming up for air after unknowingly holding my breath. I don't return to reality until I hear the TARPers arriving back at the dorms. I feel completely refreshed as I prop the canvas against the window to dry, then reorganize my desk to make room for the paints, the photo, the metal box, and the clues. In the process, I happen to group two of the handwritten items together.

Open Metal Box. Need A Pan

To know my heart, you must go to the start.
Look for the Sun when you get to No. 1.

And suddenly, with these two clues together, it becomes obvious. The handwriting is the same, but the rest is not. In fact, the clue on top feels different from all the ones that have preceded it. And now I know why.

But wait.

No.

It can't be.

I'm mistaken. I have to be.

I yank the photo front and center and stare at it. Unfortunately, it only confirms my theory.

This has to be a joke. I almost want to look around and yell, *Okay, Gong Gong, you got me!*

A knock sounds at my door, and I almost jump out of my chair.

"Yes?" My voice is as shaky as I feel.

"We're heading to the night market," Brett's voice calls out. "Wanna come?"

Of course I do. *Night market* is in the top three of my wish list for Taipei. And now I have to get away—from this photo, this sweltering heat box of a room, this ridiculous turn of events. I need to continue this hunt and find the pot of gold at the end, but how am I going to do that *and* hang on to my pride, dignity, and sanity?

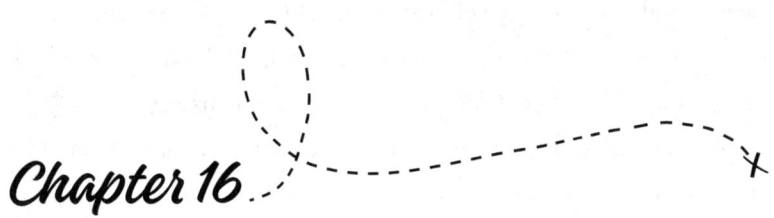

Chapter 16

As usual, I've done my research. Which is why I'm stoked to be at Shilin Night Market with my fellow TARPers by 6:00 p.m., just early enough to beat the crowds but late enough for dinner. With 539 stalls in just the main building and not including the surrounding alleyways also filled with games, stores, and food vendors, Shilin is the largest night market in all of Taiwan, with plenty to do, see, and eat. Like most Taiwan night markets, it's open every day from 4:00 p.m. to midnight.

Unsurprisingly, Brett and Jax are leading the TARP pack. And I'm glad they are because they either know the area well or they did their research too—we get off at the Jiantan metro station, which is actually closer than the Shilin station.

I think every TARPer is here tonight, including the four I haven't met in person yet. One of them, Yang, I'm excited to see because I chatted online with him slightly more than the rest. Since he's from San Diego and is attending MIT in the fall, he asked me for tips to get through a Massachusetts winter. The other three—Priscilla, Grace, and Sophia—are from the Pacific Northwest and seem to already be friends, having arrived together on the same flight.

All the chaperones are also here. The two I haven't met yet, Evelyn and Zack, don't seem to want anything to do with us, as evidenced by their only sentence of the night: "Nobody needs anything, right?" They peel off before we can even answer.

Shilin Night Market is huge, but it's difficult to get a sense of its vastness since it's mostly comprised of small alleyways. There's an adorable sign at the entrance with both the English and Chinese names painted across red lanterns.

As soon as we enter, a switch turns inside Yang. "I know what I want first," he says. "I've been dreaming about it since I had it three years ago. Follow me if you want the best noodles you'll ever have!" He charges ahead.

Because it's early enough, our massive group manages to stick together. Even though we have a promising destination in mind, I can't help looking longingly at other stands, salivating. Some are small carts parked in the street, some are kitchen-only spaces, and some are mom-and-pop restaurants with a limited number of tables.

Yang's target is a small street stand on the night market's main strip. The employees ladle out the noodles so quickly, I'm shocked no one is burned. My paper bowl of mi sua (Taiwanese), or mian xian (Mandarin), is fifty-five TWD, which is less than two dollars. After everyone has a serving, we sit on the temple steps behind the stand to eat.

The noodles are steaming hot, so I blow, waiting, even though others are digging in and chewing with open mouths to let out the heat. I'm not sure what to expect. To the eye, it's thin vermicelli noodles with squid and pork in a thick brown sauce. When I take a bite, the slightly tart, vinegary flavor pairs perfectly with the garlicky, chili-and-white-pepper spice. And it's topped off with my new love—fresh, aromatic cilantro.

"So?" Yang says, his bowl already empty.

TARP responds by chanting his name. A giant grin breaks out on his face. Passersby give us strange looks, and I'm thrilled to be in on the joke for once.

Half the group gets seconds. I loved it, but I also want to save room for the hundreds—actual *hundreds*—of mouthwatering items we walked by. I swear I walked by a chicken cutlet that was the size of my head. Who doesn't want to see what that's about?

Once we're ready to start moving again, the night market has grown busy enough that we have to divide into smaller groups. Felix and the Northwest girls wander off together, continuing their conversation from the temple steps. I stick with Brett, Trisha, Jax, and Yang. Xander looks like he's about to join, but after he sees me, he turns and takes off with Daphne and Belinda.

Good riddance.

Brett puts his arms around Trisha and me. "Where to next, ladies?"

"I've never been here before," I admit, surprising myself.

He beams, his arm dropping from Trisha as he focuses on me. "Well, in that case, we have to introduce you to all the classics. Royal treatment for you tonight, Princess!"

As uninventive as that nickname is, no one has ever called me anything along those lines before. I can't keep my heart from soaring.

Our first stop is somehow even better than the mi sua, mostly because I love any type of bun. Brett leads us to a street cart where sheng jian baos are lined up in a giant shallow pan, then steamed efficiently and perfectly, such that the bun part on top is pillowy and soft while the bottom is perfectly pan-fried crunchy. And the pork inside is so juicy it's almost soupy.

We also track down some classic Taiwanese dishes, like liang mian (cold noodles in peanut sauce with julienned cucumbers), small sausage in large sausage (pork sausage wrapped in a sticky-rice sausage), and oyster pancake (or oyster omelet) with egg, small oysters, chili sauce, and lime juice, which we share because it's so big. I'm getting so full I decide I don't need the giant fried-chicken cutlet, even if we share it.

I think we must be getting to dessert soon—and I'm eyeing the delicious candied strawberries on a stick at a nearby cart—but Yang leads us to a stand that smells like . . . feet. Not just feet, but feet with athlete's foot.

"Chou doufu!" Yang declares happily. The rest of the group appears divided. Jax seems as excited as Yang, Trisha looks curious, and Brett gives a polite no-thank-you smile.

"Stinky tofu," he explains to me. "I'm not a fan."

I read about this and could not get over that it's called stinky tofu. What kind of business model is that? Why didn't they at least call it *strongly flavored tofu* or *special tofu* or just some other name altogether? Like, mushrooms aren't called *slimy pieces of fungus* for a reason.

Part of me feels like I have to try it—it's a classic, and people claim once you get over the smell, it's delicious—but, well, I don't think I can get over the smell.

Jax gets his order first and heads over to me with a devilish grin. I'm already shaking my head. He lifts a piece with his chopsticks as he saunters closer. "Oh, come on, Blue Hill. How do you know you don't like it if you don't try it?"

Luckily, Brett grabs my hand and leads me away toward the rows of carnival games in the adjacent alleyway. The night market is such an interesting place—you never know what you're going to find around the next corner.

Jax's laugh fades away; he's not following. I breathe a sigh of nonstinky air and relief.

Once we're in the heart of the games, Brett lets go of my hand. Why does my palm suddenly feel cold?

"I'll win you a prize?" he says.

I laugh, then say more confidently than I should, "I'll win *you* a prize, Princess."

His eyes open in surprise, then narrow as he smiles. "You're on."

Unlike Xander, Brett is all in, immediately. He has every competitive cell that I do. And I find that it not only spurs me on but does so in a fun way. In fact, it almost feels like flirting as we throw darts at balloons, fish for plastic Nemos in the giant blow-up pool, and throw baseballs at stuffed Stitch dolls half-hidden behind plastic panels. Unsurprisingly, my very-not-athletic self struggles with the throwing challenges. Why are there so many of those? Brett may not play baseball or football, but curling apparently gives you muscles and hand-eye coordination because he pops all five balloons in front of him on his second try, winning a stuffed Pikachu.

"For you, Gongzhu," he says with a mischievous smile. I file the new nickname away happily, hoping it's Mandarin for *Princess* as I suspect and not *Stinky Butt* or something. Though, *stinky*—I learned that earlier. *Chou*, as in *chou doufu*.

I don't take the Pikachu. He taunts me by shaking it in my face, forcing me to smack it away.

"Double or nothing," I say even though we haven't bet anything. It just comes out of my mouth.

That finally gets him to stop waving the Pikachu. "How'd you get to be such a competitive little thing?"

"I—" My first instinct was to say *I'm not*, but I am. I so am. To a fault. And part of it is because I had no choice—it's my only way out—but also, because of a certain boy I just had to beat. But Brett can't know about either of those things. So I deflect. "How did you?"

He pauses, the teasing tilt of his lips slowly disappearing as he considers his answer. "I never really thought about it before." He lowers his eyes and rubs his chin, vulnerable. "I guess growing up with two older brothers can do that to you? They were always bigger and beating up on me or whatever, so I felt like I had to prove myself."

I want to thank him for opening up—maybe even share something about myself in return—but I'm scared to let him in. The last time I did that, the person chose a cardboard dog over me. So instead I tease, "If you think that's going to get me to go easy on you this next round, you're mistaken. C'mon, double or nothing."

Brett chuckles. Then he bows slightly. "As you wish."

I don't do any better this time. So I change my strategy. When it's Brett's turn, I distract him any way I can—making noises, grabbing his waist, bopping him on the butt with the Pikachu.

He pretends not to notice, though he doesn't always succeed, especially when I touch him. So I touch him more, tapping him on the shoulder and poking his bicep, which—whoa. Can I find a way to touch his pecs or abs too?

As soon as he's done—and he missed every time, thank you very much—he turns toward me and lunges. I yelp in surprise, which grows into a scream when he scoops me up and throws me over his shoulder.

"You're naughtier than I thought," he says.

I'm guessing he's smirking, but I can't tell because my head is bobbing up and down and all I can see is his butt, not that I'm complaining.

I squirm, but his arm clamps tighter across my legs.

"Where are we going?" I ask.

"You're in a time-out."

I spend the next few minutes trying to sway close enough to smack him in the butt. Not in a sexy way—more annoying and brat-like. I can hear and feel him laughing. I briefly wonder if he's going to smack mine, which he has easy access to. When we enter a café and he deposits me in a chair, I can't decide if I'm glad or disappointed that he didn't.

He points a finger at me. "You stay put."

A minute later, he returns with a heaping bowl of shaved ice topped with condensed milk, fresh strawberries, fresh mangoes, and tapioca balls.

My mouth is already watering (and maybe not just for the dessert in his hands).

"I don't know what your parents are like, but this is the best time-out ever," I joke. "If you were Pavlov and I was your dog, you'd only be encouraging more bad behavior."

It's too nerdy, but I don't realize until I've already said it.

But he just smiles, puts the bowl down, and slides into the chair next to me instead of across.

I take a bite. The ice melts in my mouth, and my tongue is coated in sweetness. I thought I preferred chocolate desserts, but this is up there with lava cakes.

After his first bite, Brett says, "And so what if that's exactly what I'm doing?"

And suddenly, he's turning his long legs in his chair so that his whole body is facing me, and he's leaning in.

I haven't kissed anyone before, let alone someone who makes my stomach feel like I'm on an airplane. The most Xander ever did was kiss my hand, which made me feel like I was in a Jane Austen novel then but now makes me feel juvenile. I try to quickly swallow any shaved-ice remnants.

Brett's eyes are already closing. Do I close mine too? Will there be tongue? When I set out on this adventure, I wasn't expecting *this* kind of new experience. Why didn't I do any research?

I decide to close my eyes. Then I lean forward too much, and I end up pressing my mouth into his too strongly. So I pull back slightly. Then my nerves kick in and I go slack, hoping he'll take the lead.

As his soft, slightly sticky, and very sweet lips press into mine and he cradles my head in his large hand, my mind finally turns off.

I stop thinking as his lips part mine, and his tongue gently sweeps into my mouth as if he's tasting any dessert left behind. It's surprisingly nice, and the rest of my body relaxes into him as his fingers on the back of my head weave into my hair. His other hand grazes my side. I don't know what to do with my own limbs, so I put a hand on his arm while the other hangs awkwardly.

His fist closes around my hair and tugs slightly, tilting my chin up and toward him, deepening the kiss. None of it is painful or uncomfortable. Just . . . intense.

It feels too fast and too much, so I pull back gently, and in a second he's gone. I'm still catching my breath as he winks at me, then dives back into the shaved ice, which is now a little soupy.

Did that just happen? How? Even though I just did it, I can't figure out what exactly our lips and tongues were doing or how we managed not to bump noses.

Feeling awkward, I dip my spoon back in too.

A few minutes later, I hear a chorus of *heys* coming from the street, and Yang, Jax, and Trisha join us. The shaved ice is gone in seconds, and Yang orders another.

I can't help but wonder what would have been if they hadn't found us, and that thought stays with me the rest of the night.

As we wander through the shops, I wonder, *Would Brett and I be strolling hand in hand through these? Would there be more kisses? Do I even want that?*

As Jax grabs Brett to browse clothing racks with misspelled knockoffs like "Cucci" instead of "Gucci," I stick with Trisha. Everything is so cute and cheap, I'm briefly tempted to spend money I don't have. There are personalized stickers; a wood carving store where you can get anything in any language carved on wooden key chains, plaques, pencils, or chopsticks; and even a shop where they take your photo and make a rubber stamp of your face. While Trisha stocks up, I fawn with her and stick to taking photos.

There are also random items that seem to be everywhere, and Yang talks about how fads move quickly here and whatever is popular at the time is in every store. The other TARPers spend a while at the floor-to-ceiling rack of Chinese-character key chains, which Trisha tells me is like the name key chains we have at amusement parks and tourist shops in the US. I try not to feel wistful at my lack of a Chinese name even though I shouldn't be spending the fifteen cents on a key chain anyway.

The two things I do buy are tape and a handheld paper fan—the tape so I can affix the clues into the journal, turning it into a scrapbook of sorts, and the fan to (what else?) help me combat the unrelenting heat.

And the final thing I pay for is completely unexpected, though again, it's to help with the heat.

I get my hair cut. My mom has always cut my hair, and I usually leave it long because she's not very good and the longer it grows, the less you can tell. Thus far, I've been putting it up, but even piled on my head, it's still too much here. And it doesn't help that it's black and absorbs every ray of the sun.

With Trisha's translation help, I lop off most of it, ending with a chic, chin-length bob. My head already feels so much lighter.

I keep staring at myself in the mirror when it's done. I almost don't recognize myself. New do, newly kissed, new Gemma.

Now if only new Gemma can find a way to tackle the treasure hunt without having to use the very costly clue she recently uncovered.

11:56 PM Taiwan Standard Time

Val

YOU DID WHAT

AND WITH WHOM?

I looked up a photo on the TARP website

Why can't I see his face?

Why is he curling?

Oh wait I found his social media

OH MY GOD

GOOD JOB

Also your hair is super cute, I love it!

I'm sorry I don't have time to talk,
trying to get to know other peeps

But I want to hear everything!!

Why is the time difference so brutal???

Was it good?

Gemma

Yeah, I think so.

THAT'S ALL I GET???

Are you trying to punish me?

No, sorry.

He's super hot.

It was good.

I'm just distracted by the treasure hunt.

Just wait until you hear the latest.

Ahh I have to go

You can text if you want

I'll respond when I can

xoxo

Chapter 17

Later that night, alone in my room, I alternate between staring at the metal box, touching my fingers to my tingling lips, and running my fingers through my hair, only to be surprised when they meet air so much sooner than before.

Time is ticking. And my indecision is only hurting. But I can't bring myself to do what I need to do. So instead I paint, my strokes growing more and more frustrated until, around one in the morning, someone knocks on my door. My first thought is that it could be Brett, which both thrills and scares me—does the time automatically imply a booty call? I'm not ready for that.

I open the door and smile brightly when I see Trisha. "Hi!"

"Can't sleep?" she asks. "I saw the light on. Want to go on a snack run?"

I'm already grabbing my purse before she finishes the question.

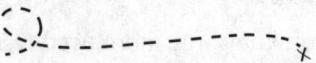

"Seven-eleven? That's where we're going?" I didn't even know they had those here.

"The locals just call it *Seven*. And I like it better than OK Mart."

"Why name it OK Mart? Shouldn't it be, like, Excellent or Best Mart? Or Number One? That's a trend I've noticed here." Like No. 1 Cemetery.

Trisha laughs.

Seven is only two stores down. As we enter, I see there's another Seven around the corner to the left, and another one down the street on the right.

"Why are there so many—" I start, but I cut myself off because, as I step inside, I get it.

Taiwan 7-Elevens are nothing like the US ones. Again, it's like they have everything in this one place. There's hot food, makeup, video games, ice cream, drinks, fancy notebooks, Hello Kitty merchandise, and so much more I can't see yet. And the store isn't even that big. We're talking mom-and-pop size, not superstore.

And there's precious, precious AC.

When the doors slide shut behind me, I'm blasted by a smell I've never come across before that makes me want to cover my nose.

"Yum, that smell makes me so nostalgic," Trisha says, and I feel like a bad Asian.

"Um, what is that?"

"Tea eggs." She points to a large vat in the corner. "Delicious. We should get some."

I try to avoid answering by picking up a drink near me. "Papaya milk, that sounds good."

Trisha laughs. "You know, my mom used to force-feed me those because she said they'd make my boobs grow. Something about a place where women ate a lot of papaya and had giant boobs."

"Double-D reason for me to like it," I joke.

Between laughs, Trisha gestures to her chest and says, "It doesn't work, though."

I shrug. "Can't hurt to try."

I glance at the price, and I'm shocked at how cheap it is. I look around—everything in here seems cheaper than it would be in the US. I'm briefly tempted to also grab some iced green tea or apple soda, but I'd have to keep them in the communal fridge and I can't afford to lose money by having someone else take them. Not to mention, money should be saved for food or calorie-rich drinks that can fill me up.

Trisha adds a tiny, round plastic dairy drink to her basket. "Yang Le Duo. You have to try it."

I'm tempted by the crispy ramen snacks, breads, seaweed rice wraps, sweet potatoes, and bento boxes with sausage over rice, but I don't need this much food right now. Then I reach the dessert section. I can't help grabbing what's labeled as a *QQ donut*, especially after Trisha explains that *QQ* refers to the chewy texture of mochi and tapioca balls.

The Lay's chips are the same logo and company as back home, but there are unique flavors here. Grilled prawn, beef noodle, seaweed, and some sweet flavors, like caramel pudding, peach tart, and strawberry. I grab a beef noodle one out of my loyalty to niu rou mian.

When we return to the dorms, we head to Trisha's room and pour out our goodies. I only got a few things, but Trisha loaded up on both snacks and beauty products. She passes me the drink I "have to try," and I offer up the beef noodle Lay's.

I sip the Yang Le Duo, which is like a sweet liquid yogurt—something I never knew I needed, but I do.

"So, are you jet-lagged?" I ask her.

"Yes. And no. I always have a hard time sleeping . . . especially away from home." She averts her eyes to the side like she's embarrassed, so I make sure she knows she doesn't need to be.

"I get that. I'm homesick too."

Her eyes light up and return to my face. "Yeah?"

I nod. "I think it's a good thing. It means we have a home we love, right?"

"Right. I do love it . . ." She sounds like she's trying to convince herself more than me.

I don't know if I should push. I offer more chips instead.

That seems to work, because she plucks one from the bag, then stares at it as she says, "I *do* love it. But does that mean there can't be room for improvement on one or two things?"

"Of course not," I answer, thinking about how much I've always wanted my world to be bigger and how I wish my mom hadn't lied to me.

"The weird part is, I've always wanted to get away—my parents have been pretty strict, really traditional, which has been hard—but now that I'm here, I miss them."

"That makes sense. It's complicated." That information casts a new light on her use of the word *freedom* to describe how this Taiwan trip is different for her. "I'm sorry—it sounds like it was hard for you growing up."

"It wasn't hard, not exactly," she says quickly, defensive, "but I guess it wasn't not hard either? I don't know. I wasn't even sure I was going to come on this trip because I have a . . . complicated relationship with the culture—well, I should say, the way my parents interpret the culture. There was so much pressure to carry on traditions, to make their sacrifices worth it. That sounds too heavy."

Here I thought an understanding of my roots and where I came from would give me the clarity I've been seeking, but for Trisha, it's been her obstacle. Similar to . . . my mom, I realize. My world feels like it was just tipped sideways.

Trisha continues, "I just mean . . . I felt like I had to be a certain way growing up, and now that I'm allowed to be whoever I want, I don't know who that is."

"I understand that."

"You do?" She's surprised, which in turn surprises me. "You seem like you know yourself, like you're not scared of anything."

I laugh. "Are you kidding me? I've been so lost this whole trip."

"In what way?"

"Ironically, in the opposite way from you. I grew up wanting but having no connection to my culture, and now I feel like I have a finite amount of time to figure that and so many other things out."

"What else are you figuring out?"

I hesitate, not sure how much to say. What's the harm in telling her about the hunt? There isn't a clear-cut reason to keep it to myself, but I don't want to let her or anyone else in. Not just because it's mine, but because it's hard to trust someone, and because I don't like sharing my story. I'm not exactly embarrassed by it, but it also doesn't feel like anyone else's business.

I simplify, cutting out the hunt altogether. "My grandfather died recently, and that's partly why I'm here. I went to his apartment the other day to clean out his stuff."

"Oh, I'm so sorry. Let me know if I can do anything. I know that can be hard."

"You've lost yours?"

"Both. The second time was especially rough. I was in the middle of finals, and my parents didn't tell me until after."

"I'm sorry." I refrain from telling her my mother lied about my grandfather my entire life. I want to relate, but I also don't want it to sound like I'm one-upping her. Instead, I try to steer the conversation by asking, "So do your parents keep other things from you, or only stuff like that, and temporarily?"

Trisha sighs. "A lot of it is health related. I'm constantly in fear that my parents are dying. I've tried to talk to them about it—how I only worry *more* if they never tell me anything—but they don't get it."

I nod, offering her sympathy and more chips.

"Did you know your grandfather well?" she asks.

I squirm. "Not well . . . or at all, but I'm trying to now."

"I didn't know mine that well either. They were kind of distant. Do you think that's a generational or cultural thing? Or both? I wish I knew more—I know they went through a lot. But maybe that's why they don't want to talk about it."

I hesitate before asking, "If there was a way for you to know more, would you? And at what cost?"

She opens a packet of dried squid and chews on a couple of strings, thinking. "I feel like yes, no matter the cost. Don't you?"

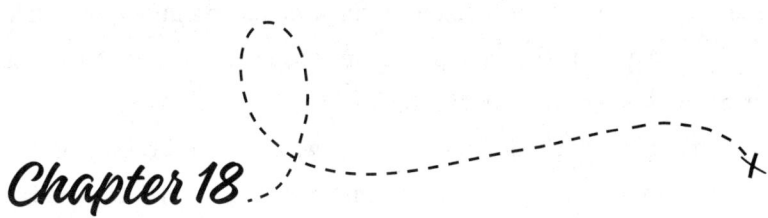

Chapter 18

I do not want to do this.

But last night, Trisha reminded me of a bonus reason to push forward on this hunt—to learn more about my grandfather and where I come from. Then this morning, a blaring wake-up call from the universe arrived in the form of an email from Amherst, letting me know that the first payment for the upcoming semester is due in a few weeks.

I don't have a choice. Yet when I find myself in front of the door—*his* door—I can't bring myself to do it. There has to be another way, no?

Xander opens the door and almost walks into me.

"Jesus!" he yells, swiveling to the side just in time.

He's in his underwear. Nothing but boxers, which are tighter than I expected. I force myself to look away, but that feels weird too, staring up at the ceiling. I get that it's hot, but where is he going half-naked?

"Hey, best friend," I say, forcing a smile.

"You scared me," he says as he darts back inside and closes the door, but the image of him in his boxers is seared into my eye-balls. He reappears in a plain gray T-shirt and navy shorts, but I just see the pale blue cotton boxers I know he has on underneath. He dressed so quickly the band peeks out, especially when he raises his arms to finish putting on his shirt.

I'm not looking in an I'm-interested way, I swear. Gross. I just . . . have hormones. But now that I remember it's Xander attached, a shiver runs through my body.

"What's going on?" he asks, impatient.

This is already off to such a great start. I should turn back, shouldn't I?

"Nothing," I mumble.

He stares at me for a second longer. When I don't say anything else, he walks off to the bathrooms. I let him go, hoping I'll be able to work up my nerve in the time it'll take him to pee and, I hope for my sake, brush his teeth. Not that I smelled anything, but I don't want to have a long conversation with him if he hasn't brushed yet. There's already enough unpleasantness in store for me—no need to add to it.

Five minutes later, he seems surprised that I'm still hovering in the hallway waiting for him.

I finally find some words. "Can I talk to you?"

He stops several feet from me and waits.

"Inside?" I gesture toward his room.

He raises an eyebrow but opens the door for me.

I step into an unexpected sea of memories. The bright blue re-tainer case on his desk that he of course packed because he had braces for three years, including when we were together. Next to the bed, the wide-rimmed glasses that he used to wear before he switched to contacts. And most overwhelmingly, the scent. The room is small and lived-in enough that it's heady with the clean, fresh, yet also woodsy smell I didn't realize I recognized as his.

I immediately go and open the window.

"What're you doing? It's hotter out there than in here."

I ignore his question as I sit at his desk, retrieve the photo of our grandfathers from my bag, and hand it to him.

His eyes widen when he looks at it.

"Where'd you get this?" he asks almost reverently, holding the photo carefully as if it's priceless.

Did Gong Gong know I would need this photo to get A Pan—more accurately, A. Pan, *Alexander* Pan—to hear me out? Not just a Pan but *the* Pan needed to open the metal box.

"From my grandfather, who's also in the photo."

"How'd you know this is my grandfather?"

Once I figured out A Pan, I saw the similarities between him and his grandfather in the photo—same eye shape, same jawline. And since then, I haven't been able to stop wondering what happened between them, these two seemingly close friends who used to make each other laugh so hard. Friends who would need a big reason to throw each other away.

Or maybe not. Xander and I were once more than friends, and look how easily he threw that away.

Regardless, there are no answers here, only more questions.

So I retrieve the folder of clues I brought, make myself forget how we used to create puzzles for each other, and spend the next twenty minutes walking him through some of the clues from the hunt. I then explain how I figured out *A Pan*. The previous riddles were written in full sentences with proper punctuation, and the one time there was an anomaly (in *Look for the Sun when you get to No. 1*), it meant something. The *S* was capitalized because it was a surname. And seeing that clue beside the *Open Metal Box. Need A Pan* made me realize that *Pan* is also a surname, and the capitalized *A*, a first initial.

I finish by pulling the metal box from my bag. And I have to force the next words out. "I need your help to open this."

Xander laughs. He didn't say a word the entire time I was talking, and now he's laughing?

"You beg me to let you into the program that you made fun of for months, then you're a jerk on the plane, and now you want me to help you? That's a lot, even for you."

I hadn't expected him to say *As you wish* and open the box with a smile, but why does he have to make everything as difficult as possible?

"I'm sorry about the plane." I don't elaborate that I'm only sorry for how strongly it came out—I still meant what I said.

He doesn't apologize back. Just returns the photo. "I think you interpreted the clue wrong. I'm not the only A. Pan." My eyes meet his as he says, "My dad."

That . . . is even worse than having to work with Xander.

I plunk the box onto the bed beside him. "There's one way to find out."

He pushes it away. "I don't even know what to enter."

"Try your grandfather's birthday." I've been thinking about it nonstop, and six digits could represent a date in the MM/DD/YY format.

"This is ridiculous." He picks up the box to give it back.

But I fold my arms across my chest. "Just try it. What harm is there?"

He continues to hold the box out to me.

I attempt another strategy. "If you're right and it doesn't work, then you win and you can gloat. As much as you want."

Finally, his arm retracts and I think I've won, but of course I haven't. "I don't know his birthday."

That I didn't expect. "Can you call him?"

"He died when I was thirteen."

"Oh. I'm sorry." I want to ask if he can call his grandmother or father, but now doesn't seem like the right time.

He extends the box toward me again. "Will you take this back now?"

"Isn't there any significant date you can try?"

He's staring off to the side, his eyes not meeting mine.

I don't hold back any of the desperation or vulnerability I'm feeling as I say, "Please?" I hold off guilting him with our past mostly because I can't bring myself to open that can of worms.

He closes his eyes. The hand with the box is still outstretched, but he's not pushing it at me as urgently as before.

I wait as patiently as I can. After what feels like an hour but is probably a few minutes, Xander plops the box onto his lap and starts turning the dials.

I stop breathing. The anticipation is too much.

When he finishes setting the sixth number, nothing happens. Only for a second. A moment later, a distinct *clink* sounds inside the box, and the entire thing falls apart. Just collapses in on itself like a dying star.

Xander jumps up as I exclaim, "What did you do?"

"It's not my fault!" he retorts as I bend down and hastily gather the sides of the box that fell from his lap. In the process, I notice another item on the floor.

"Is this yours?" I ask, picking it up.

He shakes his head. "Must've been in the box."

I absentmindedly hand him the box pieces so I can examine the new object.

It's a small metal flashlight. There's no button or switch, but there's a seam down the middle essentially separating it into two parts. When I twist it, a beam of light shoots out.

"Is this the only thing that was inside?" I ask. There must be something else—the next puzzle, a clue, some instructions.

Xander doesn't respond. When I look at him, he's examining the box sides. I snatch them back.

Six slabs total, one per side of the box. Six, six, six—is it a pattern or nothing at all? Puzzle number six, six words in the clue and numbers in the combination, six pieces. Or 666 as in the devil, because this is the worst.

Or maybe there's something else I'm missing. Using the flashlight, I bend forward to search the floor. But before I've scanned an inch, Xander grabs the flashlight.

"Stop that. There wasn't anything else." He twists the flashlight off and hands it back to me. "I did my part, so you can leave now."

"Gladly." I do one quick sweep around the floor with my eyes, then turn toward the door.

"Wait."

I pause. He's going to tell me I owe him for opening the box, isn't he?

"What do you think is at the end of all this?"

I had purposefully left out the inheritance for obvious reasons. Doing my best to be convincing, I say firmly, "This is just a way for me to get to know him, that's all."

I scurry toward the door, but Xander races in front of me. "You think there's money at the end. An inheritance."

My god, *is* my acting on par with my cap throwing?

I deflect. "My grandfather lost all his money. To *yours*. There's nothing for him to leave behind."

I keep my working theory to myself that Gong Gong involved A Pan because he wanted to lead us to the truth of what happened. To show the Pan descendants what their grandfather truly did.

But Xander believes the opposite, leading him to say, "The money he stole from my grandfather could be at the end of this. And that could be the reason why he involved me, to return it."

That . . . makes sense. Which causes my heart to plummet. If there's no money for my mom and me after this—I can't even think about that.

"You need me," he says. "The clue said so."

"Just for that one," I say confidently even though I'm already doubting it.

"Nope. It wasn't just the one, and I think you know it. And you need me for more than my knowledge about my family. I can help you with the Mandarin."

That is the last thing he should have said unless he was trying to piss me off. I take another step, and he rushes to say, "I can explain that Yangmingshan riddle to you. I figured that out immediately."

"Only because you already knew the answer."

He reaches for the folder of puzzles in my hands, but I hug it to my chest. Pivoting, he grabs his backpack and pulls out a notebook and pencil.

"The last sentence of the riddle tells us what to do: Add up the parts, line by line." He leans the notebook against the wall and begins writing. "In the first line, *listen* and *easy* are the underlined words, right?"

I ignore his condescending tone and nod, the riddle appearing in my mind.

> <u>Listen</u>, this won't be an <u>easy</u> journey for you.
> Sometimes it's as clear as—the <u>sun</u> goes with the <u>moon</u>.
> Other times, it's a <u>mountain</u> climb for the next clue.
> Add up the parts, line by line, and you'll be there soon.

On the piece of paper, he's written 阝 and 易. He points to the first character. "This is called the *small ear radical* because it looks like an ear. Technically it means something else, but that's not relevant here. It's the name of it that matters. *Ear*, as in *listen*." He points to the underlined *listen* in the clue. Then he points to the underlined *easy*. "The second character I wrote means *simple, easy*. And when you combine the two"—he writes them closer together, 陽—"that's *yang*, as in *Yangmingshan*."

"Isn't there an extra horizontal line in the *yang*?"

He's surprised. "You noticed that?" I shrug, not wanting to talk about wavelengths or patterns. Or worse, tell him I learned that character in the first puzzle, the one that told me there was treasure at the end of all this. "The right side of *yang* isn't a word by itself. But anyone who knows the language would put these two parts together and think of *yang*."

As much as I want to know more about the riddle, I can't stand hearing it from Xander like this. I turn to leave, but then he starts talking quickly.

"In the second line, *sun* and *moon* are underlined."

His pencil is scratching away, and I can't help peeking over. And again, I'm thrilled to immediately spot another error.

He's written 日 and 月 on the paper.

"I thought this was *sun*," I say, pointing to 陽.

"It is, *yang* as in *taiyang*. But this"—he points to the 日—"is an independent character also meaning *sun* or *daytime*, and it's also the radical version of *sun*."

"What the heck is a radical?"

"The symbol to denote a square root or nth root."

"What?" Because of his deadpan delivery, it takes me a second to realize he's making a math joke. And that I'd gotten used to postplane Xander, who hasn't joked with me the entire time we've been here.

But we're not totally back to before, because he just moves on and explains, seriously this time, "A Chinese radical is like a root. A base component of a character. So the word takes on a different form when they're part of another character, and they help provide context to what that bigger character means."

It sounds like he's making all this up just to pretend to solve the puzzle. But I also don't want to accuse him of that and hear him say that I should already know about Chinese radicals.

"So when you combine *ri* and *yue*"—he points to the 日 and 月, then writes them closer together as 明—"then you get *ming*."

This reminds me of the *earth also below* puzzle from before, where 土 and 也 combined to form 地. Maybe he's not making this up.

"And obviously *mountain* is just *mountain*"—he writes 山 on the page—"so by adding up the parts line by line . . ." He gestures to the handwritten 陽明山 with a *ta-da* hand motion. "The puzzle is actually quite brilliant."

That is exactly what I was thinking. A play on words and word parts is so up my alley . . . except I don't speak Chinese. I've never felt as disappointed in that fact as this moment.

At least Xander appreciates how cool this is. And my heart can't help soaring a little that he seems impressed by my grandfather. But then he immediately yanks it back down by saying, "How is the person who put this together possibly related to you, Shi Tanzi?"

"Goodbye, Alex." I walk toward the door.

"You need me."

I pause. "I don't need you because I solved the other puzzle." Well, technically Val did, but he doesn't need to know that.

"They're getting harder, and they don't all seem to have a backup puzzle. Or a backup A. Pan, not unless you want to call my dad."

I ignore the churn in my stomach warning me that his words hold truth. Then his next words flip my stomach upside down.

"If we partner up now, I'll just take twenty percent. Wait until I'm your only hope and it goes up to forty-five."

The unfairness, the pure *ridiculousness* of me giving him anything given our situations—I don't know whether to laugh or yell or cry.

I can't find any words, so I just slam the door on my way out.

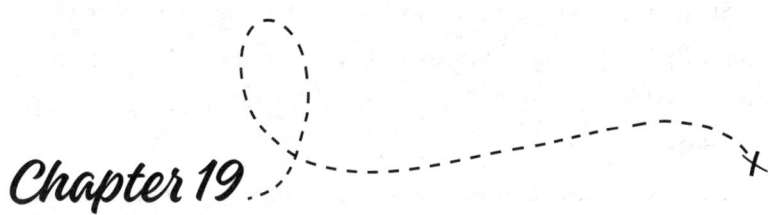

Chapter 19

I immediately return to my room, lock the door, and examine the six metal slabs that made up the box just ten minutes ago.

Is there really no clue that goes along with this? What am I supposed to do with these?

Again, they're full of small holes in random places—so many of them, everywhere—and it seems like they must be significant. But as I turn the pieces over to examine every inch, I spot something new. Letters, painted in the corners, tiny. They must have faced inward before, meaning, they weren't visible until the box deconstructed itself.

I open the journal and begin jotting the letters down.

I can do this. My weird mind was made for this, right?

Except something in my gut is gnawing at me, telling me this is useless. Not only are there too many possible combinations, but . . . if I Needed A Pan before, why would I suddenly stop needing him? The letters are not for me to solve.

Why did I have to storm out like that? Why didn't I look at the pieces while there, make him do this part too? I can't go back with my tail between my legs now.

Suddenly, a loud, urgent knock sounds at my door. I know who it is without opening it. I'm about to run to the door with gratitude until Xander calls out, "I figured something out about the pieces."

"How?" I ask warily.

There's a pause, and I already know I'm not going to like what comes next. "I took a photo of them when you weren't looking."

I run to the door and fling it open. "You had no right to do that!" My voice is louder than I mean it to be, but I'm pissed. I step into the hallway, not wanting to let him inside near the box, the clues, or any of my grandfather's things.

He doesn't look the least bit sorry. "Do you want to know what I found?"

I cross my arms over my chest. "Fine." Maybe he'll give me a hint about the letters, a big enough one that I can solve it on my own.

"Okay," he says. "Forty-five percent."

I clench my teeth so hard my temple flares in pain.

"You should've taken the twenty percent deal when it was on the table." He says it nonchalantly, like we're talking about the weather, not *money*. Survival. Which only proves how little he needs it.

"So you're extorting me."

"I'm not!" He has the gall to flush red. "I'm negotiating."

I force myself to stay calm and keep the main goal in sight, which is to get any hints possible. "How do I even know you figured anything out? Tell me first and I'll decide if you're onto something."

He shakes his head. "I'll tell you after you agree that we're doing this together. And I get forty-five."

I can't keep it in anymore. He is the worst, the absolute worst.

"Xander! Why do you . . . Why can't . . ." An actual growl erupts from my throat. I just *cannot* with him.

By now, our raised voices—fine, *my* raised voice seems to have woken up the others. Doors are opening like dominoes, and exponentially so; once the first few people have peeked out at us, the others feel like they can watch the train wreck too.

The chaperones are first on the scene.

"Everything okay?" Belinda asks nervously. She's almost deferential to Xander, which is so not fair. Just because he created her summer job doesn't mean he should get special treatment, not when she's supposed to be his chaperone too. What a conflict of interest. I should complain . . . but to who, Xander?

The other TARPers have now joined us in the hallway. They've mostly just woken up, with bleary eyes and bed head. Half the boys are still shirtless because of the heat.

Xander shoots Belinda a composed smile. "Just a private matter. Sorry for disturbing. We shouldn't have been having this conversation out here."

Xander reaches over and puts a gentle hand on my shoulder to lead me into my room. The gesture is perfectly friendly, but I don't want him touching me.

Just as I've squirmed away, a shirtless Brett appears out of thin air, his muscular torso shielding me as he pushes Xander back by the chest.

Xander retreats a step. "All right, dude, calm down. We're fine here."

Speak for yourself, I think but don't say.

Brett straightens his spine, his back muscles flexing. "Doesn't seem fine."

"Are you a shirtless knight in shining muscles or a guard dog with pants on?" Xander muses to himself. "You're either missing your top or you have extra bottoms."

Belinda walks up to them. "Um, boys, can we just . . ." It's weird to hear her call them boys when she's not that much older, but she seems to be pushing her authority.

Zack finally does something chaperone-like for the first time this trip. "Knock it off, both of you. Gemma, you good?"

I'm surprised he knows my name, but I'm grateful that someone has finally acknowledged me.

"Yup," I say quickly. "All good." Everyone just needs to go away because this moment has become a Most Embarrassing one.

There may be a few inches between Brett and Xander now, but Brett doesn't back down, crossing his arms over his chest.

Xander glances at me, and I look off to the side in a huff. His gaze briefly shifts to Brett, and then with a shrug, he leaves. But as he walks away, he calls out to me, "I saw the letters in the corners. And you will Need A Pan to arrange them correctly."

He doesn't even look back as he talks. He just speaks to the air, then disappears into his room with the softest door close of all time, probably because he somehow knew it would annoy me.

The rest of the hallway returns to their rooms, doors shutting quickly.

Eff. I have to go after Xander, don't I? But first, I have to acknowledge Brett, who's smiling at me. Easier said than done when my mind is completely elsewhere.

"You okay, Gongzhu?" He runs a hand through his hair, making it stick up in a sexy anime way.

Maybe I'm not *completely* consumed with the metal pieces. How can I be when he calls me that and looks at me like he's hungry?

"I'm fine," I say, not meeting his eye. "Xander just . . . presses my buttons. He's so annoying, you know?"

Brett laughs. Then he raises an arm and leans against the doorframe, making that side of his torso flex. "Anything else I can do for you?"

Summoning my willpower, I swallow hard and say, "Yes. I mean, no, not right now. Sorry, I'm just . . ." I can't stop staring at his muscles. "I have to get back to these six abs I have—oh my god, slabs! Metal slabs! It's a long story . . ." I continue jabbering as I slowly back into my room.

The Most Embarrassing moment continues, though Brett seems to find it funny—dare I even say, charming? Okay, maybe not charming. Cute?

As I hide behind the closing door, he calls out, "I have some experience with abs—I mean, slabs." He's chuckling to himself. Then his voice lowers as he says, "You know where to find me if you change your mind."

I lean my back against the shut door and exhale loudly. Then I have to shake my head to get the image of Brett out of there.

I try to focus on the six slabs.

Six abs . . .

Stop it.

Sitting down, I give myself ten minutes of trying to arrange the letters on my own, ten timed minutes where I'm all in, no distractions, using every resource at my disposal.

At the end, I have possible letter groupings, but no finished words. I'm not even close. From that, I conclude two things. First, the words are likely in Chinese. And second, I do Need A Pan for more than just the six-number combination.

I sigh, gather up the metal pieces, then metaphorically (and literally, by miming) put on my best negotiating hat. And I leave my hate goggles on.

Chapter 20

"Two percent, final offer."

Xander and I are so far apart on a number I don't even know why we're having this discussion. He's still sticking to forty-five percent even though I've come up from one in the past fifteen minutes.

He's been sitting at his desk scrolling on his phone, and he doesn't look up as he says, "Do you want us to wait for your guard dog to come help convince me? Never would have pegged you for someone who likes that kind of behavior."

"What do you care anyway?"

He doesn't respond to that question. Just repeats, "Forty-five."

I try to appeal to the old Xander with a joke. "Come on, two percent—you have to take it. It's the best version of milk."

Okay, that was a terrible joke. For more reasons than one because Xander responds, "I'm lactose intolerant, so forty-five, two percent—they all cause the same outcome."

Crap. Literally. (Why can't I come up with a joke like that when I need one?)

Still not looking up, Xander says, "First admit you need me, then I'll come down to forty."

I resist the urge to stomp over and yank the phone out of his hands. If I admit I need him, he'll go up to fifty. "Five percent, but only if *you* admit that the cardboard dog was a mistake."

That earns me a smirk, and I see a hint of the Before Xander. He counters, "Thirty-five percent if you admit the dog was right—*actually* admit it this time."

This is a waste of time.

"Ten percent—really, truly final offer, but only if you can promise you'll take this seriously. There's a ticking clock, and I can't have you derailing us with more cardboard dogs." *And I need this even more than I needed an A on that project.*

Finally, he puts the phone away. "Our incentives are aligned, Shi Tanzi. If we don't reach the end, I get zilch. Haven't you ever watched any treasure-hunting movies?"

He would be the villain in said movies, meaning, at the end, he's going to try to double-cross me and take everything for himself, only to lose it all. I guess I could live with that.

He's peering at me as if he wants to know what I'm thinking, but I don't let him in.

"Fifteen and we have a deal," he says. "Think of that extra five percent as my fee for getting you to Taipei in the first place."

Fifteen is so unfair, but better to give that up than retain a hundred percent of nothing. Why, *why* did the person I can't stand most, my nemesis, have to be the one with family history tying him to this hunt? Why couldn't Gong Gong just leave me whatever he had? Is he trying to punish me? Is he cruel and devious like my mother implied? But as long as there's money at the end, I'll bear it.

"Fine," I say through gritted teeth. "But since you're getting that extra five percent, then you have to admit that the dog was wrong. *And*," I add quickly, "you have to stop calling me Shi Tanzi."

He sticks a hand out, and I shake it.

"That dog isn't what broke us," he says after our hands come apart. "It was just the final straw, the symbol of how incompatible we are. The dog was wrong for you, but he was right for me and I stand by him."

That . . . is not what I was asking for, and he knows it.

The arrogant grin I haven't seen since the plane crosses his face. "But for someone who seems so adamant on where they stand, you appear to finally be having some fun. In fact . . ." He gestures for me to kneel. I stand my ground and fold my arms over my chest. He shrugs, then pretends to whip out an imaginary tarp that he uses to cover me—his version of a knighting, if you will. "You are no longer a wet blanket, as requested. You are a stiff, dry tarp."

Wait, that is so much worse.

He takes a step back, then rubs his hands together. "Okay, I'm ready to work. Where are those slabs, Number One Tarp?"

I was wrong—the old Xander is not better than ice-cold Xander. Both of them suck.

I've just made an awful, miserable, life-changing mistake, haven't I?

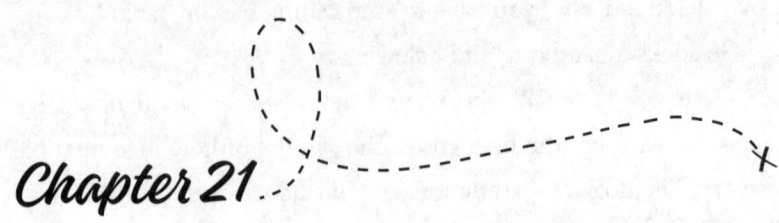

Chapter 21

This is not the partnership I was hoping for. I was expecting the worst, and somehow this is even below that.

"You said you knew it," I complain from atop Xander's bed.

"It's been two minutes. Calm down." He's at his desk examining the metal pieces and scribbling away.

"Didn't you look at the paper I gave you? I already wrote the letters on there."

"Can you just let me do this my way?"

I cross my arms over my chest. "Fine."

Five minutes later, I can't help myself. "Where are you now?"

He drops his pencil. "Maybe you should just leave these with me and I'll come get you when I'm done."

No way in hell am I doing that. I shut my mouth and he resumes. But it only lasts three minutes.

"What was the date? The one that opened the box?"

He doesn't look up. "I thought you wanted this done as fast as possible."

"Well, maybe it's related." And maybe I'm also curious.

"It's not." And that's all he says.

"You know it's likely in Chinese, right? Doesn't that help you narrow it down?"

He closes his eyes, and not because he's thinking.

We do not partner well. I knew this and still jumped in, though I didn't have a choice.

He stands. Then opens the door. "Just . . . give me fifteen minutes, okay? I need some quiet."

"I can be quiet."

He just gives me a look and keeps holding the door open.

"Fifteen," I say. *Same number as your percentage.*

I set my phone alarm, then wander into the kitchen, where Jax and Daphne are returning with breakfast for the group. I consider telling Xander to come out, but it's just fifteen minutes, right? I'll personally deliver his breakfast when the time is up.

After I sit, Brett slips next to me and hands me a cup of soy milk. My mouth is already watering. I dig into the fantuan—rice roll with meat and vegetables wrapped inside—and also mimic the other TARPers dunking their fried dough sticks into the soy milk.

"Daphne and I had to wait in line for forty minutes, but it was worth it for this place!" Jax says.

Brett starts a cheer for Jax and Daphne, and the rest of us join in enthusiastically. The TARPers love their cheering, and I'm here for it. Maybe one day I'll be on the receiving end.

Daphne beams. "This place is 'world famous,' as my dad insists. His favorite growing up. I went to be contrarian, so no matter how this tastes, I'm going to tell him that his use of the words 'world famous' is too liberal."

"Did anyone else only eat Chinese food growing up?" Yang asks.

Trisha nods but doesn't elaborate.

Priscilla, one of the Northwest girls, says, "Our dinners varied, but we always had congee for breakfast."

"We used to have a mix of Chinese and American," Jax says. "Always huge meals. Food is the only way my parents know how to show affection."

"Me too," Trisha says shyly.

Jax nods. "The more food they give you, the more they love you, right?"

"Lucky," Brett says. "My parents didn't believe in breakfast. They'd give me a thermos of hot chocolate or a candy bar on the way out."

"How did you . . . ?" I gesture in his general direction.

"Get so big and strong?" he finishes for me, and I turn red. He winks. "With two older brothers, hiding extra food in my room was my norm, breakfast included."

"No Chinese food for me," Felix says as one of the Northwest girls—I think Sophia?—passes him a fantuan. He's been coming out of his shell more since the girls welcomed him into their group. "Also, does anyone else miss cereal and yogurt right now?"

A piece of fried dough whizzes past my face and hits Felix on the side of his head.

"Boo!" chant a few TARPers. Guess it's not just encouraging chants with this group.

Felix laughs. "Come on, admit it. This is pretty heavy for breakfast, no?"

"Like muffins, donuts, and waffles aren't heavy," scoffs Jax. "Those are just excuses to eat cake when you wake up."

"Helloooo," Felix says, holding up the piece of fried dough that hit him.

With mock warning, Jax says, "Don't make this hard for yourself."

"That's what she said," says—who else—Daphne. A few people around the table chuckle.

"Na shi ta shuo de," Yang says, which garners a bigger laugh, especially from Jax and Brett. Daphne's smile disappears.

"How is that so much funnier?" Brett asks.

My phone alarm goes off. Fifteen minutes is up. I shove the rest of my breakfast into my mouth, grab some food and drink for Xander, and excuse myself from the table.

"This is it," Xander states bluntly when I return to his room. My hope soars, only to nose-dive when he hands me the six pieces stacked together.

"Are you sure?" I ask hesitantly. I don't know what I was expecting, but it wasn't a pile that still looks like a mess of dots.

"I'm sure."

The words that the stack produces are: HUI FU, MINGNA, WEI LI, and ANSHUN. I wait, but Xander doesn't elaborate.

"What do these mean?"

"They're names."

"Of your family members?" This has to be worse than pulling teeth.

He nods. Only when I give him an exasperated look does he say, "Mine, my grandparents', and my dad's."

And suddenly it comes back to me. An-Shun. That's what my mom called Mr. Pan at graduation. The other A. Pan, as Xander pointed out earlier. As for the other three, I don't know what name goes with who, but Xander doesn't want to tell and it doesn't matter for the puzzle.

So I move on. But as I start to lay the pieces on the desk side by side, Xander holds up a hand to stop me.

"They're supposed to be stacked."

"Why?" I had imagined them lying side by side to form a picture or map.

"Because they have to be."

I bite my cheek to hold my temper in as I examine the slabs closer. Picking up the individual pieces and restacking them, I watch as some of the holes disappear, blocked out by the metal from another slab. Conversely, some holes line up perfectly, remaining open.

Why does Xander have to be right?

The leftover holes after all six are stacked form three distinct groupings spaced apart. If you draw imaginary lines through the dots, in the upper left, there's an asymmetrical X that has the lower right line longer than the rest. In the upper right, there's a shape that almost looks like a lopsided tie or a misshapen vase with a triangle on top sharing a vertex with a parallelogram on the bottom. And on the bottom right, there's a stingray or bat or kite.

In the middle of the three of these, there's a single lone hole that's slightly larger than all the other holes left behind.

"What the heck is this?" I ask.

"Well, we don't know the orientation of the stack as a whole yet." Xander takes the pile from me and turns it clockwise several times.

"None of those look right," I say, completely deflated. "We need to keep brainstorming."

"Later." He returns the pieces to me. "We have to get ready."

"For what?"

"TARP is going to Yehliu today."

"Where?" I ask.

"Didn't you read the itinerary? Yehliu Geopark. It's one of a kind, with huge, out-of-this-world rock formations eroded by the sea into different shapes. It's iconic."

I push past this hint that Xander cares about things despite what he lets on. Instead, I gesture desperately at the metal pieces. "But we're so close."

"And we'll be just as close when we come back to it later. I'm not missing Yehliu."

"If you're not going to commit to this hunt, it'll be ten percent instead of fifteen." I hate the words as they come out—especially because I don't want to miss Yehliu either—but I don't take them back.

Xander sighs. "Haven't you ever played video games or written anything? Sometimes stepping away is the best thing."

A piece of our history goes unsaid between us. We used to rationalize during our library study dates that taking breaks was helping us even though we spent them giggling, watching videos online, and—the most painful one to remember—creating rebus puzzles for each other to solve, like how ICE^3 stands for *ice cube* or a drawing of a cake in a pan is *pancake*.

"I brute force it," I say.

The edge of Xander's mouth tilts downward. "This isn't a jar of pickles. And even then, you can try hot water or a knife or a rubber band over the lid. We'll find the rubber band soon; it doesn't have to be this second."

If I found a rubber band, I'd snap it in his direction. Especially because deep down I know he's right, just like how I figured out *A Pan* only after I took a break and painted, and . . . how I did my best learning when we were together.

"Fine," I relent. I wave the metal pieces in the air. "But I'm bringing these."

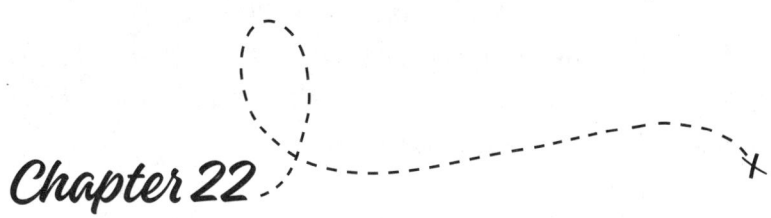

Chapter 22

When I return to my room to get ready, I see it. The flashlight. Just sitting on my desk, waiting. I practically yelp as I rush over and grab it.

How could I forget about the only thing the box held? To make it to the end, I need to stay more organized. I vow to use the journal better moving forward for notes, sketching, and keeping track of clues and inventory.

Twisting the flashlight on, it's so obvious. It's meant to be used with the slabs. What better way to see the pattern in the stacked pieces than to shine a light through the holes?

I struggle to hold them up while correctly positioning the beam of light. This is a two-man job. I silently curse Gong Gong for making me need Xander in so many ways.

With help from the piles of stuff on my desk, I manage to succeed, but the light isn't as metaphorically illuminating as I hoped. Meaning, I don't see anything new as the X, tie, and stingray shapes appear on the wall. But since the beam of light is wide enough to cover all the open holes, I think I'm on the right track.

I want to run over and show Xander immediately, see if he has any further insight, maybe rub in how quickly I found a piece we'd missed. But I only have a short amount of time to get ready.

Between showering, packing my bag, and reading the itinerary to learn about Yehliu (though I'm not telling Xander that), I'm the second-to-last one on the TARP minibus.

As I clamber in, Belinda points at me from the back row and exclaims, "You didn't dry your hair!"

My brow furrows in confusion. "Um, it's okay. In this heat, it'll dry in no time."

Belinda is growing more frantic. "But we're on a bus with air-conditioning."

"Aiyah," Yang says, clearly mimicking one of his family members. "Buneng chui feng!"

Several TARPers laugh, and my cheeks feel hot from not knowing if I'm the butt of whatever joke he just told.

There are three seats per row. The two next to Brett in the second row are empty, and he's looking at me expectantly. I briefly glance at Xander two rows back, deep in conversation with Jax. I want to tell Xander about the flashlight, but I don't want to talk over Jax (or sit next to him even though my armpits are clean). So I slip beside Brett, who beams like I've just made his day, and I can't help my stomach flipping. As I place my bag between my legs, I feel the metal pieces sliding around. I hate that they have to wait.

Trisha enters a moment later and sits beside me, and I'm both disappointed and relieved. Disappointed that Brett and I won't have more privacy, and relieved because now I can ask her, "Why is it so bad that my hair's wet?"

Daphne squawks from the seat behind me, "Your parents never

got on your case about wet hair? Lucky! That was a golden rule—not letting wind or air-conditioning blow on you, and definitely not if your hair's wet. That's, like, a death sentence."

I'm momentarily embarrassed that she heard, but I'm also grateful for the additional information even if it only confused me further.

"My mom would always talk about shi qi and your bones getting wet or something," Yang says from the front row. "Basically, the worry is you'll get sick. It's not that different from wearing a hat when it's cold or whatever."

"Yet also completely different," Daphne says.

Brett dips his head so he can whisper into my ear, "Need me to warm you up, Gongzhu?"

Already accomplished, I think as my cheeks flush.

As the bus starts moving, Belinda calls out, "Who needs sunblock?"

"I'll take some!" yells Yang, who's already wearing a large sun hat.

"Hey, Yang," Jax says as he passes the sunblock forward. "Don't tuo kuzi fangpi."

A handful of TARPers laugh.

Yang isn't amused. "I'm not taking my pants off to fart."

"What?" I blurt out in shock. That's maybe the last thing I assumed Jax said.

Yang argues, "The hat doesn't block my arms or legs, so I'm not doing anything extraneous."

"Wrong idiom, Jax," Brett says. "Yang's not tuo kuzi fangpi-ing. He's hua she tian zu-ing."

Adding just an -*ing* to Mandarin sounds so wrong to me, but no one else seems fazed by it.

Yang sounds exasperated as he applies sunblock to his forearms. "I'm not drawing a snake and adding legs either. That one's worse, Brett."

A discussion breaks out over the two sayings, with Brett claiming that the snake idiom is apt because it's about overdoing something. Meanwhile, Jax points out that when you add legs to a snake drawing, you're ruining the artwork, whereas Yang isn't ruining anything. Felix jumps in, taking Jax's side and arguing that taking your pants off to fart is about doing something unnecessary, which is more fitting here.

"It's neither," Xander says. "Wearing a hat and putting sunblock on your arms and legs are additive, not repetitive."

I notice that Sophia hasn't said anything. She meets my eyes, and I shrug as I say, "It's all Greek—Mandarin—to me."

"I don't speak Mandarin either," Felix says.

"You don't?" I'm surprised since he had been weighing in.

He shakes his head. "I'm just pontificating based on what Yang said—the idioms are pretty self-explanatory, don't you think?"

I don't respond to his question because there's a more pressing matter at hand. "How many people here speak Mandarin?" I ask the group.

Brett, Daphne, Yang, and Trisha raise their hands. Xander gives me a weird look. (As if he doesn't know why I'm asking.)

"I have like four years of lessons' worth," Jax says. "So a lot of useless idioms and history stuff, plus some conversational things."

"I speak Taiwanese," says Grace.

"Only a little," Priscilla answers. "Like, a couple of phrases here and there."

"Basically none," Sophia says. "Nihao. Xiexie."

"Still nope for me," Felix adds to a round of chuckles.

I feel a weight lifting off my chest. How did I not notice this before? I just assumed I was the only one who couldn't speak a second language.

I'm not sure what this means. There aren't a lot of Asians in Blue Hill, so I only ever compared myself to Xander. And now my world is finally getting bigger.

"Xander's Mandarin is probably the best here," Belinda says, and I can't help an eye roll. Luckily, I don't think anyone notices.

After a beat, Brett can't seem to help himself. "Not surprising for someone named *intelligent and successful.*"

That's what Xander's Chinese name means? I wonder which of the names on the metal box is his. Also, I didn't mean to start so much beef between Brett and Xander.

"Yikes, man," Felix says. "Can't even imagine the pressure you had with a name like that."

"That's almost as bad as my friend Harvmit, named after Harvard and MIT," Jax adds.

Xander smiles. "Better than being named Prince Yale or Cornmouth." His joke defuses the tension, and people laugh louder than they would have without the preceding weirdness.

Chatter breaks out as people talk about their Chinese names, and I wish I were sitting next to Sophia, Priscilla, or Felix so we could talk about other stuff. Though they seem to be joining in too. I might be the only TARPer without a Chinese name.

But then Brett turns to me and says, "Sun Bao Shi."

"What?" Is he just rubbing salt in the wound?

"That's what your Chinese name could be. *Bao shi* is *gem* in Mandarin."

It's so sweet I don't know what to say.

And then Trisha jumps in with, "Or you could be Jie Ma. Sounds like *Gemma*, and *jie* means *outstanding, prominent, hero.*"

"And the *ma*?" I ask.

Trisha hesitates. "Um, horse?"

We laugh. This outstanding horse commits both names to memory.

Then Brett lowers his voice as he says, "But I'm still going to call you Gongzhu."

Not only is my Achilles' heel less achy, but I feel warm from the inside out.

Forty minutes later, we tumble out of the minibus and stretch. Everything looks different here. Even the air smells different. Salty, like the ocean.

But I don't have time to enjoy it, not yet. As soon as Xander steps off the bus, I grab his arm and pull him to the side. I've only just told him about the flashlight when he puts a hand up to stop me.

"That's great. Let's get back into it later, yeah?"

He runs off, not letting me get another word in.

When I turn, Brett is waiting for me.

"I thought you couldn't stand him."

"I can't. This is just something we're both involved in because our families know each other, um, being from Blue Hill or whatever."

"It's okay," he says with a smirk. "I like a challenge."

I'm not sure what to make of that. Trisha joins us, and together, we make our way into the geopark. When the cape becomes visible, I stop in my tracks.

We're on the edge of a piece of land that stretches out into the ocean. The sandy surface is dotted with dark brown rocks that look like mushrooms sprouting up out of the ground, except they're giant, soaring two to three times higher than the people standing near them.

The TARPers can't contain their excitement, and Xander leads the pack, running down to the cape first while whooping. Despite all his emphasis on fun, I've never seen him look this carefree before. He reminds me of his grandfather from the photo.

Since the land curves and dips, we take care as we hike around to check out the different formations. Up close, the rocks look like honeycombs. Almost spongy even though they're obviously rock hard.

Suddenly, Trisha grabs my hand and squeals. "There she is!" She points in the distance across the water to another part of the cape, where a large crowd is gathered. Even from here, I can see why that rock formation is special—it's the crown jewel of Yehliu, sort of literally. The rock looks exactly like a lady in profile with her hair in an elegant updo. The Queen's Head, it's called affectionately. And she's perfect.

"Four thousand years," Trisha whispers. "That's how long it took the ocean to make that."

Looking at it, it's hard to believe the water wasn't a conscious artist trying to create this exact shape.

Our hands still linked, we make our way over—perhaps a little too quickly because we each stumble on the uneven ground at different points, but we right each other both times.

"The neck is so thin," I remark when we get close.

"It's broken before, and they had to fix it."

I'm completely mesmerized. I can't put into words why I love this rock. I love that it looks exactly like a queen's head, I love that it formed naturally, and I love that other people see the queen's head too.

It's like the faces in the electrical wires, I realize. I thought I was the only one who saw weird things in common objects, but here, everyone is doing it.

Trisha and I stare until the other TARPers join, after which we rotate taking pictures.

Then we break into smaller groups, with people flitting in and out, constantly evolving formations, just like the rocks. I find the Fairy's Shoe with Trisha, Daphne, and Yang, and it really does look like a fairy came down from heaven, stepped onto this magical place, and accidentally left her sandal behind. There's a long platform representing the sole of the shoe and a curved strap right where it would keep the slipper on her foot. Next, Jax, Trisha, and I locate the Sea Candles; then Brett, Trisha, and I track down the Ginger Rocks.

And my third-favorite, after the Queen's Head and the Fairy's Shoe, "Tofu Island!" Daphne yells, pointing to two long rows of rectangular rocks jutting out into the ocean. We can't get too close to those—it's dangerous and there are big warning signs—but they're so cute.

"Is that what those are called?" Yang asks.

Daphne shrugs. "How official are the names? I just know that's what my parents and I called them."

And that immediately starts a game among the TARPers where we try to find the best names for the less famous formations.

I spout off names as fast as I can see the rocks. "Turtle! Marge Simpson! Toad on a Log! Broccoli!" No one can keep up with me. This is my time to shine, and I've been training for this my whole life.

I keep going until Yang chants, "Gem-ma!" and the other TARPers join in.

My first TARP cheer! It feels as wonderful as I hoped—better, even, because it's the first time my different wavelength has been celebrated. I have never felt so at home. I want to stay here forever.

We do end up staying longer than we planned. Much longer. For the Most Embarrassing reason in the entire universe. Worse than the graduation cap, worse than my Freudian slip with Brett. By a million, maybe even a trillion.

As Trisha and I go back to the Queen's Head to look again, it starts. A rumbling in my stomach. A very painful one.

"Oh god."

Trisha looks at me, worried.

I don't have time to say anything. It's an emergency. "Bathroom!" I yell as I take off.

I have trouble finding it, and the employees I bump into don't speak English. Desperate, I do the only god-awful thing I can think of—I mime it. And just as I've squatted, bent over, and started to use my hands, I remember.

"Bian bian!" I yell—both because it's an emergency and because the words popped so suddenly into my head (in my mom's voice, asking toddler me if I need to poop).

I don't even care that others around me turn to stare. No

TARPers, luckily, but that wouldn't have fazed me either because my mind currently has one objective.

The female employee I was trying to communicate with finally jumps and leads me to the women's restroom.

Just in the nick of time.

I keep thinking it's over, but then the universe laughs at me. Enough time passes that other TARPers come to check on me.

"You okay, Gemma?" Trisha calls out. "Anything we can do for you?"

"Nothing to be embarrassed about," Daphne says in a tone that embarrasses me to my core. "Everybody diarrheas."

"I'm okay," I say as convincingly as I can. "Just . . . need another minute." Or another hour.

I hear them leave, but their whispers float back to me.

"It's a rite of passage when you travel."

"We shouldn't have taken her to the night market."

"It was probably the breakfast—we shouldn't have gotten ice in the soy milk."

"No, it was the night market! My mom says they haven't changed the oil they're using in twenty years."

"That's not true."

A male voice joins, and I want the earth to swallow me. "You all sound like Asian parents right now." I think it's Yang, which makes me feel better. As long as it's not Brett. Or Xander.

"Aw, come on, it was right there: that's what your Asian mom said," says, of course, Daphne.

And it's definitely Yang because he then jokes, "Ni de ma shuo."

I hold my breath as a chorus of laughs rings out, and I release it when the voices fade away.

I'm in there so long that by the time I come out, the sun has set. And out here, farther from the city, the stars are breathtaking. They're the same stars as back home, but somehow they're more brilliant here, clearer. Just a stunning mess of bright dots across an unending night sky.

And it hits me. Just like the food poisoning hit me earlier, though this is infinitely better.

The metal slabs. The dots are stars. What's left after we stack them together: constellations.

I almost jump in the air.

Except I don't because I have to run back into the bathroom again.

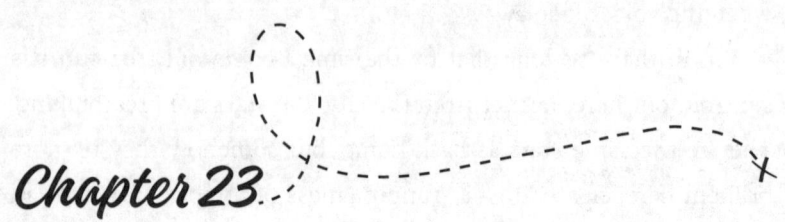

Chapter 23

This is the worst possible walk of shame. Because the only action I got was the toilet, and everyone on the bus knows it.

I climb into the minibus to another round of cheers, and I completely regret ever having wished for that.

My cheeks are probably as red as when I eat niu rou mian. I don't meet anyone's eyes as I slip into one of the two empty seats beside Trisha.

Could this be any worse?

Yang turns around and hands me a plastic bag. "Diarrhea bag," he says. "Just in case. Trust me on this."

Okay, the answer is yes. I shouldn't have asked.

I hope the conversation will turn once we're on our way, but nope. As the bus pulls out, some people ask if I'm okay; someone tells me this happens all the time when you go to a foreign country; someone else says it could've been worse and I could've been stuck in the Hualien train station bathroom, whatever that means; and Trisha gives me a few sympathetic pats on the shoulder. I don't look at any of them and just keep nodding my head while saying, "I'm fine." And when Brett asks me how I'm feeling, I pretend I don't hear him.

I almost jump out of my seat when someone sits next to me. The bus is stopped at a red light, but still—who does that? For a second I think it's Brett, in which case I'll want to disappear, but it's the last person I expect.

Xander. Looking at me with concern.

But he doesn't say anything. Just hands me a plastic bottle of clear liquid. I read the English name on the label, failing to hide my disgust. "Pocari Sweat?" In my defense, I'm very weak at the moment—it's not because my acting skills are on par with my cap throwing.

"Do you prefer this one?" He holds out another plastic bottle with green liquid. Super Supau. "Actually, you should drink them both."

He leans closer, and I instinctually lean away. He doesn't seem to mind.

"I've been there," he says quietly. "Lactose intolerant, remember?" He places the Super Supau in my lap. "They're both good. Better than Gatorade. Though Pocari Sweat isn't the best name. I think they were going for *sweat* as in, drink it after you sweat, but it just sounds like the bottle is filled with sweat."

I laugh, surprised. Maybe I'm delirious. I try to find something sinister in his motive, but I come up empty. "Thanks."

He just nods. Then he leans his head back and closes his eyes.

"Hey, Xander, do you want to switch seats?" Brett calls out.

Please no.

Just like I did, Xander pretends not to hear him.

From the front, Yang asks, "Is anyone else's parents super noncommunicative—like, our dinners are completely silent—yet they're weirdly open about bathroom stuff?"

A few yeses come from around the bus.

"Might be a cultural thing?" Daphne suggests. "Isn't there a poop café here?"

"Toilet restaurant," Jax corrects. "And it closed."

"Well, it existed for a while," Daphne says. "That wouldn't last a day in the States."

I beg the universe to make it stop, but I already know it won't listen to me.

"It'll pass," Xander says from beside me. I almost think I imagined him saying that since his eyes are still closed, but then he opens one slightly and peeks at me.

"Them talking about it or the food poisoning?"

He smiles. "Both."

Despite what's happening elsewhere on the bus and the fact that my intestines are completely empty, I feel warm inside. It must be the lingering food poisoning, right?

9:23 PM Taiwan Standard Time

Val

I'm sooo sorrrry about the food poisoning

That's so terrible

I am cringing on your behalf

And also, um, seriously?

You're working with your X now?

Gemma

Don't call him that!

Fine, your ex

How's that going?

He's surprisingly sitting next to me on the bus right now.

Oooooh

After bringing me electrolytes.

Awww

I'm leaving now.

Maybe you're reacting like that because there's some truth to what I'm insinuating

Huh? Huh?

I'd rather have food poisoning for the rest of this trip.

Be careful what you wish for

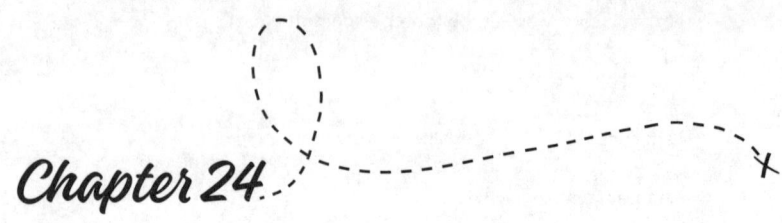

Chapter 24

I'm so distracted on the ride back, I forget about the treasure hunt. But as we pull up to the dorm and I pick up my bag, the metal pieces clink together in a reminder.

I grab Xander's arm. "They're stars!"

His eyes grow wide. "Of course."

We practically run back to our floor.

"Um, are you okay?" he asks, and I at first think he's making fun of how unathletic I am, but then I realize he's gesturing to my stomach.

"Oh. Yeah. I guess so. Your room or mine?"

"Yours," he says quickly, and I realize it's because it's closer to the bathroom.

That's probably a good idea.

"I'll be there in ten," he says.

Three minutes later, a knock sounds at my door. "I think we have to—" I say as I open the door, but it's not Xander. "Oh, Brett, hi."

"How're you feeling?"

"Oh, um, okay." He is the last person I want to talk to about this.

"Do you want to—"

I cut him off mostly because I don't want him to see Xander arrive. "It's nice of you to be concerned, but can we pick this conversation up tomorrow? I'm just beat."

His eyes soften, and I feel bad for lying. "Of course. You know where to find me if you need anything, yes?"

"Thanks, Brett. Really."

How am I kicking *that* out to make room for Xander freaking Pander? But it's not about him; it's about the hunt.

And eight minutes later, when another knock sounds at my door, I yank Xander in so no one else will see. He just manages not to spill the plastic bag he's holding filled with more sports drinks, a thermos, and rice crackers.

"Chrysanthemum tea," he says when I grab the precariously leaning thermos. "In case that sounds better on your stomach."

"When'd you get so nice?" I joke.

He looks at me strangely. "I've always been nice, Gemma." He tosses me the rice crackers. There are two kinds—elliptical and circular.

I open the circles first and take a bite. "Oh, these are so good!"

"You've never had them before?" Why is he so surprised? He knows how I grew up. "These were what I ate growing up when I was sick. This and congee."

"I had chicken noodle soup and vitamin C."

"Oh." He really does look surprised.

"Don't you know that my mom is all about assimilating? I basically had no Chinese influences growing up. I wanted them, but . . ." I trail off.

"I didn't know it was to that extent. I'm glad you're here, then."

He clears his throat. "I mean, you know, it's great that you're getting a chance to pursue your roots. Your Taiwanese American Roots. Pursuit." He grins—wide, extending to his eyes. And he waits.

"It's not a bad name," I say only semireluctantly. Because it has grown on me and I do love that I'm pursuing my roots.

"Yesss!" He pumps his fist.

I can't help a small laugh. He goes over to my window, inches the curtain back, and peers out.

"What're you doing?" I ask.

"Trying to spot the flying pigs. Gemma Sun just admitted she was wrong about something."

I grab my handheld fan and smack him lightly with it. I didn't say I was *wrong*. But, okay, maybe I wasn't totally right before either.

When he lets the curtain go, it catches on my Yangmingshan painting that's hiding behind it. He moves the curtain aside further, and I jump up.

"Oh, um . . ."

"Where'd you get this?" he asks, picking it up. "At the night market? I love it."

"Actually . . ." For some reason, I'm feeling shy. Maybe I'm scared that if I tell him it's a Gemma original, he'll point out how the flowers on the far left are a little too big or the angle of the pagoda roof isn't quite right.

But I don't have to say anything because his eyes sweep over the paint tubes on the side of my desk and he snaps his fingers.

"The group chat. You said you like to paint." He glances back down at the canvas in his hands. "I remember you were great at drawing, but I never knew you were, you know, an artist."

No one has ever used that word to describe me before. Not even me. I'm simultaneously basking in the compliment yet also overwhelmed by his mention of my drawings. He has to be talking about the rebus puzzles we used to create for each other.

I don't have time to respond before he notices the stack of metal pieces propped on my desk between books and snacks. "Oh, hey, you have everything ready for us."

My heart sinks as he puts the painting aside. Never in a million years would I have guessed that there would be any situation where Xander focusing on the hunt would disappoint me, but I would delay it just to hear him call me an artist again.

"I think you're right," he says, pointing to the holes. "These have to be constellations."

"Are there any famous stars in Chinese culture?"

We look at each other, and it comes to me the second Xander's eyes flash with recognition. *The sign in the Taipei 101 elevator. Lover's Day.* Only I can't remember the name of the folktale Daphne mentioned.

"Niulang Zhinu," Xander says, and I nod, trusting him. He types into his phone as I look over his shoulder.

"That's it!" He enlarges the picture and passes his phone to me. "Those are the same constellations as the metal pieces, right?"

Cygnus, Lyra, and Aquila—the X, the lopsided tie, and the stingray. Except, according to this website, it's a swan (how is that a swan?), a lyre, and an eagle—though I guess those designations are just what one person came up with that then became official, kind of like the Yehliu rock formations.

"It says here that these constellations were once used for

navigating—also known as the Navigator's Triangle." I nudge Xander's arm. "This is perfect! I was the president of the astronomy club!"

"I didn't know you had a passion for that until you joined."

Does he know what really happened? He didn't say that with sarcasm just now, but Xander *Pan* likes to dead*pan*. He can't know, can he?

Luckily, he doesn't dwell on it, continuing, "Don't tell me you know how to navigate using stars."

"I do. I made everyone learn celestial navigation." It was because I had no idea what else to do, and I now realize we're likely, most definitely the only astronomy club that did this.

Could my grandfather have known? How? It's so eerie how well some of these puzzles have lined up with my life, though perhaps it's just a result of genetics. Though I do not intrinsically have an interest in astronomy.

Xander isn't convinced. "Don't we need other stuff for that? Like a date? And a time? And a horizon?"

"Oh. Right."

"And that doesn't seem to make sense with the metal slabs and flashlight."

"Right . . ."

"Maybe it's something about the folktale?" he suggests.

"What do you know about it?"

"My grandparents used to tell me the story at bedtime. Prepare yourself—it's sad."

He sits on the chair, settling in. I instinctively get comfy on the bed.

"Niulang and Zhinu were star-crossed lovers—literally, in a sense, as you'll see. Basically, Zhinu, a daughter of the Jade Emperor, is a goddess who comes down to Earth and falls in love with Niulang, a cowherd. When the Jade Emperor finds out, he forbids them from being together because Niulang is human, and he brings Zhinu back to heaven. Niulang chases after her, but the Emperor creates the Milky Way to separate Niulang and Zhinu forever."

"Then what?"

"There are so many variations of the story. In some, because of their heartbreak, they turn into stars. In others, the Jade Emperor changes them as punishment."

Xander pauses to look something up on his phone. "Zhinu is a star in the Lyra constellation, the lyre, and Niulang is part of Aquila, the eagle." He returns the phone to his pocket. "Qixi, or Lover's Day, is the one day a year that the Jade Emperor allows Niulang and Zhinu to meet. A flock of magpies fills the sky and forms a bridge across the Milky Way for the lovers to cross. That magpie bridge is the Cygnus constellation."

When he finishes, it's silent for a second because I'm swept up in his retelling. Then I blurt out the first words that pop into my head. "That's so sad!"

He throws a hand in the air. "I know, right? And it supposedly rains every year on Qixi because the raindrops are the lovers' tears falling from heaven."

"That's heartbreaking! Why do you think my grandfather chose this to be part of the puzzle?" I don't expect Xander to know; I'm more thinking out loud.

"It could be nothing. Maybe they're just the most recognizable constellations, the ones with the most meaning in Chinese culture."

"Maybe," I say, though my gut is telling me there's more.

"So what are we supposed to do with these?" I ask, gesturing to the metal slabs, which Xander leans over to pick up.

As he points to each constellation, he identifies them. "Niulang, Zhinu, magpie bridge. See anything?"

Every time he says the words *magpie bridge*, I have trouble picturing it. I know it's a folktale, but I can't help wondering about the logistics. What would that bridge look like? Do they step on the birds' backs? How many would they need?

Suddenly, it hits me harder than flung fruit punch.

"The magpie bridge!" I exclaim.

"What about it?"

I pull out Gong Gong's boxes. "There's a map in one of these. Help me find it!"

In the fourth box, there it is: the hand-drawn map of Taipei *showing an arch of black-and-white-birds*. A magpie bridge!

Xander gasps. Actually gasps. As do I. Because two of the other illustrations have meaning now too. The cowherd with an eagle on his shirt is clearly Niulang/Aquila, and the fairy playing the lyre is Zhinu/Lyra.

I'm pretty sure we're already on the same page, but I say it out loud just in case: "We have to use the slabs and the flashlight to shine the constellations onto their corresponding drawings."

Xander's already in motion. Breathless with excitement, we work together. First, we lay the map on the floor. Then Xander holds the pile of metal pieces over it as I shine the flashlight through.

"To your left—no, left!" I say.

"That's my right, so you mean your left."

"Right, sorry."

He moves the stack to my right.

"No, I mean *right* as in *correct*!"

He grins. It was a joke.

I feel bad. It's normally a pun I would have liked, but the anticipation is too much right now.

It takes some maneuvering, but we eventually get the slabs and the light in the right—*correct*—places so that the constellations shine onto their map counterparts.

And in the center, the lone enlarged hole illuminates a single location.

X—or O, in this case—marks the spot.

We share a giant smile.

Next stop, National Palace Museum.

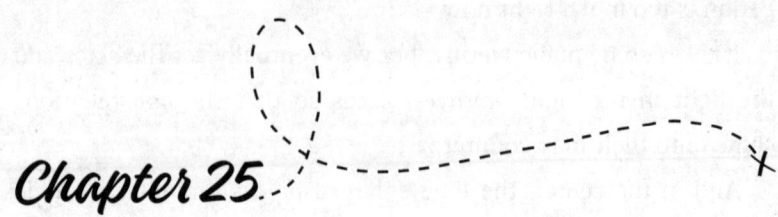

Chapter 25

I'm worried Xander will leave now that we've solved the puzzle, so I quickly blurt, "What do you think we're supposed to do at the National Palace Museum? It's huge."

He hooks right onto the line I've baited. "*Huge* is an understatement. The museum has a permanent collection of seven hundred thousand pieces, which is so big they can only display a small portion at a time."

I knew he couldn't resist an opportunity to recite from his beloved itinerary. "What if the thing we're supposed to see isn't on display?"

"Maybe that's the key. Maybe it's something they never take down."

I nod, relieved. A solid lead. Then I retrieve the journal to look at the next index entry.

"What is that?" he asks.

I don't want to, but I explain the journal. And he immediately proves why I was right to be reluctant.

"You're saying that you had a master journal this whole time?

Right, of course, if I had one, I'd save it for last too."

"Cut the sarcasm. We didn't need it until now."

He leans to look over my shoulder, but I instinctually angle away. Something in my gut tells me I can't trust him completely. And once I show it to him, I can't go back, so maybe this is a line I should hold for now. He seems offended, but the puppy dog eyes only last for a millisecond.

I try to hurry past the awkwardness by telling him, "The next index entry says . . . 'wall.'" My heart deflates. "Well, that's as nondescript as possible. So we're not even looking for an artifact or piece of art? It's just some random wall?"

"That's all it says?"

I nod. But I don't give up. I turn back to the map and examine it again, feeling like we missed something.

Meanwhile, Xander picks up the flashlight and clicks it on and off, twisting it back and forth in an annoying rhythm. Then he starts striking silly poses while shining the light onto my knee, the journal, the Supau in the corner.

"Do you have to be so . . ." *you?* I can't think of how else to finish that sentence.

"Charming?" he fills in with an innocent grin.

"You're only proving my point further," I say, but he's not paying attention to me anymore. He's sitting up straighter, his face serious, and he's examining the flashlight.

"Have you noticed there are tick marks on here?" He points to the seam in the middle of the flashlight. Before I have a chance to look, he clicks the flashlight once to the first supposed tick mark, turning it on, and then he twists it again in the same direction to the second tick.

The light disappears.

"Just another way to turn it off?" I say absentmindedly, already going back to the map.

"Wait wait wait." He jumps up and closes the curtains. "Turn the light off."

I do, and in the sudden darkness, we bump into each other.

"Oh, sorry."

Whatever I touched was *wet*. Ew. Was that his mouth on my shoulder? Or maybe I'm so sweaty I was just feeling my own moistness being rubbed in. Either way, *ew*.

After my eyes adjust, I see that the flashlight now has a purplish glow.

"A *black light*?" I ask, incredulous.

He's too excited to answer. He just aims the black light at the map still unfurled on the floor. Underneath the National Palace Museum, words appear.

It's what you can't see that matters.

Then below that, in smaller writing:

(From here on out, remember that the past always affects the future.)

He lets out a sound that's half whoop, half gasp.

Feels incredible, doesn't it? I want to say, but for some reason, I don't.

Then he reminds me why I have a wall up around him—a metaphorical one, different from whatever wall we're searching for next. "See?" he says, waving the black light. "Having fun pays off."

I was the one still examining the map, my gut telling me there was something else, but whatever. And I have to tell myself to stop thinking about how I didn't find the black light despite possessing it this whole time.

"So what do you make of the new info?" I ask, gesturing to the handwriting on the map.

"Hmm . . . it feels like the first part is the clue and the second a hint, hence why it's smaller and in parentheses."

I nod. "What do you think the clue means?"

He shrugs. "I think it'll be obvious when we get there."

"Well, where do you think we should start when we arrive? Like you said, their collection is massive."

He doesn't bite this time, standing to leave. That'll teach me to pander. "Stop stressing so much. TARP is going to the museum in a few days, so it's perfect."

Perfect? I want to throw a rice cracker at his head. We're not even halfway through the hunt—we can't afford to lose a few days for no reason!

"Can't we go sooner? Aren't you the head of this whole thing?"

"It's only a few days. We have a tour lined up and our tickets are purchased, so we can't move the date easily."

As always, Xander's coolness is driving me up the wall, ironically because he is delaying me from getting to the correct wall. He's doing this for petty cash while I'm trying to ensure my mom's and my future.

Xander tosses me the flashlight/black light. "This was fun. Thanks, Number One Tarp. We make a better team when you're more tarp than shi tanzi."

I have to fight the urge to chuck the flashlight right back at him.

1. ~~Wooden box~~
2. ~~Will~~
3. ~~Framed photo~~
    a. Answer to first riddle: 火/**fire**
    b. First line of second riddle: 火 **goes with water,
    wood, metal, and** <u>**earth also**</u>.
5. ~~Journal~~
Destination: **Yangmingshan**
6. ~~Metal Box~~
    a. Need A: **Pan**
    b. Destination: **National Palace Museum**
7. Wall
8. House gate
Instructions, first line:
9. Address
Number:
10. Poem
11. Beginning
12. Watch
13. X Marks the Spot

Chapter 26

I try to convince myself that a few days off from the hunt is fine—better than fine—because I'll get to finally enjoy TARP. But the universe heard me and laughed. Even though all the TARP activities have been funded thus far, the tickets for the dance performance tonight are out of pocket. And I need to save my stipend for food, not frivolous activities.

After telling everyone I don't feel well and spending the evening painting, it happens again the next day with an unfunded trip to the aquarium. Now I'm not only missing activities when I'm on the treasure hunt, but I'm missing them when it's on hold. I tell everyone I'm still not feeling well and feel guilty when Trisha leaves a bag of Seven goodies outside my door, but it's a guilt I'm used to. Lying is easier than dealing with sympathy or, worse, charity.

Once everyone leaves, I find all my anger bubbling toward the most logical person to blame: Xander. For making some activities an uncovered cost, for making me wait on the next step, for not needing to care about money or people's feelings or anything else except how his hair and abs look today.

When I join everyone for dinner at Din Tai Fung, I do not tell them I spent most of the day poring over *it's what you can't see that matters* to no avail. And maybe also some of it remembering shaved ice with Brett.

Knowing the TARP dinner would be covered, I only ate Trisha's Seven snacks for lunch, meaning my stomach is growling by the time the soup dumplings, spicy wontons, garlic string beans, and Shanghai rice cakes arrive.

Since Daphne is closest to the steamer basket, she doles out dumplings for everyone, carefully picking them up with chopsticks and gently placing them in Asian soup spoons. (Who knew those spoons were so versatile?)

While waiting for his, Yang mechanically picks up string beans one by one with his chopsticks. "This reminds me of eating Cheetos."

"You use chopsticks to eat Cheetos?" I ask.

Several heads nod. "Keeps your fingers clean," Trisha says.

"Great when you're gaming," Jax adds, and Brett gives him a high five.

"That's a great idea," I say. And for the first time, I don't feel like an outsider just because I haven't done something they have.

When I receive my dumpling from Daphne, I follow Trisha's lead, dripping black vinegar over it, then nibbling the top. When I slurp soup out of the tiny hole I made, my eyes widen. So hearty and flavorful. It warms me from the inside out. Then I pop the whole bite-size dumpling in my mouth. As I chew and the mixture of soup, pork, and vinegar coats my taste buds, I can't help closing my eyes and letting out a moan.

Before the embarrassment can set in, Brett winks at me, then moans as he pops his own dumpling into his mouth.

Daphne chimes in with—what else?—"I'll have what they're having."

If Brett hadn't been part of it, I would have flushed as red as the Din Tai Fung sign, but thanks to him, I feel inside the joke, not outside, and my laughs join his and the others'.

For a few blissful hours, the ticking clock fades into the background. But once we return to the dorms, it comes back louder than ever. Now it's counting down not only to the payment deadline but to the end of the trip, the end of my time with my new friends in a city I've fallen in love with. And moving forward, it'll only get harder as I'm forced to choose between the hunt and the program.

Is it fortunate or unfortunate that it isn't really a choice?

7:15 AM Taiwan Standard Time

Mom

Gemma-Bear, is everything okay?

I appreciate your sporadic texts, but it's not enough.

I'm worried.

Can you please call me when you get a chance?
Or text or email more?

8:42 PM Taiwan Standard Time

Gemma

Sorry, Mom.

I'm just really busy here.

But in a great way.

Having a wonderful time.

Don't worry, okay?

I'll call when I can.

Hope you're okay.

<Mom is trying to video call you . . . >

Sorry, I'm on the way
out the door!

Talk soon!

Love you!

Don't worry!

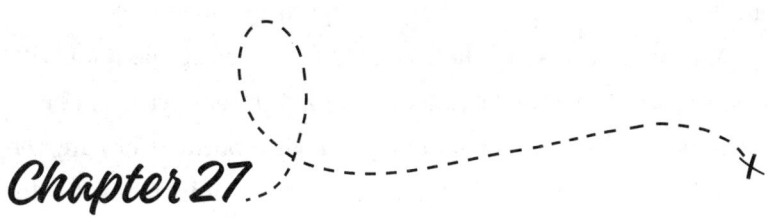

Chapter 27

*F*inally, the National Palace Museum day arrives. That same morning, I get a reminder email from Amherst about the deadline. As if I could forget! I swear I have a white hair now from the ticking clock and maybe also from the guilt of avoiding my mom. I miss her, but I don't want to talk to her about the hunt, my teaming up with Xander, or how wrong she was to keep my culture from me.

We split up into cabs, four people per car, and when we arrive, my breath catches in my throat.

I feel like I've been transported back in time. I know the building is newer, built in the mid-1960s (thanks, itinerary), but it's aptly named, reminiscent of a Chinese palace with its curved, hipped roofs. Its multiple wings are painted a bold turquoise and yellow, and the entire structure overlooks expansive grounds of meticulously kept greenery. Even the front gate is palatial, with six massive columns and matching turquoise and gold accents.

I can't imagine a grander place, yet I'm having trouble truly enjoying it because I'm in too deep, my mind cluttered with thoughts of the hunt and the looming payment.

For the first time, I'm scared I won't be able to find the next clue. It feels like the discovery of the black light was a fluke, a completely lucky break, and luck never lasts—I especially know that.

And now, because of the black light, I'm seeing the hunt with clearer eyes. There's a delicate line to toe—the answers can't be so obvious that no effort is required, yet the less obvious they are, the more chances there are of getting stuck. The journal index is helpful, and Gong Gong seems to have put safeguards in place—like having two different puzzles for that one clue—but the puzzles are growing harder. As much as I hate to admit it, Xander was right. The Yangmingshan clue was like training wheels, and now that they're off, I not only have to learn to bike but I have to win the Tour de France.

When I shuffle inside, I try to stay near Xander, who's annoyingly looking around like he's never heard of a treasure hunt. Brett inches closer to me, which I normally would welcome, but I can't have any distractions today.

Our tour guide is a middle-aged woman who has given tours to world leaders, celebrities, and Nobel Prize winners. Her vast knowledge and soothing British accent aren't enough to keep me from feeling antsy as she shows us the Mao Gong ding—a tripod vessel from the Western Zhou dynasty (ca. 1045–771 BCE) with the longest ancient Chinese bronze inscription known today. Then I'm impatient as we look at eighteenth-century revolving vases with openwork inner and outer layers that interlock and spin.

My eyes are peeled, but how can they look for something they can't see?

When we reach a bluish-green warming bowl in the shape of a lotus flower, my artist brain takes over. At first glance, it doesn't look like much, but the color is mesmerizing. Which the tour guide confirms a moment later, telling us that this is Ru ware, a rare type of Chinese pottery from the Song dynasty (960–1127 CE), and while all Ru ware is special because there are fewer than a hundred complete pieces that exist today, this bowl is unique due to its bluish-green hue that has never been replicated to this day. How? With all the new technology since, how has no one been able to? My fingers itch to try pottery, to learn how different colors are achieved.

Then we come to the crown jewel of the National Palace Museum, and all remaining thoughts of the hunt fly out the window.

A white-and-green piece of jadeite is carved into a Chinese cabbage, complete with a locust and katydid hiding in the leaves. The body of the cabbage is white and the leaves green, the perfect use of the natural color of the stone. I feel a kinship with the unknown artist who carved this. They looked at a chunk of imperfect, uncarved jade and saw a cabbage head, just like I see patterns in nothing.

It bothers me that the jade cabbage lives on but the artist's name does not. Which then has me wondering, do we create art for the world, for ourselves, or for our longevity? Despite my desire to paint, I've never thought to ask myself that before. If one of my pieces ever becomes famous, would I want my name attached?

The next carving is also by an unknown artist, and it's so awesome and perfect I have to stifle a giggle. It's similar to the jade cabbage, but this one is a chunk of jasper perfectly sculpted into a piece of meat. And it looks *exactly* like a cooked pork belly. It's so realistic I have to fight the urge to pick it up and pop it into my mouth. There are even little dimples carved into the surface like pores. The colors are perfect, and I have a hard time believing this is a natural piece of stone.

My mind with its different wavelengths does not feel weird here. I'm not eccentric, a freak. Other people saw that piece of jade, that piece of jasper, and created art from it that's now celebrated. In this room, I feel an invisible thread connecting me to my roots.

As the tour wraps up, I briefly consider asking for the guide's help with *it's what you can't see that matters*, but it feels too ridiculous. I glance at Xander, wondering if he'll say anything, but he doesn't meet my eye.

The guide leaves us in a smaller, more contemporary wing of the museum. "Feel free to browse as long as you like, and I suggest you check out the X exhibit."

It sounds like she said *X*, but maybe I misheard? I wander in the direction she pointed, mainly because it's a section we haven't seen and thus might hold whatever it is we can't see. My X—I mean, he's not *my* X, I just couldn't help the wordplay, though I now regret it—joins me.

"Did you see anything?" I ask him.

"Hi. How are you? Are you enjoying the museum so far?" His voice is deadpan, but I hear the sarcasm dripping off because it's him.

"Yes, I am. I especially fell in love with the carved cabbage and meat."

He smiles. "It learns."

"I'm not a robot. Now, about the hunt . . ."

He frowns. "But not very well."

Is he trying to be as infuriating as possible? With a sigh, I leave him to walk the contemporary exhibits. Even though I'm distracted, my artist brain does appreciate the stunning works before me. I'm especially drawn to the mixing of Eastern and Western styles, and

I think with a pang about my mom's ginger-honey rooibos tea . . . which I'm not there to make for her. Maybe I should stay in better touch than I have been.

Shaking off the guilt and homesickness, I step into the next room. I immediately recognize the first painting: *Flight of the Majestic*, a trio of cranes soaring above a lotus-covered pond, by Lee Kyung-Song. But the one I've seen has more muted colors, softer lines, and a more traditional style—my grandfather painted his own version, and it's sitting in my dorm room.

I spot several people—artists—of all ages scattered around painting at portable easels to re-create the piece before them. How many times was Gong Gong here doing exactly that? What would I give to have done that with him?

I must be on the right track because I spot several more paintings Gong Gong replicated: a school of koi immersed in what looks like a puddle from one angle and a lake from another (*Swimming Beyond*, by Chang Ying-Hom), landscapes of Chinese mountainsides and gardens (again by Lee Kyung-Song), and temples (by Huang Shufu). In his versions, Gong Gong added a classical lilt to each of these modern paintings, highlighting the old over the new. Like the reverse of Picasso's cubist interpretations of Velazquez's baroque-style *Las Meninas*. And Gong Gong changed details. His cranes were on a mountain, not over the water. Instead of his koi being in a puddle and lake, his were in a fishbowl and ocean—which makes a stronger statement, in my opinion. I take photos of them all, looking forward to comparing his versions to the originals.

When I reach the exhibit mentioned by the tour guide, I learn that X is an alias for an artist whose identity is unknown, similar to Banksy. And I recognize two of the pieces from Gong Gong's work here as well, the first of which is *Broken*, a painting of a broken flag on a stone wall. A large chunk of the actual wall has been reassembled here in the middle of the room. Gong Gong created his version on canvas with the stone wall painted as the background. The second piece is *Chengcing Lake Tea House*, a painting of two men holding hands while walking alongside a shimmering body of water. A red pagoda with intricately carved sides sits in the background, separated from the lake by an old gate.

Gong Gong's versions of X's work contrast even more than his do with the previous artists'. While X's brash, bold lines make a statement, Gong Gong's delicacy and softness appear to be passively capturing beauty, observing. Because the styles are so different, I wonder if I would have recognized these two pieces without seeing the other replicas first.

When I move farther into the X exhibit, I abruptly stop breathing.

There's an empty frame on the wall.

It's what you can't see that matters.

My eyeballs immediately jump to the adjacent wall of text. And I read everything I can, starting with the biography of the artist.

X was active in the 1960s before disappearing. They started with street art, graffiti, and murals that defied convention by expressing criticism of the government and depicting gay and lesbian relationships. While Taiwan is progressive now—being the first Asian country to legalize same-sex marriages in 2019—back in the '60s, it wasn't as accepting. X's art varied in medium and subject, but the centralizing, defining characteristic of their work was the letter *x* over people's faces—sometimes a giant one instead of any features, and other times replacing the mouth and/or eyes, depending on the message.

As for the blank spot on the wall, a painting of X's was once right here, in this frame, on display. Now it sits empty, a golden ornate border protecting nothing but the white wall paint beneath it. Six years ago, in the middle of the night, the painting disappeared. Some believe it was taken by X. Others believe it was X's descendants, reclaiming what's rightfully theirs. X never donated or sold any pieces, so there was much speculation over how they were acquired.

The museum label provides a name, *Elemental*, but no photo. However, the piece is described in such detail that, with the help of X's other works around me, I can see it in my head. The stolen piece showed two men with *x*'s for eyes and mouths, holding hands, unaware of the five elements trying to destroy them from all sides: fire, water, earth, wood (represented by a falling tree), and metal (represented by a sword).

I pause momentarily on the idea of the five elements. I thought it was four—fire, water, air, earth. A quick internet search shames me for knowing only the Greek cosmology elements used to explain nature. The elements referred to here are the Chinese elements, which represent agents of change.

Fire, water, earth, wood, metal. Where have I heard that before?

I whisper the words out loud to myself, and on the third repetition, I hear it in my head.

Fire goes with water, wood, metal, and earth also. The third puzzle. I even had to write that line out in the journal as part of the index worksheet.

And with that revelation, the last line from the previous puzzle takes on new meaning. *The past always affects the future.* The puzzles are connected. Past pieces will be used again. That's why I've been filling out that worksheet, keeping track of certain answers and locations. I'm not exactly sure how the elements tie into everything, but at least I know I'm on the right track. This empty frame is where I'm supposed to be.

Except . . . where's the next clue? I don't see anything on the front of the frame—do I need to examine the back? But I'd be kicked out just for getting too close to it.

I glance around, looking for inspiration, and that's when I see Xander standing next to me, a mischievous smile on his face.

When our eyes meet, his grin grows larger and more boyish.

"No" is all I manage to get out.

"Time to have some fun, TARPer. In fact, we may need more TARPers in on this." He rubs his hands together, and I have the sudden urge to grasp them and pull them apart. "It's time for a heist."

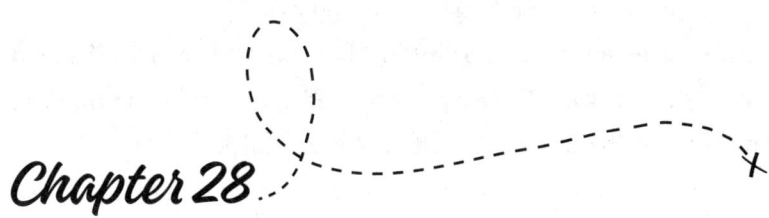

Chapter 28

Surprise, surprise. Xander and I disagree yet again.

"We're not involving the others," I say, putting my metaphorical (and literal) foot down.

"Why not?"

"Because . . ." I don't know how to articulate it. "Because."

"It'll be more fun. And we need them."

"For what?"

"We have to steal that frame, of course."

"*What?*" I had no idea that was what he'd been thinking.

"What else are we supposed to do?"

"I don't know, maybe the next clue is just . . . on the back of it."

Xander gives me a look like, *your idea isn't as fun as mine*, because, right, that's how this hunt works. "Well, either way, we can't just walk up to it—"

"And examine it," I finish for him just as he says, "And steal it."

"We're not stealing it," I hiss, keeping my voice low so no one else hears.

"It'll be the same plan for both. We need access."

I grab his arm. "I mean it, Xander." My voice is filling with panic. "No stealing. Let's take a beat. Talk this through."

"I thought you said we have a ticking clock."

Now is when he feels a fire in his pants? "Xander." I want to smack the smirk off his face as he tiptoes, then dances toward Felix and the Northwest girls. "Xander!" I hiss-whisper.

The urgency in my voice is finally enough for him to pause. *Not them,* I mouth, shaking my head. Not the ones he's closer friends with.

Then who? he mouths back.

"A treasure hunt? For real?" Trisha says in the hallway after I've given the basics to the group in front of me, which includes her, Daphne, Brett, Jax, and, unfortunately, still Xander. "This is amazing. And I told you, you're not scared of anything. You're a doer. You just go for it."

I glance at Xander, expecting him to make a joke about how I'm a doer only if there's no fun involved, but he doesn't react, except for the edge of his mouth lifting in—amusement? It can't be in agreement.

"Thanks," I say even though I don't see myself that way.

"Is this what you've been doing with him?" Brett asks me, gesturing in Xander's direction but talking as if he's not there. "Why him?"

I don't have time for this territorial BS. "Because his family is involved. We have . . . history." That's a loaded statement if there ever was one.

"So that's why you've been talking to him even though you can't stand him," Brett says as if everything makes sense now.

Xander raises an eyebrow at me, and I don't know if I want to laugh or disappear.

"Ooooh," Daphne says. "Is it time for me to get my ruler out?"

Disappear. I want to disappear.

"So what do we need to do?" Trisha says, and I could hug her.

Xander takes that as his cue to jump in. "Well, since we have the dream team together, here's what we need . . ."

"No. Absolutely not." I'm shaking my head so hard my neck twinges.

Brett waggles an eyebrow. "Come on, I know you're capable of being naughty."

That . . . is not helping, not one bit. Neither is Xander looking at me curiously, making me want to dig my heels in and tell him *yeah, I can be naughty* even though the words make me want to barf.

I ignore them, arguing, "We're basically begging to be thrown out!" I leave the other words unsaid. *I'm not being a wet blanket; this is about self-preservation, making sure we can stay long enough to find the next clue.*

"That's why we have the plan," Xander says.

"Not a very good one," Brett mutters under his breath.

"You think you can do better?" Xander challenges.

"Stop," Trisha says, surprising everyone. "Gemma, this is your hunt, so you decide. But I think we can pull this off. Together. And we want to help you."

"Agreed," Daphne says, followed by Jax, and my heart swells.

My eyes meet Trisha's, and when I see the resolve in them, I slowly nod.

I think Xander is going to be offended that I didn't trust him but agreed after just a few words from Trisha, but he simply moves on. "Everyone know their roles?"

All heads nod—Brett's reluctantly.

With a gleam in his eye, Xander says, "Should any of us be caught, TARP will disavow all knowledge of your actions. This huddle will self-destruct in five seconds. Go, TARP!"

That does not help calm my nerves. But the fact that this group feels like the exact opposite of a movie heist, let alone a Mission: Impossible one, makes me want to laugh. Case in point, we break from the giant huddle that was screaming for attention, then exit the abandoned hallway in different directions.

Unfortunately, Xander and I are stuck together. It's the most logical choice since we know best what we're looking for, but it doesn't mean I have to be happy about it. We wander over to the empty frame—Xander nonchalantly and me as if I just learned to walk this morning. As soon as we're in position, Xander pats his head as he rubs his stomach—a signal and also another metaphorical cardboard dog just to annoy me. On cue, Jax and Brett wander in, their conversation growing louder and louder. When they reach the adjacent room to our right, their words become shouts. Then the shoving begins. Of course they were given the most over-the-top, theatrical roles. The two nearest security guards run to break them up. I worry they're taking it too far and ensuring their removal from the museum; they shouldn't be kicked out on my account.

The third security guard watches from his seat but stays put. A wrinkle, but one Xander planned for. He tugs on his earlobe, and Trisha walks into the room and promptly faints. Daphne runs over, hysterical, yelling for people to help her friend. The guard jumps off his chair.

Isn't this all too obvious?

But there's no time to think. Unfortunately, it's not because things are going according to plan. The plan, as demanded by me, was to use the distractions to peek beneath the frame. Grab the bottom, lift, search the underside. "*Quick peek*," Xander promised. But I can't do that. Because Xander definitely-no-longer-pander-now-just-liar arcs his right arm in a giant circle over his head, and the lights go out. I look over just in time to see Felix exiting the pitch-black room into the lit hallway, his job done. Felix, who I didn't wanted to include but Xander brought in anyway to seemingly execute the original plan I'd said no to.

"Don't—" I start, but it's already too late. Xander's going for the frame.

Quick peek my ass.

I fumble in my bag for the flashlight. If I can just aim it at the back of the frame and show him the clue is there, maybe he'll find his brain and stop committing a crime. In my haste, I click too far, and as I shine the black light onto the empty wall within the frame, glowing words appear.

Check Leaning House gate

Thank god!

"The—" I start to say, but I'm cut off as Xander continues to lift the frame off the wall and an alarm starts blaring.

This can't be happening.

"I told you not to take it!" I exclaim, but it's too late now, isn't it? Desperately, I tell him, "The writing's on the wall!"

"You don't think I know that?"

"No, the actual writing—" I try to explain, but I'm interrupted yet again.

"Hey!" I hear from my left. The guards may have been distracted, but the alarm drew their attention back to us even in the dark, likely because the sound is emanating from right in front of us.

I quickly memorize the words on the wall, whip the black light around to make sure I didn't miss anything, then I take off.

Xander is right on my heels. *And he's still holding the frame.*

"My god, what are you doing?" He's completely lost his mind to the cardboard dog. The dangers of having fun. I've never been so frustrated to win an argument before.

Footsteps sound behind us. They're gaining. And we have nowhere to go but out into the light. Where everyone will see our faces, not to mention Xander holding the frame since he can't seem to put it down.

Should we stay in the darkness? Try to blend in with the crowd?

The alarm continues blaring, and it feels like it's somehow pointing them to us when it's not; it's just that loud.

"The flashlight!" Xander whispers urgently.

Hoping he'll have to put the frame down to use it, I hand it over willingly. And then an idea comes to mind. "Use it to find us a hiding place," I say, my head darting around. But it's too dark.

"I wish I could see," I murmur, and of course, at that moment, as the alarm continues bashing my eardrums, the lights blink on, bombarding my eyes with such a jolt I can't see momentarily. I hope the same is true for the guards. While my vision is still compromised, my hand is suddenly jerked forward and I yelp as I'm pulled from the room. It takes me a second to realize it's Xander tugging me along while shushing me. Once I see that it's him—and *without* the frame in his hands—I breathe a sigh of relief as I stop fighting and run with him, which increases our speed exponentially.

We stumble into a crowded room. Xander's pace slows so we don't draw attention to ourselves, but we're still hustling. Abruptly, he turns into one hallway, then another, and finally he lets go of my hand right before slipping behind a giant CLOSED FOR RENOVATIONS sign.

When I don't follow him—I think I'm still in shock—his hand darts out, grabs my wrist, and pulls me in after him.

There's no space. We're squished between the sign and a plastic tarp behind us. I'm not sure if there are workers inside the area, so we're trapped here. The gap is just barely wide enough for the two of us, and I'm pretty sure I'm standing on Xander's left foot. Our faces are inches apart. I can see every eyelash, every sweat bead. I think there might be a smidge of room behind him, but I'm completely stuck.

"Can't you—" I start, but he backs up only so he can put a hand over my mouth. I shake it off, and he puts an index finger up to his lips.

Footsteps sound past us.

Guards, he mouths to me.

I freeze, waiting. I lose my footing slightly—standing on someone else's shoe is surprisingly difficult—and Xander grabs my arm to steady me. My elbow accidentally pushes the tarp (*Tarp!*

Tarp! I can't help chanting in my head). As it flutters, we hold our breaths, hoping no one is on the other side, or if they are, that they'll think it was a random breeze, maybe from the AC.

I try to focus on my breathing so I'm not thinking about Xander's hand on my arm or his exhales onto my face. Or how his breath smells like mint and how he used to always use Listerine after eating—does he still?

Suddenly, the sign moves. Someone's found us. I want to scream, but there's no time.

Xander kisses me.

Except he doesn't.

His nose is pressed against my cheek, his hand covering the lower half of our faces. We're not kissing, but I'm guessing it looks like a kiss to whoever is now standing in front of us.

My eyes are wide open in surprise. And my stomach . . . did I swallow Pop Rocks? It's not even a real kiss! And it's *Xander*. Not Alex, who I used to dream about doing this with—he's gone.

I don't have time to react before I hear "Aiyah!" from beside us.

Xander immediately pulls away from me. "Duibuqi," he says, taking my hand in his and leading me out of the tiny spot.

It's a different security guard from the ones who were chasing us. He smirks. "Ah, nianqing ren. Mei guanxi. Wo haojiu yiqian gen nimen yiyang. Haoxiang jiushi zuotian!"

He laughs, and Xander laughs with him. I force a smile.

"Hao ba, hao ba. Kuai zou."

He waves us off with a nostalgic look, and Xander gives him a friendly wave before leading me away.

"He understands young love," Xander whispers to me.

My cheek where Xander's nose was a minute ago feels as hot as my palm in Xander's hand.

I don't have time to comment on everything that just went down because I realize Xander is leading me to the exit.

"We can't leave!" *I don't know what Check Leaning House gate means yet.*

"Uh, I think it's time for us to go, Gemma." He grips my hand tighter, and the frustration builds in me as we scurry outside.

Once the fresh air hits, I explode. "Why'd you make us do that? You only see the fun, and that's so dangerous. Can you take this hunt seriously now? Was that enough to show you how wrong you've been?" About this, about the cardboard dog.

"Hey, we didn't get caught, right? We're okay."

"Just barely! Where's the frame?"

"I left it in that room. They'll find it and put it back up, no big deal."

"It's a *huge* deal! We didn't need to risk any of that! I told you, the clue was written on the wall—"

I stop talking when he reaches into his back pocket and produces a piece of cardstock. He holds it out to me with that arrogant grin of his.

"What . . ." I trail off as I take it from him.

Five illustrations. I recognize the artist immediately, as if they had been drawn by my own hand.

"Where was this?" I ask, my heartbeat racing for a different reason now.

"In the frame."

"In?"

Xander nods. "I felt a loose corner and asked for the flashlight so I could look behind it. This was stuffed inside."

That's why he ditched the frame. He'd found what we needed.

"And it makes sense with the clue too, right?" he adds. "It's what we couldn't see that mattered."

Feeling grateful to him is somehow worse than wanting to throttle him—I don't know how to deal with it. But I wouldn't have found this without him, especially because I had thought the writing was all there was.

Maybe we make a better team than I want to admit.

"Told you cardboard dogs are necessary."

Or maybe he can go to hell.

I ignore him and check my phone. Texts from the other involved TARPers assure me that everyone is fine. Brett and Jax didn't even get thrown out.

Breathing a sigh of relief, I turn back to the cardstock. But I can't focus on the images when the same thought keeps going through my head.

"Why would my grandfather make us do something like this?" The black light was clever and harmless, but the frame?

"It's an adventure. Why have you do any of it? He's whimsical, fun, sending you out to do things you never would have otherwise. Isn't that the whole point of this?"

Is it? Well, that's a giant can of worms I can't deal with right now. The point of all this needs to be money at the end. If there's other stuff along the way, fine, but that can't be the only thing. And whimsical, fun? That does not sound like the man my mother described. Not to mention, I don't find anything whimsical or fun about breaking the rules at a museum (though I do love my ragtag heist team minus Xander Pander).

Luckily, Xander doesn't ask me again how I could be related to this person, and we focus on the cardstock:

At the top is the word *Instructions*. Below that, there are five images—three in the first row, then two in the second.

The first three images: a giant nose and a finger inside one nostril (I mean, what?), an arrow pointing up, and a golf tee.

The two images in the next row: a plus sign and the number one.

They remind me of the rebus puzzles Xander and I used to love. Not exactly the same—it's not one image representing a single saying—but close enough. They're memories I do not want to relive with Xander, though I'm also upset when it becomes clear he's not thinking about the same thing.

"Is that someone picking their nose?" he says, chuckling as he points to the first drawing.

As much as I don't want to, I can't help a small laugh. "Appears so." But there's no time for giggling. I concentrate on the two images next to it. "Pick up—"

"Tee," Xander finishes for me.

"I know what a tee is."

"I didn't say you didn't."

Except he's always making fun of my lack of athleticism, and this feels adjacent to that. For the sake of the hunt, I let it go. "What does it mean? Are we supposed to find a golf tee?"

Xander shrugs. A lot of help he is.

"Well," I say, motioning to the handwritten word at the top. "It looks like these are instructions for what to do when we get to the next place."

I glance at the index and confirm it.

8. House gaTe
Instructions, first line:

"*Check Leaning House gaTe* must be our clue for where to go next," I say.

Xander points to the second row of images. "What about this *plus one?*"

"I'm not sure," I say, but I fill in the journal index so we can move on to the where.

8. House gaTe
Instructions, first line: **Pick up tee**

"And what's this about a leaning gate?" Xander asks.

Annoyed, I tell him yet again, "It was written on the wall in the empty spot. Black light."

Instead of sensing my irritation, he holds up a fist. I do not bump it. Unfazed, he says, "Good going, Number One Tarp," as if I returned his gesture.

"Thanks," I mumble as I open a clean journal page and jot the clue down exactly how it was written on the wall.

Check Leaning House gaTe

"Hmm . . . was there a gate on the way in here?" Xander thinks out loud.

"I don't think so," I start, but then I remember the grand gate at the front of the entire complex. "Wait, there was!"

We rush down there, which takes a long time because the place is so huge. When we reach the bottom, we're both out of breath and sweating. Okay, fine, I'm the only one panting.

"Looks perfectly upright and straight, no leaning," Xander says, examining the gate both from a distance and closer.

I can't talk.

"I don't think this is it," Xander concludes. "Must be a different gate."

I manage a nod.

Xander walks twenty feet to a bench in the shade, and I follow. When he reaches into his bag and hands me a bottle of water, an embarrassing groan rumbles from my parched throat.

As I gulp desperately, Xander says, "Um, sorry about the stage kiss. I panicked."

Suddenly it's like we're fourteen again, sitting next to each other in the library after school, alone, and his fingers grazed mine. After I smiled, he leaned down and kissed my hand. So minor, so small, yet it was bigger than my entire world at the time. I thought about that tiny peck for weeks, maybe even months, which is more embarrassing than how winded I am right now.

Ignoring the memory, ignoring the curiosity over whether Xander ever pictured us kissing for real the way I used to, I simply ask, "Where'd you learn to do that?"

"I did the high school play sophomore year."

"You played Romeo?" I don't remember that.

"Chorus member number twelve, thank you very much, but I did see them teaching Martin and Laura how to stage kiss."

"Why'd you do the play? For fun?"

"Why'd you do the astronomy club?"

"Not for fun," I say, which is as close to the truth as I'll get. I change the subject immediately. "Are there any other gates here?"

"Yes, but maybe we should walk to the next one?"

I ignore his jab and refuse to admit I can't even walk right now. Instead, I pull out the cardstock and journal.

Even though I need to focus on the *Leaning House gaTe*, I can't help my eyes wandering back to the illustrations. They feel like a piece of Gong Gong, even more so than his handwriting. These drawings are just black ink on paper, but they remind me of his paintings, with similar shading techniques and line angles, almost like a signature. I think I could recognize his work anywhere, just like his handwriting. He managed to put his distinctive mark on the famous paintings upstairs . . .

Wait.

"We need to go back in," I say, standing.

"Gemma . . ."

"We have to."

I retrieve my phone and pull up the photos I took earlier in the museum. More specifically, the *Chengcing Lake Tea House* painting by X. Even though it's completely different from Gong Gong's in terms of style, they both have the same important feature. On the right side of the canvas, there's a gate. Only, it's not leaning. Like the gate in front of the museum, it's upright and straight.

"My grandfather painted a version of this," I tell him. I wish I could remember his painting better, but it only comes to me in unhelpful, fractured pieces.

I text the photo to Xander, which he then examines while tilting his head this way and that. Meanwhile, I swipe to the next photo in my roll. The painting's plaque. Nothing too helpful here—it was created by X in the '60s and, like all his works, the name was given purely by description.

Chengcing Lake Tea House. Check Leaning House gaTe. Is the *house* in the clue short for *tea house*? Are we supposed to do something with the gate in the painting? Maybe examine it with the black light?

We need to get back in. I want to scold Xander for his impetuousness, but I can't when that's what got us the instructions.

Xander reaches over and opens the journal in my lap to the page where I've written the clue.

Check Leaning House gaTe

And then I remember.

"Look." I point to the *T* in *gaTe.* "I noticed this when I first saw it. There's weird capitalization." And if the past has taught me anything, it's that capitalization mattered to Gong Gong.

The *C, L,* and *H* are also capitalized—is that significant? I place the phone screen on top of the open master journal, the plaque photo now beside my handwritten clue.

And then my brain sees the pattern. With the clue and the plaque side by side, it becomes obvious. The capitalized letters: *C, L, H, T.* Or better yet, *C, L, T, H. Chengcing Lake Tea House.* I scribble frantically in the journal, crossing out letters.

Bingo!

Check Leaning House gaTe is an anagram for *Chengcing Lake Tea House!*

I whoop, so excited that I forget my previous hesitations (and infamous cap-related experience) with the action. It comes out naturally, and, turns out, it's more of a noise than the word *whoop.*

"It's an anagram!"

Xander's eyes ping-pong back and forth between my phone and the journal. A moment later, they grow wide and I realize he was confirming the anagram. But instead of being merely excited, he looks . . . incredulous?

"How did you figure that out so quickly?"

Slightly embarrassed, I shrug. "I don't know. My brain just . . . sees patterns sometimes."

"What does that mean? What kinds of patterns do you see?"

No one's ever followed up before, though I guess I've only ever told my mom and Val, both of whom had seen enough to understand.

"Um, it's not important." There's no way I'm telling him about the faces in the electrical wires or how I tend to rearrange letters and numbers even when I'm not on a puzzle hunt.

"Is that why you're so good at this stuff?"

"I'm not," I deflect.

He grins. "You always have been, M Game."

I ignore the question that arises—*Is he thinking about the rebus puzzles?*—and focus on the weird nickname he called me. I assume it's along the same lines as Shi Tanzi, but after a second, I realize it's an anagram too. It's easier when I can see the letters in front of me—I'm such a visual person—but luckily it's only five letters.

"Too bad I have that extra *m* in my name sticking out in front, Ax Nerd."

He chuckles. "Ax Nerd? That's not a thing."

"You're right, Ex Nard."

"Okay, that's way worse. I'd rather be Ax Nerd."

"Are you sure, Ex Red Anal?"

His eyes bug out as he laughs. "No fair! There are so many more letters in my name."

I shrug as if to say *not my problem.*

"All right, M Game. Mega M. What does your genius brain say we should do next?"

I internally blush at the compliment but force myself to focus on the hunt. "Is Chengcing Lake a real place? If so, maybe we need to go there. To that tea house."

"It's a real place, but doesn't that seem too simple?"

Simple? After he was just impressed by my figuring out the not-simple anagram?

But before I can respond, he says, "Maybe the mention of the gate was just a way to get us to the right painting." He holds up the photo of the original *Chengcing Lake Tea House.* "Does this look off-kilter to you?"

I tilt my head. "Maybe like a degree. Why?"

That boyish, excited, this-is-going-to-be-epic grin appears on his face, and my stomach drops.

"Why?" I ask again, nervous this time.

"I think we need that painting."

I burst out laughing. "Good one." It's the first of his jokes I've ever found funny.

"I'm serious." He gestures to the frame. "The painting is *leaning.* And the clue had the word *leaning.* Coincidence? I think not."

Just when I thought we were starting to get along . . . I close my eyes and count to three. Then I ask, "Haven't you learned your lesson?"

"No, I'm sure of it! Just listen—"

"You are no longer allowed to be in charge of any more plans."

I storm off, my chin held high.

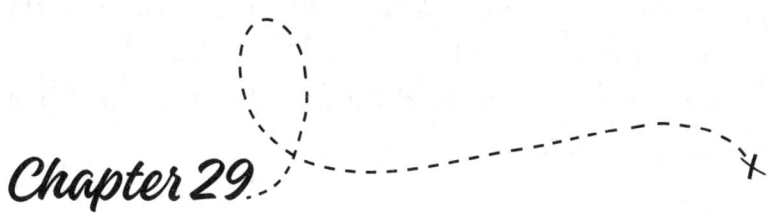

Chapter 29

Back at the dorm, Xander, Brett, Trisha, Jax, Daphne, and Felix listen enraptured as I tell them about the anagram. Part of me feels like the group is too big now, especially with Felix, whom I didn't invite, but it's also hard not to enjoy their enthusiasm.

"This whole thing is so cool, Gemma," Trisha says. "I mean, your grandfather has found a way to, like, show you himself. To make up for not knowing you."

I smile and nod, wishing I didn't have to cover up how I came here for the money.

Brett is deep in thought. "I never really thought about my grandparents as . . . I don't know, people, until now. Does that make any sense? Like, I know they immigrated and it was really hard and they came with just the clothes on their back and they used to have to walk uphill ten miles to school"—a few people chuckle—"but they're *people*. Like us. They had loves and losses."

"That they never talked about," Daphne adds.

"Because it was too hard," Trisha says, her eyes sad.

"And it's too late now," says Daphne. "Mine are all gone."

"My grandparents talked to me all the time," Brett says, "but I still just thought of them as, you know, my grandparents. Like how you see your parents when you're small. I guess I didn't grow out of that since they passed when I was ten."

Trisha puts a hand on mine. "Gemma, this is so special. You should treasure it."

Treasure the treasure hunt. The hunt itself is a sun, a treasure, from Yong Ping Sun. I hadn't thought about it that way before.

A quiet, reflective moment passes over the group. I have too many emotions, so I shove them all away.

"I'm going to call my grandpa!" Jax blurts out, retreating to his room.

I'm so surprised I'm still staring at his closed door when Felix pipes up. "I never thought of my parents as people either. They've been fighting. A lot. And instead of spending the summer with me, they decided to send me away. They applied to this program for me, and I've been bitter. But . . . I guess it hasn't been easy for them either." He takes a breath. "I don't know what I'm saying. Just that, it was fun today. Thanks for including me. And sorry if I've been tough."

He turns and leaves before any of us can say anything.

I guess you never know what other people are going through. Here I thought Felix was simply a curmudgeon, but there was so much more to him. Just like how none of the other TARPers know what I'm going through, and how I hid so much from my high school classmates. I make a mental note to check in with Felix later.

Before, I didn't want to let anyone other than Val in on this, but now, looking at their supportive faces, I can't remember why I felt that way. I've been scared to let people in, and maybe my world being so small is partly my fault. Sure, I wasn't born into a huge family, but aren't Val and the Gonzalezes my family? I should already know how rewarding it can be to form connections, to trust. What happened with Xander—Alex—made me focus too much on the potential pain and forget the possible beauty.

"Gemma," Trisha says, "can we see the painting? Your gong gong's version?"

I beam, then let them the rest of the way in by retrieving the *Chengcing Lake Tea House* replica from my dorm and displaying it on the common room table. Xander pulls up the original on his phone.

At the same time, we all spot the most notable difference.

"Leaning gate!" we yell in unison. The gate in Gong Gong's painting is crooked.

"And the people aren't present," Xander adds. The two men were the focus of the original, but in Gong Gong's, it's the tea house.

"That's not as important as the leaning gate," Brett argues.

Maybe it wouldn't be so bad if one of them left.

"I still think we need that original painting."

Maybe it should be Xander.

"There's no way he would have wanted us to steal a piece of art," I say.

"How do you know? It was a good thing Xander took that frame off the wall," Daphne says, and I'm annoyed that she's enabling him.

"I don't think you're supposed to steal it," Trisha says to my relief. "Maybe you just need to use the black light again, like you did with the empty frame."

I thought that earlier too, but . . . "He wouldn't have defaced the original with UV paint," I say. But even as the words come out,

I wonder, *Would he have?* I don't know him. Though to do that, he would have needed his own ragtag team, a huge one.

"Oh my god," I exclaim suddenly, realization dawning on me.

"What?" ask several of them.

I reach into my pocket and retrieve the flashlight. Xander immediately turns off the overhead light. Gong Gong wouldn't have defaced a priceless painting no matter how whimsical he was, but there was another painting he could alter.

When I shine the black light onto Gong Gong's replica, the tea house comes to life, glowing. A beacon. Highlighted now not just by its central positioning but also color. The leaning gate is also glowing.

This is exactly the confirmation I needed. I want to shove it in Xander's face and gloat. Like I learned back at Taipei 101 with the damper—sometimes the simplest answers are the best ones. I need to write that in giant letters in the journal so I don't forget again.

Xander still hasn't accepted it yet, saying, "Surely that can't be it."

"Don't call me Shirley," says—who else?—Daphne.

Brett holds up his phone. "That's a real tea house at Chengcing Lake. I found the exact match here."

I open the journal to write down our destination. And I see the instructions again—*pick up tee*. "Of course," I say, pulling out the cardstock to show everyone. "We have to go there to buy tea."

"We should have known," Trisha says.

Daphne nods. "Chinese people love their homophones."

"What's the *plus one*?" Brett asks, his eyes darting to Xander.

The others run through possible meanings: "Maybe you're supposed to play golf there—hence the golf tee—and shoot plus one?"

"Or maybe it's a cross, not a plus sign?" "Is it possibly a romantic thing?"

I don't want to consider that last one, so I raise my hand. I'm shocked when the entire group hushes. "Um . . ." They're all looking at me expectantly. "I hope it'll be clear once I'm there. But I think we're agreed that my next step is to get to that tea house."

The group breaks out into cheers. I join in until Trisha says, "So when are you leaving for Kaohsiung?"

1. ~~Wooden box~~

2. ~~Will~~

3. ~~Framed photo~~

   a. Answer to first riddle: 火/**fire**

   b. First line of second riddle: 火 **goes with water, wood, metal, and <u>earth also</u>.**

5. ~~Journal~~

Destination: **Yangmingshan**

6. Metal Box

   a. Need A: **Pan**

   b. Destination: **National Palace Museum**

7. ~~Wall~~

8. ~~House gate~~

Instructions, first line: **Pick up ~~the~~ tea**

9. Address

Number:

10. Poem

11. Beginning

12. Watch

13. X Marks the Spot

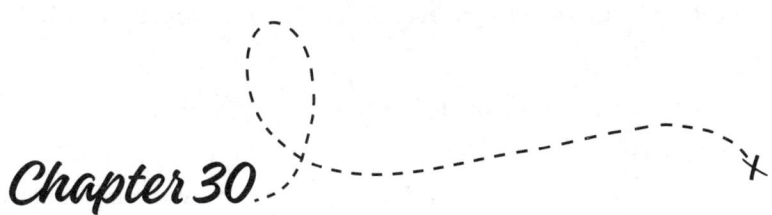

Chapter 30

Xander is not excited about traveling to Kaohsiung. Neither am I, for the record. I'm not only going to miss more TARP activities, but I just brought my friends in and now I have to leave them. It's a subtle reminder why I'm hesitant to let people in—because it never lasts.

But I'm going, no question. The Amherst reminder email is still fresh in my inbox, and Kaohsiung is only a few hours south on the high-speed rail.

It is, however, a question for Xander, who catches up to me in the hallway.

"I'm not sure I can leave TARP."

I'm scared he's going to ask for a higher percentage, but he doesn't. That was the end of his sentence.

"And I wouldn't ask you to." Which is true. Xander's show-ing a rare glimpse of himself in how much he cares about TARP. I wouldn't take that away from him no matter how much I want him to come with me.

"So you'll go alone?"

I can't help wondering what subtext is there—does he think I can't do it by myself? I hate even more that I'm wondering if he's right.

"I have to see this through," I say.

"Of course."

I try to lighten the mood. "It'll go faster anyway without you getting me in trouble or kicked out of places."

His face falls. "I was just trying to help." After a beat, he says, "Good luck, M Game," and then he slinks to his room.

When will I learn that I shouldn't be attempting jokes?

I tell myself I'll be fine. I tell myself that all Xander and I do is fight anyway, so this is for the best.

But I've never been a good liar.

Before I go to bed, I slip a note under his door thanking him for his help and promising to keep him in the loop, especially if there's any information about his grandfather.

At the crack of dawn, my friends wake early to bid me adieu. Xander's noticeably absent, his door shut. I try not to look at it as my stomach flips upside down.

Trisha especially seems glued to my side, and I wonder if I should ask her to come along. If I'm being honest, I'm scared—fine, utterly *terrified*—of doing this alone. But I also don't want to put that pressure on her because why would she choose this random, unpredictable journey over TARP?

"We're here if you need help," she says, and I do feel better. But only for a second because she follows that with, "Not just on the puzzles, but if you get lost or need a translation . . ."

"And if you get lonely," Daphne adds, "I can pretend to be the two apes fighting over you."

I almost choke on my own spit that she would interpret Xander's actions that way. As for the other one, I look over at Brett now. He hasn't offered to come, and I haven't asked.

He ignores Daphne's comment and chucks me lightly under the chin, so soft I almost don't feel it. "Go get 'em, Gongzhu."

I'm partially disappointed, partially relieved. The idea of so much one-on-one time only stresses how little I know him and how wildly this could veer off the rails at any moment, especially when I'm at my most high-strung and vulnerable. At least I know exactly where he stands, not willing to give up TARP activities to come— which, why would he? Again, we barely know each other.

I give him a brief nod, then address the whole group. "Thanks for all your support. Truly. It means so much."

A chorus of *good luck* and *keep us updated* rings out.

I'm halfway down the stairs when I hear Trisha call out, "Wait!"

I stop breathing. Could it be? Maybe. I check my watch. I can't spare much time, but if she packs quickly . . .

Footsteps sound behind me.

I turn, hopeful. Pounding down the steps, brimming with excitement . . . is Xander.

Xander.

My heart soars. But I also don't want to count my chickens yet.

"Are you . . ." I start but then stop because the question feels ridiculous. But at the same time, I need to make sure. "I didn't think you were coming."

He grins at me—boyish and almost puppylike. "The puzzles say you Need A Pan."

I blink rapidly to keep tears from forming—that would be Most Embarrassing. "That's really . . . I can't believe . . . *Thank you.*"

This is above and beyond. He's not just helping me, he's sacrificing TARP, the only thing he's ever cared about enough to let it show.

He gestures to the overstuffed backpack slung over his shoulder as he says, "Don't worry, I've packed the grappling hook, shovel, and sword—the last one in case we have to slay a dragon. One can never be too prepared on a treasure hunt. Do you have our snarky parrot wearing an eye patch?"

His joke brings an unexpected smile to my face. Before, I would have been annoyed that he wasn't taking this seriously, but he is. He's here. And given that, maybe there's room for some fun after all.

"I didn't have space for him," I answer, not knowing how to joke back. Should I have named the parrot? Though all names suddenly elude me. Except George.

Xander grins. "No problem, we'll pick up Captain Jack Not-Sparrow on our way."

That name is so much better than George.

I can't stop staring at him. This Xander that defied all my expectations. Maybe I need a new perspective. Maybe I've been too stuck in the past. It's exactly as Gong Gong said, the past affects the future, perhaps too much sometimes.

In my head, I take the hate goggles off.

"Ready, partner?" he asks me.

"Yes, *parrr*-tner," I say in my best pirate impersonation.

He holds a hand up, and for a second I don't know what he's doing. I put my hand against his awkwardly, and he looks confused before he decides to squeeze it.

When he turns and leads our way out the front door, I realize he was holding his hand up for a high five. A move that is so far out of our usual interactions I didn't recognize it.

The hand squeeze was even further out of our world, even when we were dating. So why did it feel so nice?

I exhale in relief when our train pulls out at 6:26 a.m. on the dot. I feel like a hero departing on an epic journey. And I'm thrilled to be with my partner in crime, metaphorically, and, after yesterday, literally. After all, X marks the spot.

I try to ignore Daphne in my head saying, *That's what she said.* And I also try to ignore the strange flutter that ripples through me.

As I settle deeper into my window seat, my phone buzzes with a text. My eyes widen when I see it's from Brett.

> Do you need me to come save you?

I'm confused for a second. Save me? I respond.

> From Mr. Annoying. Pressed your buttons yet?

I'm suddenly glad I didn't say *Xander Pander* to that steel trap. And picturing Brett here in between us, I have to stifle a laugh. That would be fun for no one.

"Guard dog rearing his head?" Xander says coolly, his eyes amused.

Ignoring him, I quickly text Brett that I'm fine, then put my phone away.

"Did you tell him to heel?"

I roll my eyes and don't dignify him with an answer. Instead I say, "Thank you for coming." The words don't feel like enough, so I open a bag of rice crackers and offer that as well, though of course that's not enough either.

"This maker of cardboard dogs doesn't turn down an adventure." He takes a cracker. "Also, um, are you okay?"

At first I think he's still talking about Brett, but then his eyes shift to the cracker, and I realize he's asking about my gastrointestinal tract. Kind of him but also embarrassing.

"Fine. I just like them."

He nods. "So much better than saltines."

"So much."

There's a strange energy between us I can't quite place. Maybe it's because there's so much we're not saying. Or maybe it's because we're both thinking about how I had diarrhea.

"Speaking of Yehliu," I say, "other than, you know, it was awesome. You seemed to enjoy it too?"

His aura turns wistful. "Yeah. I was looking forward to that excursion the most."

Which explains why he was so adamant to not miss it.

"My dad used to tell me about it when I was young," he

continues. "We'd read these Xiao Bai Ke books when I was little—these Chinese educational books about science—and one of them was about Yehliu. It just . . . looked fun. I've always wanted to go."

There is so much packed beneath what he just said. The fact that his bedtime stories with his father were Chinese science books, that he spoke as if they didn't have much else to bond over, thus making Yehliu special . . . I suddenly feel bad for him. My mom was absent because of work, but she was close. Warm. Open.

I'm suddenly reminded of something else from the Yehliu trip—the bus, when Brett made fun of Xander's Chinese name.

"Does your Chinese name really mean—"

"Yes. It does." He doesn't even let me say it.

The questions fill my brain. *Did you feel pressured? Is that why you pretended not to care, as a coping mechanism? Or did something happen in ninth grade that changed you, changed us, and you didn't tell me about it?* I suddenly realize that as much as I feel like I know Xander, I don't. I might have known him four years ago, but after that, I only saw the act he projected at school. I have no idea who he's become or how he's changed.

As if to prove my point, the next thing out of Xander's mouth is the last thing I would have guessed. "You know, I just realized that your grandfather would have loved my Chinese name. Hui Fu, based on the actual characters, means *intelligent* and *successful*. But *hui, intelligent*, is a homophone for *will be*. So even though it's not the same character, *hui fu* also sounds like it means *will be successful*."

That sounds exactly like something my grandfather would love. Not only am I getting to know Gong Gong, but so is Xander. And *Hui Fu*—I finally know which of the names from the metal box is his.

Now it feels like I'm looking through the holes of the metal slabs at Xander, at Hui Fu, a black light shining on him, illuminating parts I couldn't see before. Parts he wouldn't *let* me see before.

"Is your English name related to your Chinese one?"

Xander shakes his head. "My parents picked my English name and my grandparents my Chinese one. Or . . ." He nibbles his lower lip in deep thought. "Do you think there's a chance your grandfather was involved in my Chinese name? I never thought about that before, obviously, but, I mean, they were close once. Business partners. Friends, it seemed, from the photo. And my grandfather was not whimsical in the least." He pauses. "Do you know when their falling-out was?"

"Not a clue. Do you know what business they had together?"

"No. But my grandfather was in toy manufacturing. So maybe something with that?"

Of course a toy manufacturer would like puzzles. I press my lips together to keep from saying, *How do you know that exact business isn't the one he stole from my grandfather?* I wonder if he's thinking the same thing.

"Anyway," he says, "it wouldn't be that far out of the realm, right? If they were still speaking then. Maybe I even met your grandfather."

"How funny would that be, if you met my grandfather and I didn't."

"You didn't?" His shock in turn shocks me.

"I thought you already knew that."

"I didn't. And I'm sorry. That's really sad."

I shrug. "Your family isn't the only one who disliked him."

"Your mom?"

I nod. "They were estranged. So it was always just my mom and me." *Against the world.*

"Now it makes even more sense that you came on this journey to get to know him."

"Does it?" I blurt out. But instead of regretting it, I want to talk about everything with this newly illuminated Xander, the one who knows about the hunt and my family history. I haven't been able to talk about my confusing emotions revolving around Gong Gong with anyone since I got here, not fully.

"I don't know where this hunt is leading," I say. I worry he'll bring up the treasure and his cut, but he doesn't. "I wasn't even sure there was anything to follow before I flew across the world. I mean, who puts a puzzle in their will? But also, who flies across the world on a hunch?"

"You do." He's talking as if this all makes sense when it doesn't. "That's exactly the Gemma I know."

"Is it?"

"The one who bulldozes forward, full force, regardless of what other people say? Who laser focuses on something she believes in? Yeah, that's you."

I can't tell if it's a compliment or a dig, but his face is soft, a gentle curve to his lips. *You're a doer,* Trisha told me. I've never felt like one, but here is another person telling me that.

Because I don't know how to take a compliment (I don't get many), I say, "Well, if that's true, I get why you're so annoyed with me all the time."

His eyebrows arch in confusion. "Gemma," he says, his voice serious. "I'm not annoyed with you all the time."

Is he joking in his deadpan way? Except he's staring at me intensely like he's trying to look into my soul.

He leans forward until his face is inches from mine. Goose bumps rise on my arms, not from fear, but from something else. Something foreign. Anticipation?

He opens his mouth to say something.

But just then, the train conductor taps Xander on the shoulder, and he startles, his arm bumping into mine and pushing me away.

"Huoche piao?" the conductor says.

Xander fishes his train ticket out of his pocket, and I do the same. With a nod, the conductor continues down the aisle.

Whatever moment had been there before has passed. Xander digs into his backpack and emerges with the Hello Kitty pack of cards. How far we've come from when we first got those.

"Want to play?"

I can't help wondering, *Play cards or whatever game seems to have started between us today?*

And how do I win?

Chapter 31

I step out onto the streets of the sun—I mean, Kaohsiung.

"How in hell is it hotter here? I mean that literally—are we in hell?" I normally wouldn't have said that out loud, but maybe it's the heat, or maybe it's because something has shifted between us and I feel more open with Xander now.

"It's even hotter farther south of here," he says. "My grandfather used to say Ping Dong is the land of two suns. That's where he did his military training."

I wonder if Gong Gong was in the military. He had to have been, right? Mandatory conscription? When did that begin?

I can't decide whether a cab or public transit is better—a cab is more expensive but also saves us twenty minutes. Luckily, Xander quickly hails a cab, then pays for it without letting me chip in. I feel bad, like a charity case, but it passes quickly because we're *here*. Chengcing Lake.

We enter through a grand gate that is not at all crooked—we both checked, just in case. The tea house is a ten-minute walk from here, which sounds close but feels long, especially with so many distractions on the way. Lush green trees and stunning purple flowers flank a path that winds around the gorgeous, expansive lake. The water glimmers with multiple shades of green and blue, reflecting a sun that is way too hot but is at least pretty.

Xander seems just as awed as I am, his head turning left and right to take in every detail. We pass two aquariums, one of which is free, and I'm dying to go in—especially after being forced to miss the TARP aquarium trip—but I don't want to slow us down. Maybe later?

We come to a long white bridge that cuts across the lake, zigzagging back and forth at right angles like a snake or dragon crawling through the water. The wooden sign at its head says NINE-CORNERED BRIDGE in English and Chinese.

"You look like you want to," Xander teases me. Calling out my shi tanzi ways without actually calling me a wet blanket.

But I can't lose any time. Not when the stakes are this high and I needed money yesterday.

"Come on, it's hot," I say, which isn't a lie, but it's not the main reason I'm leading us away.

Luckily, he follows without cracking any jokes.

The first thing we notice when we arrive is the gate.

"It's leaning!" Xander exclaims, his eyes lighting up.

It's crooked, perfectly matching Gong Gong's painting (but not X's).

Together we examine it. I'm too afraid to touch it—it feels wrong, like a crime—but Xander goes right in. And when he pulls in the direction that the gate is leaning, it moves with a groan.

I want to yell at him to be careful, but that seems rude when he's the one doing all the heavy lifting, literally. So I bite my lip and hope we won't be kicked out for destruction of property.

Xander heaves until he lifts the gate post out of the ground. Underneath, there's a thin metal box.

"Oh my god," I whisper.

"Uh, Gemma?"

"Hmm?" I look up from my trance to realize Xander is still holding up the gate and is now sweating profusely. "Oh! Sorry!"

I swiftly bend forward and pick up the metal box. As soon as I'm out of the way, the gate slams back down. I hold my breath. The entire gate shakes, but it doesn't collapse. Just remains leaning there, like this is the only position that makes it happy.

"Good job," I say even though I wonder if there's a more graceful, less stressful way we could have done it. But at least it's done, and quickly to boot.

The box is so well sealed it takes me a minute to get the top off. Inside is a folded-up piece of cardstock. On it are gorgeous illustrations interspersed with handwritten symbols that look like a language I've never seen before. I'd like to think I can at least tell if characters are Chinese by now, and these are not. As for the drawings, some are obvious—I immediately note a cloud and a moon, even a self-portrait of Gong Gong—but others are trickier. The longer I look, the more details I notice, including mathematical symbols. Mostly plus, minus, and equal signs. No multiplication or division.

"What in the world is this?" I ask.

"Must be the next clue."

"Already? What about picking up tea or the plus one? Or maybe they're related? There are plus signs on this."

"Only one way to find out," Xander says, heading toward the tea house.

When we arrive, it's empty. No customers, not even an employee. Is it too early? I hope we won't have to wait until the afternoon.

The tea house is airy and adorable. Sunlight streams across wooden tables and stools in intricate patterns created by the carvings on the side of the pagoda. In front of a giant wall of teas just waiting to be steeped is a counter set with teacups and teapots. Beyond that, in the back, is a closed curtain.

I try to focus on our next steps while we wait. Pick up tea, plus one. The former we can definitely do, though easier said than done because the menu is completely in Chinese.

"Just pick out some tea for me," I tell Xander.

"What do you like?"

"I don't know." I've liked all the tea I've had here, but I can't remember what's what.

"That's not the right answer," calls out a voice from behind the closed curtain.

A moment later, a woman in her seventies appears through it. "A person should know what tea is their favorite. Otherwise, how do you know who you are?"

That feels . . . erroneous, but I don't say anything.

"We're here to pick up tea," Xander says, emphasizing the last three words, and I'm glad he's here. I would've been too shy to do that.

Recognition sparkles in her eyes. "Ah, zhendema? That's good. I'm Jiayi."

"Jiayi!" Xander exclaims. He looks at me and gestures to her. "She's Jiayi!"

"Um, yes. Hi, Jiayi, nice to meet you." I don't understand why Xander's so excited.

"Sorry, right," he says, a little frazzled. "Jiayi. That means *plus one*."

From the puzzle! She's who we're looking for, apparently.

She grins widely. "That's what your grandfather used to call me. Plus one."

"Her grandfather or mine?" Xander asks.

Jiayi ticks her head in my direction. "I think yours."

"I'm Gemma Sun."

"Yes, Sun. Nice to meet you."

"And I'm Xander Pan."

Jiayi's eyes widen. "Pan, as in Pan Wei Li?" Wei Li—I remember that from the names on the metal box. And I make a mental note that she said the surname first.

Xander nods. "That's my grandfather."

"Wei Li used to call me Good One, in English, which is the direct translation of Jiayi, and of course Yong Ping had to take it a step further and use the homophone. Always with his games. Just like how, whenever he came to pick up tea, he would say, 'I'm here to inspect the tea!' Because in Mandarin, 'pick up,' *jian*, plus 'tea,' *cha*, is a homophone for 'inspect.'"

I look at her blankly. I don't know any of those words, so the joke is lost on me. My Achilles' heel has let me down again, and this time, it makes me feel like I'm not my grandfather's true lineage.

"He did love his games," I force out.

That's enough to earn a smile from Jiayi. "And that's why you're here! I just didn't know to expect both of you, together."

"We're not together," I say quickly, then feel bad. I refrain from looking at Xander. "Anyway, you knew we were coming?"

"Yes. And now I can finally fix my gate. You got the thing?"

I nod, then ask, "How long has it been crooked?"

"So long I can't remember when it was straight. Wei Li had just started his job delivering to us when he backed into it."

I can't help a small smile. The way she talks about them . . . they feel alive.

"Why so urgent now?" Xander asks.

Jiayi puts her hands on her hips. "Because Yong Ping told me months ago I couldn't fix it, and now it's all I can think about. Apparently, it's the most crooked gate in all of Taiwan—people are traveling from across the world just to see how ugly it is!"

I stifle a chuckle. I'm already falling in love with Jiayi. And then I realize what her words imply—my grandfather started planning this months ago. He knew his time was nearing the end, and instead of reaching out, instead of trying to see me before it was too late, he put together this elaborate hunt that feels more ridiculous by the second. He went to so much effort to do everything *but* see me.

The disbelief, frustration, and desperation ball together in my stomach, forming a knot that sinks to the bottom. I don't know if I will ever understand how Gong Gong could choose not to meet me. He had eighteen years. How did my mother phrase it that day? *It's not like he fought for us.* This taints the hunt and almost makes me want to stop on principle.

Jiayi comes over and gently pushes on my shoulders to get me to sit down. "You need to try all the teas," she says. "To figure out which is your favorite. Yong Ping would have it no other way. Then that will be the one you 'pick up' and take home with you."

I'm not sure if she could see the emotions on my face. Xander, on the other hand, is staring at me intently. I look away. He would never understand. He grew up with his grandfather, not to mention a huge family.

For the first time on this hunt, the pressure of the ticking clock disappears. If only it was for a different reason.

I've tried several greens and whites as well as three oolongs harvested from different Taiwan mountains.

"The higher the tea grows, the sharper and better it tastes, and thus more expensive," Jiayi tells me.

"So our grandfathers called you nicknames in English?" I ask as I sip a Dragon Well. Wow—that is fantastic, maybe at the top of my list for now. It's floral, umami, almost a little nutty.

Xander reaches a hand out to grab the next porcelain teacup, and Jiayi smacks it. "Thirty more seconds," she says to him, then turns so she's facing both of us. "Your grandfathers taught me English. They were young, in their twenties and thirties when they lived and worked here, at Chengcing Hu, and I was just a child, spending my days doing schoolwork in this tea house while my mother ran it. They were learning English because they were determined to get out of here, to go to the land where everyone said you could find gold in the streets."

Their business. So many questions pop into my head, but I keep them to myself as Jiayi continues her story.

"They made me learn English with them. Their lessons were dumb, didn't work." I stifle a laugh. "But *I Love Lucy* and *I Dream of Jeannie* worked. Now, reality TV. Have you seen *Love Island*? So juicy!"

This time I do laugh out loud.

Xander hesitates before asking, "Did you keep in touch with them?" I know he's trying to ask if she knows what truly happened between them—a.k.a., who was at fault.

"Wei Li I never saw again after he went to America. But he sent letters, photos." She retrieves a stack and hands it to Xander. "For you. Even though the photos you've seen—most are of you."

I glance over, waiting for Xander to open the letters, but he doesn't. He just grips them tightly in his hands. Which rubs me the wrong way. I've shared everything I know about my grandfather with him.

Jiayi's eyes ping-pong from Xander to the stack to me. I assume she's going to let it go, but no, not Jiayi. "What's wrong with you? Why aren't you looking?"

"I'll look later," Xander says, pretending he doesn't care, but I can see through his fake armor. Is he scared to show us his real self, or is he scared to find something he doesn't want to know? Like a hint that his grandfather was the one who took everything, and that it wasn't bagel seasoning?

"We're all family here," Jiayi says.

"Maybe back then." It's the most Xander is willing to show.

"Do you know what happened between them?" I ask Jiayi.

"What do you mean? Yong Ping still spoke fondly of Wei Li when I saw him recently."

Xander's eyes flash. The rest of his face stays bland, neutral, but I already know what he's thinking. That if Yong Ping still spoke fondly, then most likely his family's story is true: my gong gong was the villain.

Is that why my grandfather made this hunt and included Xander? To atone for what he'd done? That certainly feels more and more like a possibility as I'm getting to know the heartless man who never wanted to meet me. That would just go hand in hand with my luck, wouldn't it? To crave family my entire life only to learn that my one extended family member was a bad person.

Oblivious to our inner storms, Jiayi asks, "So what was the clue that sent you here?"

Xander tells her about the painting, finishing with, "Do you know why X painted this tea house?"

Jiayi sips her tea, cocks her head to one side, and says pensively, "This tea house has meant a lot of things to a lot of people."

"Did you know X?" Xander asks.

"Briefly. He was gone young. Quite the loss. He regretted his work. Felt he created them when he was too naive, trying to make sense of a world that can't be made sense of. He was just trying to express himself and didn't mean for his paintings to become what they did."

Xander leans forward. "Who is it?"

Who cares? I want to say but don't.

"I promised to never tell." She begins pouring the next round of tea.

"Did Gong Gong paint when you knew him?" I ask Jiayi, trying to steer the conversation back.

"If he did, he kept it a secret from me. He was just a fisherman back then."

"Really?" I don't know why, but I wasn't expecting that.

Jiayi nods. "Among other things. He did anything, whatever jobs he could get. He was conscripted into the army, and after his service, he was lost. That's how he ended up here, and how he and Wei Li met. Two lost souls after their service, trying to find their next step."

Xander nods. "My grandfather never talked about his time in the military." He hesitates before adding, "Though he didn't talk about much, really."

Jiayi slides new teacups in front of us. "Jasmine. My personal favorite. Gan bei!"

"Gan bei," Xander says, toasting. "Dry cup," he translates for me.

I would be thinking about how adorable that phrase is if Jiayi's eyes hadn't turned judgy when she realized I didn't understand Mandarin.

I want to tell her I'm judging myself enough for the both of us, but I just sip the tea.

"This one," I say. "My favorite." I don't know if it actually is or if I'm just changing the subject. At least this lie won't hurt anyone but me.

Chapter 32

We leave Jiayi with our hands and stomachs full. Jasmine and Dragon Well tea for me—how did she know I wasn't being completely truthful when I said *jasmine?*—high Alishan oolong for Xander, and a bag of dried mushroom snacks each. All on the (tea) house, pun intended.

Right before we part, Jiayi asks, "Where are you headed next?"

I show her the cardstock, and she laughs.

"Classic Yong Ping. I don't know what it says, but that seems too long for where I thought he'd send you."

"Which is . . . ?"

"Aihe. One of his favorite places here."

"Love River," Xander says for my benefit.

Jiayi raises her eyebrows at me, and to avoid her gaze, I pull my phone out and look up Love River—a tourist destination with gondola rides, boat cruises, and even a night market in a connecting park. The river itself is the spine of Kaohsiung, not only holding cultural significance but also playing a crucial role in the city's economy and tourism.

When I reach the section about how Love River received its name, my heart drops. When I first heard *Love River*, I pictured a sight for proposals, anniversaries, declarations of love. But the origin of the name comes from tragedy, in honor of a pair of lovers who died there by suicide in the '40s.

"Why was it Gong Gong's favorite place?"

"You love what you understand," Jiayi says. Then she shuffles us along, telling us to get moving on our adventure.

Outside, I pause.

"Should we find a place to solve the clue?" I say at the same time Xander says, "So should we make our way to Love River?"

"Why?" I ask.

His brow furrows in surprise. "Don't you want to see it?"

"Only if it's where the next clue sends us."

"Don't you think your grandfather would have wanted you to? I thought you came here to get to know him."

The payment email flashes through my mind. "I . . . think he'd want me to stick to the hunt."

"Isn't the point of this not just to get to the end, but the journey to get there?"

Said by someone whose life isn't about survival. But I bite my tongue.

He continues, "If he simply wanted you to have an inheritance, he would have just left it to you. Why send you on this hunt if not to show you beautiful places and have you trod the same steps he did? You charged to the tea house without appreciating anything. Look at where we are!"

All I hear is that there might not be an inheritance at the end of this, and that would break me. But instead of admitting that, I just say, "My grandfather's entire life was trying to survive; he wouldn't have had the luxury to sit around looking at the view."

"Or maybe that's precisely why he's making you look. Maybe it took him a lifetime to learn how to cope, how to appreciate what's important, and he's trying to pass some of those lessons on to you, like how to find the beauty even when it seems impossible."

I ignore the niggling memory of Gong Gong making me pay respects at Yangmingshan. I don't want Xander to be right. "Stop trying to mold everything into a cardboard dog."

"That's not what this is. Well, not completely," he adds with a smirk, which I don't return. "Look at the evidence. Don't you feel like every step of this hunt hints at something else, something bigger? Like after Jiayi said your grandfather understands Love River, I'm looking at the Niulang Zhinu constellations in a new light. Did your grandfather experience a tragic love story?"

I nod reluctantly. His wife died young, leaving him to raise his daughter alone, and then he lost her too, in a different way.

It makes some sense, but . . . "Why wouldn't he just tell me about his life?"

"Not everyone can just say what's on their mind." I know there's meaning behind his words, that he's referring to himself, but now does not feel like the time to unwrap that.

"Let's just figure out the next puzzle," I say instead.

"You're hopeless."

"And your head is in the clouds." The words escape before I can think, and I immediately regret them.

"Is that how you picture me, walking around singing *la-di-da* in my head? Because you're wrong. I'm singing *ob-la-di, ob-la-da.*"

Ob-la-di-hell, I'd like to ob-li-ter-a-da that joke from my memory.

Xander stands. "You can work on the hunt if you want. I'm going to go enjoy myself."

"Wait," I say. Xander turns, hopeful. I swallow the words that were about to come out. *I don't even know where to start with this puzzle.* And in its place, I say the only word that pops into my head. "Please." Then I try a little harder. "Let's walk around the lake, enjoy the sights, and find a place where we can sit and figure out the clue. If that sounds good to you."

I think we both know that I haven't changed my position, but after a moment, Xander sighs. "Fine."

We don't have time for the aquarium, but I lead Xander back to the nine-cornered bridge and walk onto it first as if to prove how *ob-la-di* I suddenly am when really I'm hoping for a better vantage point.

And I'm not disappointed. I can see so far out from here, and the fact that the bridge turns gives me so many different views—is that why it's designed this way?

I halt in the middle and lean over the railing. Xander stops beside me. All I hear is the clock ticking in my head, but not him. Not a care in the world as he drinks it all in, taking a deep inhale, then sweeping his eyes over the entire scene before closing them to presumably listen to the water and birds around us.

I stare at him with envy. Maybe my life could be that carefree if I wasn't constantly worrying about me and my mom surviving. But there's no use in wishing, so I shade my eyes with a hand and survey the surroundings.

And moments later, I find it. A few feet out from the other end of this bridge, there's a two-story open structure. I can't tell if it's made from real bamboo or just painted to look like bamboo, but it has a roof to block the sun and a table inside—the perfect spot to work on the next puzzle.

Suddenly, I do feel relaxed. I close my eyes, enjoying the breeze on my face as I listen to the chattering of nearby birds and insects. When I open them a few seconds later, Xander is smiling at me.

Just as planned, he doesn't argue when I lead him straight to the table at the end of the bridge.

The cardstock sits between us, looking just as confusing as before. The only difference is that now, after meeting Jiayi, I recognize her as one of the illustrations.

I tackle the only task I can—I write descriptions of the illustrations to try to simplify. But once that's done, I fear my usefulness has run out. Now the puzzle is half-English, half-gibberish:

$$\frac{\triangle}{\rightharpoondown} - - = ?$$

[hashtag] [hashtag]

$$\frac{\sqcup}{\rightharpoondown} / - \sqcup^{\checkmark} + \frac{\sqcup}{\pitchfork} \setminus = ?$$

[cloud] [rain] [moon]

$$\frac{ㄅˋ}{ㄠ} - \frac{ㄅ}{ㄠ} = ?$$

[hug] [fluffy bun]

$$\frac{ㄐ}{ㄚ} - ㄖㄣˊ + \frac{ㄒ}{ㄥ}ˊ = ?$$

[portrait of Jiayi] [stick figure] [thumbs-up]

$$\frac{ㄍㄨ}{ㄥ} - ㄅㄚ + ㄎㄡˇ = ?$$

[portrait of Gong Gong] [hashtag] [mouth]

$$\frac{ㄓㄨ}{ㄥ} - \frac{ㄒ}{ㄣ} = ?$$

[handshake] [heart]

While the puzzle is making me want to lie down and take a nap, Xander is just getting started. I can almost see the caffeine pumping through his veins.

I hand him the journal and pen. He's surprised but takes them without complaint. After examining the puzzle, he begins scribbling.

"It's Bopomofo," he says. I rub my eyes, too tired to ask. Luckily, he explains, "The Taiwanese phonetic system."

My head pops up. "How come I haven't seen that anywhere?"

"It's not used on signs or, well, anywhere public, really. It's what you learn in your first year of school, and it's mostly in schoolbooks to help kids sound out characters they haven't learned yet."

I don't even know what every young child in this country knows. Jiayi's disapproving face appears inside my head to judge me some more.

"I think we should start here," Xander says, pointing to the second line. "Combining the Bopomofo with the illustrations, we're supposed to take *yun*, 'cloud,' subtract *yu*, 'rain,' and add *yue*, 'moon.'"

He writes something out and shows it to me:

$$雲 - 雨 + 月$$

"Wait," I say, pointing to the first two characters. "That second one is included in the first. Is this . . . Chinese-character math?"

Xander smiles. "I think so. How fun!"

"But how do we know how the remaining pieces fit together? I assume there are several different possibilities?"

Xander nods, his bottom lip between his teeth. "But only some of the arrangements are actual words . . ." His voice trails off as he begins writing again.

My eyelids grow heavy. As much as I hate it, I have no value to add here. And as Xander continues to scratch his pen against the paper, it's like ASMR, and I can't keep my eyes open any longer.

I see Bopomofo letters and my grandfather's drawings on my eyelids as I drift off.

"What's going on?" I startle awake in that way that happens when you were trying not to fall asleep.

"You're okay," Xander says distractedly, still focused on the puzzle.

"I fell asleep," I say, still waking up.

He chuckles. "You did? Here I thought you were just showing me your interpretation of *The Tempest* where you play the storm."

I sit up, alert now. "Was I snoring that loudly?"

He smirks. "I'm just teasing."

Thank god. "So I wasn't snoring."

"Oh, you were. But I exaggerated the volume. It was kind of nice. Almost like a white noise machine. Asian noise machine?"

I don't want to, but I laugh. I can't help it. That's exactly my kind of joke.

Peeking over at the journal, I suck in a breath. It's filled with Xander's handwriting, and even though I can't read any of it, a single word appears in my head: *progress!*

The paper with the puzzle is much neater, only holding his final answers.

"Amazing job," I say, eager to hear details. "What does it mean?"

He finishes writing his current thought, then excitedly explains what he has, step by step. "The hashtag drawings in the first line signal that the words are numbers, and if you take the character for three and subtract the character for one, you get the character for two."

$$三 - 一 = 二$$

"Of course that's also mathematically correct."

My mind must still be shaking off the last dregs of sleep because the character for *two* looks exactly like an equal sign and the *one*, a

minus sign. I simply nod, hoping it's not important for the answer
to the whole thing.

"It's an address. Two is the number. And the next three lines
make up the street name."

I look where he's gesturing to see that he's solved all but one of
the equations for the street name.

$$雲 - 雨 + 月 = 育$$
[cloud] [rain] [moon]

$$抱 - 包 = 才$$
[hug] [fluffy bun]

$$佳 - 人 + ? = ?$$
[portrait of Jiayi] [stick figure] [thumbs-up]

"I was having a really hard time overall," he says, "until the
equation with the cloud, rain, and moon helped me realize the
answer isn't always an exact match. Like how this line turned into
a short stroke?" He gestures to the top of the 育 character. I nod
even though I don't know what he's talking about. "So that helped
me realize the next equation also isn't an exact match. This half
of this character"—he gestures to the left side of 抱—"is used as
the radical for the word *hand*. But the answer"—he points to the
才—"is not a radical. It's by itself. So it's actually a different word
with a different meaning even though they look the same."

Is he speaking nonsense on purpose? Again, I just nod.

"I haven't figured out this third equation yet, but we'll come back to it," he says. Then he taps his pen on the final two equations, both of which are solved.

$$公 - 八 + 口 = 台$$
[portrait of Gong Gong] [hashtag] [mouth]

$$忠 - 心 = 中$$
[handshake] [heart]

"These tell us the city. Taichung. And by the way, your grandpa used seemingly specific characters in this puzzle. Like this one?" He points to 公. "That's *gong* as in *gong gong*. Grandfather."

He points to different words in the puzzle, translating them as he goes. "This one means *loyalty* . . ." He pauses, and neither of us says what we're thinking—*Who was the loyal one out of our two grandfathers?* "This is *jia* as in *Jiayi*. This one means *heart*. This one means *mouth*, maybe in reference to communication or lack thereof . . . It almost feels like he's subtly telling us a story—maybe his story—within this puzzle. It's brilliant."

I ignore that this supports Xander's previous theory about my grandfather's intentions for the hunt and say, "He's also calling back to previous puzzles." I point to the 人, which I recognize from the puzzle at Gong Gong's apartment when I had to add a stick and a rock to it to get fire.

I think Xander's going to ask me for more details, but he's too excited. "Since we have almost everything, I think I can . . ." He trails off as he searches on his phone. "Bingo."

He finishes the last equation.

佳 -人 + 行 = 街

"That . . . does not make sense visually," I say.

"It's the radicals," he explains again. "When *ren*"—he points to 人—"is part of a word, it turns into its radical form, which is the left side of the first character here." He points to 佳. "So in other words . . ."

He writes 佳 - 人 = 圭.

I still don't get it, but it doesn't matter. "So the place we're going to next is . . . ?"

Xander writes it neatly at the bottom of the page.

2 育才街, 台中

I pump my fist in the air. "You're a genius." I'm surprised that I mean it.

I'm scared he's going to suggest we head to the aquarium or continue walking around the lake, but he gathers our things and stands.

"Shall we?"

I nod excitedly. And as we leave, I don't slow my pace.

It's okay, I tell myself. Because it's for survival. Once I reach the inheritance, then I can stop and smell the purple flowers.

1. ~~Wooden box~~

2. ~~Will~~

3. ~~Framed photo~~

   a. Answer to first riddle: 火 / **fire**

   b. First line of second riddle: 火 **goes with water, wood, metal, and** <u>**earth also.**</u>

5. ~~Journal~~

Destination: **Yangmingshan**

6. ~~Metal Box~~

   a. Need A: **Pan**

   b. Destination: **National Palace Museum**

7. ~~Wall~~

8. ~~House gate~~

Instructions, first line: **Pick up** ~~tee~~ **tea**

9. Address

Number: **2**

10. Poem

11. Beginning

12. Watch

13. X Marks the Spot

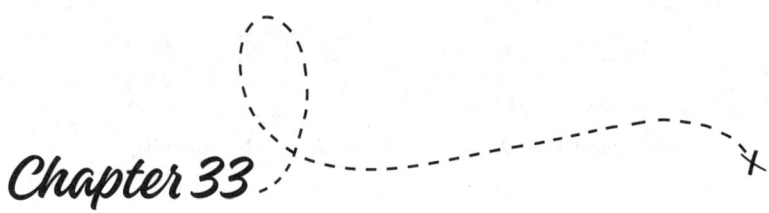

Chapter 33

"So, did it kill you to take a second on the bridge?" Xander asks once we're on the train to Taichung.

Maybe it could have if it keeps me from getting to the money I need. "Did the view change your life?" I counter.

"No, but I probably had a better time than you did."

He's right, but I have no regrets. Perhaps one day my life will include cardboard dogs. Maybe after I find the inheritance.

I don't want to fight with him anymore, not after he sacrificed TARP to come with me, so I retrieve my last dried seaweed pack and hold it out as a peace offering.

He takes a few sheets. I'm not sure if peace has indeed been made or if he's still salty—emotionally, that is. Physically, he's licking the seaweed's salt flecks from his lips. Lips that I never noticed before as being just a shade darker on the lower half—maybe because he nibbles on it when he's thinking?

Not that I'm noticing that. Or his lips. It was just because of the salt, that's all.

"Do I have something on me?" Xander asks, watching me watch him. His tongue swipes a lap around his mouth. His full, soft, now-wet mouth.

"Did I get it?" he asks, his tongue still licking.

"Yes!" I blurt out too forcefully.

"Jeez, okay, sorry. You were just staring really intently."

Please, dear god, don't let my cheeks be red.

Luckily, Xander doesn't notice, and he's apparently not emotion-ally (or physically) salty because he retrieves the Hello Kitty cards from his backpack. "Jian Hong Dian?" he asks, already shuffling.

He taught me Jian Hong Dian, or Pick Up Red Dots, earlier, in which the objective is to, of course, pick up as many red cards as possible.

As we begin our first round, his eyes are focused on the cards as he says, "I used to play this with my grandfather." He didn't tell me this earlier.

"Did he like games?"

"Not usually. But there were a few exceptions. This, sudoku, KenKen—though maybe he was just tricking me into doing more math."

I wonder if Gong Gong liked any of those, or if he and Xander's grandfather played any games before their falling-out.

After a few back-and-forths, a red ace appears—the most valu-able, coveted card. And Xander flipped it over, meaning it's mine for the taking if I have a nine.

I slap down the nine of hearts. Thirty points in one go.

Xander groans, then throws three of his cards onto the tray table face up. "Seriously? I had three nines, and you just had to have the last one?"

He playfully makes a grab for the red ace, and I spring for it. We're pushing, grabbing, laughing. When I manage to snatch the red nine, red ace, *and* two of Xander's nines, I extend my prizes in the air as I use my other elbow to push him back by the chest.

His arm wraps around me, reaching for the cards. His face is inches from mine.

When I realize just how close we are, I freeze. Then he freezes. Even the air around us seems to still.

His mouth slowly curves into a smile. One I last saw four years ago. It's not confident or mischievous or playful. It's . . . shy.

It's not at all what I expected. Is it possible I'm not the only one who can hear my heartbeat in my ears or is aware of the location of each and every one of our limbs, hairs, cells?

"Gemma," he says, low, husky, almost guttural. I can practically feel each syllable. I've never heard that timbre from him, much less when he says my name, and it raises goose bumps along my skin.

I hold my breath, both from anticipation and from not wanting to move a muscle, lest it spook him.

His phone rings. The sudden sound and vibration startle us both.

He moves away first. "Sorry," he says as he checks his phone. When he sees who the caller is—which I can't see because of how he's angling the screen—he frowns.

"I have to take this." He stands swiftly and walks out of the train car.

After a few minutes, I can't take the curiosity. Screw the cat—it's Xander. I have to know. With the excuses *bathroom* and *snack* tucked away in the back of my head, I follow after him.

He's standing in the space between our railcar and the next, his back to me. I catch the tail end of his conversation.

"Dad, stop it. I've got it handled." Pause. "I won't let that happen. Just trust me."

Then he turns around, and our eyes meet.

"Gotta go. Bye." He hangs up swiftly and, his face completely neutral, asks me, "Everything okay?"

I nod. "Just . . . bathroom." Why—*why* didn't I choose the snack excuse instead? Is he going to think I have diarrhea again?

He points behind me. "Over there."

"Thanks."

When I return to my seat, our next rounds of Jian Hong Dian feel different. Whatever heat that was briefly there before is gone. Not just on his end, but also mine because his words from the call are still ringing in my head. There are a million reasons why Xander could have said those things to his dad, but there's one possibility that sticks out.

All those days ago, he was the one who brought up treasure-hunting movies. And if those movies have taught me anything, it's that Xander has an incentive to be on my good side now, especially if he wants to double-cross me later. At one point, I would have thought even he wouldn't do that, but maybe Hui Fu would under the pressure of his family. Wasn't it just earlier today that I remembered I don't really know Xander Pan?

I need to have more walls up. Assume the worst. Because I won't be able to forgive myself if I lose much-needed money due to carelessness. I not only fix the hate goggles back in place but I also add a metaphorical fortress around me. Nothing's getting through, not even Super Supau, Captain Jack Not-Sparrow, or Jian Hong Dian.

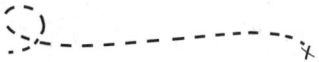

After we arrive in Taichung, Xander leads the way to 2 育才街. I hate how dependent I am on him, but it's also just easier. The apartment building before us is midsize with buzzers out front. Since we weren't given a person's name or an apartment number, I was expecting a single-story house or even a shop.

"Are you sure this is it?" I ask.

He glances at his phone, then nods.

Wondering if we missed something, I unzip my backpack to retrieve the puzzle just as Xander grabs the journal and flips to the index.

9. Address

Not much information there.

But Xander disagrees, his fingers immediately going to the buzzer for apartment 9 and pressing.

A female voice comes out of the speaker. "Wei? Shi shui?"

"Sun Yong Ping yao wo men lai," Xander says, and I wait, but he doesn't translate. I also note that he said the surname first, just like how Jiayi had called his grandfather *Pan* Wei Li. That must be the convention.

There's a long pause during which I wonder if we have the wrong apartment. Just as I'm about to revisit the puzzle, the front door buzzes open.

When we reach apartment 9, the door is still closed. Xander and I share a confused glance as we wait three, four, five minutes.

Then when the door finally opens, my heart skips a beat.

I'm looking at a familiar face. Yet I've never met this woman before. She looks to be in her sixties, and she's tiny; the top of her head comes up to my chest.

Xander looks from her to me, and I know what he's seeing. This woman and I share the same round face and high cheekbones. What he doesn't see on her but I do: my mom's thin eyebrows and low hairline.

My mouth dries out completely. Is this Gong Gong's sister? Am I finally meeting an extended family member? But then I remember my great-grandparents' obituary. It didn't mention another child. Could this be a *long-lost* sister of Gong Gong's?

"Lai lai," the woman says, motioning us inside. But while her hands are welcoming, the rest of her appears reluctant.

We sit at the dining room table. Her apartment isn't fancy, but it's homey, with photos of a large family and grandchildren's drawings and trophies littered between books, magazines, and the usual lived-in clutter. I don't recognize a single face or name.

Xander speaks first. "Qing wen ni shi shui?"

"Ni shi Yong Ping de sunzi ma?"

Xander shakes his head. "Wo shi Pan Hui Fu." He points to me. "Ta shi Sun Gemma."

Something flashes in the woman's eyes. She's silent for ten seconds, five of them spent looking at Xander, five at me. "Wo shi ta de waipo," she says finally, her gaze still on me.

Xander's eyes grow wide, and I want to stomp my foot for attention like a toddler. I only caught the names, nothing else.

"Do you speak English?" I ask her.

The same look that Jiayi gave me crosses her face. Then she

holds a finger up. "Keyi . . . aiyo, deng yixia. Yes. Hao, hao. Ah, yes. One moment. Must . . . switch my brain."

Xander nods knowingly, and now I not only wish I was bilingual but that I also understood the feeling they're talking about.

She looks right at me as she says, "I am your waipo. Grandmother."

My heart stops.

When it resumes, I shake my head. "That can't be. But—no. How—no."

She didn't say those words with any warmth or love. It was a fact, stated simply like she was telling me her age or name. That's not how a real grandmother would act, right? So something's off?

Is she my father's mother? That would explain the lack of emotion.

But she looks like my *mother*. And just her, I now realize. Not my gong gong.

All the evidence points to her telling the truth, yet it also can't be true.

"I marry Yong Ping, your grandfather. Many decades ago. Have a baby girl."

"I was told my grandmother died. Right after my mom was born."

"No, I *leave*," she corrects me. "After I give birth."

Too many questions flood my brain. I'm drowning. *Is this real? Does my mom know? Did she lie to me again?* And the biggest question of all that only the woman before me can answer . . . "Why?" I ask.

"No reason to stay."

The amount of sudden hostility I feel toward this person is too much. I know the details elude me, but right now, hearing that she abandoned my mom because there was *no reason to stay*, I stand and walk right out of the apartment.

Footsteps pound behind me. I don't want to talk to her, but of course it's not her. She didn't follow; she doesn't care.

"I don't want to talk right now," I say to Xander as I speed walk toward the front of the building.

He catches hold of my elbow and turns me to face him.

"Don't," I say. "Let me go. I can't."

"Just wait one second. Take a breath."

I don't want to, but I automatically mimic him as he inhales deeply, then releases. And we do it again. And again.

My heartbeat in my ears grows slower, fainter.

"Okay," he says gently, leading me to a lone chair in the hallway. "I'm sorry. About your grandmother."

I wipe away the tear that's running down my face. "How could she just leave my mom?"

"Well, I know it won't be easy, but there's only one way to find out."

"What if there's no reason? What if she's just a horrible person?"

"Wouldn't you rather know that?"

No. If I don't know, I can still have hope that there's another explanation.

Xander squats so he's at eye level with me. "I think you'll regret it if you leave now. If you want to go, I'll go with you—but I think you just need a minute. If we go back up, I'll be there with you, okay? The whole time. And if you suddenly want me to come up with an excuse to leave, just rub your stomach and pat your head."

I can't help a laugh.

But I'm not ready to go back. Not yet. So I sit in silence for a few minutes until I worry Xander's legs are cramping.

"Why is it important for me to know?" I ask. "It was better before when I knew less."

"Wouldn't you rather know the truth even if it hurts? You have a rare opportunity to talk to her."

I think back to what Trisha said to me. I think about how before this trip, I wanted to have a bigger family so badly. It had just never occurred to me that you not only can't choose how much family you have but who they are.

As much as I don't want him to be, Xander is right. I have to know the truth. I came this far.

"Okay," I say, standing.

When we reenter the apartment, she—my *grandmother*—has made oolong tea and set out pineapple cakes. Xander grabs my hand and squeezes, then lets go much too soon.

We sit at the table again. My grandmother starts from the beginning.

"I go to America for school. To Massachusetts. I meet Yong Ping at the grocery store he work at in Chinatown. He always slip extra turnip in my bag—my favorite. We date, we marry. Soon, pregnant. Same story as others, right? Wrong." Her eyes darken. "I find love letters. So many. From before we meet, from after. So many after. He say he write them to get his feelings out, that he will never leave or cheat, but is that not cheating? His heart with another. He tell me, we are family, we stay together, feelings don't matter. But they matter to me. He never love me. His heart completely belong to Pan

Wei Li." She turns to Xander. "Wei Li is your grandfather?"

Xander's jaw drops open. Meanwhile, on this side of the table, I'm so overwhelmed I can't remember my own name.

She just nods, then continues. "Yong Ping and Wei Li fall in love in Taiwan. But back then, is not like now—love anyone, be anyone, marry anyone. They hide. Always hiding. They go together to America for opportunity, for money. But still hiding. And now in new place. Wei Li grow scared. Yong Ping think different, want them to stay together, but Wei Li say no. He leave Yong Ping, find someone, get married, have kids. Yong Ping meet me after. He never talk about his past, about Wei Li. Only after I find the letters. But too late then. Love means no lies. After I learn truth, I have baby, then leave. Come back home to Taichung."

She just . . . left? Because her husband was in love with someone else? How could she do that to her own child?

Xander's mouth is still open. My hands are clenched so hard I have fingernail indents in my palms.

"Did you . . ." How do I even ask this? "Did you ever reach out to your daughter?"

"Why would I? My life, my family here." *Now* the warmth fills her voice, her face ironically glowing like the sun because she left the Suns. "Four kids—three boys, one girl." She reaches behind her, grabs a framed photo, and tries to show us.

I barely glance at it. Xander's mouth closes. I don't feel a single connection to this woman in front of me. Sure, I feel for her, she's been through a lot, but how could she just abandon my mom?

"I cannot live a lie," my grandmother says as if she senses me judging her. And I understand that, but there was a child involved.

"So . . . they were both life and business partners?" I ask.

"What? No business," she says. "Yong Ping work at grocery store, Wei Li at a company. Toys, I think?"

"We were told that they started a business together." I leave out the swindling part.

She shakes her head. "Lies. So many lies. No, this is the truth: Yong Ping stop by a lot because he want to see Wei Li. Wei Li want it to stop, so he lie, tell his family, don't let Yong Ping in because he a thief. Steal everything from him."

Xander finally speaks for the first time since my grandmother began telling her story. "You're lying. This can't be true."

"Xander," I warn. I'm not defending her, but we shouldn't be calling her a liar either.

She shrugs. "Believe what you want. I don't care. I just tell my part."

I consider asking her again if she wants to reach out to my mom now, but I don't have a chance before Xander stands.

"Excuse me." He runs out of the apartment.

I chase after him, shocked at how much of a hypocrite he's being. In the lobby, I manage to block his way. "I thought you said this was a rare opportunity."

"But what she's saying isn't true."

"What reason does she have to lie?"

"I don't know, but she has to be!"

"Why?"

He throws his hands in the air. "Because! If she's right, did my grandfather love my grandmother? Their relationship—which I admired my whole life—can't have been a lie."

I hadn't thought of that, but the answer isn't to just ignore my grandmother's story either.

"And none of this makes sense," Xander says, clutching his head. "It's just—it doesn't compute. My grandfather was always telling me to be myself, to be brave. Even when I was constantly bullied in junior high, he said, *It's because they're jealous. Don't change anything.* And then he died. I've been feeling guilty for years that I changed everything. From Alex to Xander, to pretending I don't care so people would leave me alone—and what does it mean that it worked? Everyone suddenly thought I was cool."

I had no idea that *that* was why he changed his name and acted the way he did. I don't know how to reconcile that with Xander Pander causing the end of our romantic relationship.

I don't have time to dwell on it, though, because he feints right, then darts left past me when I fall for it.

"Wait!"

"For what? I'm out. I can't do this anymore."

"What about the hunt? The fifteen percent?" I say when I mean, *What about me? You said you would be there with me the whole time.*

"You think I care about the fifteen percent? I never did."

"What do you mean?"

"Why do you think I'm here, Gemma? You think it's about a percentage? I wanted to help you, be a part of this, but I knew you'd never let me unless I made a stink about what I get. Because you'd never believe me otherwise."

"That's not true," I say, but he's right. I would have been suspicious, wondered what other angle he had. Wasn't I just worrying about him double-crossing me on our way here? "What were you talking to your dad about on the train?"

"Really, Gemma? After everything we've been through, you still don't trust me?"

"I . . ." My words catch in my throat.

His face falls.

"I do, I trust you," I finally get out, but it's too late.

"I should have known better than to think things were different between us. What's one or two days compared to four years of you rejecting and spitting on all my olive branches?"

"What are you talking about?"

"I'm always the one who made the effort, tried to smooth things over, tried to be nice, be friends, get you to smile, and all you ever do is hate me."

"I didn't . . ." They weren't olive branches. He was pushing my buttons, needling me. Wasn't he?

"And just for the record, my dad keeps calling because he's mad at me for being nice to you. He says you're going to stab me in the back just like your grandfather did. I defended you, but maybe I shouldn't have."

Xander turns and leaves.

I was right not to trust him, I tell myself. Because in the end, he didn't stay with me like he said he would.

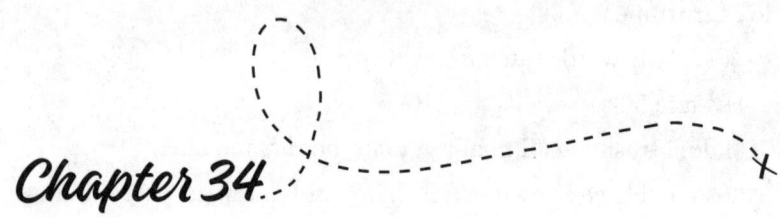

Chapter 34

I'm alone. Completely alone. No Mom, no Val, no TARPers, and now I've just lost Xander, the only ally, however unlikely, who came with me. There's "family" upstairs, but now I understand blood does not make someone family. That word is more special and earned than genetics.

The tears fill slowly at first, then spill onto my face.

This is not what I was expecting when I set out on this journey. At the beginning, I knew so little about Gong Gong, and I filled in the gaps with my mother's stories. I pictured him to be cold, calculating, and tough, making me go through these steps to get to the inheritance as a test, maybe even a cruel joke. Yet, as Xander pointed out, this hunt has shown him to be whimsical, fun, eccentric. And that wasn't the only thing Xander was right about. I fought him when he brought it up, but now it feels obvious. The hunt was a way for my grandfather to show me himself and pass on lessons like *the past always affects the future* and how to find the beauty in life. Didn't I pick the paintbrush up after experiencing that transcendental moment in the Yangmingshan garden? Even when I was fighting it, the changes were happening in me.

At the same time, I want to yell at Gong Gong's ghost, *Why didn't you just say those things? Why put me through all this?*

But I already know the answer to that too. It's exactly as Xander said: *"Not everyone can just say what's on their mind."* Gong Gong was a man who didn't know how to communicate. One who sent his granddaughter across the world to collect pieces of him in lieu of seizing the opportunity to meet her. With all that he went through, maybe the only way for him to tell me that he had a tragic love life was through the story of Niulang and Zhinu, another love that could never be.

My phone buzzes. My heart leaps into my throat.

It's not who I thought but still a pleasant surprise. A text from Trisha, asking me how things are going. My thumb hovers over the telephone icon, wondering if I should call. Would she come meet me? But for what? To take over being my partner in the hunt?

Then I realize something else: I don't have the next clue.

I retrieve the journal and flip to the index.

10. Poem

Not helpful.

There's only one path forward if I want to keep going. And since I don't know what else to do, I trudge upstairs to the stranger who happens to share some genes with my mother and me.

My grandmother lets me back in. Now we're staring at our teacups and filling our mouths with pineapple cake so we don't have to talk.

Eventually, I can't dam the flood of questions any longer. "Did you keep in touch? Did you want to know how your daughter was doing?" *Did you care at all?*

"Yong Ping send letters and pictures." She gets up, disappears into a room, and after what feels like a year, returns with a dusty stack. Clearly put away, seldomly looked at, and not of importance. As I thumb through, a couple of them don't even appear opened.

"Yours, if you want," she says, which doesn't surprise me.

I run my fingers over the familiar handwriting on the envelopes.

"He always write so beautiful." Her words imply nostalgia, but her tone is emotionless.

"Makes sense for an artist."

She looks confused but doesn't ask.

So I do. "Did he paint when you knew him?"

"No," she says firmly, like it would have been a problem if he did. "We not have money for silly things. Silly even if you have money."

Is she trying to make me dislike her as much as possible?

Oblivious to my thoughts, she sips her tea, then asks, again with no emotion, "You tell your mama about me?"

"Not yet."

"Because of time difference?"

"Yeah," I partially lie. Then I find myself blabbering, "That's the only reason, though, because we're really close. She's great—so communicative, open—the best mom."

My grandmother sips her tea slowly, then puts her cup down with a soft *plink*. "Why you mad at your mother?"

"I'm not, I—"

And that's when it hits me. I am. Really mad. I have been since I found out she'd kept Gong Gong a secret from me. It's also on Gong Gong for not reaching out, but she's *my mom*. She holds my whole heart in her hands, and no one can hurt me like she can. But because she's my mom, I let it go. I didn't want to hold a grudge, but we also didn't talk about it enough. Whether it was because I was leaving or because I always had to be the one to let things go first, it doesn't matter. I've been feeling alone because there's a knot in the thread that connects me to her, and we haven't even tried to untangle it.

How did my grandmother know what I was feeling? For some reason, it frustrates me. She doesn't know me, and the person who abandoned us doesn't get a window into my heart.

"So my mom doesn't know about you," I say, hating that I need confirmation. I'm clearly not over her previous lie, not at all.

My grandmother answers with one firm, deliberate shake of the head. Then she says, "Never good to sweep things under rug. That is why I leave."

I do not want to take advice from her, but the confirmation that my mother doesn't know this humongous thing that *her* parents lied about . . . I stand.

"You can use bedroom," my grandmother says, pointing.

"Gemma-Bear, is everything okay?"

Tears stream down my face. Despite her having been asleep, she picked up my video call after only one ring.

"Why are you crying? Are you hurt? I've been worried sick!"

Weirdly, with so much going on, the first thing I say is, "I lied to you. About Xander. We dated a while ago. And . . ." I don't know what else to say. And what? He was the worst person in my life and now . . . it's somehow even more complicated than before? "Anyway, I don't want any more secrets between us, so I just wanted to get that out of the way."

"I figured," my mom says. "About you and Xander."

"You did?"

"I'm your mother." Those words mean so much coming from her, and my heart squeezes at the thought that she will never know how I feel right now. "And, Gemma-Bear . . . just so you know, people are not their parents or grandparents or any other relative."

It's the perfect opening for me to tell her about her mother, but I don't get a chance before she says, "Xander went above and beyond to get you into that program. No one dropped out. That's why An-Shun was so upset at the airport."

That . . . cannot be true. But they were arguing in Mandarin, and as much as I forget it sometimes, my mom can understand.

"There were only supposed to be ten participants total, and I'm not sure what he did to make a spot for you, but it didn't sound easy."

I can't deal with this right now. "Mom, I didn't call you this late to talk about Xander. There's something else. Something really big."

In one giant mess of word vomit, the facts come out: the truth about Gong Gong and that her mother is still alive.

I may have just learned a big chunk of that myself, but it didn't come at me all at once in the middle of the night. My mother blinks at me once, twice, a third time.

"I . . . didn't know any of that," she says eventually. And then tears fill her eyes. "I can't believe he went through that. I can't believe he didn't tell me about her."

I want to say something petty along the lines of *now you know how it feels*, but I don't need to.

"I'm sorry I didn't tell you about your grandfather," she says. "I should have. I should have let you decide for yourself if you wanted a relationship with him."

My instinct is to say *that's okay, I forgive you*, but this time, I don't. "You should have. But more than that, I feel betrayed, Mom. Here you were stressing open communication while holding on to this giant secret yourself."

She nods, her eyes squeezed shut. "I know. I'm sorry. So sorry. I wish I could hug you right now."

"It makes me wonder what else is a lie, what else you haven't told me. It makes me question everything. It makes me feel like I don't know you." It's all coming up now.

"I understand. And I'm glad you're telling me." She smiles through the tears. "You've grown so much in the time you've been there."

"By telling you how mad I am, I've grown?"

She wipes her eyes. "Yes. Humans have feelings, Gemma-Bear. You've been trying to be an adult since you were five because of our circumstances—and I'm so sorry it's been difficult for you—but being an adult doesn't mean being devoid of emotions." I can't help thinking of my grandmother. "It means being able to

confront, communicate, and work through them, often with someone else."

"Not always," I say, now thinking of both my grandparents.

"Well, that's what I think it means, and I couldn't be prouder of
you."

Here I've been so worried about what's going to happen to her
when I move away for college, but maybe I shouldn't have been so
concerned. My mom often seems like a mess, but now I'm seeing
her in a new light—one that makes her glow like the beautiful sun
that she is.

"I forgive you," I say. And I truly mean it.

"It's okay if you're still mad."

"I'm not. I promise." And with that one obstacle overcome,
there are only a thousand left. "So, um, are you okay, Mom?"

She sighs. "Are you sure it's her?"

"I mean, I'm pretty sure. Do you want to—"

"Just . . . give me a second."

When she still hasn't spoken a few minutes later, I say, "Your
father didn't leave you. He stayed." I may not fully know him, but
I know enough to defend him in this moment. "I can tell you more
later, but I've been learning bits about him, and, Mom, he sacrificed
so much. He lost everything and everyone, multiple times. That has
its effects on a person. I think he might have been trying to protect
you in the only way he knew how, and I know that may not have
been right for you, but maybe he was doing his best?" I don't say
the obvious, that she should understand that better than anyone.

She doesn't respond, merely shifting her eyes away from the
screen.

"Do you think if you'd known his real history, what truly happened to him, you wouldn't have had the falling-out?" I ask.

She hesitates, and I'm scared of what's held in that pause.

"Gemma, I didn't tell you everything about our falling-out. I was trying to protect you, to shield you from potential hurt, and I told myself before it was okay because I wasn't lying, I was just withholding something, but . . . no more half-truths. I promise this is the last thing I haven't told you yet." I wonder how much of this is because we're having a heart-to-heart and how much is because the truth about her own mother has shaken her. "So here it is. All of it. And I wish we weren't doing this from opposite ends of the world, but you know I'm here, right? And I love you. I love you, you are my sun, my treasure, my everything, and I wouldn't change that for anything in the world."

"Mom, you're scaring me."

"The reason your grandfather and I had a falling-out is because . . ." She takes a breath, and then it comes out in one fell swoop. "He once told me that if I got pregnant before marriage, I shouldn't come home. That was the extent of the sex talk I got. And he meant it. So when it happened, I didn't. And he let me go. I was only eighteen! He didn't try to find me, didn't try to help. Not until you were three years old. *Three.* By then, I was done. I didn't want him back in my life, and can you blame me?"

No, I really can't. My voice breaks as I say, "Just you and me, against the world."

She places a hand over her heart. "Always."

Even though we're on opposite sides of the globe, more than seven thousand miles apart, I feel like she's sitting right beside me, her hand warming my heart because of that unbreakable thread connecting us.

Why did I ever wish for a bigger family? Everything I could need or want is already in my life. *Family* is a single word that encapsulates the world, transcends every ocean. And I'm just lucky enough to have it.

Chapter 35.

After having the most vulnerable, illuminating conversation with my mother, I sit through the most awkward, painful, soul-crushing one as a bystander. My mother-daughter relationship couldn't be any more different than the one I'm witnessing before me.

I asked my mom if she wanted to talk to her mom, and she said yes. After I handed the phone to my grandmother, I wasn't sure whether to stay or go, but the call only lasted five minutes.

"Nice to meet you," my mom says in farewell.

"Yes" is all my grandmother says before she hands the phone back to me.

I knew they weren't going to say *I love you* and *I love you more, my sun, my treasure*, like my mom and I did, but . . . that's it?

The conversation had mostly been my mother asking a few questions and then an exchange of phone numbers so awkward I wouldn't be surprised if my grandmother gave a fake one. The entire time, she didn't ask my mom a single thing.

"I have to go," my grandmother says, and for a second I

wonder if she's talking to my mom still, but then I realize she's talking to me.

"Oh." I stand.

She doesn't elaborate. Does she actually have somewhere to be, or is she done with me, with her past? Gong Gong seemed to think the past always affects the future, but maybe my grandmother is trying to outrun that. So far, it appears to be working.

"I have something else for you," she says, and as much as I don't want it to, my heart inflates with hope.

She disappears into the closet, then returns with a medium-size box about ten inches tall and five inches wide. She gives it to me, and I'm about to open it when she holds a hand up to stop me.

"That's your gong gong."

I almost drop it, but thank god I don't. That would be a mess of epic proportions.

"They give him to me because he not have anyone here, but I do not want."

Would it have killed her to leave that part out? She could've just said something nice, but no.

"Okay," she says awkwardly. "Be safe." While the words feel like something family would say, it's not. She doesn't ask if I have a place to go, if I have money for the train, if this box is a burden—which it is, in all senses. I don't want to carry it around, and I'm also not the right person to decide what to do with it. Though if I don't, who will?

Despite my grandmother's behavior thus far, I put Gong Gong down so I can hug her. She stiffens and just stands there, only patting my forearm after a few seconds. And that's all I get.

I pick Gong Gong back up and show myself out. Then I collapse into the chair in the lobby. My grandmother doesn't walk past me. Maybe she didn't mean she had to go somewhere physically, but let's be honest, it was a made-up excuse to get me out of there.

My grandmother can't even spend an extra twenty minutes with me. And Gong Gong didn't want me either.

Suddenly, the aftermath of my mom's reveal hits me like a high-speed train. Not only did Gong Gong cast me aside, but I was the reason for their falling-out. I was the root of their estrangement, the cause of my mother's struggles.

I know she said she wouldn't change anything, but it's hard not to feel that her life would have been easier without me.

The sobs rack my body. I cry until there are no tears left.

Once I'm completely spent emotionally and even physically, the panic sets in.

Where am I going next? I don't have a clue (both meanings). Not to mention, there's a bigger question at play now.

If the purpose of this hunt is for Gong Gong to tell me his story, is there any money at the end? The only goal may be 4 me 2 NO him, just like the will stated clearly in the beginning. The "sun" at the end of the adventure could just be him, Sun Yong Ping, the true him. And that's it. That's the simplest, most likely answer.

Which would mean I shouldn't be banking (double meaning) on a payout. How is it possible that the tuition payment is a much bigger looming problem than I previously thought?

I'm so overwhelmed I want to lie down on the floor. More than that, I want my mom. I want her to hug me, tell me it'll be okay, and brush my hair like she did when I was a child. Which makes me feel like a child who can't do anything for herself, not the adult my mom saw on our call earlier.

Except . . .

I used to think being an adult meant handling things on my own. But maybe I got that wrong too. Maybe being mature means knowing when you need to lean on others, especially the ones who love you.

Finally, I make myself do something I've been avoiding for too long. I open my email and forward my mom the payment information. I've been feeling alone, but I don't have to. I didn't want to burden her, but she wouldn't want me carrying this by myself.

The solution is still lacking—even more so than before—but after the email *swooshes* into the ether, I feel lighter.

Pushing that aside, I now ask myself the other important question hanging in the air: If there's no inheritance at the end, do I want to keep going? Do I want to get to know this person who didn't want me?

Or is the hunt a sign that Gong Gong changed his mind toward the end of his life? And that's when I realize. There's no indication this adventure was meant for me. He might have left it for my mother. In fact, isn't that the most likely story? There hasn't been a single sign that he cared to know me.

I want to yell at the wooden box of ashes next to my backpack. Then run back to apartment number 9, bang on the door, and yell at my grandmother.

I can't stay here any longer. I debate leaving Gong Gong behind, but I can't do that either. With him in my reluctant arms, I wander out of the building and just walk.

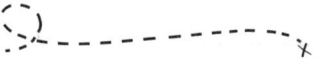

I end up in a café a few streets down with a picture menu on the wall. I have no appetite, yet my stomach is rumbling, so I decide to order just two small items for now.

When the server brings the dishes over, she says the names of each, which I file away. And I dig in immediately, my hunger taking over as the savory scent of food overwhelms my nostrils.

The gua bao is a white fluffy bun filled with tender pork belly that looks almost identical to the jasper one sitting in a glass case on the other side of the island. It tastes better, though. And the mix of salty meat with fresh cilantro, pickled vegetables, and ground peanuts makes me devour the entire bao in three bites.

The zongzi is a pyramid-shaped bundle of sticky rice wrapped in bamboo leaves. Opening it feels like unwrapping a present. My chopsticks spear through to discover Chinese sausage, pork, salted egg yolk, pickled vegetables, mushrooms, and dried shrimp in the center. I try to scoop a little of everything into each of my giant bites.

Then I wash it all down with a boba milk tea. Pure heaven.

Now that my stomach is full, I can think more clearly.

But the same thoughts fill my mind. About how angry I am at my grandparents. Though . . . I'm not angry at my mother anymore. The most important relationship, the only one that matters to me, was strengthened by the truth coming out. There's power in the truth—both for better and for worse. Knowing what my gong gong went through, what he and Wei Li and my grandmother went through, doesn't justify his actions and make them okay, but it at least helps me understand them better. I'm glad I know more.

So despite the frustration, rejection, and sadness filling my insides, I decide that I want to see where Gong Gong is taking me. For myself, for my mom, and maybe even a little for him.

Except . . . where am I supposed to go next?

Forcing myself to stay calm, I look through the journal and the rest of my stuff. And it comes to me. It's the only possible option, other than opening the wooden box, which I wouldn't do even if that turned out to be the path forward.

From my backpack, I retrieve the letters my grandmother gave me and tear into the most recent one, dated a few months ago.

There are two pages. The first is, I hope, a puzzle, but I can't tell for sure when all that stares back at me is a wall of Chinese. The second page is completely blank. I immediately cup my hands around my face to create darkness, then shine the black light. Nothing. Then, thinking back to the stick-and-a-rock puzzle, I make a mental note to try a heat source as soon as I'm able (I don't think the café would like me standing on a chair to reach their ceiling light).

Focusing on the first page, I open the translation app on my phone. And for the first time this entire trip, it struggles. The English words that pop up don't make sense together. I read them again, and it somehow grows more confusing.

I push it away in frustration. I *just* decided to keep going on the hunt, only to immediately get stuck?

Why did I think I could do this? I'm not Chinese enough to complete even one step on my own. I was foolish to have felt like I belonged here, no matter how briefly. But then where do I belong? I'm too Chinese for America yet too American here. Before I arrived, a naive part of me thought I'd complete myself here. But now it just feels like there are more missing pieces than ever.

In an act of desperation, I take a photo of the page and text it to Xander. No reply, of course.

The thought of Xander sends a pang through my stomach. I think back to all the things we said—flung at—each other right before he left. Is what he said true? Is it possible that the hate goggles have been distorting everything, and I've been misinterpreting his actions this whole time?

Then I remember my mother telling me the great lengths he went to just to get me into TARP. And he made me go back and talk to my grandmother. Yet when he couldn't face the truth about his grandfather, instead of supporting him like he did for me, I picked a fight.

I send Xander a flurry of texts, apologizing.

No response.

I push the disappointment aside and do the only thing I have control over: I take another look at the puzzle.

First, I inhale a deep breath, then close my eyes for a few seconds and pretend I'm at the Yangmingshan garden. When I open them, the puzzle doesn't look any different—it's still gibberish—but I feel calmer.

I reopen the translation app, and this time, I write the English translation beside the Chinese characters.

觀魚碧上，	Watching fish on blue,
木落潭水清。	Muluotan clear water.
暮紫鱗躍，	Twilight purple scales jump,
圓波處處生。	Circular waves are born everywhere.
涼煙浮竹盡，	The cool smoke and floating bamboo are exhausted,
秋照沙明。	Autumn shines on the sand.

| 何必滄浪去， | **Why bother to go to the sea?** |
| 茲焉可濯纓。 | **How can I wash my tassels?** |

And reading the translation again, it almost sounds like . . . a poem, I realize. With that structure and mentions of *twilight purple, circular waves, floating bamboo*—that has to be it. And then I remember:

10. Poem

Okay. Maybe I can do this.

I study the English words, trying to find meaning, but then I worry I'm wasting my time because this may not be an accurate translation, especially with poetry, which needs translating even in its own language.

Is Gong Gong trying to show me more beauty? Make me appreciate another art form?

Feeling stuck with the English, I turn back to the original, this time focusing on each individual Chinese character. Should I look them up one by one? Maybe the translation would change if I did. Or should I look at them as pictures and try to find a pattern that way?

And that's when I spot it. Every line has five characters, except for one, three, and six. I immediately change gears.

In the app, I copy the entire poem in Chinese. Then I paste it into an internet search.

An exact hit. A website claims the poem is by Li Bai, one of the most famous Chinese poets from the Tang dynasty, the golden age of Chinese poetry. And in the version on the site, there are five characters in *every* line.

Three missing characters! Comparing the original with my grandfather's, the missing ones are: 潭日月. I recognize 日 and 月 from when Xander wrote them out—so smoothly, I can still picture it—to explain the Yangmingshan riddle. *Sun* and *moon*.

Throwing the three characters into another search brings up Sun Moon Lake, or 日月潭. A beautiful alpine lake right in the middle of Taiwan, so named because the east side is in the shape of a sun and the west side a moon.

Poetic. Beautiful. And it has *Sun* in the name. Exactly the kind of place Gong Gong would send me to. And it's seventy-eight kilometers (forty-eight miles) from here, accessible by bus.

Sun Moon Lake, here I come.

I just wish my partner was still with me.

1:23 PM Taiwan Standard Time

Gemma

I'm sorry.

Not just about the fight, but the past four years.

And I should have supported you back at my grandmother's apartment like you did for me.

I'm here if you want to talk.

2:45 PM Taiwan Standard Time

Just because your grandfather didn't tell you everything doesn't mean you didn't know him.

You did. And maybe you know him a little more now. Maybe it makes sense why he told you to be yourself. But if he couldn't do that in his own life, you shouldn't be too hard on yourself either.

Anyway, this is terrible to do over text. When you're ready to talk, if ever, I'm here.

Again, I'm sorry.

4:02 PM Taiwan Standard Time

I wish you were here.

Not for your puzzle solving skills (which are impressive, but I managed to figure out the next puzzle and am on my way there), but as my partner.

5:21 PM Taiwan Standard Time

I hope you'll accept the following as my sincerest apology:

You were right about the cardboard dog. Not because I need something from you, but because you're right. Finding the fun is just as important. This wet blanket is a full on tarp now.

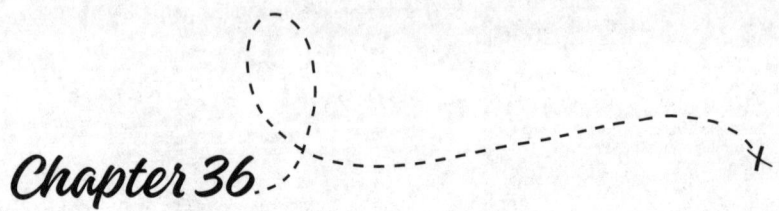

Chapter 36

I can't stop thinking about Xander on my way to Sun Moon Lake, hence all the texts. Maybe I'm exhausted and a bit delirious too—it's been an incredibly long day that started at 5:00 a.m. and has included multiple life-changing moments.

Even though Xander doesn't reply, I don't regret what I said. Because I mean every word, and maybe some additional words I didn't write. There's only so much you can say in a one-way text chain.

My money is dwindling, which is an even bigger problem now that there probably isn't an inheritance at the end. But I've come this far, Sun Moon Lake is on the way back, and with everything that happened, my resolve is strengthening—even more so after a power nap on the bus. When I wake, I immediately hope I wasn't snoring. Then I both curse Xander and curse that he's not here. Especially when I see the shining Sun Moon Lake comprised of indescribable shades of teal. The surrounding mountains and trees are reflected in the clear, rippling water, and the air is filled with the chirping of birds. My god, would he have loved this.

I walk around, just enjoying the view, the fresh air, even the sun on my skin. It's hot, but I've never felt so alive. On the way here, I read about how this is one of the top thirteen most scenic areas in Taiwan and how it's home to the Thao tribe, who consider the island in the middle of the lake to be holy ground.

I sit on a bench near the water and drink in every detail. Lalu Island is visible in the distance, separating the lake into its crescent-moon and round-sun shapes. The real sun reflecting on the water lights it up as if by magic.

I wonder how much time Gong Gong spent here. What significant milestones he might have experienced. Did he work here? Did he stop by on his way elsewhere? How I wish for more details, but I know they're not coming.

The sun is just beginning to set, and the image is breathtaking. Purple, pink, orange streaks across the sky. Almost like I'm on another planet.

This is it, I realize. This is the perfect place for my gong gong to be laid to rest. Even though I don't know what role this setting played in his life, it was important enough that he sent me here. I had previously considered putting his ashes with his parents at Yangmingshan, but this is what he would want. To be one with nature, to be part of the beauty he found despite his pain.

I leave the walking paths and venture into the surrounding greenery. Halfway to the water, the emotions catch up to me and I have to stop. Staring out at the gorgeous water in the distance, I suddenly can't understand how I missed moments like this before.

"Thank you, Gong Gong," I whisper into the wind. "I finally see it now."

Wanting to have a moment with him, I try to remove the top of the box, but it's jammed on there—ordinarily a good thing for a container of remains, but a perfect movie moment this is not. After a few seconds of grunting and sweating, the lid moves a millimeter. Hallelujah!

As I keep pulling, I continue with what I hope is a nice send-off. "I wish I could have met you, but hopefully you're at peace now—"

The lid pops off suddenly. I shriek as a cloud of ashes explodes into the air and the box drops top down into the dirt. Thank god I clamped my mouth shut in time, but the ashes are picked up by the wind and whipped all over me. I frantically shake my limbs in what probably looks like a freakish dance. I've gotten most of it off—I think it's just soil now—when my back rams into someone.

"Sorry!" I blurt out before realizing they may not understand.

The person grabs my arms to steady me. "Are you okay?"

I know that voice. I whirl around. "Xander?"

He's here. He came back.

For . . . me?

Xander grins. "I leave you alone for a few hours and you decide to have a dance party without me? A weird one, I'll say, but looks fun."

The most Xander greeting if there ever was one, and I welcome it.

But then he says something I'm not expecting. "Is this why you stood me up at the ninth-grade formal, because you thought I couldn't keep up with you?"

"Wait, *what*—stood you up?" Did I hear him correctly?

"How can you not remember?"

"No, I didn't—we were broken up."

"We had a fight. Couples fight. I never wanted to break up. But I got the message when you didn't show up at the dance."

Is that true? Did we not actually break up, neither of us having said those words? "I just assumed, and I was so mad . . ."

"Oh, I knew that."

I can't help a snicker.

"You didn't talk to me after the project either," I point out.

"I—I know. But I was going to apologize at the dance. Might have even brought you flowers and everything."

Seeing how embarrassed Xander looks now, I can't imagine how hard that was for ninth-grade Xander. It had never occurred to me that he had been hurt too, or that his act might have been to cover that up.

"I had no idea. I'm sorry."

"Well, let's try to do better than our fourteen-year-old selves moving forward, yeah? I regret how I handled things too."

Xander gives me a small smile, and when I return it, the energy between us shifts, from regretful to hopeful. I don't know how to interpret it, but I don't have a chance before the wind picks up again, sweeping some of the ashes onto my arms and the front of Xander's shirt.

I immediately resume my dance, then swat at his chest.

"Ouch! Calm down, it's just dirt."

"Um, it's actually my grandfather."

Xander yelps, then mimics my ridiculous dance. I can't help a small giggle.

"Is he off me?" he asks, patting his shirt even though it's completely clean.

I nod. He relaxes.

"Your grandmother gave you that?" he asks as I pick up the now-empty box.

I nod. "I see it now. What he—and you—wanted me to see. And I thought he might want to be laid to rest here."

"Makes sense. Since this is where they fell in love?"

"Wait, what?" I knew there was something significant about this place, but I didn't expect Xander to know what it was. And, more important, his comment means he must have accepted what my grandmother told us.

"My grandfather used to talk about Sun Moon Lake fondly. I've always wanted to come. He said it's the perfect place to fall in love."

"So you're okay with . . . ? You've accepted that—"

"Before, I was scared to read the letters Jiayi gave me. I didn't know if I wanted to see what was in there. Which was hypocritical of me, I know. I'm sorry. After what your grandmother said, I was *terrified*. But your texts gave me the push I needed. And reading through them . . . You were right. About my grandfather. I do know him even if there was one part he kept from everyone, even himself. And maybe I knew him well enough that a part of me subconsciously knew that your grandmother was telling the truth."

He pauses, then looks out into the distance as he continues, "His letters brought back memories. Like how when I came home from school one day with a busted lip, he told me that physical wounds heal more easily than emotional ones, and that I'd be okay. And when my parents forbade me from dating until college"—they did?—"he told me it was for the best, that you have to be older to know who you're supposed to be with. And . . . the date that opened the metal box? It was December 31, 1975, the day he came to America. He used to tell me the story often, about how he left that day because it was cheaper, and how it felt symbolic to him— starting 1976 in a new country, a new world. And he mentioned coming over with a love that he lost. I assumed at the time it was another woman who died, but obviously I was wrong. He was talking about Yong Ping."

I reach over and squeeze his forearm briefly.

Xander tears his eyes away from the water to meet mine. "I can't fault him for not telling me something he wasn't ready to face himself. But maybe he tried to tell me in his own ways."

We share a sad but understanding smile.

"Thanks for the texts," he says sincerely. "I'm sorry I left."

"But you came back. Why didn't you tell me you were coming? Or that you solved the puzzle?"

He grins. "Where's the fun in that? You said yourself you're Team Cardboard Dog now."

"About that . . ." I pause, then force the words out. Words I should have said many years ago. "The reason I cared so much about that dog is . . . I needed that grade. I didn't see the fun because I felt like I couldn't. When you grow up the way I did"—I can't stand to give him the details; I don't want his pity, which is why I hardly ever talk about this to anyone—"when you don't have much, it changes your perspective. And that might also have been why I believed my mom's story over yours. Anyway, I never wanted the dog to break us. I just . . . didn't know how to deal with it."

Xander chooses his words carefully. "I'm sorry. I didn't know."

"Because I never let anyone see."

"If I had—"

"That doesn't matter now." We were fourteen, we were different people, and what matters is who we are now.

"So that's why—" he starts to say, and again, I don't want to hear him list all the details he might have noticed.

"Why that grade and all the grades mattered so much," I cut in. "Why I was so angry at you I didn't go to the dance, why I couldn't buy a new dress after you spilled fruit punch on it."

"After I what?"

Is he serious? But he looks genuinely surprised.

"You spilled fruit punch on my dress. When we presented our science project. You were . . ." I flail my arms exactly like he did that day.

"I did? I'm so sorry. I didn't realize."

"Are you telling me you were just that excited about the dog?"

He looks sheepish. "Maybe. And maybe I felt like I had to justify it after it, well, as you said, broke us."

A heaviness hangs in the air. Unlike before, I decide to be the first to put it all behind us.

"I'm really glad you're here," I tell him.

He smiles, the tone shifting now that we've aired our dirty laundry. "But you don't need me; you solved the puzzle yourself."

"That's not the main reason I want you here."

"So you said."

An electrical charge passes between us.

"I'm glad I'm here too," he says.

My mouth quirks up. "And you apparently wanted me here so badly you created an extra spot in the program?"

Xander's cheeks flush uncharacteristically. "I—well—" I've never seen him at a loss for words before.

I save him from his misery. "Thank you. Truly. I know it couldn't have been easy."

"I had to find another donor. And I had to change some of the activities."

It takes me a second to realize what he's saying. "Is that why the dance performance and aquarium were suddenly self-funded?"

He scratches the back of his head. "Yeah."

I had no idea. I feel awful that the other TARPers had to pay more so that I could come on this trip. "You didn't need to—"

"I wanted to."

Our eyes lock, and warmth blooms inside me. But then another couple walks by, breaking the moment.

We make our way back to the path.

"Where are we headed next?" Xander asks.

"You just got here," I tease. "Don't you want to enjoy the view first?"

"No, I desperately, urgently need to know where to go next!" he demands, and I push his shoulder. I'm sure he's making fun of me, but it only seems to be partly a joke because he follows up with, "Seriously, though, do you have the next clue?"

Maybe I'm rubbing off on him too. It's a two-way street, just like our fights and our breakup, all of which I previously blamed on him unfairly due to my pain, insecurities, and prejudices.

But now the hate goggles are off. Way off. Which is why I mime taking them off and flinging them into the water.

He looks at me like . . . well, like I've just mimed pulling goggles off my head. But then his eyes widen when he realizes what I'm doing.

"I'm sorry about everything from before." I hold my hand out. "New leaf?"

"Not that one, it's got a piece of bird poo on it. This one." He mimes picking up a different leaf, then holds his hand out.

"You know, you really do make it hard sometimes," I say, but I'm laughing.

"Oh stop, you love it." He grasps my hand with his, and we shake.

I can't stop smiling.

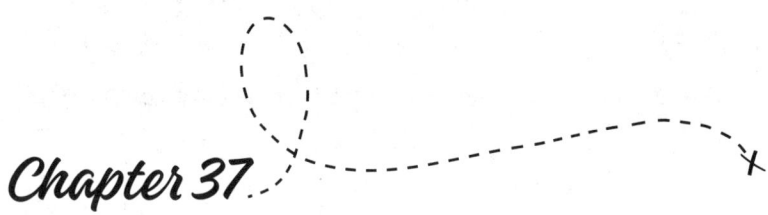

Chapter 37

Once Xander and I are partners again, everything feels back on track. On the main strip, we fill up on delicious street food, including fried cabbage buns, fish rolls, and mochi. And as we sit on a bench and munch away, we brainstorm.

"So this feels like a detour like the Yangmingshan garden," I think out loud. "And with that, there was just an extra direction to go there—I already had the clue for the next location. Which means!" I shove the last of the mochi into my mouth and retrieve the letter from my backpack. "This blank page holds our next destination."

Xander is staring at me in awe. "It's fun to see your brain in action."

I wait for a joke to come, but that's it, he's done. "Oh. Thanks." I suddenly feel shy. "Only, I don't know how to make the clue appear. It's reminiscent of when I used heat in the third puzzle, but I had instructions to do that. We can still try it, though."

"Maybe the instruction is in the poem."

That would make sense. Except the poem doesn't make any

sense. Xander holds a palm out, and I gladly hand both papers over.

A second later, I say, "Well?"

"Well . . . I'm not a poet, that's for sure. This is gibberish to me in both languages."

Weirdly, that makes me feel better. Though I of course would have preferred him to know the answer immediately.

"There's a lot of mention of water," he points out. *"Fish on blue, clear water, waves, the sea, wash.* What are tassels, you think?"

I shrug. "Is it a bad translation?"

He shrugs back. "No idea what the Chinese words are."

I wait patiently as he taps a finger on his chin.

"The last two lines are jumping out at me," he says.

I reread them: *Why bother to go to the sea? How can I wash my tassels?*

"What are you thinking?" I ask.

"I think we have to get the paper wet. We're not going to the sea to wash the tassels, we're washing the page right here." I'm pretty sure if this were happening a week ago—maybe even a day ago—Xander would have already grabbed his water bottle and poured it over the paper. But this Xander says, "If we wet it and we're wrong, though, we'll be destroying the clue."

"What if we just try a drop, right in the middle, and if nothing appears, we at least won't be destroying the whole thing."

"Of course. Brilliant." He beams.

I wish I had my paintbrushes. Both because it would deliver the perfect small streak of water and because I have a burning desire to paint the scene before me, and not just because of the landscape.

Xander sacrifices the corner of his shirt, pouring a little water onto it and then wiping it across the page.

The faintest line appears. We share the look of two treasure hunters finding the next piece of the map.

"Eureka!" I grab my water bottle and pour.

"Wait!" Xander exclaims. He frantically shakes the excess water off the page. But he's laughing, I'm laughing.

The page is so wet it's on the verge of tearing, so we lay it on the bench between us. Ink slowly appears out of thin air like magic.

The top part forms first, which Xander reads aloud: "A box inside a box, a hog under a roof."

"Um, okay." Not sure what to do with that. As the words at the bottom finish forming, I read them out loud: "Once you have done the above step right, look at the beginning in a new light. Don't forget what you've learned along the way; all that you've seen, gathered, found is fair play."

The instructions feel almost meta because I'm already looking at so many things in a new light, including the boy in front of me.

"Box in a box," Xander mutters to himself, and I hand him the journal so he can brainstorm. "Has to be *hui*. Hog . . . well, roof has to be . . ."

I let him work, feeling bad I can't help but also enjoying the beauty of the lake at night. The building lights are reflected on the water, and the stars above make me feel like I'm far away from home yet also close. I've just grabbed a blank sheet of paper to begin sketching when Xander says, "I've got it."

Despite his words, his face looks sad.

I lean forward to see what he's written.

回家

I don't recognize the characters, but the first one looks exactly like a box in a box, and the second has a clear "roof" on top of what I assume is the character for *hog*.

"Hui jia," he says. "Return home."

"Really?" I understand his look now. "We're done here?"

I flip to the index in the journal.

11. Beginning

His smile is wistful. "We're done here."

We spend a few more minutes taking in the beautiful scenery, and then we look up how to get back to Taipei.

1. ~~Wooden box~~

2. ~~Will~~

3. ~~Framed photo~~

   a. Answer to first riddle: 火 / **fire**

   b. First line of second riddle: 火 **goes with water, wood, metal, and earth also.**

5. ~~Journal~~

Destination: **Yangmingshan**

6. ~~Metal Box~~

   a. Need A: **Pan**

   b. Destination: **National Palace Museum**

7. ~~Wall~~

8. ~~House gate~~

Instructions, first line: **Pick up ~~tee~~ tea**

9. ~~Address~~

Number: **2**

10. ~~Poem~~

11. Beginning

12. Watch

13. X Marks the Spot

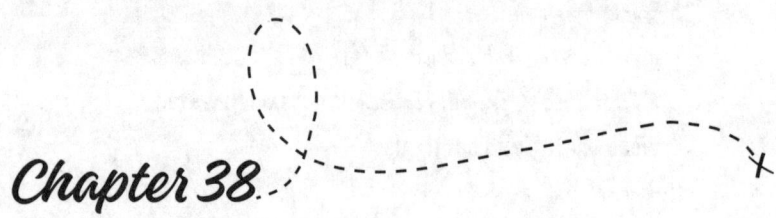

Chapter 38

We travel late into the night to return to Taipei.

As we sip chrysanthemum-tea juice boxes on the train, Xander says, "I can't believe our grandfathers hid who they were for so long."

"I wish they didn't feel like they had to." I'm not just talking about them either.

Xander puts down his tea, which makes me follow suit. "You never hide, though. You're always yourself, even when it's difficult or embarrassing. You show your passion, even when others make fun of you for trying. Not everyone can do that. I admire you, Gemma."

I'm frozen, not sure what to say.

He takes a deep breath, then finally admits, "I've been hiding. Just like our grandfathers."

I give him a tight smile. "I know."

"What do you mean, *you know*?"

"I mean, I know you haven't been yourself. Which is a shame, because your true self is not so bad. Less annoying, for sure."

He chuckles.

I hesitate, then I tell him, "I may have been calling you Xander Pander in my head."

He laughs. "Why didn't you call me that out loud?"

"Um, because it's mean?"

"I would have thought it was funny!"

I don't get that personally—I would have been upset if the tables were turned—but it makes him more tolerable, maybe even likable.

He lowers his voice, and his eyes dart away as he says, "Though I liked it when you called me Alex. Maybe because I subconsciously knew you could see the real me."

That surprises me. "Good to know. Are you going to go back to being Alex?"

His face grows pensive, as if he hasn't thought about it yet. College would be a good time to start fresh.

"No," he says eventually. "I like Xander. I need to be myself no matter which half of my name I'm going by."

"Or you could go by Alexander, your *whole* name."

"Symbolic, but that's too long for anyone to say comfortably all the time." He pauses, his lower lip disappearing for a moment as he chews on it. "Maybe . . . I just like when *you* called me Alex."

"Oh. Um, okay." Except in my head, calling him Alex was an insult. I'll have to figure something else out. I don't address him by any name as I say, "You know it's okay to care about stuff, right?"

"Yeah. I know."

"I'm sorry you did that to protect yourself. I didn't realize people were—"

"It's okay," he interrupts. He doesn't want to talk about it.

"I think your grandfather would be proud of you."

He turns toward the window. "Thanks." When he turns back, his eyes are glassy. "And thanks for seeing me all along."

I nod.

He clears his throat, then shifts the focus back to the hunt by asking, "Should we try to figure out the next part of the clue?"

He gestures to my backpack, and I have no choice but to pull out the slightly damp, no-longer-blank page.

For the first time, I'd rather put the hunt aside. I can't help wondering if Xander feels the same way because as we hunch over the paper together, he continually grazes my shoulder with his, and our fingers touch more than they need to.

Another first: I have a very hard time focusing on the clue in front of me.

Despite my lack of focus, we figure out the instructions before we arrive in Taipei.

> *Once you have done the above step right,*
> *look at the beginning in a new light.*
> *Don't forget what you've learned along the way;*
> *All that you've seen, gathered, found is fair play.*

The most important line is to *look at the beginning in a new light*. After we return to Massachusetts, we have to examine items from the beginning of the hunt with the black light—an item we gathered along the way. This feels fitting, coming full circle. The adventure through Taiwan has changed me, just like how Gong Gong's travels changed him, and now we'll be reexamining the past, the present, and the future in a new light.

The plan is to start with the will and newspaper clippings from the first two puzzles, and to keep going from there if it's neither of those, though my gut thinks we won't have to go too far down the index.

And because I'm so me, I brought the will and clippings to Taiwan. Meaning, we don't have to wait until we're in the States. As soon as we get back, Xander and I race to my dorm. Since it's the middle of the night, the rest of the floor is asleep, and it's almost spooky as I dig through the silence and the mess that is my room. When I emerge with the will, wooden box, and newspaper clippings, Xander is ready with the black light.

"Back to the beginning," I say even though it's not completely true. This journey has been so many steps, twists, and turns that when I look back, I can't even see the starting point.

Xander shuts off the overhead light, and we work efficiently—me shuffling through the items while Xander shines the black light. Nothing in the will, but the newspaper clippings begin lighting up. I write all the illuminated words in the journal.

After we turn the lights on, we laugh, and I rewrite them so they're legible.

The words that glow are *day, a, cosmic, put, for, lily, look, of, agent, change,* and *care.*

"*Look for* goes together," Xander says, and I write them on their own line before crossing them off the original list. "Followed by *a,* maybe."

After a few tries, my eyes spot a familiar pattern. "A cosmic agent of change," I say. "Where have I heard that before?"

Xander shakes his head, unsure.

It comes to me as suddenly as the words explode out. "The elements!"

I cover my mouth, afraid I woke up Daphne or Trisha on either side of my room. "The Chinese elements," I say, quieter this time.

Xander snaps his fingers. "Wuxing. The five agents. Fire, water, earth, um . . ."

"Wood and metal," I finish automatically, my mind already elsewhere. Because as Xander said *fire* and *water*, I remembered how those two elements were used to make clues appear on previously blank pages. "That's an underlying theme throughout this hunt. They keep popping up."

Xander's nodding. "Brilliant. And what do you think these last four words mean?" He points to *day, put, lily, care.*

When it's down to just those, my brain sees the pattern immediately.

"Lilliput Day Care. That's where I went as a kid." Why Gong Gong would choose that particular destination eludes me, but it doesn't matter because Xander's smile is so wide I can see his molars.

"Then that's where we're going next."

We've done it. Completed the Taiwan leg of the hunt. And after we go to Lilliput Day Care, there are only two puzzles left, *Watch* and *X Marks the Spot.*

I'm so excited I let out a whoop. Just as I'm about to throw myself into Xander's arms, Daphne pounds on the wall we share.

The noise startles me into freezing.

"I should get to bed," Xander says quickly. He's gone before I can even respond.

What was I thinking, wanting to jump into *Xander's* arms? And why do I feel like a piece of me left with him?

Despite an incredibly long and eventful day, I lie awake that night listening to the beats of my own heart, which I may not fully understand anymore.

Chapter 39

We still have five days left on the TARP trip. At first, it feels unfortunate because the end of the hunt is so close I can taste it. But then I realize there's nothing I can do about the tuition money right now. Meaning, this is the first time in my life where the only thing I have to do is *enjoy*. So I throw myself into that objective with full Gemma Sun force.

The day after we get back is a beach outing, and I jump in with gusto, borrowing a swimsuit from Trisha and packing up some of my favorite snacks.

Once we arrive, our giant group sets up in the sand with makeshift umbrellas and way too much food and drinks. As the boys pull off their shirts, I pull my sun hat low so no one will see me peeking. And surprisingly, my eyes are drawn to Xander. His skin is smooth and tan, and as he reaches to yank his T-shirt over his head, his ab muscles flex and glisten in the sun.

A just-as-toned but longer and lighter torso steps into my view, and I'm grateful for the hat blocking where my eyes were aimed.

"Need sunblock?" Brett asks.

"Oh, um, Trisha already got me, but thanks."

A few other TARPers call out that they need some, and Brett has no choice but to go over to them. I settle back under the shade of my umbrella, only to feel a tap on my shoulder. Startled, I turn too fast and almost bump noses with Xander. But instead of backing up, he shifts his head closer to my ear to whisper "I see elements" in the I-see-dead-people way.

A shiver runs through me, and it's not because of the allusion to *The Sixth Sense.*

Xander points into the distance. "Ocean water, metal beach umbrella, wooden washed-up branch."

I giggle with him, wanting more than anything to contribute something fun and witty. But all I come up with is, "We're missing fire and earth."

He smiles, the conversation dying. Time of death is when Jax waves him over to play volleyball.

I look over at Felix digging through his backpack beside me. "How are you doing?"

He seems to understand the subtext because he gives me a solemn smile as he says, "Better, thanks. That day was a turning point for me." He doesn't seem to want to share more.

Before I can tell him he doesn't need to, the Northwest girls run up and drag him off. He pretends to be reluctant, but a grin peeks through as he scurries away with them.

As the rest of the group sunbathes, snacks, reads, and plays games, I close my eyes, inhale the delicious saltwater smell, and feel the other elements—the sun on my face, the breeze in my hair. I have no idea how much time passes before I hear, "You look content."

Xander is back, shading his eyes to peer at me from across the blanket.

"No complaints here," I say, stretching my legs out as I sip a still-cold papaya milk.

He tilts his head at me. "You look kind of hot, though."

For a second I stop breathing. Did that just happen? Did he say he finds me attractive in front of the entire group?

I learn a second too late that he meant the other kind of hot. Because right after he says it, he jumps to his feet, rushes toward me, and scoops me up in his arms.

"Wait!" I yell, worrying about my hat getting wet.

Xander pauses, his arms tightening around my back and legs, but he stays in place. He lowers his voice so no one else can hear as he asks, "Do you not want to go in the water?" His tone is gentle and soft, worried.

I throw my hat onto the blanket. "Okay, now I'm ready."

As soon as the words are out, Xander takes off running.

"Hey, what happened in Kaohsiung, you two?" Daphne calls after us.

I don't know if Xander heard, but since he doesn't acknowledge it, neither do I.

Xander jumps into the ocean with me still in his arms. The temperature of the water is Goldilocks perfect—not too hot and not too cold. I clutch his neck tighter. His arm under my knees releases, and I move away, thinking he wants to separate. We're already apart by the time I realize he had been shifting so his arms could go around my waist.

A splash sounds behind me. A second later, I feel a different arm around my shoulders.

"Anyone want to chicken fight? You and me, Gongzhu," Brett says. "Against this one." He points in Xander's direction.

Xander doesn't look fazed. Maybe he's even amused. "I'm good," he says.

"Aw, c'mon, don't be a chicken."

"I thought you just asked me to be one," Xander deadpans.

Brett looks confused. I can't help a small giggle, which seems to annoy Brett.

"Maybe we should chicken fight just the two of us, without anyone on our shoulders," Brett challenges Xander, who doesn't react.

When Brett pushes further, even splashing water in Xander's direction, I suddenly feel nauseous.

I'd been seeing the signs all along, but it didn't come together until now, similar to how you can be on the right track with a puzzle, but you need that *aha* moment to see it clearly.

And now I see Brett clearly. I understand exactly why he's been flirty, and it's not because he likes me.

Feeling like a fool, I wade toward the beach, wanting to be away from this. Both Brett and Xander follow, Brett closer.

"Gemma, wait!"

I whirl around in hip-deep water, accidentally splashing Brett as he catches up. "I'm not interested, and neither are you, not really," I tell him matter-of-factly.

"What? Of course I'm—"

"It's nothing but a competition for you. You're only interested when someone else is. It has nothing to do with me."

"No, I—" he sputters. "No, I like you because we're similar. We're both competitive."

I used to think so too, but what a laugh that feels like now.

And while it used to annoy the bejesus out of me, maybe it's good that Xander doesn't give in to that. And maybe it's attractive that he doesn't give in to Brett either, even if it likely means he's not into me.

"You were just being competitive with whoever else was talking to me."

"I—" Brett is still struggling, but his resolve is weakening. "Maybe, I don't know—"

He never saw me. He barely even knows me. And from the way his expression is shifting from determined to confused, I know I'm right. He knows it too. He just can't admit it yet.

I hold a hand out. "Just friends," I say, not acknowledging that we weren't exactly dating before. But I want it to be clear that there will be no more flirting or kissing or et cetera.

He doesn't take my hand, not wanting to accept defeat, but I grab his and shake limply. Then I leave and wade over to Xander, trying to convince myself with every step that this will be good for Brett in the long run. It's definitely good for me, as much as it hurts.

From a few feet away, Xander flashes me a tight-lipped smile, but I don't have time to read what's beneath it before Trisha, Daphne, and Jax join us.

I'm happily surrounded by friends, but I wish it had taken them just a few more minutes to join us.

That night, Trisha shows up at my door with beauty masks.

"You know, because of the sun," she says.

I excitedly let her in. Trisha insists we go all out, first with eye masks, then whole-face ones that make us look like different animals—tiger for me, kitten for her.

"So do you feel like the hunt led you where you wanted to go?" she asks.

"Yes and no. It didn't go where I thought it would, but it went where I needed it to."

"Do you feel less lost?"

"Yes, but partly because I realized that not knowing things and feeling uncertain are just a part of life."

She sighs. "Yup. An important but hard lesson."

"You know," I say slowly, venturing out on a limb. "Even though she hasn't been here, my mom went on a journey too."

I proceed to spill it all—telling her about meeting my grand-mother, about my complicated feelings toward everything, and, most important, how my mom was tangled in it. I tell my mom's side without bringing Trisha into it directly, but at the end, she has tears in her eyes.

"That sounds . . . familiar," she says. "The complicated relation-ship with culture and family, the struggle to distinguish between family expectations and your own wishes . . ."

"My mother came out the other side."

Trisha seems to understand what I'm saying. "Maybe I shouldn't be so scared to try to communicate with my parents. Even if it doesn't go well, I'll have at least tried."

I nod. There isn't much else to say.

She hugs me so tightly the serum from her mask mixes with mine. (All good; tiger, kitten—both felines, right?)

We're interrupted by Val calling.

"Can I introduce you?" I ask Trisha. "I think you two will get along."

My worlds are coming together. Because there's just one world. There's just me.

Trisha and I aren't the only ones feeling more comfortable with ourselves and each other.

Over the next few days, when we hit the clubs at night, I bust out my nerdy dance moves without worrying how I look. Meanwhile, Daphne and Jax nail the latest TikTok dances, and Yang shows off his popping and locking skills.

At karaoke—which I prefer, not because I like singing but because it's more intimate—Trisha joins me in belting pop songs while the Northwest girls dance backup. Jax, Brett, Yang, and Xander sing a boy band medley accompanied by semiaccurate dances, with Felix joining in on the last one.

"Glad to see you coming out of your shell," Jax says to Felix.

"What are you talking about?" Daphne says. "He's still as curmudgeonly as before. He complains about everything." In fact, he just finished complaining that our private karaoke room was taking too long to bring us our ordered food.

"I'll have you know," Sophia says, "that it took me three days to convince him to do *one* song tonight. So the fact that he did *and* danced—I think he deserves a trophy. As do I."

We of course chant both their names in response.

At the New Taipei Gold Museum, Xander spends the first few

minutes telling us how we're seeing real offices, living quarters, processing plants, and gold-mining equipment.

"Xander, I don't need an audio version of the itinerary," Daphne says.

"This is additional info," he argues.

"Well, I didn't read the itinerary for a reason."

"I was enjoying it," Yang says, shushing her.

Daphne tries to start a *Nerd! Nerd!* chant, but Yang drowns her out with *Tarp! Tarp!*, which I join in on. Xander flashes me a grin as wide as when we solved the most recent puzzle. If only pretrip Gemma could see me now.

Once we're inside the museum and people naturally divide into groups, I stick near Xander and ask him questions. He delights in being a personal museum guide to Yang, Trisha, and me. I can't say every single detail is riveting, but I'm thrilled he's being himself. I act my butt off, and by the end of the hard-hat part of the tour, Xander's face is glowing.

While I'm more comfortable in some ways, I still have some hangups. Like how at the museum, I try to ask an employee where the bathroom is, but instead of saying *cesuo*, I accidentally say *lesuo* instead. After staring at me for a confused second, the employee points me to a garbage can.

Brett can't hold his laughter in. "Don't shit in the trash can, Gemma!"

Arrow to my Achilles' heel. And it doesn't help who it came from.

Shockingly, Xander swoops in. "You're the only piece of *shi* here that belongs in the trash can," he says to Brett, who shuts up immediately.

From that point forward, for the rest of the trip, I stop trying to say *cesuo* and use *bian bian* instead. I don't know if it's *poop* the noun or the verb (or maybe both?), and it's so much more embarrassing, but it always does the job, and urgently.

My other attempts at Mandarin don't go any better except for phrases that sound like other English words. Like, I will never forget *to not have* because it sounds like *mayo*.

"Don't people get confused if there isn't any mayo?" I ask the other TARPers after I learn it. *"Mayo mayo."* I get a big laugh—my first one where I'm not only on the inside of the bilingual joke, I *said* it.

Thanks to the TARPers and my own evolving experiences, I'm finally starting to realize that we all have different relationships with our culture. There is no "right" way to do it. Before, I thought the only way to be Asian was to be like Xander. But I'm Gemma. Gemma, who struggles with Mandarin but can still make a joke in it, who will never eat Cheetos with her fingers again, and who is still a work in progress as to how she feels about her roots. And that's okay.

Two days before we leave, Xander helps me pack up Gong Gong's belongings to mail back to the US. My original strategy was to simply seal up the boxes they came in, but Xander insists I ship my dirty clothes (which are lighter) while keeping the most valuable items on me (photos, jewelry, art supplies, and any paintings that can fit in my luggage).

He's right, but I can't help joking, "But then that'll be so heavy for me."

"I'll help you," he says like it's a no-brainer. "I can give you a ride back from the airport too, if you want."

"Oh, that would be great. Thanks."

We return to packing like that conversation wasn't out of the ordinary even though two weeks ago, we pretended to be strangers on the way here.

Xander also offers to mail some of the items for me in the packages he's sending back to his house.

"My parents are making me ship them five-cent crackers and ramen. I keep telling them we can order this stuff online, but no, they make me do all the work. I'd feel better if these have more purpose than that, truly."

Before, I would have worried about not getting the items back, but I know Xander will take care of it (though I do still choose the items carefully in case his dad gets his hands on them first).

In the end, we manage to pack everything but the books, which are too heavy, so we donate them, but not before I hit every page with the black light just in case (which yields nothing).

"I can't believe it's almost over," Xander says.

"It went by too fast. Thanks again for letting me into the program."

"Of course, M Game. Wouldn't have been the same without you." He smiles, but it's wistful.

Things won't be different once we return home, will they? I assumed I'd still see him around Blue Hill over the rest of the summer, but maybe not. Once the hunt is over, there's no reason to keep meeting up. And regardless, in a month, we'll be going our separate ways to Amherst and Harvard.

For the first time, I'm not sure I want the hunt to end.

The last big TARP meal is my favorite, not just because I've gotten to know everyone so well, but because Peking duck and luobo si bing turn out to be my favorite foods ever. For the former, the crispy skin and moist, perfectly seasoned meat are wrapped in a thin bing with scallions, cucumber, and tianmian sauce. I'm convinced there's no better combination of flavors. And I never thought much about radishes before, but whoever invented luobo si bing is a genius. Seasoned julienned strips of radish stuffed into a flaky pastry with a juicy inside that's reminiscent of soup dumplings—I will be fantasizing about these for years to come. I'm told that not all luobo si bing come so soupy, and I thank Xander for doing his research while planning the program, not just because of the soupy luobo si bing, but also not *not* because of them either.

When it's time to say goodbye to the TARPers, I feel like I'm saying goodbye to friends I've known my whole life. Especially Trisha.

Just before we part, I hand her the painting I've made specially for her: a collage of Taipei 101, the damper, Yehliu, and 7-Eleven. She clutches it to her chest.

"You'll keep in touch?" she asks.

"Of course."

"NYU isn't all that far from Amherst."

I beam. "We'll go out for niu rou mian."

We hug for a full minute.

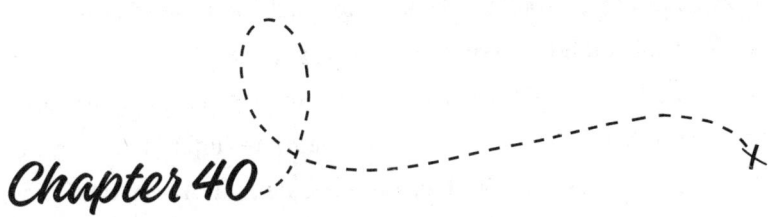

Chapter 40

This time, I'm beyond grateful that Xander and I are sitting next to each other on the flights home. We form a plan of when to sleep to try to readjust to Eastern Time.

"Also," Xander adds, "we're landing in the afternoon. Which means . . ."

We can go straight to the day care center.

"Is, um . . ." I don't know how to ask my question without sounding rude.

"My cousin Sean is going to pick us up, not my parents."

I nod, relieved both by his answer and by the fact that I didn't have to elaborate.

"Your mom was okay with us carpooling?" Xander asks.

I told my mom the day before we left. I thought she'd resist, but she just said, "Okay, if you're sure." When I checked again later, she said, "I trust you."

"It was no problem," I tell him. "Honestly, it's a big help. Now she doesn't have to take any time off work."

He nibbles his bottom lip. "She wasn't . . . upset?"

I shake my head. "Things have been different . . . better . . . between us since I told her what we learned about her parents."

He exhales loudly. "I'm so glad. For you, of course, and . . . it makes me hopeful for when—if—I tell my dad. But, I guess, also not that hopeful because he couldn't be more different from your mom." He pauses. "You're lucky to have her, you know that? The way you talk about her . . . it's clear how close you two are."

"Thanks," I say even though that word doesn't feel like enough. "It was sweet of your dad to read you bedtime stories. And your grandparents. You're lucky to have a large family—I've always wanted that."

He gives me a small smile.

I nudge his elbow. "And that big family is going to benefit us today because Sean's coming to take us to day care."

Xander covers my hand with his as he chuckles. I can't tell if it was an accident or on purpose, but he leaves it there a second longer than necessary. It's reminiscent of yet completely different from all the times our hands touched in the past. And because it's so different, I don't know what I should do. Turn my palm up? Definitely not put my other hand on top—we're not making a hand sandwich.

Turns out it doesn't matter because he promptly removes it to power on the screen in front of him.

"Movie?"

I force a smile and nod.

We spend the rest of our awake time on the flight playing cards, watching movies (Xander is especially good at pressing both our screens at the same time so we can watch simultaneously), reminiscing about the trip, snacking, and planning a giant TARP reunion in the States for next summer.

Our hands don't touch again.

Sean is in his early twenties, a programmer, and too cool to be into a treasure hunt. But he's still happy to swing by the day care center.

Instead of feeling embarrassed, I'm just glad he won't be accompanying us inside, opting to grab a coffee instead.

Lilliput is so much smaller than I remember, which makes sense—*I* was so small the last time I was here.

We're standing in front of the outdoor play area, which has two swings, a slide, a sandbox, and a homemade wooden playhouse. Surrounding that are benches, a water fountain, and some trees and shrubbery. I'm not sure how busy Lilliput is nowadays, but no kids are currently playing. Maybe because it's too hot and they're inside.

"You used to come here?" Xander asks, looking around.

"Every day for years."

"Isn't this kind of far from where you live?"

"Yeah, but we came because of Greta, the owner. She was so good to us." Even though it was outside her job description, Greta taught me to read, and as soon as I learned the word *great* and how to spell her name, I told her it made sense because they have the same letters in them. "My mom works at the nursing home where Greta's mom was, and Greta was so kind to us, basically letting me come here for almost nothing. Otherwise, we never could've afforded it. Even when we didn't have electricity or heat, I had a safe place to go and my mom didn't have to quit her jobs. And of course my mom slipped Greta's mom extra french fries and mashed potatoes, though we obviously got the better end of the deal."

Xander puts a warm hand on my shoulder, and I feel the affection traveling from his heart to mine. "I'm sorry."

"Nothing to be sorry about," I say, then change the subject. "Do you see any cosmic agents of change?"

"Several. Earth all around us, metal chains on the swings, wooden play structure, wooden benches, trees . . ."

I'm briefly transported back to the beach, when he whispered in my ear about seeing elements. It's so vivid a small shiver runs through me now, and I hope he doesn't notice.

"Do you think there's a reason why the agents of change are the main theme throughout, the thread connecting all the puzzles?" I ask. "Like, do you think it's a sign that my grandfather wishes he could change things? Go back and do some of it differently?"

Xander ruminates for a moment. "I think you'll never know for sure, but it's a strong possibility." I like that he's honest but wish his answer was more definitive. He's right, though. I'll never know for sure what meaning I was supposed to glean from each step, not unless there's a detailed letter from my grandfather at the end, which isn't happening.

"I've been thinking about the elements for a while now," I tell him. "Especially how they relate to the puzzles. Not only do they keep coming up as answers, but they've been serving as agents of change."

"What do you mean?"

"Like in the third puzzle, using fire or heat changed the piece of paper so the ink appeared. And in the first puzzle, the wooden box physically changed to reveal the next clue—a piece of its side came off."

Excited, Xander chimes in, "And the metal box with the holes fell apart, and then we rearranged the pieces into something else."

"And then water revealed the most recent clue."

"What about earth?" Xander asks.

"Maybe when we looked under the gate?" That box was buried in the dirt.

"That feels different. The earth didn't change or cause change. We just moved the gate, and the box was there." He glances at the earth around us. "Do you think that's what we're supposed to do here?"

"I doubt he wants us to dig this whole place up."

"Maybe we have to find a specific spot."

"Maybe."

My head is only half in the hunt. The other half is thinking about how there are only two puzzles left. Two more steps until Xander and I no longer have to see each other.

"Let's start examining," I say, gesturing so we'll split up. I need a second.

From the bench, Xander calls out, "Do you think we're looking for multiple elements in one place?"

I think for a moment. "No, he said look for *a* cosmic agent of change. He picks his words carefully, so I think we're looking for just one." Which makes it that much harder.

A few minutes later, Xander waves me over. "I think I found something."

I join him in front of the wooden playhouse. "This was my favorite when I was little. Because of . . ." I take a step toward the fake mailbox, and I gasp.

Xander is watching me, waiting. He knows there's more to the story. But I'm speechless. Because I don't understand how this is possible.

The mailbox sticks out from the front of the house, a simple box that is more for a child's imagination than functional because the pieces are fixed. The top flap doesn't open. I don't know how much extra it would have cost for some hinges, but this entire house looks more like a DIY project made from leftover scraps than a prefabbed kit.

But as a child, I found that one of the mailbox's sides was loose. And if you jiggled it just so, you could slip it off and on, making it the perfect hiding spot. I used to stow all my treasures in there— my favorite rocks, the pencil Greta gave me, candy—always waiting until other kids weren't looking to access it.

And now, on that precious jiggly piece, there's a sun carving with a circle for the body and wavy lines for the rays. A design I've seen before. No, a *carving* I've seen before. On my mom's necklace. The one she never takes off. But that's not even what I'm focusing on right now.

"How did he know?" I whisper. No one knew about my secret hiding spot, not even Greta.

I quickly explain this to Xander as my fingers curl around the bottom of the wooden piece. It comes off immediately, so much easier with larger, stronger hands.

Something's inside. I reach in with shaky fingers, still not quite believing this is happening. It's cool to the touch. Round. Small enough to fit in my palm. Clutching it tightly, I pull out a silver pocket watch.

The same sun design is carved on the front, a matching set with my mom's necklace. Growing up, I just assumed it was special because of our last name and Slugger. But now I realize there's more to the story.

Before I can tell Xander about the necklace, I hear my name from across the outdoor area. "Gemma?"

I turn, and tears immediately prick my eyes. Quickly, I replace the side of the mailbox, then jog to the schoolhouse and into Greta's outstretched arms. Her face has a few more lines and her hair more gray, but it's Greta, and all I feel when I look at her is safe.

She cups my head with her hand. "Gemma, you're all grown up. It's so good to see you." She doesn't seem surprised by my visit.

"Did you know I was coming?"

"I had a feeling," she says with a twinkle in her eye. "A while ago, your grandfather came and asked if he could add a small design to the playhouse."

"You met him?"

"That was the only time I talked to him, but he used to come here when you were little. He'd watch you from that bench." She points to the other side of the play area.

And with those words, I remember. An older man sitting on the bench, a giant hat pulled low, a newspaper open in front of him. I saw him many times.

That's how he knew about the hiding spot. He *saw* me.

"Why didn't he come talk to me?" I asked.

Greta's eyes are sad. "Your mom asked me to keep you away from him. I don't know the story there, but my job was to protect you."

That's right, Greta would call us inside when he was there. And right before we went in, I would hide my trinkets in the mailbox so no one else could take them from me.

Gong Gong saw me. Because he wanted to. And by placing the watch here, he wanted me to know it.

I will not forget that he didn't want me at first. That I'm the reason for his estrangement from my mother just by existing. But maybe everything is grayer than I previously realized.

Gong Gong made mistakes and didn't always come from the right place. He was human. He will never be family the way my mom, Val, Señora Gonzalez, or even Greta is. But maybe it doesn't have to be so black and white. He was a product of the tragedy he experienced, the relentless hardships he had to face over and over again. They shaped him, just like my hardships have shaped me. He needed help but didn't know how to get it, and I won't be like him and dismiss him because of his mistakes.

And by showing up at Lilliput, by putting together this puzzle hunt, he was trying, perhaps in the only way he knew how. He didn't know how to tell his daughter or granddaughter about his life, but he found an imperfect way to try to explain, maybe even ask for a little understanding and forgiveness. And this time, at the end, he was completely honest, revealing his true self to us, warts and all. Perhaps the hunt was his way of showing remorse or how his story is gray, muddled, and complicated, just like all of life.

I feel the hardness of my heart begin to soften.

Xander comes over, and I introduce him to Greta, who invites us inside.

I linger behind for a second, deep in thought. Right before I enter, I turn toward the bench.

"I forgive you," I whisper to my gong gong.

I take a mental picture of the playground, imagining him there again, and then I leave. I don't look back.

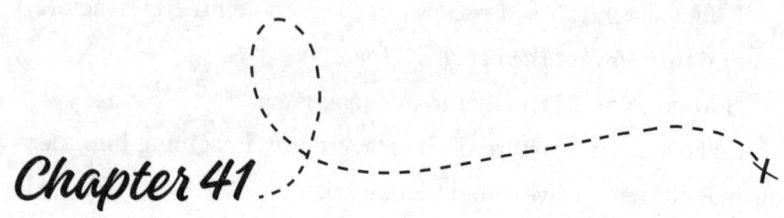

Chapter 41

We don't stay long because we don't want to keep Sean waiting. When we meet up with him again, he's waving his phone at Xander.

"Your family's freaking out," he says. Then he turns to me. "I didn't know you were Gemma *Sun*."

Oh no. Did they just find out about the ride, or did they learn about the whole hunt?

"His parents see *everything*," Sean says spookily, then laughs. "Sorry, man. Next time tell me we're on a secret mission."

Xander looks annoyed but less upset than I would have guessed.

"Sorry," I say.

He shrugs. "It's fine. They've been bugging me this whole trip."

"Beginning at the airport," Sean adds as he starts the car. "I heard about the fight."

"Yeah, they were pissed he went above and beyond to get me into the program," I say as I buckle into the back seat.

"So much so that they wanted Xander to kick you out on the spot."

"Really?" It was already such a big deal that he added me, but he also had to deal with that?

Xander glances at me over his shoulder as he says, "I'll always have your back, Gemma."

I . . . don't know what to say to that. But I believe him. And I wish I knew how to tell him what it means to me, and that I feel the same way.

Sean peers at me in the rearview mirror. "Yeah, Gemma, I'm telling you, Xander's the one you want in your corner—he'll go down swinging. When we were kids, I broke into my parents' liquor cabinet, and when they found out, I was deader than dead. Then Xander here jumped in and convinced them we needed it for an extra-credit chemistry experiment. Can you believe it? No one but him could've pulled that off. You know, it's too bad you didn't throw your graduation hat before his speech, because he would've found a way to turn that around too."

How weird it is to be back here after I've changed so much, only to be reminded of old mistakes that will haunt me forever. In fifty years, at our reunion, are people still going to be making fun of me for that?

"So what comes next?" Xander asks, and I'm so lost in thought it takes me a second to figure out what he's talking about.

"Oh! Right!" I retrieve the watch from my pocket.

Running my fingers over the sun, I wonder if Gong Gong carved this himself. Did he make the necklace too?

"My mom has a necklace with the same design," I tell him. "I'll ask her about it." I consider calling or texting right now, but this feels like a bigger conversation. Though I still text her that I'm fifteen minutes away, as she asked me to before I left Taiwan.

A tiny button sits at the top of the watch, and I press it. The cover springs open. A folded-up page is wedged inside, and on top of that is a tiny slip of paper. I unfurl the slip first.

I never stopped loving

No end punctuation, which is abnormal for him. All the other clues had proper punctuation. It must mean something, just like his use of capitalization.

I pass the slip to Xander, then ask him the question that pops into my mind. "Do you think he meant your grandfather? Or my mom? Or . . . me?"

I already know his answer. Which is the same as what he said earlier on the playground: there won't be a way to truly know.

I hold up a hand before he says anything. I don't want to hear it. Not yet. I just want to fantasize for a second longer that Gong Gong meant all three.

Before I can look at the folded-up page or show it to Xander, Sean asks, "What's this about your—maybe our—grandfather?"

Xander passes the slip of paper back to me. "Oh, uh, it's kind of a long story, but . . ."

As Xander begins telling Sean, I stare at Gong Gong's handwriting.

I never stopped loving

Before, thinking about Gong Gong's life ushered in a cloud accompanied by mournful music. But with these words . . . now I'm thinking about how he tried. He went for it. He loved and lost, and never stopped loving. Even with how everything turned out, he never gave up.

I used to think that I dove into everything full force—even if I'm going to accidentally be the astronomy-club president, I'm going to go all out and make us learn celestial navigation—but I'm now realizing that this isn't true for *all* areas of my life. Sometimes I've been too scared to try.

If Gong Gong could do it even after all he went through, why can't I?

I don't want to be scared anymore.

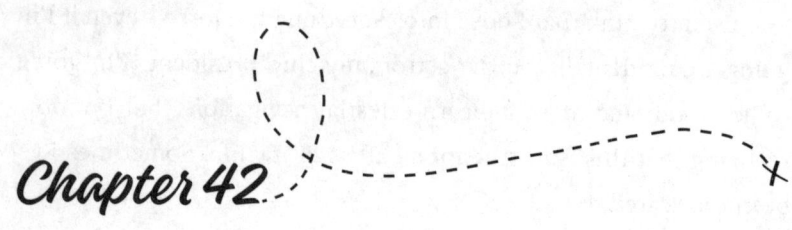

Chapter 42

When I arrive home, my mom is waiting for me with a steaming cup of ginger-honey rooibos tea.

"Mom! Why aren't you at work?" I say into her shoulder because she tackled me with a hug as soon as I entered.

"I took my break now so I could see you. I missed you too much!"

That explains why she asked me to text when I was fifteen minutes away.

I try to ask another question, but she's squeezing me so tight I can only get muffled noises out.

She finally lets go so I can talk.

"Only one cup of tea?"

"Sorry, I can't stay. But I just had to see you." She tucks my hair behind my ear. "I love this new hairstyle. It suits you. And, honey? I'm proud of you, you know that?"

I know she's pressed for time, but I have to bring it up now. "Mom . . . are we . . . ?"

I run out of words. I don't know how to tell her that despite knowing better, I put all my eggs into the treasure hunt basket, and now it's looking like none of them are going to hatch. I'm not sure how we're going to get the money for tuition.

She cups a hand to my cheek. "I don't have an answer yet, but I'm trying. We'll figure it out like we always do, right? You and me—"

"Against the world," I finish.

She removes her hand, and some of the hope I momentarily felt vanishes with it.

"One more thing." I reach into my pocket and retrieve the watch.

Upon seeing it, she sits down, a hand over her mouth.

"It matches your necklace," I say. "Did Gong Gong make that for you?"

A slow smile appears on her face. "Gong Gong—is that what you've been calling him?"

Right. I forgot she hasn't heard me say that yet. "That phrase came up at some point and it kind of stuck."

Her eyes are shiny with tears as she slowly, reverently pulls the necklace off over her head. "Gong Gong gave me this when I was a little girl to remind me who I am and where I come from. Because . . ." She takes a breath. "Because this is the best gift of all. Sun represents family, the most valuable treasure."

"Slugger," I whisper, my voice filled with emotion.

She nods wistfully. "Gong Gong never went anywhere without that pocket watch."

Just like you never go anywhere without your necklace.

"Here," she says, standing and coming over to me. "This should be yours." She loops the necklace over my head. "To remember who you are and where you come from."

Which I'm finally beginning to understand.

I squeeze the pendant. "Thank you." Then I remove the two

pieces of paper before handing the watch to my mom. "And you should have this."

She takes it from me gingerly, as if she doesn't quite believe it's real. Then she grips it tightly in her palm.

"I love you, Mom."

She leans over and kisses the top of my head. "I love you more, my sun, my treasure."

Those words mean even more now than ever before.

Once she heads back to work, those words, my necklace, and Gong Gong's slip of paper not only remind me to be brave, but they fuel me past the jet lag to begin planning. I forgot to tell Xander about the second piece of paper inside the watch, and now I have the perfect way to continue our hunt together stateside. I just hope he'll find it perfect too.

1:19 PM ET a day later

Gemma

There was another piece of paper in the watch.

The next puzzle.

Meet at the high school football field in an hour?

Xander

Of course

You don't have to sneak out or anything, do you?

Yeah I'm going to need you to wait below my window to catch me

Use your knees, okay?

Don't worry, I ate a light breakfast

If you ate a Taiwanese breakfast, that's not light.

Just aim for the hedges.

In all seriousness, I do have to sneak out

Oh, seriously?

Sorry, that sucks.

We can call it off if that's easier.

Where's the fun in that?

Don't worry, I threw the cardboard dog out first to break my fall

I told you he would serve more purposes

Do you seriously still have that?

Of course I do

Bring it.

Are you telling me to bring the dog or challenging me to a cheer contest?

Um, both?

Don't be aggressive,
B-E compassionate

Doesn't quite have the same ring to it.

See you soon

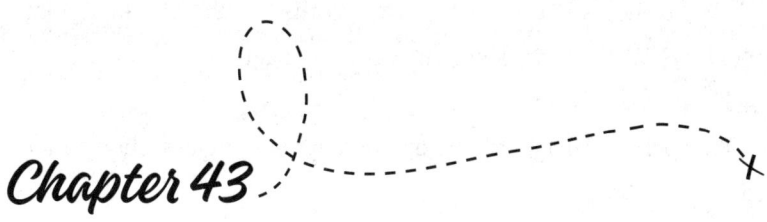

Chapter 43

"Oh my god, you really do have it?" I greet Xander when he shows up on the football field with the cardboard dog.

Seeing it again is so jarring I almost drop the water bottle and bag I'm holding. I remembered it being bigger, maybe because of how much damage it caused.

"He caught me when I jumped out the window," Xander deadpans.

"He must be tired, then. Let's leave him in the locker room," I say so we don't have to carry him around.

Xander obliges, and when he returns, I reach into the bag and hand him a piece of paper.

"Next clue?" he asks as he examines it. There are numbers at the top, then an equation with two images below. "Okay, the numbers at the beginning seem to be a location—coordinates for longitude and latitude. I assume they're here?"

I nod. "Exactly where we are."

He shifts his focus to the equation, which combines two images with a plus sign, then ends with an equal sign and question mark.

"Is that a pan and a sun?" he asks.

I pass him the bag. "This stuff is also needed."

"Were they somehow connected to the watch? Or your mom's necklace? We're supposed to use all this together?"

I nod.

He opens the bag and retrieves a magnifying glass, then a metal pan with an object taped to its center.

"Wait." He inspects the item on the pan. "Is that a—"

"Yup."

He furrows his brow at me, confused, but a moment later, he shrugs. "I guess we gotta do this, huh? Your grandfather knew how to have fun. He would've liked the cardboard dog."

I just smile.

"So you solved all this without me, then waited so we could do it together? I'm touched."

He hands me the magnifying glass, but I shake my head. "You do the honors."

We take a simultaneous step back. Then Xander angles the magnifying glass so it concentrates the sun onto the pan. Pan + Sun = ? We're about to find out.

A few seconds later, a spark ignites and the firework bursts into the sky.

We both whoop, with Xander jumping in the air.

When the smoke clears, he says, "So pan plus sun equals fireworks? Is he talking about his relationship with my grandfather . . . ?" He trails off, and then his eyes meet mine. "Or is this not . . . ?" He can't bring himself to say it.

His eyes turn serious, the most serious I've ever seen. "Gemma . . ."

I look up at him, my face just as serious but with excitement dancing at the edges. "You're missing a couple agents of change."

His eyes widen. Then he begins thinking out loud. "The pan is obviously metal. And using the sun, that was fire, and maybe the firework can count as that too—I mean, *fire* is in its name. Earth?"

"Maybe the ground below us?" I suggest.

"So we're missing wood and water." When he says the last word, his gaze locks on to the water bottle in my hand, and he grabs it, then pours it over the pan. The heat melted a coating on top, and the water washes it off to reveal . . . nothing.

But Xander has been on the hunt almost as long as me, and he's already digging in the bag I handed him. A second later, he's shining the black light onto the pan.

The words *my amusing go-to* appear.

"*My amusing go-to* what—joke? Story? Nickname for you?" He's stumped for a second but then seems to remember the last time we shone a black light and words appeared. "It's an anagram!" He stares at it intently for a few minutes, then declares "Go to gymnasium!"

We're off like two bullets.

"The gym is indeed my go-to," he says as he keeps up an effortless jog. "Which I know you find amusing. And annoying."

I can't help a laugh because he's right on both counts.

Xander enters the gym first, and as soon as he crosses the threshold, the lights go out. He's in full puzzle mode, his hands whipping up and shining the black light everywhere. On the opposite wall, a drawing of two M&M's playing Monopoly appears.

Xander stares at it, no expression on his face. Just when I can't handle the suspense any longer, he turns to me.

"I don't think I'll ever fully understand your brilliance."

That is not at all what I thought he would say. How does he keep finding ways to make me feel so . . . deserving. Special. Worthy.

"This is the best rebus puzzle of all time," he says, gesturing to the drawing. Then he declares the answer. "M Game. You must have my next clue."

He extends a palm out, and I drop a mint with teeth marks into it.

"Um, thanks?" He examines it. "Did you have to bite it?"

"That's part of it!"

"A chewed mint?"

Excitement balloons in my chest. "Yes, exactly!"

He looks at me, then the mint, then back again, a boyish grin on his lips. A second later, he retrieves his phone and types away.

Rearranging letters, I hope.

Five minutes later, his eyes soften. He puts his phone away, then holds a hand out to me.

"Yes, Gemma, I'll dance with you."

A chewed mint, an anagram of *dance with me*.

As soon as he says that, a disco ball turns on, "Ob-La-Di, Ob-La-Da" begins to play, and the cardboard dog drops down from the ceiling—the last agent of change, wood.

His mouth falls open.

"I've got my eye on you, Half Package," Val yells from the other side of the gym. "She's too good for you, you know. And I'm still her partner in crime, not you!" She sneaks out the door closest to her, her jobs now done, the last of which was to grab the dog from the locker room and hang it up.

"You did all this?" Xander asks, his arms wrapping around my waist.

"With Val's help." I place my hands on his shoulders, and we begin swaying together. "Sorry I unknowingly stood you up at the dance four years ago. I'm hoping I can rectify that—and many other things—now."

"I can't believe you found such an elegant way to connect the puzzles we solved with our past—the rebus, the dog, the dance. Except I'm also not surprised." He gently brushes my hair aside, his fingertips caressing my forehead as he says, "I adore how your mind works."

I doubt he knows just how much those last words mean to me. My whole life, I've felt like my weird wiring was something to hide and be embarrassed by, and this is the first time anyone has spoken about it as a strength. Something to be loved and appreciated, not hidden away.

He smiles. "So Pan plus Sun equals fireworks, huh?"

I bite my lip, trying not to blush. Was that too forward? No use questioning it now.

He raises an eyebrow. "I thought you weren't physically attracted to me."

"What? Why would you . . ." And then I remember. All those weeks ago at graduation, he overheard me with Val. That feels like another lifetime. "No, that's not true. At all. In fact . . ."

I pause, the words suddenly feeling too scary to say even though I've basically already said them. But then I remind myself why I went to the trouble of this grand gesture.

Because it's Xander. And because the treasure hunt showed me a side of him I would have never known otherwise. What better way to declare my feelings than with what brought us close enough for me to fall all over again? Except this time, we know ourselves and each other better.

"I like you, X." A nickname so much better than Alex or Xander or Xander Pander. "More than luobo si bing and niu rou mian and rice crackers. So, a lot."

A smile slowly takes over his face, one that's so bright it's like he's the sun. But he's not—I am.

"I like you too, Sunshine." That nickname is worth the wait. "More than Yehliu and art heists and cardboard dogs."

I faux gasp. "That much?"

I think he's going to make a joke, but his intense eyes meet mine as he simply answers, "Yes."

He stops swaying to cup my face with both hands. Deliciously slow, like we have all the time in the world—which, we do—his eyes roam over my face, taking in every part of me. It's somehow more intimate than physical contact. His gaze dips down to my lips, and I find myself watching as the corners of his mouth curve up. He takes a breath, his lips parting, and I lean forward first.

Our kiss tastes like sunshine. He feels like home.

Pan + Sun = Fireworks, indeed.

Chapter ~~44~~ 45.

(In honor of Taipei 101, of course)

Five minutes later, I'm embarrassed when Mrs. Nelson turns on the gymnasium lights and asks what in god's name we're doing. But the second she sees Xander, she beams like she's just spotted a celebrity. Then when she realizes who he's embracing, she pauses and says, "Oh! Hmm. Well . . . I guess that makes some sense."

Then she follows that up with, "Are you sure, Xander? You remember the . . ." And she mimes me throwing my graduation cap in the air. "Anyway, none of my business, have a good summer, kids."

Her brief appearance takes the magic out of the moment. But Xander still leans over to kiss the top of my head. No clearer sign of how things have changed.

"Your dad is going to kill us," I joke as we start cleaning up. "Or just one of us. Me."

"He's . . . not talking to me right now."

"Because of me?"

"Because of me. I told him about, you know. My grandfather, what we learned."

"I'm so sorry."

"He needs time, and that's fair. I think he'll realize the truth like I did eventually, and when he does, I'll be here."

"He's lucky to have you," I say.

Xander gives me a small shrug. Then he changes the topic. "So none of this had to do with the other hunt?"

I beam. "Not at all. It was just for you."

He grabs my palm and squeezes. "I'm honored. Thank you."

I reach into my back pocket and pull out the actual paper that had been inside the watch. The real next puzzle and, according to the master list, the *last* puzzle.

"Ooh, what's it say?" he asks.

"I didn't look," I answer honestly.

"You waited for me?"

"Of course. The index for the last puzzle is *X Marks the Spot*. I assume that means you, X." *My* X. Val was right all along.

I shove the paper at him. "Good luck."

He laughs. "When did your humor get so dry? I love it." I blush. "Seriously, though, thanks for waiting. That means a lot."

I lean over and kiss his cheek. Because I can. He beams like I've filled him with sunlight.

Together, we unfold the last puzzle.

It looks like gibberish.

[(6b.) – (national) – (lace) – (museum)]

+

[(5.) – (gingham) + (3a.) + (were) – (answer) – (fine)]

+

[(8.) – (in)]

+

[(9.) + (6a.)]

=

?

And remember (3b.)

"Um," Xander starts to say, but I'm already grabbing the journal from a side pocket of the bag. I have no idea what any of this means, but I recognize *3a.*, *3b.*, *6a.*, and *6b.* from the index.

"Brilliant," Xander says when he makes the same connection. "I mean, seriously, how cool is this?"

I nod. "The last puzzle is a culmination of everything."

We settle on the gym bleachers and lay the puzzle beside the journal index, whose final filled-out version looks like the following:

~~1. Wooden box~~

~~2. Will~~

~~3. Framed photo~~

   a. Answer to first riddle: 火 **/ fire**

   b. First line of second riddle: 火 **goes with water, wood, metal, and earth also.**

~~5. Journal~~

Destination: **Yangmingshan**

~~6. Metal Box~~

a. *Need A:* **Pan**

b. *Destination:* **National Palace Museum**

~~7. Wall~~

~~8. House gate~~

Instructions, first line: **Pick up ~~the~~ tea**

~~9. Address~~

Number: **2**

~~10. Poem~~

~~11. Beginning~~

~~12. Watch~~

13. *X Marks the Spot*

I'd been writing in the extras as we went along, just waiting for this moment.

Comparing the two, we sub in the answers from the index, starting with the first bracket, *[(6b.) − (national) − (lace) − (museum)]*, which turns into *[(National Palace Museum) − (national) − (lace) − (museum)]*.

"We're left with two letters," Xander says.

I nod as I write them below the puzzle. "*P-a.*"

Then I squeeze his hand excitedly, loving how we're on the same page (literally and figuratively).

Tackling the next bracket, *[(5.) − (gingham) + (3a.) + (were) − (answer) − (fine)]*, we get *[(Yangmingshan) − (gingham) + (fire) + (were) − (answer) − (fine)]*.

"Should we start crossing off letters?" Xander says just as I start crossing out *g*, *i*, *n*, et cetera. Our minds are in sync.

We're left with three letters this time: *y*, *r*, *e*. I add these at the bottom as well.

"The longer ones are done," Xander says, and we stop for a quick high five.

We're feeling pretty great about ourselves, which is exactly why the universe decides to throw us a wrench.

As we tackle the next line, we run into a hiccup. A big one.

The line *[(8.) − (in)]* translates to *[(Pick up tea) − (in)]*, which doesn't make any sense because there isn't an *n* in *pick up tea*.

Xander remains calm, but I'm frustrated. "What are we missing?" I ask.

His steepled fingers are pressed into his chin as he thinks. "Okay, puzzle eight was at the tea house, with Jiayi, and our instructions were to pick up tea. Let's walk through our experience there."

We trade off talking, throwing in whatever tidbits come to mind. And as soon as he begins repeating Jiayi's comments about my grandfather's games, it hits me.

"What was the word my grandfather used to say when he picked up tea from her? The homophone or whatever?"

"Right. Um . . . pick up tea . . . I remember it being an unusual translation . . ." I hold my breath as Xander thinks out loud. "Pick up—*zhua*? That can't be it. Oh wait. Pick up. *Jian. Jian cha.* Which sounds like . . ." He closes his eyes and scrunches his nose, which is adorable, but I don't have time to appreciate it because I'm willing the word into his head. His eyes snap open. "Inspect!"

"Which has the right letters in it!"

Inspect minus *in* leaves five letters—*s, p, e, c, t*—which pair perfectly with *p, a, y, r, e*.

"Pay respect," I say, rewriting it with the added space.

The next bracket, *[(9.) + (6a.)]*, is also confusing. The *(9.)* corresponds to just a number, 2, and *(6a.)* is just the word *Pan*, both of which we're simply adding on to what we already have.

"Pay respect to Pan," I say aloud, and it's so obvious I feel silly for not seeing it before. "Or pay respect*s* with an *s*, same thing. Pay respects to Pan."

It all makes so much sense. The index for this puzzle says *X Marks the Spot*. And maybe just like Val always jokes, *X* really means *ex*. Gong Gong's ex is going to mark the final spot.

I look up at Xander. His eyes are cloudy with emotion—exactly what, I can't quite tell. "Are you . . ." I trail off.

He nods. "Let's go see my grandfather."

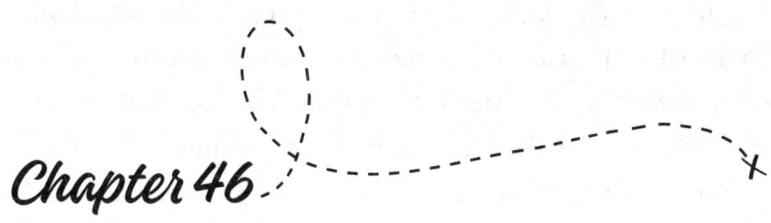

Chapter 46

Pan Wei Li rests in a columbarium about twenty minutes away. Xander drives since Val brought me to the high school earlier.

The car ride is slightly solemn, but not in an awkward way. In a paying-respects way, just like Gong Gong instructed.

"He wasn't exactly warm," Xander says out of nowhere but also not out of nowhere; he's obviously talking about his grandfather. "And he wasn't very happy or expressive. More . . . reserved. I guess now I know why." He pauses. "I think he cared about my grandmother, though. That's possible, right?"

"Of course," I say sincerely. "And he of course cared about you."

Xander nods a few times, as if he's convincing himself. I hope he'll feel it more with time.

After a beat, he adds, "I get what Jax and the other TARPers were saying before. About not seeing our grandparents as people. I know it's better that I know all this now. It's just . . . hard."

"I know. I'm sorry." I reach over and give his shoulder a supportive squeeze.

The columbarium is completely different from Yangmingshan.

There are no employees at the front, no niches that open, no keys. Instead, the niches are sealed off and covered with marble plaques. I try not to deflate as Xander leads me directly to Wei Li's plaque, carved with his name, dates, and BELOVED HUSBAND, FATHER, GRANDFATHER. This won't be like my last columbarium visit, where the hunt items were in the mementos section.

Xander closes his eyes, and we pay our respects with a moment of silence. As I stand there thinking about Wei Li, I feel like we've met in passing. Not exactly ships in the night, but more like a person I've read a biography of, understand certain parts of, and wish to know more about. When Xander's ready, I hope to hear more stories to piece together a fuller picture. By knowing him, I can know Gong Gong and Xander better too.

I also can't help thinking about how much sense it makes that we're here now. It's brilliant, as Xander would say. The hunt was designed for the Pan and Sun families, so of course the last two steps required both of us. And thanks to this journey, Xander is finally here in front of Wei Li's true self, and I'm here to meet him for the first time.

Xander teaches me how to pay respects the way he learned. I follow his lead, raising my clasped hands once; then getting on both knees and bowing my head three times; then finishing with one final clasped hand raise.

We share one last look at each other, then at Wei Li, and we exit the columbarium. Outside, I hold a hand out to Xander, and he shakes it with confusion.

"Thanks for being my partner for this." That's all I can bring myself to say—I'm too emotional.

"Wait, is this it?"

"That was the last puzzle. No more steps."

"There must be something else, no?"

The old Gemma might have lost it here, torn the entire place apart searching for more, but I feel a surprising sense of peace. This hunt took me to places I'd never imagined—physically, emotionally, even romantically.

I loop my arm around Xander's. "I already won my prize."

He blushes, then tenderly kisses the top of my head. "So if this wasn't about an inheritance . . ."

"I think it was about him telling his story, the one he wasn't able to before his time was up. He wanted us to know the truth, and how he loved your grandfather until his last breath." My own breath hitches as I say this. A love so powerful, hidden away for decades. It's so consumingly sad, my lungs feel full of water.

Then I say something that's been niggling at the back of my mind. "It bothers me that he told you something your grandfather didn't seem to want you to know."

"I've thought about that too. But he didn't tell us, not really. Your grandmother did. He couldn't have known she would do that. I think your grandfather was merely trying to clear up the misunderstanding about the business and swindling, which makes sense. That's heartbreaking, to have your family and your love's family think you're a villain when you didn't do what you were accused of. And in that sense, I'm grateful to him. I doubt my grandfather would be upset about him setting that record straight."

I nod, his words easing my worries.

He turns in the direction of the car. "Hard to end this epic adventure, isn't it?"

"Well, we'll always remember—"

Xander's hand shoots out to stop me from taking another step. "Remember," he repeats.

I wait, not sure what he's getting at.

"We forgot a part of the puzzle," he says, and my heart skips a beat. *"And remember three b."*

With those four words, my mind kicks back into high gear. "Three b. Fire goes with water, wood, metal, and earth also."

We look at each other, and at the same time, we exclaim, "The elements!"

Of course there's an elements component to the last puzzle. This whole hunt has revolved around them.

We hurry back into the columbarium, eyes pinging all over the place and pausing on the plethora of metal and wood everywhere.

Not helpful.

We exit the columbarium to brainstorm more, not wanting to disturb the dead, and we settle near the entrance on a bench.

"Think," Xander says encouragingly. "Is there anything else we might have missed?"

I take a mental step back. It feels like everything has been coming together with the puzzles linking to each other in multiple ways. So as Xander reexamines the last puzzle, I retrieve the journal and flip through the sketches, notes, and answers interspersed with the clues I've painstakingly cut and taped inside. Seeing all of it at once only emphasizes how this journey was one of a thousand steps.

My hand pauses midflip, and I let out an excited yelp. Too overwhelmed with thoughts to explain, I merely tap frantically on the page.

"What? What is it?" Xander asks.

I suddenly have sympathy for dogs who can't talk and desperately want something. I'm half-surprised Xander didn't say, *What is it, girl?*

"Pay respects," I say, still tapping. "When I visited my great-grandparents at Yangmingshan, I was supposed to pay respects by appreciating the other sun."

Xander is blinking at me, confused, which is fair because my words sound like gibberish even to me.

I try again. "I had to walk through the gardens outside to, I now realize, appreciate life. My grandfather wanted me to pay respects by appreciating what only the living can. And that's what we have to do now. The instructions at Yangmingshan were partly to help me see the beauty and meaning in life, but also for this moment, right here, to direct us once we got to the end. Because the past affects the future, just like he said."

I'm rambling. It's all too much. Xander is still staring, completely befuddled by what just came out of my mouth—and maybe I am too. But deep down it makes sense.

I try to simplify. "There's something out here!" I exclaim, gesturing to the land surrounding the columbarium.

That, Xander finally understands, and he jumps up.

We try the left side of the columbarium first, which is a graveyard full of tombstones. Backtracking, we go to the other side, and a few feet out, connected by a dirt path, is a park.

"That's it," I say, sure. It's not that similar to the Yangmingshan garden (no pagoda, no Taiwan landscape), but it's the American version of it—not Zen-like but still peaceful and beautiful, with tall trees, rows of white and pink flowers, and an elegant birdbath.

"Are you sure?" Xander asks. "I think that's not part of the cemetery anymore. I think that's just a public park."

His words instill a seed of doubt, but then he points to a group of trees in one corner. "Wood."

Right, we're looking for agents of change.

"Water," I say, pointing to the birdbath in the opposite corner.

Two trash cans sit in the remaining two corners. "Um, metal trash cans?" I say, a little unsure because it seems lazy to use the same item twice. "It's weird that all of these things are in the corners, right?"

Xander approaches one of the trash cans, then puts a nostalgic hand on it. *Germs!* I want to call out, but I'm relieved when he says, "It's not a trash can. It's a joss-burning station."

"A what?"

"A place to burn paper items for the dead in the afterlife. Food, money, clothes. My dad requested these so we could do that for my grandfather."

"That's metal *and* fire," I say, incredulous. "All we're missing is earth."

And all at once, everything comes together.

I grasp Xander's hand. Then I open the journal to the index and point at the last line, number thirteen.

"X marks the spot," I say.

I should have known. This is my grandfather's game, after all. And no one loved double meanings more than him, not even me.

His ex marks the spot, but it's also marked by an actual X. If we connect the four corner elements with two lines, they form an X across the park.

"X marks the spot," Xander repeats, getting it. His eyes are shining now. "The last missing element. Earth."

I nod. "We have to dig."

Earth is the last element that hasn't yet served as an agent of change in a puzzle. So of course we have to complete that here. And in the *3b.* line, *earth also* was underlined, which translates to 地, which means both *floor* and *ground*. And while in puzzle three I had to look below the floor, now we have to look below the ground. The past indeed affects the future, and we needed it to get to the end.

"Everything has come full circle," I whisper. Full X? There must be a joke in there somewhere.

Xander beams as he looks over the park. "Just brilliant."

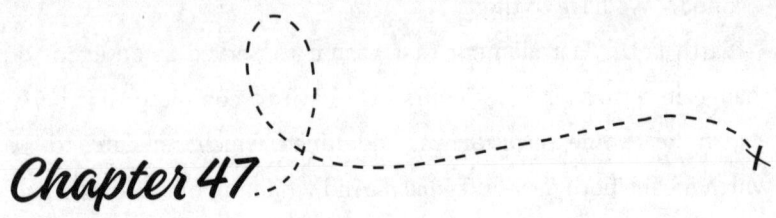

Chapter 47

After we figure out what we have to do, we run into a problem immediately.

"What are we going to dig with?" I ask.

"You don't have a shovel in your bag?"

I giggle. And it's not lost on me that before, I would've wanted to hit Xander with said bag. But I now know him well enough to know he's also trying to think of a solution, and that joking is his way of brainstorming, coping, enjoying life, everything.

"Maybe we should come back later anyway, when it's dark," I say. "It can't look good if people see us digging, right?"

"Or it'll look infinitely worse if we're found digging a hole next to a cemetery *in the dark*."

I didn't think of that. "At least it's not *part* of the cemetery? And since when are you one to say no to an adventure? This is way less incriminating than *stealing* from a museum."

"Well, there's only room for one fun person per situation. Otherwise, we'll end up constantly running from security."

"I don't know, that was kind of fun, wasn't it?" I inch forward until we're as close as when we were hiding from the museum guards. Then I gently place my shoe on top of his without putting weight on it.

This time is completely different from then. Xander nuzzles his nose into my hair, and a low, delighted hum rumbles in his throat as he kisses me behind the ear. His breath against my skin sends shivers down my spine. And there's nothing fake or staged about the kiss we share.

When we finally come apart, Xander says with a sigh, "We have to go get a shovel, don't we?"

Thirty minutes and two stores later, we return with a shovel that's cheap but not so cheap it looks like it'll break as soon as it hits the ground.

Using an app, coordinates, and GPS, we locate the exact middle of the X. The earth itself doesn't give us any hints; it's completely smooth, no signs of disturbance, meaning whatever we're after has likely been here for a while, possibly years.

I hold the shovel out to Xander.

"What?" he says innocently.

"Go ahead."

"We should've bought two," he teases.

"We'll take turns."

After one turn each, we hit something.

A couple of feet down, placed horizontally, is a long metal scroll tube. I switch to digging laterally.

I'm jumpy with anticipation. I need money desperately, but along the way, this hunt became about so much more. And even though I don't want to, I can't help hoping for not just an inheritance but a letter. A message in Gong Gong's own words to me or my mom so I can stop guessing at his thoughts.

When I've freed it, Xander takes the tube from me, then extends a hand to help me out of the hole.

This is truly the end of the hunt. We both feel it, taking a deep breath while staring at what we've found, the supposed 太陽 at the end of the adventure. And this moment is the last time we can dream, fantasize, guess about what's inside. Once we open it, there's no going back.

He hands me the tube.

"Together," I say. Because it's what Gong Gong would have wanted.

I grip the tube, and Xander pulls the top off. Tilting the opening toward us, we peer inside.

I half expect a mouse or some other animal to pop out and surprise us, but, nothing. I reach in and feel something stiff yet soft. Bendable. Grasping as gently as I can with just my fingertips, I slowly pull. Xander helps by grabbing the tube and pulling in the opposite direction.

A long piece of canvas appears. When I see handwriting, I can't help it, my heart is in my throat.

Without speaking—it's like we're of one mind—Xander holds one end of the canvas and I the other. We unfurl, walking away from each other. The writing faces us.

My voice shaky, I begin reading, "'My Forever Ping . . .'" and my heart sinks to my pelvic floor. This is not from my grandfather. Which I already knew because it wasn't his handwriting, but I didn't fully believe it until I saw those three words.

Shaking off the disappointment, I keep reading. "'I know this was taken from you. So I found a way to get it back, don't ask how. Consider this my last grand gesture. I don't have much time left. I wish it had been different, but I don't regret my life. I wish you the very best.'" That's all there is. No name. "Is this from—?"

Xander nods. "That's my grandfather's handwriting. I don't know if *forever* is a play on the direct translation of his name, Yong, or if it's, you know, a declaration."

"Or maybe all of the above," I suggest.

"So what is this?"

Simultaneously, we turn the canvas over.

We both gasp.

It can't be. Yet it also makes sense.

It's the stolen painting from the museum, the one that used to sit in the now-empty frame.

Tiny clues along the way had made me wonder about this possibility, but it was too wild to believe without proof.

Well, this is giant indisputable proof staring me in the face.

My grandfather was X, the Banksy of Taiwan. But only for a short period of his life when he was younger, it seems, after which he stopped painting for a long time, maybe because he had come to America or because he had lost the love of his life or because all his hardships made him stop fighting. When he picked it back up in his older age, his style was so different it didn't resemble X's at all, perhaps because he was a completely different person then.

And this painting before me, the one with two men being attacked by elements of change—they are Gong Gong and Wei Li. And Wei Li's last act to show Gong Gong that he still cared about him in some way was to retrieve the painting for him.

Looking at it now and knowing Gong Gong's history, I see it in a completely new light. The *x*'s over their eyes and mouths seem to represent their forced anonymity, having to hide who they are. They can't speak, they can't see, they can't be themselves.

And the fact that the painting is here at the end of the hunt— this is the sun in multiple respects. It's priceless, an actual treasure in the literal sense, and it's also an act of love. Gong Gong saved that painting for us, then led us to it. It's proof that he believed family to be the most valuable. The best treasure of all, just like Slugger's gift.

X certainly marked the spot, in more ways than one.

"I can't believe my grandfather took this from the museum," Xander says. "It's so unlike the version of him that I knew."

"I didn't realize heisting was in your blood. Now the National Palace Museum incident makes more sense."

He chuckles.

We continue to stare at the painting, drinking in the details.

"This feels like a representation of his life, doesn't it?" I say.

"A masterpiece," Xander agrees.

"Oh my god, and we're touching it with our grubby dirt-encrusted fingers and exposing it to the sun," I suddenly realize.

We quickly and carefully refurl it and return it to the tube.

"You know what this means?" Xander asks.

That I can sell this and Gong Gong's other paintings for money. And I'm descended from a famous, groundbreaking artist. And that Wei Li still had feelings for Gong Gong, though he seems to have also loved the life he lived.

"What?" I ask dreamily.

"That if we had stolen the Chengcing Lake painting at the National Palace Museum like I'd wanted to, we would've been just taking back your grandfather's work! We would've been heroes, not criminals!"

I laugh. Even with how well I know him, Xander still has the ability to surprise me. And I wouldn't have it any other way.

~~1. Wooden box~~

~~2. Will~~

~~3. Framed photo~~

   a. Answer to first riddle: 火/**fire**

   b. First line of second riddle: 火 **goes with water,**
wood, metal, and earth also.

~~5. Journal~~

Destination: **Yangmingshan**

~~6. Metal box~~

   a. Need A: **Pan**

   b. Destination: **National Palace Museum**

~~7. Wall~~

~~8. House gate~~

Instructions, first line: **Pick up ~~the~~ tea**

~~9. Address~~

Number: **2**

~~10. Poem~~

~~11. Beginning~~

~~12. Watch~~

~~13. X Marks the Spot~~

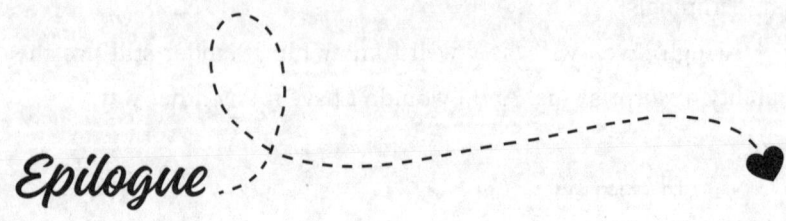

Epilogue

5 MONTHS LATER

I take the steps to the Chinese restaurant two at a time.

"Ji wei?" the employee greets me.

"Wo de nan pengyou yijing daole," I say, gesturing to Xander on the other side of the room.

A second later, we're running toward each other. It's been two weeks since I've seen him, a longer stretch than usual because we were both taking finals. When we meet, he loops his arms around my waist and lifts me in the air. I kiss him like I need his lips on mine to live.

"Whoa," he says when we break apart, out of breath.

"I missed you," I say.

"I missed you too."

He puts me down, helps me out of my coat, and we slip into the same side of the booth.

"I like your dress."

"It's still stain-free," I say with a grin. Xander bought this for me as a start-of-semester gift to replace the one he spilled fruit punch on. I've been wearing it frequently, regardless of the weather, pairing it now with an undershirt and thick leggings to combat the New England winter.

"How'd you do on your finals?" I ask.

He raises an eyebrow. "Trying to compete with me?"

I chuckle. "No, I just want to make sure they went okay."

He grins.

"Aced them all?" I ask.

He waggles his eyebrows. I hold a hand up and he high-fives me.

"You as well?"

"Do you have to ask?" I say, though really, he also knows how hard I've worked this semester. College has been a whole other level, and most of our dates were study sessions. And while there were plenty of rebus puzzles and contraband hot chocolate, there were also kisses, snuggles, and new puzzles, like anagrams and Chinese-character math, the latter of which I can now do, thanks to the Mandarin class I'm taking.

After we order all the dumplings, I tell him, "The Boston Fine Arts Museum is in."

It took several months, but I managed to prove my grandfather was X. Once his work was authenticated, I sold off one of his paintings to cover this year's tuition, and another so my mom could quit her night job. The rest I decided to loan out to museums. His work made me truly feel the power of art—how it can make us think, understand, even change—and I want to share that with the world. A sixth agent of change.

Gong Gong's masterpiece—now renamed *Agents of Change*—was graciously gifted to us once the truth came out (and it helped that Wei Li's message on the back exonerated us from the actual theft). Boston was our top choice to display it so we could see it from time to time, so I'm thrilled the Museum of Fine Arts just agreed.

"Let's go as soon as it's up," Xander says. "Maybe there will be a Gemma Sun original next to it soon, but not the one you made for me. That's mine."

I blush, still not used to the praise he heaps on me in excess. I'll be taking art electives as soon as there's room in my schedule, but I'm painting as much as I can in my limited free time. And because Xander refused to take any money from the sales of Gong Gong's work—not even one percent—I painted him Sun Moon Lake, which hangs above his bed in his dorm room now.

"How's it going on your museum project?" I ask. He narrows his eyes, and I quickly correct, "Sorry, your super-secret, undisclosed project."

Smiling now, he leans forward to divulge, "I think I might've tracked down someone who was involved."

Xander's been looking into the art heist, and we suspect that since Xander's grandfather didn't travel to Taipei in his later years, he must have hired someone to do it for him.

"It's a good lead, but I need help from my favorite puzzle master." He nudges my elbow with his.

"Aren't you the heist expert, though?" I giggle, thinking about him patting his head and rubbing his stomach in the National Palace Museum.

"I need someone who has a different and better way of thinking."

The different wavelength still embarrasses me here and there—I might have accidentally gotten myself elected treasurer of the Agriculture Student Advocates instead of the Asian Student Association—but there are also perks to being me.

Our food arrives, and Xander and I click our chopsticks together in a toast.

"Gan wan!" we joke, our play on *gan bei*, saying *dry bowl* instead of *dry cup*.

"So, Jax texted wanting an update on how the TARP reunion plans are going—oh, and he said he loves the new logo you designed—"

I bite into a dumpling, and soup squirts sideways onto Xander's shirt—almost exactly in the same spot as the fruit-punch stain on my old dress.

"I'm so sorry!" I blurt as I rush to grab napkins. "I swear that wasn't payback."

But he blocks my hands from reaching the liquid. "Don't! You're going to ruin a Gemma Sun original!"

I chuckle. "That's what you think my art looks like? A splotch?"

"It's not just a splotch." He circles his finger around the wider part, then follows the thin extension to the side. "It's a pan. You drew a pan on A. Pan. It's perfect. A masterpiece. One that might be stolen and displayed in a museum, making us need to break in to get it back . . ."

I can't hold it in anymore. The laughs break free.

How did I not see Xander's sense of humor before? How did I miss out on years of this?

Better late than never.

I think if our grandfathers could see us, they would be as happy as we are.

Somehow, this hunt turned out to be so much more than I could have dreamed. I found the sun at the end of the adventure, in all meanings. There was literal treasure and familial treasure—getting to know Gong Gong and the love of his life, deepening my relationship with my mom, even meeting my grandmother. And the delicious cherry on top of the shaved ice was that I got to know my treasure hunt partner, the real version of him, and it turns out he's family too.

Now, for the first time in my life, I don't feel too American or too Chinese. I am a mix of all my experiences. While it's fine to want to know more about my roots, it's not a burden anymore. It's evolved from an embarrassment and weight to a curiosity and privilege. And now that I know the hardships of my family's older generations, I feel in my core, in my roots, that this makes up a piece of me as well. They're human and made mistakes, and everything about their experience made them who they are. *That* is where I'm from. It's not a place or culture, but people. Thanks to this journey of a thousand steps, I have a better sense of who I am, where I came from, and now where I'm going.

And this is just the beginning.

TARP Evaluation

Name: Gemma Sun

1. Why did you join the TARP program?

   To annoy my mortal enemy, mwahahahaha. I think I succeeded too.

2. What did you get out of the program?

   A partner in crime—scratch that, no crime. We didn't commit any crimes, I swear.

3. Any suggestions for future years?

   The TARP creator is kind of a genius, isn't he? And he's hot. But it also feels like a conflict of interest for him to be a part of the program, you know? Some kind of power imbalance. Maybe if he goes again, he should bring a girlfriend to keep that in check since the chaperones won't do it.

4. Any last comments?

   I really hope no one else is reading these other than you, X. Also, you know this whole thing is one giant cardboard dog, right? And another thing, should we name the dog? How about George?

Acknowledgments

I am so grateful to be writing the acknowledgments for my fifth book. I can't quite believe it! Thank you, dear reader, for going on this adventure with me, Gemma, Xander, and the TARPers. I hope you had as much fun reading as I had writing. In this book, I wanted to draw from my love of puzzles and my love for Taiwan, and in many ways, this is my love letter to both. And I have never been so hungry while writing before! To both new readers and those who have stuck with me through multiple books, thank you, and know that I write for you. Hearing from you is still one of the best parts of this dream job, and I'm so grateful for all your posts and messages.

Kathleen Rushall, my rock, thank you for your wisdom, support, and guidance. I am so lucky to have been working with you since the start of my career, and I can't imagine this journey without you in my corner. Thank you for everything.

Jenny Bak, what kismet it was to learn that you love puzzles as much as I do! Thank you for your enthusiasm from day one and for bringing out the best in this book. Thank you for being so support-ive of my vision, for our great brainstorming sessions, for helping me dive deeper, and for always wanting the best for the book, the characters, and your authors. This story wouldn't be what it is without your brilliant insight.

AZ Hackett, thank you for your fantastic ideas and your wonderful attention to detail. You helped elevate the characters, the puzzles, and this story, and I'm so grateful for your input.

Jordana Kulak, thank you for being so competent and kind. I appreciate all the hard work you put in, and I'm so thankful to get to work with you.

Kaitlin Yang, thank you for designing two covers that I deeply adore. I am in awe of your talent and brilliance.

Jacki Li, thank you for creating a stunning, fun, eye-catching cover illustration! You perfectly captured Gemma, Xander, and Shilin Night Market.

The entire Viking team: how I love working with you all. Thank you for your enthusiasm, talent, and collaborative spirit. I am so grateful for how open, passionate, and hardworking you all are. Please know I appreciate each and every one of you.

Special thanks to Penguin Teen, Felicity Vallence, Shannon Spann, Summer Ogata, James Akinaka, Kelsey Fehlberg, Marinda Valenti, Opal Roengchai, Bri Lockhart, Gaby Corzo, Vanessa Robles, Krista Ahlberg, Christine Ma, Abigail Powers, and Alicia Lea.

Kim Yau, thank you for all your hard work. I'm so grateful to work with you!

Thank you, Rachel Lynn Solomon, for being so excited about this idea early on. Thank you, Samira Ahmed and Lizzie Cooke, for all the boba dates. Thank you to the following for your ongoing support: Ann Liang, Ali Hazelwood, Julian Winters, Kat Cho, Rena Barron, Ronni Davis, Anna Waggener, David Arnold, Kate

Hannigan, Susan Blumberg-Kason, Mia P. Manansala, Susan Lee, and Marianna Leal.

A huge thank-you to librarians, teachers, and booksellers. Signing at ALA was such a highlight for me, and there is no place more wonderful than a room (or convention center) full of librarians. Thank you for everything that you do. And for being so kind to us authors. You all are the best! Special thanks to Rachel Strolle.

Thank you to all the wonderful indie bookstores for your continued support. I'm especially grateful to Women & Children First, Old Firehouse Books, Belmont Books, Porter Square Books, the Silver Unicorn, the Novel Neighbor, Parnassus Books, the Book Cellar, the Book Stall, and 57th Street Books. Special thanks to Kathleen March, Karlee Nussbaum, Sarah Hollenbeck, and Suzy T.

Thank you, friends and family, for your support! Diana, Lexi Klimchak, Melissa Richart, Javier Burgos, and Benjana Guraziu—all the hugs. Pete, you are missed.

Mom and Dad, I love you. Thank you for your love and support. And for your help with my books. And thanks for all the adventures in Taiwan. I hope you know this is my love letter to your home. And I hope you enjoy all the Easter eggs I put in for you—Jian Hong Dian, all our favorite places in Taiwan, all our favorite foods. I hope this is as much a trip down memory lane for you as it was for me to write it. It was so fun looking through all our photos for inspiration and descriptions.

Dan and Matt, thanks for your support. And thanks, too, for all the Taiwan fun through the years.

Anthony, this is always my favorite part of writing acknowledgments. It's also the hardest because it feels impossible to put everything I want to say into words even though that's my job.

Thank you for always believing in me, for loving my stories as much as you do, for talking through every tiny detail and caring as much as if they were your own words. Thank you for making my books and me better. Thank you for being the first to understand my wavelength and loving me for it. Thank you for always being up for an adventure, for finding the fun in everything even when we're in line at the post office, and for your endless jokes, just like Xander. Unlike Gemma, though, I've loved them and you since the start. You are my sun, my treasure, my everything.